VASILY MAHANENKO

I0562212

A CHECK FOR A BILLION

Books are the lives we don't have time to live,

Vasily Mahanenko

GALACTOGON
BOOK #3

MAGIC DOME BOOKS

A CHECK FOR A BILLION
GALACTOGON, BOOK THREE
COPYRIGHT © VASILY MAHANENKO 2019
COVER ART © VLADIMIR MANYUKHIN 2019
ENGLISH TRANSLATION COPYRIGHT ©
BORIS SMIRNOV 2019
PUBLISHED BY MAGIC DOME BOOKS
FIRST PAPERBACK EDITION 2019
ALL RIGHTS RESERVED
ISBN: 978-80-7619-082-5

THIS BOOK IS ENTIRELY A WORK OF FICTION.
ANY CORRELATION WITH REAL PEOPLE OR EVENTS IS
COINCIDENTAL.

ALL BOOKS BY VASILY MAHANENKO:

The Way of the Shaman LitRPG Series
Survival Quest
The Kartoss Gambit
The Secret of the Dark Forest
The Phantom Castle
The Karmadont Chess Set
Shaman's Revenge
Clans War

The Alchemist LiTRPG series by Vasily Mahanenko:
City of the Dead
Forest of Desire
Tears of Alron

Dark Paladin LitRPG Series
The Beginning
The Quest
Restart

Galactogon LitRPG Series
Start the Game!
In Search of the Uldans
A Check for a Billion

Invasion LitRPG Series
A Second Chance
An Equation with One Unknown

World of the Changed LitRPG Series
No Mistakes
Pearl of the South

**The Bard from Barliona LitRPG series
(with Eugenia Dmitrieva)**
The Renegades
A Song of Shadow

You're in Game!
(LitRPG Stories from Bestselling Authors)

You're in Game-2!
(More LitRPG stories set in your favorite worlds)

TABLE OF CONTENTS:

CHAPTER ONE

THE PRECIAN CRUISE SHIP PLOWED PLACIDLY THROUGH THE VAST VACUUM OF SPACE. The captain glanced at his console and turned back to the porthole. For the last five years, he had ferried tourists to the system's asteroid belt and he still found himself mesmerized by the spectacular vista. His passengers' security did not worry him: the Zatrathi fleet was on the other side of Galactogon, and the treacherous Qualians were blockaded in their home systems, posing no threat to his cruiser. They were deep in allied space, not a single enemy within a radius of twenty parsecs. Of course there was always the chance pirate raid. But even this was less likely than colliding with a stray asteroid. The pirates were weak, fragmented and lacked the resources to mount a raid this deep in Precian space. And if some minnow risked it, the cruise's escort of a dozen destroyers would be sure to put him in his place.

"Captain, three asteroids straight ahead!"

The Precian glanced up at the bridge's screens with

1

---

displeasure. It was rare, of course, but this had happened before — the asteroids in the belt would sometimes collide with one another, ejecting debris from the belt. And sure enough — three tumbling cliffs were currently hurtling at his cruiser.

"Give me a detailed situation report!"

"Three asteroids with average diameter of fifty meters. Risk of collision with object number three is 98%. The remaining objects do not pose a threat. Trimming our course should avoid collision."

The captain frowned — any abrupt change of course was not desirable. There were a number of Precian VIPs on board. Any discomfort due to the inertia involved might result in the captain's own discomfort as he tumbled down his career ladder. He could easily end up the captain of some rusty transport on a sandy backwater.

"Maintain current course," ordered the Precian after a brief pause. He could only hope that the danger would pass. "Destroy object number three. We will arrange a small show for our passengers."

Three torpedoes shot out of the cruiser in the direction of the dangerous asteroid. Meanwhile, onboard the cruise liner, the ship's intercom burst to life with the captain's voice:

"Esteemed passengers! This is your captain speaking. I would like to draw your attention to your cabin's screens. We are about to conduct a minor demonstration of the power of Precian weaponry!"

The asteroid flared into a little sun for a few seconds. A salvo from the cruiser's beam cannons pulverized what remained. Nothing could be allowed to interfere with the peace and tranquility of the important guests.

"Report!"

"Target terminated. The two remaining asteroids are projected to pass fifty meters to starboard. Shall we destroy them as well?"

"Leave them."

The captain wiped the sweat from his forehead with a trembling hand. The obese Precian's body did not handle the tension of the last few seconds well. He had begun to worry: Would the Precian VIPs enjoy his little bit of improvisation? Or would they resent his waste of torpedoes? What if, upon their return, he would be court-martialed for wasting ammunition instead of simply taking evasive action? Such were the new worries that lodged themselves in his mind.

"Bravo, captain!" One of the guests entered the bridge as if it were his living room. "I appreciate your ingenuity. A mesmerizing spectacle! I must say, we almost believed it to be real. To launch an asteroid at the cruiser to tickle our nerves, and then to destroy it in such a spectacular fashion! Bravo! Would you like a reward?"

"The asteroid emerged from the belt on its own, Sir Grandar." The captain's back wasn't used to bending, but this was one of those instances when one had to overcome one's sizeable belly and bow as deeply as one could. The emperor's favorite was not the type of individual with whom one could even hint at a lack of respect.

"Do not hold me a fool! I am well versed in the gravitational fields at work within asteroid belts! These boulders could not have come flying out on their own. Someone helped them and it seems to me that you did it. Would you maybe have us believe that pirates were behind this?"

In the peace and quiet of his own head, the captain recited everything he thought about Grandar's intellectual abilities; naturally, what came out of his mouth was something else entirely:

"Sir Grandar, there have never been pirates in this area." And, just in case, the captain bowed once more as deeply as he could and looked up only when he'd reached the bottom. What the hell was this fop talking about? *What* pirates?!

"Maybe, this isn't such a good idea?" I looked over at Eunice who was holding onto the space rock as tightly as she could. Her helmet's visor concealed her face, but the biometric sensors indicated that her pulse had accelerated. Training and exercise is one thing, but a true raid where you come in riding in on an asteroid, tumbling through open space at a Precian cruiser — is quite another thing altogether. We had reached the most critical part of our operation — the one where we no longer had any control over what would happen next. Just hurtling on this asteroid, praying the Precians won't waste a torpedo on an object that posed no threat to them. My wife had never done this kind of thing before and she was understandably nervous. Once the cruiser was ten seconds' flight from us, the time had come for me to decide — go alone or go with Eunice. After all, a nervous pirate is a dead pirate.

"It's a fine idea," my wife reassured me with a note of stress in her voice. "I'm calm — I'm ready."

"All right," I nodded, accepting her decision. "Brainiac, what do you have?"

The rhino's roar blared across my speakers, signifying that the boarding party was eager for battle and wasn't just sitting idly by waiting to retire. Next came the snake's lazy yawn and indistinct murmur. Despite her seeming boredom, the engineer was ready to start screening *Warlock* with shields at any second. The gunner rapped a paradiddle as usual, and only Brainiac deigned to reply intelligibly:

"Captain, the team is ready. We await your orders."

"Let's do it then!" I ordered. Crouching, we waited until the asteroid rotated around its axis. As the Precian cruiser rose on the gray horizon, I jumped as hard as I could. Eunice jumped behind me. The shot of adrenaline after the long wait blurred my vision but then settled into a mellow buzz. The time had come at last! At stake was a prize check with a one and nine zeros!

Far behind us, a vivid explosion bloomed deep inside the asteroid belt, spraying fine, colored dust in an iridescent sphere that deformed as it encountered the other asteroids. The Precians' sensors would be sure to detect it, and I really hoped that aboard the cruiser, everyone's attention would be directed that way. We had packed a lot of reagent on that asteroid and now as it encountering the debris and ice particles drifting in the belt, a large area of space exploded in a breathtaking riot of color. The vision was an impressive one for anyone uninitiated.

The hull of the cruiser approached faster than I expected and I hurriedly fired reverse thrust to slow down. This was another weakness in our plan, another point that was down to circumstances. If at least one Precian did his job and maintained close watch over the ship's perimeter sensors — instead of gawking at the fireworks display — we were sure to be noticed. Eunice had been opposed to running this risk, but I had insisted. Aren't we soldiers of fortune, or what? Plus, Galactogon had taught me to believe in the locals. If NPCs act stupid, they act stupid in the grandest way possible. Did they detect us during our initial approach? No. So they shouldn't detect us now either.

As I looked for the best place to land on, I was constantly distracted by Eunice. I did not like the trajectory of her flight from the very beginning — the deviation was too great. It was possible to adjust course using the suit's thrusters, but this required a certain amount of skill which, according to my prior observations, Eunice did not have. As soon as I got close to the cruiser and attached myself to its hull with magnets, I rotated myself and put my feet on the hull. Pausing a moment until my wife's boot came flying past me, I grabbed it with both hands and pulled with all my might.

"Kill the thrusters!" I yelled, but Eunice, overwhelmed by her suit's controls, did not hear me. The second of confusion cost us dearly — the magnets failed and we went tumbling back into space.

"I got it! I got it!" Eunice fired her thrusters again, sending us in a roll. Time rushed on and her movements became impulsive and abrupt. As I tried to compensate with my own thrusters, we slammed back hard against the hull and began sliding along its length.

"Kill the throttle!" I yelled, trying to grab onto whatever slid

---

past us. "Cut your throttle!"

One of the myriad antennae slipped past my hand. I grabbed it, and my suit's servos whined from the stress — Eunice's suit was blasting at full thrust.

"Brainiac! Shut her off!" I pleaded, realizing that Eunice wouldn't do anything on her own. Poker has the concept of 'tilt' when a player loses his head and makes error after error trying to make it right. For all intents and purposes, Eunice was now on tilt.

"About time you asked me," the ship's computer said pedantically, and the tension in my arm dissipated. Eunice's armor had finally gone still. The magnets snapped on again, attaching us to the cruiser's hull. But before I could breathe a sigh of relief, Brainiac announced:

"Two fighters are heading in your direction. ETA is ten seconds."

So they'd noticed us after all!

"Let's get out of here!" I pressed myself to one of the spires, pulled my immobilized wife to me and jumped, deactivating the magnets. A couple of seconds of weightlessness and we were again drawn to the hull. Attaching Eunice to the base of the spire, I leaned on top of her and activated the protective screen. Hopefully we look more like a sensor array than a couple of pirates out spacewalking around their prey.

"How are you? Eunice?" There was no reply. "Brainiac, turn on her comms. Eunice, can you hear me?"

"Get off my foot, you oaf!" my wife snapped angrily. "Yes, I'm fine!"

"Are you going to panic again?" I asked in as neutral a tone

---

as I could muster, resisting my urge to curse and yell. We had almost blown the entire operation.

"No. I was just a little confused," the girl replied with irritation. She sounded embarrassed by her unprofessionalism.

"You can't argue with hormones," I agreed, recalling the books about pregnancy I had read in preparation for our child, but then I hurried to change topics. "Brainiac, what's the status of those fighters?"

"They've gone. They scanned the hull and returned back to their hangar. Everyone seems fixated on the light show we put on. Hang on...I don't like the look of that antenna that just popped out of the hull. It looks like a close perimeter sensor."

"Roger. We'll cut through the hull right here then."

Eunice nodded and began setting up a small force field that would prevent the air from rushing out when we broke through the cruiser's hull. Brainiac had explained that the hull integrity sensors were very sensitive to any drop in pressure aboard the vessel. I had seen this device in use aboard Aalor's ship and couldn't help but wonder: Why could physical objects pass through it, but not air? The answer turned out to be simple — the system was one of the most important additions to any spacecraft. Whenever beam cannons overwhelmed ships' shields, the plasma would perforate the hull causing a myriad holes and therefore air leaks. Not all captains liked to work in armor suits — in fact, I was particular in my affection for the hunk of iron I was constantly encased in. Many other captains preferred to stand on the bridge and show off their beautiful physique. You can't breathe much without air, so especially powerful cruisers would expend one of their integration slots on this force field system to ensure that hull integrity would be maintained during battles. I had no idea whether a luxury cruise ship would carry one of these or not, so I decided to play it safe. Relying on dumb luck was the last thing I wanted.

Having finished installing the device, Eunice activated the plasma cutter. I waited nearby, looking away from the bright sparks. The Precians were vigilant and any sudden movement could ruin our boarding operation. This was also why I removed the camouflage field generator from my armor suit and attached it to the place where we were working. The 'antenna amplifier' that concealed us, should remain even after we'd boarded the cruiser.

"Ready!" Eunice pushed in the hull segment she'd cut out and stepped aside, allowing me to enter first. 'Ladies first' was not a principle we observed in our family. I squeezed through the opening and plunged three meters to the deck floor. Though my armor suit softened the fall, activating its stabilizers, the blow still jarred me. Eunice dived in after me and I managed to catch her near the floor. A pirate has to be a gentleman sometimes too. My spatial scanner modeled the cabin we were in and Brainiac helpfully identified it as the utility closet. Since the trip to the foggy asteroids lasted only a few hours, most of these facilities were typically empty. Why take on unnecessary cargo, after all?

"Brainiac, help us out! Where should we plug you in?"

"The right wall, lower plug. I will highlight it for you!"

A thin laser beam pointed at the wall I needed. I took a remote terminal configured for Brainiac out of my inventory. It would let my ship's computer interface directly with the cruiser's systems, as if they were linked by a cable. A handy little piece of gear whose main drawback was how incredibly expensive it was. On the whole, I have to mention that this entire operation had turned out to be ridiculously troublesome and costly. We had had to attach rocket engines to the asteroids, aim one of the rocks at the cruiser, have time to remove the engines before the asteroids came out of the belt, buy and deliver a lot of colored dust, pump it into several harvesters and, well, buy the harvesters themselves. The credits had poured with cosmic speed and, looking at the explosion we had engineered, I knew exactly where they had gone. But even that was nothing. The biggest blow to my gaming account was incurred by the information, or rather the list of passengers and the coordinates of this particular cruiser. If it weren't for my new partner Vargen, who had turned a tidy profit selling the loot from the Uldan base, I would've never dared getting involved in such a dubious enterprise. However, we had the cash and we had to use it intelligently.

"I'm in the system." It took Brainiac about a minute to deal with the cruiser's security system. "Projecting the ship layout to your HUD now. Identifying the passengers on board. Highlighting your objective."

The individual we needed was located in the other end of the cruiser. There were a thousand and a half Precians on board altogether, of whom two hundred were crew. Of course, a cruiser of this size could accommodate more, but everyone loved comfort.

"You are now engineers of the third rank, with the access of first rank personnel." Brainiac worked his magic, adding two new crew members with high level access to the cruiser crew. Becoming an officer didn't interest me. There weren't that many of them on the ship and their movements would be monitored more closely.

But who's going to pay attention to some maintenance staff? Especially of the third rank? Especially humans? We were mere handymen of the bring-that-here-and-take-that-there type. Who knew where we came from or how we'd ended up on the ship? And no one cared. The NPCs' logic would oblige them to look away, diligently keeping them blind to us.

"Well this is uncomfortable," Eunice mumbled, putting on the uniform of a Precian cruise janitor. But there was no other way — we had to look the part to a T. The gray suit fit her snugly, emphasizing my lady's fine curves. It was a good thing Brainiac had spent three days contemplating the meaning of life. Eunice and I had things to do in the meantime on our deserted planet.

I placed the ID card to the lock and the door panel slid up. The way into the cruiser's interior lay open before us.

"To the right along the corridor, then straight one hundred meters to the elevator. You need deck number three."

The cruise ship's interior turned out to be entirely different from what was the norm aboard cruisers. The corridors were all absurdly wide, there were screens and paintings hanging everywhere, and here and there we even came across aquariums and statues. It felt like instead of being on a space cruiser, we were visiting the country estate of a Precian billionaire. A kind of ostentatious chic that forced the underlings to feel their inferiority and poverty.

"Watch over us, Brainiac," I asked the ship's computer to keep an eye on the video feed and alert me if anything. Approaching the nearest wall, I shamelessly tore off a painting hanging there. Pleased with my chance loot, I turned and stumbled onto Eunice's look of disapproval. "What? It's for our family! The enemy doesn't deserve it. On the black market, they'll pounce at such an item so fast they'll tear your hands off in the process!" My wife just shook her head, failing to appreciate the finer points of my pirate's worldview. I guess stealing loot was shameful in whatever game she used to play. No big deal. She'll get used to it. She didn't marry me for nothing.

"...because, Sir Oleander, you simply had no opportunity..."

Everything went cold inside me — this voice was perfectly familiar to me. The strange thing was that the cruise's manifest hadn't listed this passenger. I cast around, looking for somewhere to hide. If the third adviser of the Precian Emperor sees me here, we'll be done for on the spot!

"What is it, Lex?" My wife did not fail to notice my agitation.

"Stand in front of me. The adviser is here! He doesn't know you." I finally found a small nook behind a statue and huddled into it, screening myself with the painting I'd filched for good measure. It didn't work out very well, but my panicked brain could not come up with another option. Judging by the voices, the adviser was approaching. I peeked through a crack, observing the procession. The adviser was escorting a Precian in shackles. Three armed guards followed behind them.

"My brother's policy is mistaken. No good will come of it." Oleander had a deep voice, the kind that women fancy between the ages of eighteen and infinity. Judging by her narrowed eyes, my wife too was an admirer of baritones.

"Our empire..." The adviser began to respond — when his

gaze strayed across Eunice. She had stepped aside to the wall in order to let the Precians pass, yet still failed to escape the local's clingy eye.

"A human?" the adviser said with surprise. One of the guards approached Eunice and I heard the squeak of her ID being scanned. "A cadet of the Precian marine academy. Her name is Nurse…Your name seems familiar to me. Have we met?"

"No, sir, your lordship." Eunice bowed curtly, showing deference.

"Yet I definitely know you from somewhere…"

"I cannot say, your lordship. After graduating from school, I continued my studies in engineering and found a job with this cruise line. Perhaps you have heard of a design I developed? A stability system for marine mechs. The Hansa Corporation found it interesting enough to give it a closer examination."

Eunice lied without hesitation and did it beautifully. It was good luck that she had started out with the Precian Empire. It made our cover story all the more plausible. Naturally cruiser personnel could speak the common tongue, but this would raise questions and attract unnecessary attention. As a former Qualian, for me, the speech of the Precians was a chaotic torrent of strange sounds and only Brainiac interpreting in real time allowed me to understand what was being discussed.

"Perhaps, perhaps," the adviser frowned. "Yes, most likely I came across your name in one of the reports. Well, it's nice to know that such talented warriors are fighting for the Precian Empire. Here, Mr. Oleander, take a look. Is this what you wish to rid us of? Humans are useful allies of our empire."

A CHECK FOR A BILLION

The prisoner did not answer and merely measured Eunice with a scornful look.

"Come along. The brig awaits. Today the emperor will render his sentence. I am afraid I will miss your poetry."

The procession went on its way and I climbed out of my improvised cover. Examining the painting that had so successfully saved me from having to explain myself to the adviser, I threw it in inventory. I won't sell it. I'll hang it up in the orbship for good luck.

Our subsequent journey brought no surprises. The passengers did not notice us. Some of the crew cast us menacing looks, evidently thinking about what they could make us do. To solve this problem, we held tablets in our hands with a warning blinking red on their screens. Coupled with our fast pace and serious mugs, we looked like we were on a very urgent mission. No one bothered us until we reached the elevator, but as soon as we ascended to the third deck, our troubles returned.

"Halt!" A marine in an armor suit barred our way. "Your ID!"

We obeyed and held up our plastic cards to the scanner. The scanner flashed green. All clear. But the guard did not back down.

"Deck three is off limits to junior personnel!"

"The HVAC in section 37 is busted," Eunice explained. "Feel free to verify with the custodial ops. Either let us pass or go repair it yourself. The captain won't be happy when the guests start complaining about their stuffy cabins."

The guard pressed a few buttons on his tablet. Brainiac had done his job perfectly and the onboard system indeed reported a malfunction. Nothing so critical as to arouse the interest of senior engineers. A straightforward replacement of some condenser units.

"Val, escort them!" The guard stepped aside, but another guard immediately replaced him beside us. I sighed with displeasure. This wasn't part of the plan. And yet, there's no arguing with a blaster muzzle.

"Let's go." Eunice hurried onward. "We need to finish soon, before the guests return."

I must admit that our escort turned out to be useful. We encountered a few more checkpoints, but now the procedure was limited to a perfunctory ID scan. The guards could see our status and though they did not understand why such low-ranked staff had been sent to repair the cabin of a nobleman, they did not hinder us. And if anything, we always had Val's imposing presence. My hands were constantly itching to pocket a few more expensive goodies, but the presence of a guard protected the cruiser's decor from my paws. In this manner, we finally reached the door we needed. Under escort, under constant supervision and without any loot. This last part upset me the most.

As soon as the entrance door closed behind us, Brainiac said:

"Captain, there is no one in this area."

For poor old Val, this meant one thing only — his clock cycles in Galactogon's AI stack were about to expire. An EM grenade appeared in my hands — a miniature bomb with the same effect as an EM cannon. Attach one to an armor suit and press a button, and every electronic device in a one-meter radius sizzles and fries. Quite a reliable way to neutralize an unsuspecting space marine encased in an armor suit. Oh the toys you'll discover when

A CHECK FOR A BILLION

Hilvar gives you permission to trade with the pirates…

"Can you hear me, Brainiac?" I took a new comm from my inventory. The EM blast knocked out not only Val, but my old comm as well.

"You're coming in loud and clear. There is no interference. The Target is currently located in the next cabin. Warning! The Target is not alone."

"We can't wait," Eunice interfered. "The cruise will enter hyperspace in half an hour."

"You're right. Let's just deal with it." I removed a blaster from my inventory. The Precian on the floor twitched, making another attempt to overcome the weight of his armor. Eunice turned away, leaving the matter entirely to me. Leaving a witness behind was not in our rules. There was too much at stake. A shot — and all that remained of the guard was a shimmering crate of raq and elo. My rapport with the Precian Empire did not change because it was already at zero.

"Let's go." I pulled out my manipulators and, unable to resist, tossed another painting from the wall into my inventory. There was just something so unusual about it, so catchy. A complete abstraction, but it was hard to look away. It'll make a nice gift for Hilvar. He likes that kind of stuff.

While I was filching the art, the Target came out to meet us voluntarily.

"What are you doing here? Scram!" I heard a cry of indignation. I suppose there was something to sputter about: Two armed junior engineers were expropriating the local decor as if they were in their own house. How could you not be indignant? My

16

---

manipulators snapped into action and Duke Narlin, the nephew of the Precian Emperor himself, flew up into the air, flailing his arms comically. A quick shot of sedative and he calmed down and went limp. I carefully placed the valuable little body in a chair and pointed Eunice to the door. Our unexpected guest was on the other side and it was time to get rid of him.

"Surgeon?" another voice exclaimed. The guest had come to us himself, having heard Narlin's outburst. Eunice raised her blaster, about to send the stranger to the other side, and I barely managed to shove her elbow, sending a plasma bolt at the wall. I was all too familiar with the newcomer.

"What are you doing on this ship? You're an outlaw! If you wanted to meet with me, you should have simply called...I must say that our past business turned out to be quite profitable for me!"

I did not allow my wife to shoot Grandar, the former junior adviser to the deputy weeding assistant to the gardener of the Third Palace of his Imperial Highness, the Emperor of the Precian Empire. Back in the day he had done me a huge favor — he had gone to the emperor and passed on information from me. Later I had asked the emperor to show his favor to this Precian who was able to help me in difficult times. But I could not even imagine that Grandar would rise so swiftly in the ranks. The bands on his robes suggested that I was looking at an intimate of the emperor. An imperial favorite who carried his master's blessing and all that jazz. Basically, he was now a bigwig who had been at the right time and place to help me. I could hardly allow Eunice to shoot him. Not at all, in fact.

"I have some business with the duke," I replied.

A CHECK FOR A BILLION

"What business can a pirate have with a member of the imperial family? I should call security, but…my intuition tells me to hold off. I must admit I am confused. Help me, Surgeon. Explain what you are doing here."

"I need to get onto Zalva, the imperial capital. It's nothing criminal, I assure you," I answered honestly, causing Eunice to scoff. She did not like improvisation.

"What does Narlin have to do with it? He will not help you." Grandar closely examined me and the sleeping duke. "He is only the tenth in line to the throne!"

"I have every reason to believe that it is for this reason that he will help us." I had to act quickly, so I decided to share my plans with Grandar. It was not for nothing that he had appeared in this room. You don't just encounter locals randomly along your way. Everything has its reasons. And anyway, I can kill him at any time if something goes wrong.

"Trade fraud?!" Grandar exclaimed when I showed him the data I had. I finally managed to use the compromising evidence I'd found on the viceroy's tablet. Vargen had told me that the deceased Precian was about to be honored as a hero who had traded his life for that of Lumara, the uncrowned empress of the fallen Delvian Empire.

My plan was embarrassingly simple. If the quest for the check was on again, we would have to start from the point we'd left off our earlier journey. In my case, I had to find my way into the ship of Rrgord, the Precian prince, and get the coordinates of the seven planets he had discovered. One of them should contain my final prize. I found the weakest link in the list, found out when the duke would take a cruise and then arranged an operation that would force the Precian to take us to Zalva. The only problem now was this Grandar, who could spoil all our plans.

"I am loath to upset you, but Narlin will not agree," the Precian said to my chagrin. "His duty to the empire has always been dearer to him than his own life. The compromising material you have will merely push him back from tenth to like twentieth in the line of succession, and even that is not a fact. The emperor might even praise him for his resourcefulness. After all, these are mere financial machinations, not actual treason. The duke tried to increase his wealth. What member of the imperial family does not seek to do the same?"

"How much do you want?" Eunice suddenly asked.

"Have we met?" Grandar walked up to my wife with evident interest, as if he had just noticed her presence. I was forced to introduce her.

"Surgeon here once helped me out a little," the Precian deigned to explain himself. "I think I owe him a favor and we can be useful to each other. For a modest two billion, I will take you to Zalva. However! The ticket is one way. You will have to arrange the return leg on your own."

"Deal!" I didn't bother haggling and shook the Precian's hand. It didn't really matter to us who would take us there as long as we made it.

"You will need to dispose of this one," Grandar pointed at the duke casually. "If he wakes up, he will ruin all our plans. Narlin is bound to the planetary spirit, so killing him won't do. I imagine a sojourn on some distant backwater should do the trick. Can you do it, or will you need help?"

I looked over at Narlin sprawled out on the deck floor. I doubt we'd manage to drag him to the other end of the ship without getting noticed.

"I see. Right, don't overexert yourself. I see no problem in helping a partner." Grandar called some servants and ordered them to bring a container for food waste with them. "When do you expect this body to wake up?"

'Partner.' 'Body.' How deftly Grandar had learned to play with words and change his shoes on the go! After all, he had been with Narlin for a reason and had most likely wanted something from the duke. Yet seeing a chance to make some extra money, this Precian had immediately scrapped whatever plans he'd just had. He would surely go far. It was clear to me now how Grandar had risen so high in the ranks of court.

"Without the antidote, he should sleep for a few days."

"Excellent. I must say, I like how you do business. I imagine we can be helpful to each other. Where shall I send the container?"

At that moment, two Precians ran into the room. Grandar pointed at the duke, and without any further formalities or fanfare, the servants stuffed him into a small crate they had brought.

"Put the container in the back room and wait for Surgeon to appear," Grandar ordered. "Now get to it!"

The servants did as ordered and left us alone.

"I have many slaves now. I love it when they don't know anything. Unnecessary knowledge is the leading cause of headaches," said Grandar, sentencing his servants to death. Formally speaking, it'd be a cinch to eliminate two Precians.

Although, a plan of my own had just occurred to me when it came to that business, but I wasn't going to let the emperor's favorite in on it. It couldn't hurt to have an extra ace in my sleeve.

"Isn't it just swell when everyone sees eye to eye?" Grandar took our silence for consent. "I need two days to prepare your transportation. Send half of the payment to my account today. I will share the information with you right this instant. Aren't you a pirate, Surgeon? Would you mind doing a small chore for me? Naturally, I would like to see what you're capable of before I decide whether we should work together or not."

"What do you want?" I stiffened, expecting some new chore.

"Nothing too complicated. I just need you to make your way into one of the cruiser's compartments and steal the 'Oblivion of Jarullah' for me. It should be a mere trifle for a pirate like you. Isn't that so? For my part, I will make sure that the ship does not jump to hyperspace in the next three hours."

Grandar's hand casually reached for his PDA. I had seen one like it before. A mere touch and an impenetrable shield would appear around the Precian. And, I imagine prior to that, an alarm would be sent to security, notifying them that the emperor's favorite had been attacked, at which point, our little raid would come to an inglorious end. It seemed I had no choice.

"We will get you the Oblivion — as soon as we find out what it is and where it is."

CHAPTER TWO

THE PRETTY AND TEMPTING NAME OF 'THE OBLIVION OF JARULLAH' belonged to a mysterious artifact which the Precian Emperor had personally presented to his third adviser for destroying the Zatrathi flying fortress. The emperor had been impressed by the courage of his subject, who had rushed into the thick of the fight, risking even his binding to the planetary spirit. For this as well as other numerous services, the emperor presented the adviser with a jewelry box and commanded him to open it at least once a day. Then he sent his empire's most dedicated workaholic on mandatory leave. That is, right from the award ceremony, the adviser had been taken under his blue armpits and escorted to the departing cruise cruiser.

Not daring to oppose the will of the emperor, the third adviser went on the vacation, yet he did not hurry to use the artifact, just as he did not hurry to share with others why exactly this imperial gift was so valuable. Upon arrival on board, he simply handed the jewelry box over to be stored in the ship's vault with the explanation that he was fearful of losing such an important object.

The natural question was what did Grandar have to do with any of this? Well, the imperial favorite harbored a deep envy of the adviser and could not forgive the imperial honor and respect bestowed upon his rival. His plan was to steal the mysterious artifact, find out what its value was, and then let it slip as court gossip that he had seen the adviser scorn this incredible present. Such are palace intrigues.

But I do have to say that this time, my intuition failed me thoroughly. I should have blasted that toady as soon as he walked in on us without any further conversation. I mean, this situation was the last thing I needed!

"Ideas?"

"Seems impossible," Eunice said what we were both thinking. The vault was impregnable.

"That's why I made you the offer." My wife's negative mood did not bother Grandar at all. "If anyone on this ship can pull off this little heist, it's you and no one but you."

I stared at the schematic again, meticulously searching for non-existent gaps. Brute force wouldn't work, even with my upgraded armor suit. Two automatic beam cannons were a good impediment to trying the strong-arm approach. Brainiac already explained that he couldn't disable them. And these cannons were the same reason we couldn't just come in from the hull side. Goddamn beam cannons. Should I cut a hole from the neighboring cabin? Not an option — I'd have to get in there first. And the cruiser's bridge was no place for a stowaway like me. Which reminds me…

A CHECK FOR A BILLION

"Listen, the items from the vault...Do they have to be picked up by their rightful owners exclusively or do you think that some authorized representative could retrieve them?"

"Come on, Surgeon, what a stupid question! As if the aristocracy would deign to wander around the ship in search of a glorified storage locker! Of course we have our proxies to deal with such matters!"

"What would we need to prove our authorization?" Finally something resembling a plan began to take shape in my head.

"Access from the personal PDA of the owner," said Grandar and then, seeing the satisfaction on my face, quickly added: "Hacking it won't work. I have tried."

"Is it biometrically protected?"

"No." The imperial favorite waved his hand. "Just a password, no fingerprints."

"Well...Do you have anything valuable in the vault?"

"Me?" Grandar echoed, puzzled. "No, I keep my valuables on my person."

"Well then you need to authorize me to deposit something for you. That'll get me into the vault. Then I'll barricade myself and try to find the adviser's jewelry box. After that, you'll report me and claim I killed your servants and snuck into the vault. By the way! Tell them that Narlin was the one who told you to send your servant into the vault. We'll blame the whole thing on him. We need to look out for our rapport — we still have to work together after all. While I am busy with the jewelry box, Eunice will drag the duke into space and wait until the cruiser jumps into hyperspace. After that you can handle the rest yourself."

"I'm not going anywhere without you!" my wife objected, but I stopped her.

"As soon as I have the jewelry box, I'll respawn. We'll meet up in two days at home." I made sure to emphasize the last word.

"Wait!" Eunice refused to relent. "I can do a better job with the vault and the jewelry box than you! Women are more trusted. I already have a cover story and I speak Precian! So why not?"

"Because we can't have you showing up on their radars," I snapped. "You will be the one to go to Zalva with Grandar, not me. You will infiltrate the prince's ship and download the coordinates with Brainiac's help. You were training to become a marine, so get on with it! Meanwhile, I'll make a ruckus in another part of Galactogon to draw any suspicion from Grandar. No one should be able to connect today's raid with your appearance on Zalva. Any more questions or objections?"

"It seems to me that this is the beginning of a long and fruitful partnership," said Grandar. "I am heartened. Now I won't have to turn you over to the cruise's security."

"That was your plan?" I asked without the least bit surprise.

"Who do you take me for? Of course that was my plan!" said Grandar astonished, as if this was the most obvious thing ever. "I was going to send you into the vault and then hand you over. Why not? I'd be rewarded for my heroic deed and honored as defender of the empire!"

"And what about the trip to Zalva?"

"One thing doesn't interfere with the other. How would you know that I betrayed you? Security would shoot you on the spot and that's it. No questions asked. I can solve the problem of Narlin

---

on my own."

"What exactly did the duke do to displease you?"

"Why I almost lost my current status because of that fool. But now, it does not matter!"

"And in the meanwhile you wanted to turn over Surgeon to security?" Eunice refused to believe Grandar's story.

"Of course! Betray and conquer! We are losing time! Come here, number 10."

The door immediately opened, and the next servant came running in.

"I need you to deliver a gift of the Emperor to the vault." Grandar removed the medallion hanging around his neck. The servant bowed low, accepting the errand, but did not have time to take the object from the Precian's hands. A shot from the blaster turned him into a shimmering crate of loot — which contained a set of Precian servant's clothes.

"Snap to it! Your new garb awaits!" ordered Eunice, replacing the blaster in her inventory. She had interpreted Grandar's actions accurately. If anything happened, he had asked his servant to take the medallion — not me. And he could testify to this under oath without fearing discovery.

"It looks good on you Surgeon! Really! If you get tired of piracy, I will gladly accept you into the ranks of my slaves."

"Doesn't seem like a very long-term position," I muttered, adjusting my snow-white robe with the emblem of an imperial favorite. Throwing a hood over my head, I took the medallion, imagining myself a courier, not a slave.

"I'll start worrying about my servant in ten minutes,"

Grandar warned. "You must infiltrate the vault within this time frame. Meanwhile, I will go look for the captain. I need to delay the cruiser. Let's get to it then!"

"I don't like that jerk." Eunice stared suspiciously at the door that had closed behind the Precian. "He's a bit too overwrought for a simple 'local.' There's an advanced AI running him."

"That's precisely why you need to get out of here urgently," I agreed. I rummaged through my inventory and pulled out two armor suits. Boy do I love convenient game mechanics and an expanded inventory! "Take this. We need to cover our asses. We'll freeze Grandar's servants and store them with Narlin. They may come in handy later on, if this whole business goes sour. Never hurts to have an ace up our sleeve."

A grin appeared on my wife's gloomy face. She liked this scenario better than a simple murder.

"Don't be late. I'll wait for you on Blood Island."

Eunice pressed her lips to mine, wishing me good luck in my coming adventure, and busied herself with the unconscious bodies. Understanding the importance of her assignment made the girl compliant, affectionate and tuned to the cause.

I looked at the duke's chambers with melancholy. So near and yet so far! Grandar, that bastard, even managed to spoil things here. He knew that I was suffering from an advanced stage of kleptomania, and yet no: "In ten minutes, I'll…" He sure had learned the intricacies of surviving at the highest levels of power quickly.

It turned out to be much easier to move through the cruiser in the habit of a servant than an engineer's uniform. I should take this as a lesson for future escapades. The guards just watched me

A CHECK FOR A BILLION

pass, without bothering to ask for my papers, please. I even entered the bridge deck without any trouble, merely showing the guards the medallion and explaining that its owner wanted it deposited in the vault. The vault itself was a separate room at the back of the bridge. In addition to various instrument panels and consoles, the main crew of officers piloting the cruiser was stationed here. Brainiac howled in grief when he saw the network integration panel. If I could connect him here to the ship's mainframe and buy him a minute or two of calm intercourse, the cruiser would be ours. However, I was not allowed to linger and examine anything in detail, but was hurried along with a careless wave to a corridor where there was already a group waiting in line. Three people were allowed inside the vault at a time, while the line to deposit or retrieve property from the vault consisted of about twenty Precians. Since I was the only human, I naturally drew everyone's attention. Fortunately, they limited their discussion not to my immodest person, but the eccentricity of Grandar, who allowed himself to have a human slave.

The line moved slowly. I fretted and fidgeted and kept glancing at the time. Three minutes. Yet my persistent desire to scatter everyone aside and simply rush into the vault was preempted by the guard's watchful eye. Grandar's deadline approached inexorably and I had only advanced halfway.

"Let me pass!" I heard a demanding voice. Just in case, I pulled my hood tighter over my head and hunched in an attempt to appear smaller and less conspicuous. The imperial adviser suddenly burst onto the bridge deck. "Everyone out! I must enter the vault immediately! This is an emergency!"

"Step aside!" cried the guards, rushing to clear the way.

The line parted, but suddenly the third adviser stopped and tilted his head to the side, as if listening to something. I glanced around uneasily. The crew members and guards froze for a second with him. My time had run out and Grandar had turned me in! No doubt there was an alert active on the internal communication system.

With lightning speed, I sidled up to the adviser. Puzzled, he looked up from Grander's patch to my face. His blue Precian face gaped in amazement. It looked like he refused to believe what he was seeing. I reached into my inventory and pulled out a Zatrathi grenade, one of my prizes from their base. Its explosion could break the binding to the planetary spirit and send any NPC to permanent oblivion. A player would simply respawn at the nearest respawn point. This last bit would be very inconvenient for me at the moment, but Grandar had left me no choice.

"Everyone step back or the adviser gets it!" Before the Precian could react, I quickly turned to him and explained: "This grenade annuls planetary spirit bindings. Don't bother using your personal shield, I'm much too close to you. If you turn it on, I will set off this grenade and that will be the end of you forever. Now order everyone to step back!"

"Do not shoot! Everyone step back!" The adviser had enough presence of mind to quickly grasp the situation and gesture to the guards rushing at us. "What do you want?"

"I want to get inside," I pointed to the vault. "We can talk inside."

Just in case — so that the Precians didn't get any ideas — I took out my blaster and shot both beam cannons to splinters. If anything, this'll make me feel calmer.

A CHECK FOR A BILLION

"Do not interfere!" the adviser barked with a sidelong glance at my grenade. Yes, he had definitely recognized it. His nervous sigh was further proof of this.

Your access to the Precian Empire has been adjusted.
You have limited access to the trade planet Belket in the Precian Empire. You may visit the planet once a week for a period of no more than five hours.

"The Precian Empire will not forgive you for this," the adviser added irritably as my rapport with him dropped to zero.

"Step inside. We can talk about forgiveness later." I gestured at the vault. After ordering the servants out, I shut the door and barricaded it with a massive table. "Your sidearm, adviser..."

The adviser reluctantly tossed me his blaster. Then he vacillated for a moment and added a second one.

"Now we can talk in peace. Tell me, adviser, why were you in such a hurry to reach the vault? It's not like you to be in a rush."

"A human named Nurse. I recalled where I had encountered that name. She was with you when you came to Zalva. It did not take me long to understand the obvious — she is a pirate just like you!" A knotty blue finger pointed in my direction. "What could a space pirate be up to on this ship? The only possible answer is to steal something. So I immediately rushed here, too late, alas!"

"I must praise your perceptiveness," I cast him a conciliatory smile. "Let's not beat around the bush. I propose we get to business right away. I need the Oblivion of Jarullah. I will get it anyway, with or without you. It will be easier with your help and there won't be any consequences for you. We have worked together a lot. I wouldn't want to spoil a nice memory."

"So this is all over the Oblivion?" The advisor craned his long neck in amazement. I nodded silently. "What do you know about the properties of this artifact?"

"Nothing, but it does not matter. Let's dispense with the small talk. Hand the item over to me and we can conclude this mutually unpleasant encounter."

"Let me remind you, Surgeon, that at the moment, you still have access to Hansa. It may only be once a week, but that's better than nothing." The adviser had turned into an ice sculpture, full of cold pride and frosty dignity. "If you plunder the emperor's gift, the Precian Empire will be closed to you completely!"

An unpleasant weight settled on my chest — the adviser had struck me where it hurt. The new orbship I had obtained at the Uldan base was good but not perfect. I had already upgraded its hull and navigation system, and even shared a few gadgets I'd found on the base with the Hansa engineers — so that they could consider how to give me the third list of upgrades in circumvention of the ban. Vargen explained that only a few guilds had such access, so it was worth gaining it at any cost. Yet the other side of the scale was weighed down by a check for a billion credits. Damn! Grandar stated unequivocally that he would not work with me without the emperor's gift.

"Adviser, let's be honest. I have been contracted to obtain the Oblivion of Jarullah by a third party. Maybe we can negotiate…"

"A third party?! The name!" the Precian cut me off. "I

demand you name the scoundrel!"

"The pirate code prohibits divulging the names of our clients," I began to argue.

"Do not treat me like an idiot, Surgeon. There is no pirate code! I want the name!" the adviser repeated with even greater irritation.

I vacillated a little more, making a show of it, and then said:

"Duke Narlin. He was the one who helped me get on board the cruiser."

"How and when could he do so if even I myself had no idea I would be traveling aboard this tub until the last possible moment?" the Precian asked incredulously.

"Well as you just pointed out, you didn't know. Others, especially others who happen to be tenth in line to the imperial throne were well aware. I imagine this whole thing was arranged a while ago."

I was going to insist on my side until the end. Since Narlin has been knocked out of the game for a long time, why not make him the scapegoat? The adviser's face turned into an impenetrable mask, and only his dilated pupils suggested any doubt or shock. This was natural enough — the duke was almost the last person you could suspect of being a traitor.

I frantically ruminated what to say if the adviser doubted my words and began arguing that Narlin had no motive — and why would he need a gift from the emperor anyway? But to my surprise, the adviser did not ask these questions at all.

"Arrest Duke Narlin!" said the Precian loudly enough for the guards on the other side of the door to hear him. I hadn't considered

---

the possibility that we could be heard. I frantically replayed the conversation in my head and sighed with relief — I don't believe I'd said anything important. After a couple of moments, the answer came through the speakerphone.

"Adviser, Duke Narlin is not on board the ship. Our systems find no trace of him. We have discovered two corpses in the duke's chambers. Guard Val, from the fifth battalion, and a servant of Sir Grandar."

I couldn't help but start fretting again. The fact that the locals could see the disappeared bodies of the NPCs we'd killed was unpleasant news. There had been no mention of it in the game guides.

"Have you examined the surveillance camera footage?"

"The cameras have been disabled. We are currently working on identifying the reason."

I could not hold back a sigh of relief — Brainiac had cleaned up our traces in the system.

"Where is the duke?" The adviser forgot all about the grenade in my hands and loomed over me as if he was about to thrash the truth out of me. Having put together two and two, I guess he decided that I had some more information.

"Adviser, I don't know anything more than you do. I am a pirate — and one who has his pride by the way. I am not a personal secretary," I replied defiantly.

"How did Grandar's servant end up in Narlin's cabin?" the adviser continued to pry. We had somehow reversed roles. In theory, I was supposed to be the one pressing him, demanding a code to the storage box that held the Oblivion. Nevertheless, I replied:

"Your question is misdirected. I can only say what I saw. Narlin was threatening Grandar until Grandar agreed to his demands. Everything else does not concern me."

"Who killed the servant?"

"I did. Narlin ordered me to do it. He wanted me to take his clothes and medallion."

"It's not adding up, Surgeon. You are a pirate, and yet you've just betrayed your client quite easily. Doesn't this dishonor you? What if I publish this conversation with you?" The Precian changed topics abruptly and began to threaten me again. I was ready for this:

"My ability to access Hansa is at stake. I do not want to lose it, so I made a deal with you voluntarily. I hope you will meet me halfway. Without threatening my reputation. Narlin said he was going to leave the ship. Do not ask me how, I do not know."

"Adviser, we have detected an unauthorized launch. A scout! There is a Precian on board. We could not identify him, our monitoring system is malfunctioning."

I grew worried again. Either there is another team working aboard the cruiser or Eunice is improvising. Damn! I can't even call her to clarify. I can't put on my armor suit — I'm not the only one with EM grenades. Hell, I can't even unclench my hand without this grenade going off.

"Don't let him escape!" the adviser ordered in a steely voice. "Stop the scout! If it refuses to obey — attack it!"

"The ship is heading for the asteroid belt!" Everyone seemed to forget all about me and turned their attention to their own affairs. "Contact in ten seconds!"

"I am granting you authorization to destroy the scout! The fugitive must not escape alive!"

"Narlin has a binding," I reminded just in case. "In a minute he will be reborn on his own planet, and you won't be able to prove anything. He will deny everything, claiming that he was framed, and that he was never even aboard this cruiser."

"You will help bring him to justice!"

"Me?!" My astonishment knew no bounds. "Have you forgotten who I am? A pirate, an outlaw who has no place in the Precian Empire. Stop constantly threatening me! What is my word worth against the word of a duke? No, adviser. I would rather give up on this job and return the money I've been paid than get involved in your court intrigues."

"And if you succeed in obtaining the Oblivion of Jarullah?" The adviser looked at me pensively. "Where and when are you supposed to hand it over to your client?"

"I am to be contacted," I replied, indicating with my tone of voice that I did not intend to delve into this topic. "I have no further information."

"Narlin has been playing with fire for a long time now." It seemed that the adviser was talking to himself. I think that my story about the duke's betrayal had found fertile ground in the mind of the Precian patriot. "He and Oleander both sought the removal of our ruler but we did not have evidence against the emperor's nephew. And now this…Such an opportunity…Surgeon, you simply must help us!"

"Why is that? You've just cut off my access to the Hansa

A CHECK FOR A BILLION

Corp and threatened my reputation," I recalled. "I don't owe anything to anyone at the moment. Except for Narlin, but I will return the money to him."

"No!" the adviser began fretting. "There is no need to return anything to anyone! You will receive the Oblivion of Jarullah, but you will have to hand it over to Narlin in person. Only to him — no servants. Haggle, argue, threaten, do what you must, but insist on a personal meeting! Then we'll grab him and tighten the thumbscrews."

'A personal meeting' means that the adviser will either keep a close eye on me, or there is a beacon in the Oblivion that will track my movements. Either way, carrying this item around should be hazardous to my health.

"What do I get in return?" I asked in turn. "I'm not big on charity."

"We will graciously restore your right to visit Hansa once a day," the adviser replied.

"You give me a guarantee that nothing will hurt my reputation, grant me access to the third tier upgrades list and give me another five percent discount on Hansa products," I immediately countered. "Otherwise, I wash my hands of this whole thing here and now."

"I will need to discuss this with the emperor." The adviser cast a sidelong glance at the grenade in my hand. "And for that, I will need my armor suit."

"No discussions, adviser. Either you make a decision here and now or no deal. I know that you have all the authorization you need. The emperor trusts you like he trusts himself!"

The adviser looked at me angrily but no sooner did he calm himself and make his decision, than we received the next bit of news.

"There is trouble! Adviser, sir! Sir Oleander has vanished!"

"What do you mean, vanished? Where did he vanish to? Why have I not been notified?" This new blow was too great for the adviser and he simply collapsed into the nearest chair.

"The guards have been killed, the brig is empty. The recordings from the surveillance cameras are corrupted."

The adviser's helplessness lasted only a few seconds. Composing himself, he began to issue orders:

"Locate the human named Nurse. She should be somewhere on the cruiser. Organize a control center. I want reports every five minutes. Turn the ship upside down!"

"Hold it!" I slowly uncurled one finger, indicating that I was about to blow us all up. What is Eunice doing? What does she want with this Precian? "Adviser, we weren't done talking!"

"We are done talking, Pirate Surgeon. On behalf of the Precian Empire I hereby contract you to perform a secret mission. Did I miss any of your terms?"

New mission available: Double Agent.

Description: Give the Oblivion of Jarullah to your client and notify the third adviser of the Precian Empire. Rewards for completion: daily access to Belket; access to the third list of Hansa updates; -15% on Hansa equipment. Penalty for failure: Access to Belket will be revoked forever. Deadline: 7 days. Do you wish to accept this mission?

A CHECK FOR A BILLION

"It's all there. I accept." I glanced over at the grenade in my hand, while the Precian shook his head disapprovingly.

"You will be allowed to leave the cruiser unhindered. You can put your grenade away. I never believed you would use it. The Pirate Surgeon that I know is made from a different type of stuff. I am sorry that you betrayed the interests of the Precian Empire for a passing fancy. You didn't end up helping the Delvians and you set yourself up too. We know that you managed to steal the crystal and the pedestal. We will not continue to work with such an unreliable partner."

The adviser stepped over to one of the strongboxes in the vault and took out a jewelry box. An ordinary, plain, wooden, entirely unremarkable jewelry box. My engineer could make a hundred of these in minutes.

"I want to know everything you know about Nurse." The adviser handed me the box, but did not let go.

"I have little information. We met on a training planet, traveled together to meet the emperor, then I fell ill, and when I woke up, she was already gone. Where she went is not a question I can answer."

"Adviser, there is no trace of a human named Nurse on board." A note of bewilderment sounded in the reporting voice. "We studied all the cameras and searched most of the premises. The human you ordered us to find is not on this vessel."

"This is some kind of nonsense!" The Precian exclaimed, outraged. "What's going on here? Why do people keep disappearing from this ship? This is a disgrace! Is this a spaceship or a black hole?! How could two Precians and a human simply vanish?!"

We emerged from the vault to these outraged cries and immediately ran into a very worried-looking captain.

"I could not...I could not know..." said the unfortunate captain, stuttering. Sweat flooded his face, and his triple chin trembled with fear. Three disappearances and two infiltrations. Nothing of the sort had ever happened to him during his career and I didn't have to try very hard to imagine how he felt. No doubt he was already praying that this was all just a nightmare he'd wake up from any moment now.

"What I know is what will happen to you if you *don't* find them. Surgeon, why are you still here?! Get off my cruiser! I have enough problems here without you underfoot!"

"My ship. She needs to dock with the cruiser to pick me up."

"Did you hear that, Captain? Immediately issue docking access to Orbship *Warlock*. Surgeon is on urgent business. As for the rest of you, anyone want to explain to me what's going on here?!"

I tossed the jewelry box into my inventory, whipped out my marine armor and jumped into it, finally feeling like I was coming back home. This game is way more enjoyable when you have a reliable barrier of raq between you and the rest of the gameworld. Eunice's voice sounded in my headset.

"You're back online at last, Lex. I'm outside on the cruiser's hull, will you pick me up?"

'Why even bother making a plan if no one ever sticks to it?' I asked myself a purely rhetorical question.

CHAPTER THREE

SHORT WHILE LATER, I found myself standing in the main hangar of the Precian cruiser, impatiently barking orders at my various subordinates.

"Brainiac, give me a sitrep. Have you received permission to dock?"

"Yes, Cap'n. Everything is in order, I can head your way."

"Wonderful! First pick up Eunice and the Precians with her. Set your flight approach near our breaching point. Fly as close as you can without raising any suspicions. Is that clear?"

"Crystal clear, Captain. I'm on it!"

"Eunice, are you in position?"

"Well, yeah, I've been here a while now."

"You will only have one chance so make sure to coordinate with Brainiac. You can't miss your jump! Jump directly at *Warlock* — the engineer will catch you."

"Should I jump alone or with the rest? There are three others here with me."

"Everyone jumps, obviously. Fasten them to yourself with something or have everyone hold each other's ears or something. Remember, you cannot fire your thruster, otherwise they will notice you. Brainiac won't be able to brake very well. Anyway, I'm counting on you! After that come pick me up and we can go home."

Out of the corner of my eye, I noticed some movement at the far end of the corridor and turned my head. The cruiser's crew suddenly began scurrying about in a panic. It was like the emperor himself had appeared for a surprise inspection. The soldiers clambered into their armor suits, while the captain came on over the intercom and began ordering all the passengers back to their cabins. I looked out of the nearest porthole and saw a squadron scramble from the cruiser and take up a defensive formation. I had a bad feeling about this.

"Brainiac, what do you see?"

"What do you mean?" the ship's computer asked puzzled and then went quiet for a second. "Trouble, Captain! Three cruisers and thirty destroyers have entered the system! Pirates!"

"Brainiac, get us out of here!" I ordered immediately, trying to think of a reason for why pirates would suddenly ambush a cruise ship deep in Precian space. "Can you break through?"

"Three cruisers? Hmm..." came the computer's underwhelming response. "It will take some work. Of course I could risk it but..."

I see. Despite the upgrades, the orbship still remained an ordinary scout. According to the current vessel food chain, this placed *Warlock* a little above a frigate, yet well below a destroyer. And here I was calling for a standoff with three cruisers at once?

A CHECK FOR A BILLION

No thanks. We could flirt with one, assuming I was on board. But at the moment Brainiac had calculated everything correctly — taking a risk like this without the captain on board wasn't worth it.

"Okay, maintain your position. Eunice, you will have to sit tight and enjoy the view."

"What view?" my wife countered. "The one of the container, the hole in the hull and the two armor suits? Their armor never vanished."

"Use your imagination, my love. I'll be back in a bit — I need to deal with the locals here," I reassured her. "I'll go find out why the hell the pirates have decided to attack this cruiser."

"Keep me posted," was all I heard in response.

It was as if the ship had been abandoned. The passengers had been escorted to their cabins, and the crew members were all either at their battle stations or out in space. Everyone was busy, so I reached the captain's deck without incident.

"Stranger on the bridge!" As soon as I entered, I heard a warning cry.

"Arrest him and take him to the brig. He is a pirate spy!" the captain instantly shot back. The fat Precian had really lost his marbles. A security guard popped up out of nowhere and pointed his blaster at me. Yet still faster responded a small utility droid: The barely noticeable critter zipped out of the wall and without any further ado stuck two electrodes right into my foot. I felt a short sharp shock and then went tumbling out of my armor suit, which collapsed next to me in a shapeless heap.

"In the name of the Precian Empire you are hereby placed under arrest!" said the guard. I didn't have time for him though. I darted back over to my armor suit and quickly placed it into my virtual inventory. Was I about to give up a legendary item? Never! Then again, this little maneuver ended with a change of poles for me — that is, I went tumbling upside down. The guard's blaster had a built in manipulator, which, fortunately, he used a second too late to stop me from saving my armor.

"To the brig with him!" The captain repeated his order and turned back to the bridge's giant projection screens. One quick glance at them was enough to see that the cruise's situation was a bleak one indeed. The entire screen had filled with a swarm of red dots denoting Precian destroyers and fighters. Red meant that they had been destroyed. I didn't get a further look. The door to the bridge returned to its place, and I was dragged along a narrow side corridor. There was no thought of resisting. I just tried to shield myself from taking any painful blows against the walls. Life without an armor suit was sad and painful.

"Eunice?" I called my wife. It came out a bit piteously, because at that moment I was carelessly slammed against a comms box.

"What?" My wife replied instantly. I cursed mentally. I need to let her know that I've been detained in some gentle manner. She shouldn't get agitated after all!

"How are you doing?"

"Fine. Just sitting here," replied Eunice a bit puzzled and fell silent in expectation.

"Then I will keep you company."

"Where?"

"In the brig…"

A CHECK FOR A BILLION

"Where?!" came an indignant cry, but I did not have time to answer. The guard dragging me had reached the brig. He tossed me inside and locked the door. A squealing erupted in my ears and the earpiece grew incredibly hot. Swearing, I pulled out the overheated comm unit and threw it away. It instantly smoked and melted with a quiet hiss, leaving behind a barely noticeable stain on the floor. I guess electronics don't work inside the brig. A sad discovery, but if things get really bad I can always fall back on Lumara's present. Figuring that I would be able to use the gadget only once in the cell, I decided to save it for an emergency. And this wasn't yet an emergency. The important thing was that I'd gotten a warning off to Eunice.

A few minutes of compulsory idleness went by and then the ship shook noticeably, at which point the lights in the brig went out. Hoping that maybe the signal jammer had gone out with the lights, I tried to use another standard comm. Nothing doing. The device met the same fate as its fellow, melting on the floor. I groped in the darkness until I reached the iron bed and lay down. If you have no control over the situation, the best thing to do is relax and wait.

From the other side of the door came the sounds of quick footsteps, curses, and shouting. Without Brainiac's live interpretation, I had no idea what was going on. Suddenly, a siren howled. I was surprised that there was even such an alarm on board such a luxury cruiser. A captain in charge of such important passengers should be afraid of even breathing loudly, much less sounding an alarm. The screeching howl lasted only a couple of minutes, after which it broke off just as abruptly as it began. The silence that ensued was even scarier however. I sat up in my bed

---

and listened intently — no running, no screaming. Suddenly, the front door swung open, and two locals appeared in the doorway. The pauldrons of their armor suits had human skulls painted on them in neon paint. Well, at last we meet. These were the official and scariest pirates of Galactogon — the Brotherhood of the Jolly Roger, headed by the legendary Corsican himself.

"Welly, welly, welly, well…what have we here then?" lisped one of the newcomers. "A scallywag in Precian captivity? And this small fry calls himself a pirate? Ugh. What a repellant sight."

"Well then stop gawking and take him to the captain!" replied the second pirate. "He will figure it out! Let's go, darling! You're free!"

A pair of familiar manipulators appeared in their hands, and I was dragged out and made to count the corners again. The pirates proved to be some pranksters. They were too bored to keep me in front of them so they bounced me down the corridor in a zigzag fashion, passing me from one manipulator to the other like a Ping-Pong ball. They weren't very good and so sometimes one'd miss and I'd go flying past the catcher's beam into the wall with a loud thunk. Stars danced around my head and the system kept announcing new debuffs. This bit of exercise had a beneficial effect on my brain and as a result, I understood two things. First, the Corsican will not talk to me as he would have no need of a weak pirate. Second, I absolutely cannot tolerate this kind of treatment. As the pirates were talking to each other, arguing over how long I would last as a Ping-Pong ball, two small grenades appeared in my hands. The locals kept me at a distance from themselves, but not far enough. Three meters was all that separated us, so I pulled the pins and tossed the EM grenades. The pirates turned into iron idols, immured in their legendary armor suits, like in coffins. I got to my feet, calmed myself down and pulled my blaster out of my inventory.

"I hope you boys are on good terms with your planetary spirit," I muttered and fired a shot into each one's head. Two shimmering crates fell to the floor, but I was much more interested in the notification that accompanied this:

Your rapport with the Corsican has grown. Current Rapport: 2.

One point of Rapport for each dead pirate? Why this changes matters! A blood-thirsty smirk spread across my face as I activated my comm.

"Brainiac, are you here?"

"The cruiser has been captured. The pirates destroyed all the Precian destroyers," reported my ship computer. "You'll have to sort it out without me Cap'n! I'll wait for you here."

"Don't panic. Are you in the system?"

"Yes, but they haven't found us yet."

"How many 'guests' are there on board the cruiser and where can I find them?" I asked the most pressing question. Much depended on it. If the cruiser's surveillance system couldn't track the pirates, I'd be helpless.

"There are forty-three…no, forty-one pirates on board. Two have vanished somewhere."

"Not somewhere, but to the digital underworld," I grunted, delighted with the news. "Mark all the pirates' locations on my HUD and make sure to keep me updated about their movements. By the way, what are they doing here?"

"Judging by the comm chatter, they are looking for someone named Oleander."

"They can't have him!" barked Eunice. "He is my trophy. I dragged him here all by myself!"

"And right you did. Brainiac, has the hull taken any critical damage?"

"Yes, the cruiser has lost its integrity in several places. All the damaged compartments have been sealed."

"Seal any compartments that lead to Nurse and set their status as 'depressurized.' We don't need any uninvited guests."

"Done. Oh…"

Brainiac disconnected. A second passed, then another second and a third — and still there was nothing from my ship.

"What happened?" I called on my PDA.

"They found us," came Brainiac's displeased reply. "The locked on and jammed my comms. You're on your own, Captain. I'll wait for further orders but if you die…We will head back to Blood Island."

After calling Eunice to apprise her of the situation, I pulled out my armor suit. Deprived of elo, it resembled the fossil of an ancient monster that had mysteriously appeared on a space ship. The EM shock blew its powercells beyond recovery, so I simply dumped them where I stood. The replacement powercells snapped into place and the armor suit came to life, winking at me with its initialization sequence. Its servos whirred, recovering stability and with it its upright position. My other body had assumed its customary place and was ready for use again. I'll have to prod Hansa to fix this emergency ejection mechanism. Surely they have something that will solve the problem.

I turned my attention to the pirates' locations in my HUD. About twenty of them were located not far from me, on the captain's bridge. It occurred to me that perhaps I can encounter the Corsican himself there. After all, who knows? Just in case, I decided to head there last. There were four more enemies on the deck below me. They're the ones I should start with. But before that, let's check this loot.

Killing pirates from the Brotherhood of the Jolly Roger turned out to be a profitable business. Not only did I find a legendary blaster in each box, but they came with a full set of equipment, that included everything from comfortable shoes for sneaking to a tactical vest and helmet made of raq. A perfect outfit for an operation that required not only armor, but also agility and stealth. And yet, surprisingly, this was not the main piece of loot. Both pirates also dropped a small black metal token with the emblem of the Jolly Roger. Proof that I had destroyed the enemies of all empires.

I immediately put on the new equipment, saving the second set for Eunice. An armor suit doesn't solve all your problems and it's nice to have a backup option.

The elevator did not work, so I moved toward the stairs. Since I had plenty of elo, I decided to fly instead of clanking about. Here they are, the advantages of ground marine armor over space armor. There is no room inside the ships for air maneuvers, and as a result many players and NPCs prefer to dispense with thrusters and equip their suits with some other, more necessary device. The snake had complained several times that she had no space to install the newer systems she had developed, but I remained implacable. The thrusters were my main 'competitive' advantage — no one would hear the stomping of my huge marine armor if it just flew. The pirates didn't hear me either.

I flew up to the second deck fully armed. The blasters on my shoulders were locked and ready, the EM gun in my right hand was aimed and ready to disable any resistance, and in my left hand, just in case, I carried a grenade. Who knows, after all? Finding some cover behind a bulkhead, I paused to assess the situation.

The pirates of the Jolly Roger worked cohesively, clearly understanding each of their tasks. Two of them were going from cabin to the cabin, flushing the Precians out into the corridor where they'd be searched and robbed. Another pair was busy identifying high-born hostages and corralling them for transportation to the pirates' ship. They didn't stand on ceremony with anyone — at gunpoint, the hostages were collared and chained to the collar of the next hostage in line. The hostages were forced to lean the back of their heads against each other, but prudently kept quiet, fearing for their lives.

I waited for the first pair to enter the next cabin. Then I aimed and fired. And aimed again and fired. Two more pirates turned into loot crates. Nobody expected me and their carelessness came at an immediate price.

"What's going on out there? Is someone resisting?" Hearing the shots from my blaster, a third pirate popped his head out of the cabin.

A CHECK FOR A BILLION

I aimed and the total was now five pirates.

Your rapport with the Corsican has grown. Current Rapport: 5.

From here on, hiding didn't make much sense. I flew out of cover and approached the hostages. My appearance was like a trigger. Panic swept across the Precians. Not knowing what to expect from this new menace, they rushed in the opposite direction from me. The danger now was that someone would stumble and fall. Then the collars would work like nooses and strangle the lot of them.

"Freeze right there!" I hollered at the Precian nobility and fired at the floor. The Precians calmed down and froze. Several Precians fainted from fright, but their neighbors instantly grabbed them, keeping them from falling and pulling the rest down.

This gave me a chance to take a breath and turn my attention to the open cabin door. The fourth pirate did not hurry to emerge. Most likely, he was smarter than his partner and realizing that something was amiss, had taken up a defensive position. On top of this, he'd probably also warned the others that things had gone bad, so I'd better get out of here quickly.

Three more sets of clothes, blasters and Jolly Roger tokens went into my inventory, and I began to slowly move to the other side of the open door.

Reaching the stairs, I flew back up to the first deck. I did not manage to reach it unhindered. As soon as I flew up to the landing in front of the door, the door opened revealing three pirates

---

rushing to reinforce their dead mates. I didn't even have to aim — a point-blank shot from my EM gun cut short the brave warriors and they noisily collapsed into a heap. No defense could save them — they were too close and too unprepared. The blaster cannons on my shoulders came alive and my rapport with the Corsican grew by another three points.

Somewhere above, I heard heavy stomping. I grinned as I left the landing. Let them look. Some time should pass before they figure out what's going on. The door closed silently and I flew farther along the ship. The pirates had finished their work in this part of the cruiser — all the cabins had been turned inside out and anything of value had been plundered.

It was unfortunate, but there was no loot left to be had on the first deck. All the nobles lived on the third deck, and here, if there were items of artistic value, then the pirates either took them away or destroyed them. Several paintings had been mercilessly charred by blaster fire. Judging by their remains, the Brotherhood did not have a liking for postmodern art.

The elevator still did not work, yet I didn't want to go back to the stairs either. Opening the elevator's doors, I jumped into the shaft and descended down to the engineering deck. Before he'd been forced offline, Brainiac had identified a dozen targets down there, which would be invaluable to increasing my rapport with the big boss. I didn't manage to exit the shaft silently and soon heard quick steps approaching. There was nowhere to hide in the empty compartment, so I flew up to the ceiling, settling like a spider among the lattice of pipes and conduits.

Six pirates appeared from around the corner. Five of them

rushed to the elevator, while one remained as a sentry. It was immediately obvious that he was their commander. The soldiers opened the doors and carefully illuminated the shaft.

"What's happened?" asked the one left behind. Now I was sure that he was the squad leader.

"It's empty!"

"Search the premises! Arcana reported that he descended to this deck! Find him! There will be a five percent loot bonus to the one who brings me this freak!"

Inspired by the bounty, one of the pirates climbed into the shaft in the hope of finding the sinister foe. I had no doubts about whom they were looking for. If Brainiac could hack the cruiser's mainframe and force it to display the locations of everyone onboard, then the pirates could do the same. I just hoped there weren't any cameras on the engineering deck. Otherwise, all my careful sneaking would go to hell.

Three EM grenades clicked quietly in my hands. One went flying at the commander, the other two at the group crowded around the shaft.

The explosions came almost simultaneously. Deactivating the magnets holding me to the ceiling, I glided and aimed my blasters at the pirate caught between the elevator doors. The EM blast had caught him partially, immobilizing the upper part of his armor suit. I killed him first so that he couldn't report back to the bridge.

Your rapport with the Corsican has grown. Current Rapport: 14.

The corsairs hadn't dropped anything interesting or unique, yet the commander made up for it. In addition to the usual set of equipment and blaster, he also had seven torpedo detonators. I have no idea why he brought them to the ship, but the sabotage plan lent itself of its own accord. Among all the other systems housed on the engineering deck, there was the torpedo assembly system. I doubt the Precians allowed the pirates to board without a fight, so surely the cruiser had fired several torpedoes at the enemy.

And I was not mistaken — ten deadly missiles lay right there on the floor. The Precians had not had time to deliver them to the conveyor that led to the launch tubes. The corsairs' appearance had put an end to the operation.

I inserted the seven detonators and the torpedoes entered their setup mode. With Brainiac's guidance, telling where to find the buttons I needed to push, I set the timers to twenty minutes, after which I dragged my makeshift bombs to various parts of the engineering deck to maximize their destructive potential. After a little thought, I also smashed the deck's comm unit. Now no one would be able to reprogram the torpedoes. However, just as I was putting the last torpedo in its place, I heard an unexpected invitation over the speakerphone:

"Surgeon, this is the Corsican! I am waiting for you on the bridge. You have five minutes, the clock is ticking."

The voice coming over the speaker was so unpleasant and strange that my face contorted. I had imagined the Corsican as brutal and fearless, his voice full of imperiousness — not at all the voice I had just heard.

A CHECK FOR A BILLION

"Don't go Lex. It's a trap!" Eunice instantly warned me. The pirates hadn't found her yet, which was definitely good news.

"I know, I know," I replied. "But this is one of those invitations you can't ignore."

Figuring that my fourteen points of rapport was enough to ensure that they wouldn't try to kill me immediately, I cautiously moved towards the elevator. The chance to see this legendary NPC in the flesh was just too tantalizing to pass up. There were no new pirates to deal with. It was as if the Corsican had ordered them to stand down. Reaching the elevator shaft, I flew up to the third deck and jerked the doors apart. Again, I encountered no resistance or aggression — the corridor welcomed me with a hospitable emptiness.

A few meters from the bridge, I climbed out of my armor suit and replaced it in my inventory. I didn't want to deal with any unnecessary surprises. Adjusting the trophy body armor and checking its level of elo just in case, I walked resolutely to the captain's deck. Then again, when the doors parted, the dozen blaster barrels pointed at my person did shake my resolution. An electromagnetic pulse passed through my body, frying yet another comm unit and turning my advanced armor vest into an ordinary plate of raq.

"A prudent decision," snarled a Pyrrhenian, emerging from the bridge. He was a mirror image of Hilvar, minus a few pounds. The flying barrel circled around me, scanning me with some sort of device. "He's clean! There's no trace of Oleander on him."

I stepped onto the bridge. Both the adviser and Grandar were already here, sitting on the floor, each inside his respective

---

force dome. Not a bad decision when you have an endless supply of elo on hand. They were the only Precians here, however.

"What do you think you're doing on my cruiser, henchling of the Traitor?"

The captain's chair spun around its axis, revealing the great Corsican. My heart, which had been beating faster and faster from the anticipation, stopped like a jammed motor. The pirate leader looked exactly as his voice had suggested — my earlier impression had been an accurate one. I was off only in the dimension of appearance. The pirate leader was so disfigured that he looked more like he had stepped out of a children's horror story than a pirate legend.

The first thing that caught my eye were the stumps he had instead of legs. The Delvian had not bothered attaching prostheses, preferring to flaunt the consequences of his dangerous profession. The second thing that caught my eye was his lower jaw or rather its absence. The pirate leader did not mind at all that his long red tongue was just hanging down out of his throat, endowing his overall physiognomy with an unforgettable expression. It was immediately clear that, given these disabilities, the Delvian could not possibly speak, and thus the third thing that caught my eye was the speaker on his chest with a cable that looped up and straight into the Corsican's cortex — voicing his very thoughts. Yet all these striking details were forgotten as soon as I encountered the eyes of the mighty pirate. They were absolutely black and piercing, as if they could scan your mind for thoughts you didn't even know you had. The cumulative effect of the Corsican's appearance suggested that this was a character you dealt with as quickly as possible and through a dozen intermediaries, if possible.

"I was working on this little heist I'd been contracted to do," having finished my inspection, I answered the question.

"You were discovered in the brig. Explain yourself." It was clear that the Corsican had no problems whatsoever using his terrible appearance to gain an advantage in conversation. I'd bet that he could even get answers from a deaf-mute.

"I completed my job and was about to get out of here when you appeared and ruined all my plans. The fat Precian who claims to be the captain around here, decided that I was one of your spies and threw me into the brig. I imagine you know everything that followed. It's true I caused a slight ruckus and sent a couple of your boys to meet their planetary spirit, but they themselves are to blame! When you summoned me, I came."

"Very well," the Corsican accepted my explanation without a trace of emotion. "What about that thing? What is it? Give it here."

"This is a present from the emperor to that Precian there." I nodded in the direction of the adviser. "I can't hand it over. It's the reason I came here."

"Sure you can," replied the Corsican with something like a chuckle crossed with a sneer. "I'll give you five seconds."

Everyone around us pointed their blasters at me yet again.

"Sure I can, sure I can!" I backpedalled. "Here it is!"

I took the jewelry box out of my inventory and held it up for everyone to see. Falling to one knee and raising the emperor's gift over my head, I solemnly proclaimed:

"Allow me to present you with this humble gift, oh head of the Jolly Roger!"

GALACTOGON BOOK THREE

Your rapport with the Corsican has decreased. Current Rapport: 0.

Why look at that! The pirate likes it when I kill his warriors, but he doesn't abide toadies… I'll take it into account for next time. The Delvian wagged his tongue in a peculiar gesture of disapproval but said:

"Let him pass!"

I slowly stood up and carefully approached the Corsican, trying not to provoke anyone. He stretched out his fingerless hand. Bowing one more time, not quite so reverently this time, I pulled off a trick available only to players and their virtual inventory. The object in my hand abruptly changed to another, and I stuck it into the Corsican's hand, pressing his other hand on top of it. Before anyone could realize what was happening, I whispered with unvarnished anger:

"This is one of those Zatrathi grenades that disrupts your planetary binding. You know what this means!"

I'd wager that the Jolly Roger had captured their share of Zatrathi weapons and had encountered one of these grenades before. There's no way they were that rare. Accordingly the Corsican should be familiar with its operation. The Delvian's reply confirmed my hunch. He yelped sharply and started, but kept his eyes locked on mine.

"Don't shoot! What do you want?"

"I want to get out of here. I want to get out of here in one piece, without any further hassle and with my rightful loot in my possession."

A CHECK FOR A BILLION

Your rapport with the Corsican has grown. Current Rapport: 100.

The Delvian's upper lip twitched. I guess this was like him smiling or something.

"Very well. I like daring people. You will be granted safe passage. Hell, we'll even escort you. You don't have to fear anything, Surgeon — but we will still meet. I promise." The pirate leader cackled for emphasis.

"We most definitely will meet again," I nodded, not taking my eyes off his. "I have big plans for the Jolly Roger."

To my bewilderment, now all the pirates around us exploded in raucous laughter.

"You have a minor problem with the company you've chosen to keep, pirate! The Jolly Roger is no place for Hilvar's henchlings. Let Surgeon pass! I permit him to leave the ship!"

"Twenty million for the adviser," I nodded at the Precian in his bubble. "I want to get some bonuses from him."

"Do not try my patience." The Corsican stopped laughing abruptly. "You have ten minutes to vacate my cruiser!"

I did not bother hanging around any longer. Cautiously turning away from the head of the pirates, I expected to be shot in the back at any moment. His word was good, however. No one dared lay a finger on me, though as I was leaving, one of the pirates approached me and announced that I could use the second hangar. As soon as the doors to the bridge slid shut behind me, I broke into a run and clenched my trembling hands into tight fists. I did not really believe that I could pull off this ruse until the very last moment.

"Brainiac pick me up in the manner we discussed." I was being escorted by two pirates, so I didn't openly tell the ship that we had to pick up Eunice & co. from the hull. I hope Brainiac's AI can decipher insinuation. Five minutes later, my orbship was hovering a couple of meters from the cruise cruiser and, receiving permission, I left the hijacked ship. Eunice was already aboard *Warlock*.

"Let's get out of here! Step on it! Step on it, I said! The twenty minutes have almost expired! Set course for Qirlats."

"This is not possible," came the measured reply. "Our hyperdrive is currently being disrupted. Torpedoes inbound. Missile approach velocity equivalent to seventy percent thurst."

The pirates were still pirates. The Corsican's word was trustworthy up until I got off his ship. No one had promised me anything after that.

"Throttle to 80% and let's scram!" I collapsed in my captain's chair, not taking my eyes off the timer. One minute. I need only a minute.

"Multiple bandits inbound! Fighters!"

"Shoot them down. Snake, send a couple torpedoes their way to distract them."

"Torpedoes away. Oh, there is even a hit! They missed one!"

The torpedo had slammed straight into the destroyer's bridge deck, decapitating it. This cost the pirates what little initiative they had, and I calmly flew past the damaged ship into open space.

"Thrust to 90%. We're outta here!"

A CHECK FOR A BILLION

The minute expired and somewhere behind us, far away, in the very depths of the Precian Empire, a little sun flashed into existence and was snuffed out by the vacuum. The torpedoes' detonation reached the backup reactor and triggered a chain reaction. The explosion vaporized the cruiser where she was. I did not see any of this, of course, but the results of my hard labors appeared as a notification before my eyes:

+10,000 Rapport with all empires.

The Precians, Qualians and Delvians wish to work with you.

Your rapport with the Corsican has grown. Current Rapport: 1000.

You have attracted the curiosity of the leader of the Jolly Roger. You may meet with him in three days. Access granted to the Silmar System.

CHAPTER FOUR

UNICE HAD DONE HER JOB 100%, EVEN 150%. Besides she and I, there were now three more creatures on *Warlock's* bridge deck: Duke Narlin, still in his container; Grandar's servant, terrified of having fallen into pirate captivity; and Oleander, the brother of the Precian Emperor himself. My lovely wife captured him solely due to her natural greed. Passing the cell that held the prisoner, Eunice decided it would be a waste to leave him to the Precians. She quickly dealt with the guards, sending them to respawn. His Excellency proved more finicky. Sir Oleander did not wish to leave his apartments voluntarily. Having resorted to tranquilizer darts, Eunice shoved him into an armor suit and dragged him to her extraction point. She planted Grandar's other servant on the shuttle that the adviser saw fleeing the cruiser. May he rest in space…In the end, everything turned out for the best and maybe even a little bit better. At least that was how my wife saw it.

"And what are we going to do with him now?"

A CHECK FOR A BILLION

"What should anyone do with a lucrative investment?" Eunice shrugged.

"Lucrative?" I countered. "The Corsican raided pretty deep into Precian space to get this guy. We need to know why and how we can make a nice buck from this, before we start throwing words like 'lucrative' around."

Oleander silently regaled me with a look full of utmost contempt. Then again that was about what I expected from him. I'm a pirate and a human to boot, which, in aggregate, put me on par with a cockroach — in his kindest taxonomy of creatures. Would you like it if a cockroach rescued you from certain death? It was clear from the Precian's face that he would decline given the chance, and yet nor could he do anything about it.

"All that can be sold for profit must be sold for profit!" I said with exaggerated gusto and slapped Oleander on the shoulder. His face twisted further into a frown from such familiarity. "I don't have mutual contacts with the Corsican, but I know those who do. Don't despair, your Excellence! You shall soon be rid of our disagreeable company."

"Do as you wish. Your petty machinations do not concern me," the Precian spat and shrugged my hand off his shoulder. His ill humor amused me. I had achieved my goal — Oleander had deigned to open his mouth. A first step to a fruitful partnership, you could say.

The engineer popped up through a hole in the deck. I had ordered her to examine the jewelry case earlier. Oleander's façade of condescending revulsion cracked; fear stiffened his noble features. Over his shoulder, Grandar's servant outright fainted from terror. Well sure, it's not every day you encounter a giant, talking, three-eyed snake with a pair of arms. Tactfully, the snake preferred to ignore our prisoners' reactions.

"You know, Cap'n, I can definitely say that you need to get rid of this item. And the sooner the better. It contains three beacons and you can't jam any of them. All we can do is destroy them, along with the case. Right this instant."

To illustrate her point, the engineer brandished a large hammer.

"Hang on, hang on…" I grabbed the jewelry case from her. "We'll always have time for that. Have you figured out what's inside?"

"No," said the snake. "I didn't want to break it, and I haven't had time to generate the code. If it's urgent, I can use some ancient techniques I've picked up over the years — a hammer and a chisel."

"Bring them and let's try it," I agreed, but before the engineer could disappear, Oleander deigned to open his mouth again.

"Do not try to force the emperor's gift. It contains an automatic self-destruct mechanism. The contents is very important for the third adviser. My brother is very diligent about his choice of gifts and does not make them lightly."

Without further ado, I held out the case to Oleander.

"Open it. I want to know what's inside."

"I will not do this," snapped the noble and folded his arms across his chest. "And yes: I know how to open the case — but I shall not, human scum."

"As you wish," I did not insist. "My client can figure out

what's what on his own. I'm just the help."

"Then you are acting on another's orders?" Oleander's face became even more contemptuous. When it seemed like things couldn't be worse, my admission knocked the bottom out from under him.

"Not exactly. Some things I did based on personal initiative, others I was paid for. I abducted Duke Narlin myself." I proudly nodded at the container.

Only now did Oleander notice it. He jumped up abruptly and flung off the lid. Having examined the container's contents, the Precian turned back to face me and now his contempt had given way to anger.

"What have you done to my son?! Remove him right this instant!"

My astonishment caused an Indian raga to play in my head and my jaw dropped of its own accord. This was a turn worthy of a Bollywood script!

"I ask you again: What have you done with my son and why is he still in this…this box?!"

A true grandee stood before us, looming over us with his aura of authority. His eyes turned bloodshot, his nostrils flared, even his skin grew darker, darkening from blue to a nocturnal black. I'm sure it was a terrible sight, though I wasn't impressed. I had seen my fill of these types in my day. Now, I didn't even bother raising my voice:

"Shut your gob and take your seat, your…blueness. Otherwise, I'll stuff you in there with Narlin and jettison the lot of you into space like a family crypt! I'll count to three!" I

---

demonstratively placed my hand on a manipulator.

"What do you want, pirate?" At last it began to dawn on Oleander who was really in charge around here. He stepped back and sat down in his chair. "Is it money? Planets? Concubines?"

"Oh! I want concubines, please," Eunice jumped in.

"None of the above, your lordship. First of all, I want to know why the Corsican was looking for you. Second, I want to know what's in the case. I would also like a nice ransom for you and passage to Zalva. Something like that."

"Caaaap'n," said he snake, extending her head into the bridge. "You can deal with the Precians later. Look here."

The engineer brought up a projection of the sector we were in. Everything seemed clear and calm, but then Brainiac zoomed in and outlined one of the nearest stars. I was about to ask what I was supposed to be looking at, but stopped, my mouth half-open. The point of light grew in size until it dawned on me that this wasn't a sun at all, but a huge spaceship in the shape of a perfect sphere. Almost like an orbship but much larger.

"This is a battlesphere," Brainiac explained, as if reading my thoughts. "The main combat vessel for a single Uldan. According to the current classification, it is comparable to a destroyer, but it may be piloted by a single Uldan with a full crew of ten."

"Have you tried hailing it?"

"You bet! I've used all the frequencies available to me. There is no reply. It is maintaining position nearby and staying silent," the snake answered.

"Has it been there long?" It seemed that Brainiac wasn't

telling me everything.

"I noticed it right after I set you down on the asteroids. We were too busy to warn you though. It didn't seem like a threat, so I left it alone. Anyway, I took it for some kind of UFO initially."

"Turn around and head in its direction."

"We're already headed that way. Speed is at eighty. Although, the distance between us has not diminished. I do not think the battlesphere wants us to approach it."

"Change course then!" I ordered. "Ninety degrees to starboard!"

"Roger ninety degrees to starboard…The distance to the battlesphere has not changed. We seem to be moving in parallel."

"Brake then, Brainiac. Full stop!"

"Roger full stop! Captain…maybe we should jump into hyperspace while we can? I have a bad feeling about this."

The battlesphere also stopped and so synchronously that it could have been our shadow. I sat down in my chair with a bad sense of foreboding. This was the last thing I needed. Of course, I was pleased to encounter a living Uldan, but given our recent discovery about the Zatrathi and the Uldans, this was probably not a good thing. Who knows what this one wants from me?

"Brainiac, calculate a route to Qirlats. We'll go meet with Hilvar. We need to get rid of this dead weight."

"What should we do about the battlesphere?" Eunice asked, alarmed.

"Maintain distance. Damn…This is all so inconvenient…"

"I agree. We need to get to Zalva as quickly as possible!"

"You will not set foot on Zalva, human," said Oleander

unexpectedly, having correctly understood that by 'dead weight' I was referring to his lordship. He addressed me exclusively, refusing to acknowledge Eunice. "You have no invitation and therefore cannot enter the capital."

"I've already been promised safe conduct to Zalva, so the issue is resolved."

"Safe conduct?" The Precian grimaced. "You are truly a human if you believe that! The only ship not subject to inspection is the emperor's. Our border troops scan any incoming ship entirely. There is no way to hide somewhere or be shielded. The one who offered you this is a fool. Or he deliberately misled you, pursuing his own interests. Perhaps he intends on turning you over to the empire for a bounty. Such an act would earn him both praise and a reward!"

I cursed. My interactions with Grander were limited to a few minutes' total, but I was sure that this was exactly his plan.

"There are still people loyal to me on Zalva, who have the required level of access," Oleander went on. "If you need to get something, we can arrange for it to be delivered."

"I thought you don't deal with humans," I said.

"I'm not doing it for you. I'm doing it for my son. In return, you will let him go! What do you need on Zalva?"

"I need the logbook of the prince's scout that the Zatrathi captured."

"Is that all?" Oleander asked with surprise. "The log from Rrgord's vessel?"

"Yes. Zalva itself is of no use to me. All I need are the entries for analysis."

A CHECK FOR A BILLION

"Rrgord's ship is neither unique nor secret. It is located in one of the hangars and undergoes daily inspection. If all you need is the logbook, I am ready to make a deal. But only for the sake of my son! As for my own fate, I don't care what it is. I do not need the help of a human!"

"It's a deal then. Whom should I contact?"

"No one. Set course for planet Valtor in Confederate space. The planet is loyal to me, and the adviser won't dare follow me there."

"I'll show you this just in case." I took out the Zatrathi grenade and tossed it into the container with Narlin. "If there are any problems, your son will die his final death. His binding to the planetary spirit will do him no good."

"My word is not enough for you?! This is precisely why I wish to cleanse the Precian Empire of all humans," said Oleander with hatred. "You have no place in Galactogon. You need to be destroyed like the rodents that you are before you manage to destroy yourself and us with you!"

Ah! I have risen through the ranks to the level of a rodent! Excellent! I am no longer at the very bottom. Although it would be better to make sure. I handed Oleander the jewelry case again:

"What's inside?"

The Precian resisted taking the emperor's gift as long as he could, but it was already clear from his expression that he would help eventually. I pointed at the container with Narlin, forcing Oleander to act faster. The Precian snatched the case from my hand, and his fingers danced along its surface, touching protrusions and indentations known to him alone. A click sounded and the case's lid flipped aside. A bright red light flooded the bridge deck.

"It's so beautiful," Eunice whispered, pulling out an intricate statute of some creature. Made of some kind of glittering material, the emperor's gift cycled through every shade of red, radiating a pleasant and soothing light. A leaden heaviness filled my eyelids. I began to nod off and quietly slipped into a dream.

I woke up to someone roughly brushing my cheek with cold metal.

"Cap'n, you better wake up on your own or I'll be forced to give you a kiss!" The snake's tail swayed before my eyes. The statuette had already been returned to its rightful place inside the case.

"What was that?!" I said indignantly, looking over the 'damage.'

Eunice was slumped against Oleander's shoulder, sleeping, while he, in turn, snored loudly, his head resting on hers. My exclamation caused everyone to snap back to their senses.

"Did you do that on purpose?" I loomed over Oleander.

"What? I merely did as you commanded, pirate! What are you dissatisfied with now?"

"You could have warned us! What was that?"

"The Oblivion of Jarullah, as I understand it…The emperor gives each subject what he lacks. This was the third adviser's reward. Everyone knows that he is a recalcitrant workaholic. He performs his duties fanatically — to the detriment of his own health. My brother gave him this to force him to rest. I suppose the message is that sleep too is good for the empire."

A CHECK FOR A BILLION

I nodded. This made a lot of sense. The adviser was always in a hurry, wanting things done yesterday. He was insatiable. Naturally, given his pace he'd have to sacrifice sleep. Otherwise, he wouldn't have enough time. And at some point, his lack of sleep would hamper his health. It was not for nothing that he had suffered so much in the Barrens of Zalva's moon. Age and his extreme workload had had their effect. It was a pity that the adviser did not heed the imperial order and deposited the gift into the vault immediately upon arriving at the cruiser. I would need to make sure and return this sleeping pill to its owner, before his fatigue overwhelmed him.

"Are the beacons attached to the jewelry case or the statuette?"

"The case."

"I have a job for you, snake. Find me a way to block the artifact's effects. Without the case. We will hand it over to our client. He still does not know what lies inside. Brainiac, set course for Valtor! Oleander is our guest."

A large and motely welcoming party came out to meet the brother of the Precian Emperor. It turned out that Precians of various classes supported the official opposition. There were merchants here and soldiers and even some of the local nobility. The first dock could barely accommodate those who wanted to ensure the safety of the Leader of the Resistance, as Oleander called himself. And I suppose after his dramatic demonstration of defiance before the emperor and the bust-up that followed, his supporters were right to be concerned for the Precian's life.

"I need a day to get the records," Oleander warned, as the official reception drew to a close. "Wait for me planetside."

"We'll wait, as will the grenade next to Narlin. Keep in mind that an EM pulse won't disable it," I reminded just in case.

Fortunately, my fears were unfounded. Early next morning, Oleander handed me the data stick. Brainiac scanned it and confirmed that he could extract the coordinates of seven planets that had never been located before. We had succeeded! Rejoicing, I let Narlin go and didn't even demand that his father return to the orbship. Gossip had it that it was his supporters who had contracted the Corsican to free their leader from the Precians to begin with.

Sitting in my orbship, I was finally left alone with my own thoughts. Eunice had gone off to the local market to buy some provisions. You couldn't call Valtor a popular planet, but there were still plenty of merchants around. Considering that Oleander was not an official representative of the Precian Empire, I assumed that contraband was in high demand too.

I spent a long time staring at my PDA, deciding what to do. Anyway you spin it, Grandar had reached his elevated station with my help and, given his proximity to the emperor, it would be a pity to kill him. And yet! That impudent, narrow-minded, bourgeois scoundrel had wanted to turn me in for a bounty! I could not forgive this. What was more important? The vain thought that one of the locals had made his fortune thanks to me, that I had some influence on the lore of Galactogon — or two billion GCs in my personal account and a positive rapport with the third adviser?

A CHECK FOR A BILLION

'What a dumb question,' I said to myself as I dialed an old acquaintance. I knew the adviser much better than Grandar and our partnership had always been productive.

"Adviser, this is Surgeon speaking! I am glad that the incident with the pirates is behind us. Do you have a minute to spare?"

"You have the audacity to call me after your awful deeds on that cruiser?!" came the irate reply. "A thousand deaths! A thousand valiant Precians cast into oblivion because of you, Surgeon!"

"Which of my emotions are you currently appealing to?" I clarified. "My conscience? You've got the wrong human. Would it be better if your nobles had become the pirates' hostages or slaves?! Things worked out the way they did because of the Jolly Roger! I wasn't working with them."

"We could have managed without your involvement!"

"Lies!"

"Lying is *your* business. Tell me that you're not on Valtor right now or that you aren't the one who delivered Oleander there!" the adviser pressed. "He's already announced that neither the Precian Empire, nor the pirates, nor even the Zatrathi can oppose the freedom of the word and his message to cleanse Galactogon of the human plague. Are you digging yourself a grave?"

"Adviser, what's the difference what type of hole I'm digging and for whom? I am calling you about another matter altogether. I want to tell you the truth of who hired me and return your artifact to you. We can be useful to each other. Let's not ruin our partnership."

"I have already surmised that Narlin is not behind this," said the adviser after a long pause. "You have a minute."

"Grandar," I said, without any introduction or explanation.

A florid Precian curse sounded on the other side and I grinned widely. This situation was starting to look lucrative indeed!

Rrgord turned out to be a hardworking type. In his brief life he had managed to acquire a fame that reached almost all of Galactogon. The complete fruits of the Precian astronomic community were at his disposal and as a result, random jumps often brought unexpected and pleasant results. For example, not every experienced explorer could boast of the discovery of seven star systems with one or two planets each. Yet the prince had managed this in his paltry 20 years. He was a born explorer.

The system closest to us was just a ten-minute hyperjump away, so we immediately set out for our prize.

"We are emerging from hyperspace. Planet detected! Attention! Uldan battlesphere detected in our vicinity!"

The silver ball was still shadowing us. It had left us alone as we approached the Valtor system and then reappeared as soon as we had strayed from the populated center.

"Brainiac, broadcast the following on the public frequency: 'Your constant presence is beginning to irritate me. If you do not explain the reason for your pursuit, I will be forced to attack!'"

"Done...There is no response."

"Lex, let's deal with the planet, first, huh?" Eunice placed her hand on my shoulder soothingly, reminding me of our main objective. I nodded in agreement, sending the ship to land. The battlesphere followed us at a respectful distance.

A CHECK FOR A BILLION

You are the first player to land on the planet Zartamin (Precian Empire). This planet's second name is 'Rrgord the Almighty-4.'

Do you wish to claim this planet for yourself? Warning! Claiming this planet will decrease your rapport with the Precian Empire.

There was no planetary spirit as such on this rock. In fact, there was nothing on it at all — neither an atmosphere, nor minerals, nor water, nor our prize check. It was even more barren than the Moon. In accordance with the rules, we would have been notified that it was here as soon as we'd emerged from the ship. Everything was clear here though. A heaviness weighed on my soul. It had been too simple to get those coordinates and it had been too simple to reach the planet too...I had had to jump through numerous hoops to get to Rrgord, while in this case, all it took was a simple deal with Oleander and that's it. This kind of effort wasn't worth a billion credits.

"Nobody said that it would be easy," Eunice encouraged me when I shared how I felt with her. "We might even have to fight our way to one of those planets, who knows. Anyway, there are only six remaining. Let's go! We can visit all of them before we meet Grandar!"

We visited three more planets and encountered similar disappointment. The planets were all identical. I didn't claim any one of them because I had just begun to recover my rapport with the Precians. Launching into orbit from the fourth, I lost my cool and swore loudly — the battlesphere remained with us. My anger and frustration boiled over.

"No, this is too much," I muttered. "Brainiac, broadcast the following: 'This is your last chance to communicate before I attack. You have a minute!'"

"Message broadcast."

"Battle stations! Snake, ready ten torpedoes for launch!"

I gave our annoying tail a minute and a half instead of one. There was no answer. Eunice did not object to the attack. Like the rest of the crew, she had grown sick and tired of our stalker.

"Throttle to a hundred! Brainiac, let this bastard have it!"

Warlock burst forward like never before. It was the first time I'd ordered the engines to full thrust and even the inertial dampeners couldn't deal with the force. We were imprinted in our chairs, as Brainiac displayed our ETA to the battlesphere on the screens: 2 AU. A minute passed yet the distance did not change. The enemy matched our pace easily, causing further irritation.

"Snake, launch the torpedoes!"

"Torpedoes away!" the engineer reported as *Warlock* shook noticeably — running at full throttle had its drawbacks. The deadly missiles shot away with much greater speed than the ship and rapidly closed the distance to the enemy. I was eagerly expecting contact. Ten seconds remained.

"Something's about to happen," Eunice muttered impatiently.

Seven seconds.

"Brainiac maintain our speed. We need to finish him off."

Three seconds.

"Everyone get ready!" I clenched my armrests, expecting

to see the silver sphere ignite before me.

Contact! The torpedoes continued on their way, burning through their fuel, while the battlesphere vanished.

"Bandit portside!" Brainiac announced in a panicked tone. "I am detecting an EM cannon tracking us. Brace for impact!"

For a split second, the light in the captain's deck blinked.

"Power supply restored!" reported the engineer.

"Gunner, fire at will!" I ordered. The Uldan had made the mistake of entering our beam cannons' range and my orangutan responded with a flamacue of plasma.

"Torpedoes away! Time to contact is five seconds...No! I don't believe it!"

I could understand the snake's disappointment — the battlesphere had just been to starboard and a bit below us — yet now it had appeared on the opposite side.

"Brainiac?"

"I don't know!" the computer said with resignation. "What is this? Instant teleportation? He simply vanished and immediately reappeared in a different place!"

"Brace for impact!"

The lights flashed again and the engineer announced the unpleasant news:

"Captain, we have enough elo reserves to take five more such shots."

"I see. Turn us around then," I ordered, frustrated. Looks like we picked up the Losers debuff somewhere. "Brainiac, set course for Belket! I need to speak with the Hansa people!"

"Calculating now," said the computer, relieved, and

displayed a countdown timer. We danced with the battlesphere for a full minute before the stars turned into long lines. And I should say that our enemy did most of the dancing, amusing himself and shooting at us with his EM cannon. He used neither torpedoes nor beam guns.

"We only have three planets left," Eunice reminded just in case.

"I don't want to go anywhere while that jerk is on our tail with a clear advantage," I shook my head. "He was openly mocking us!"

"Why do you even care? So he's there...big deal. He wasn't bothering us! Notice that there was no aggression on his part. You started it first."

"And to no avail," the snake intervened. What are they, best friends all of a sudden? "Twelve torpedoes down the drain! I'll need an entire hour to restore them."

"Brainiac, request permission to land on Belket. We'll head to Hansa straight away."

After I gave Hansa some of the equipment I had plundered from the Uldan warehouse, they had become easier to deal with. Not so much when it came to their new systems, as with their corporate representatives who became more hospitable. Although, I confess, the list of devices that they offered me under the table pleased me too. Here, in particular, was some camouflage for my marine armor, which could create a cloaking field that would hide me across all known spectra. The perfect disguise for a thief, and worth some twelve billion credits. Which is like three, motherfracking, B-class cruisers! Had everyone gone mad in

A CHECK FOR A BILLION

Galactogon? And I know for sure that at least one player bought that upgrade. I'd seen it work in person.

"Impossible!" the eggheads crowed in unison when I showed them the video of the battlesphere toying with *Warlock*. To celebrate my new discovery, the Hansa Corp even went so far as to offer me some tea. After a couple of hours of brainstorming, one of their engineers came to me with an unpleasant verdict:

"We need more time to study the problem. At the moment, we can confidently say that what we observed were localized, micro-hyperjumps. Modern technology does not allow us to calculate hyperdrive instructions with such precision. And speed. We need time and further data. It would be beneficial if we managed to examine the ship somehow. If you manage to arrange this, we will give you a fourth list of upgrades."

"You have a fourth one too?" I asked surprised.

"But of course," grinned the Precian. "Who do you take us for? The fourth list is dedicated to unique prototypes. These are singular devices that have not been mass produced. If you want it, you must deliver the battlesphere to us. That is all for now. We are busy."

I was carefully shooed out and a message appeared on the wooden door of the reception room: "The Corporation is not available for the next 72 hours." I glanced at the countdown counter and was impressed with how seriously the eggheads had taken to their new task!

Eunice now and then suggested we explore the remaining planets, but I decided to play it safe. The first thing I did was have my wife pick up the fighter she had bought back when she started her game and fly it over to Blood Island. For, if we were shot down, we would respawn on the planet, while the orbship would be sent to a ship graveyard a good distance from it. In that case, getting over there to recover the orbship without any transport would pose a problem. And then, suddenly, Grandar appeared on Belket before the designated deadline.

For our outing to Zalva, the imperial favorite had assembled an impressive fleet consisting of a legendary cruiser, five destroyers, hundreds of frigates and a whole swarm of fighters. The Precian had his own personal palace on Belket, which I entered without any inspection. When I saw my host's cordial demeanor, it occurred to me that I could be wrong in suspecting him of a playing a double game. But as soon as the doors shut behind me, this nonsense instantly cleared out of my head.

"Surgeon, store the orbship in my cruiser's hangar. My engineers must go over it. You're still a pirate after all!"

The Precian's tone did not brook any objections. He himself was sitting in a jet seat, so as not to belabor his feet with having to walk. And he was barking out orders, poking his finger here and there, telling people where to go and what to do. If one of the servants did not understand his orders, then he would receive a lashing. As I noticed, there was a special affection for this activity around here. Even the personal bodyguards, circling a couple of meters above the ground, did not neglect to apply lashes to any slaves who seemed sluggish. I examined the properties of the archaic whip: the creator was a human engineer named Marat. Here they are, the ample opportunities for self-realization that a game offers: Beyond the endless base raids, gunfights and dogfights, the game also offered an elaborate economic and social environment. In pursuit of pleasure or profit — and frequently just to stave off boredom — players could take on any number of at times peculiar roles and occupations.

"Brainiac, do as he says, but don't allow anyone to board the ship," I ordered, prompting Grandar's displeasure.

"Right, this I don't like one bit!" he objected. "I must be able to dispose of all the property on my ship! Otherwise we will not be able to pass customs!"

The Precian had changed entirely since our last meeting, even in his tone of voice, which had become arrogant and condescending. It was as if in deigning to speak to me, Grandar was showing me mercy or something.

"I will grant access to *Warlock* only once we're in orbit around Zavala," I replied. "That is where I will pay you the second billion as well."

"Quiet!" Grandar hissed, glancing around. "No one should hear this! The walls have ears! Zander! Change the slaves!"

The head of Grandar's security swooped down to us, casting down chains to five of the slaves. They obediently attached the chains to their collars and Zander abruptly pulled the poor fellows toward him, knocking them all together. Using the same chains to fetter their bodies, the guard departed, leading the slaves away. Others immediately took up their places, waiting on Grandar with all the zeal they could muster.

"Fine then," the Precian grimaced in displeasure. "You will grant me access later. Now get on with it!"

Once I had seen my orbship tucked away in one of the

hangars and set my rhino as a sentry, I joined Grandar in the cruiser's mess hall. Eunice stayed prudently back on the orbship. If they tried to disable it with an EM blast before taking it by force, she would have time to set off the self-destruct mechanism. We entered hyperspace, and the captain reported that we would reach our destination in six minutes.

"Your jewelry case." I pulled out the emperor's gift and offered it to the Precian. In turn, he placed his hands behind his back and demonstratively indicated the desk with his eyes. Remembering the adviser's instructions, I just shrugged, replacing the jewelry case in my inventory.

"No, Grandar, this won't do. The transfer must take place from hand to hand, otherwise I haven't technically fulfilled your order. Will you receive the item or should I look for a more reliable buyer?"

"Come now, Surgeon, what is this? This is an unpleasant surprise," Grandar clasped his hands affectedly. "Are we not partners?"

"Sure we're partners," I said easily. "Did we not have a deal? We did. Have I done as you requested? Nearly. I merely wish to hand you what you ordered and no more. That is the only way this mission will be complete and you won't be able to complain later. This is a strict policy of mine, surely you understand. I am risking my reputation with future clients."

"All right, hand it here," Grandar twitched impatiently. "What's in there?"

"I have no idea," I answered honestly, taking out the jewelry case again. The snake did not bother to say what she had put in there. "Can we consider my assignment fulfilled? For the sake of paperwork?"

"Are you sure you haven't opened it?" the Precian asked, squinting suspiciously as his hand hovered over the case.

"Of course not," I confirmed, recalling that Oleander was the one to open it. Grandar still hesitated.

"Swear it!"

I took an oath with a clear conscience and waited for Galactogon's system to confirm it.

"In that case," the imperial favorite sighed, "I confirm that you've completed my assignment. You have done well and all that! Hand it over!" He snatched the box out of my hands, fumbled with it for a while and then looked at me with puzzlement: "Now what? How do I open this thing?"

I just shrugged. Grandar went on:

"Doesn't matter. I'll deal with it later. I want my second billion now!"

"Once we're on Zalva," I reminded him. "That was the deal."

"Plans have changed!" Grandar barked. "Zander!"

The head of security entered the mess hall.

"What is the status of the orbship?"

"Everything is ready, master. We have identified the self-destruct mechanism's detonators and set up the EM field."

"Very good. Now listen here, Surgeon. Either you give me my two billion credits now, or you say goodbye to your ship!" It looked like the Precian had decided to clean me out thoroughly before we reached Zalva. "Why are you silent? Make your decision. There is not much time left!"

I just sighed and shook my head. Realizing that the second billion was out of the question did not upset Grandar too much. He was already beside himself with his delight at the ruse he had spun. He had deceived a pirate, stripping him of his money, the jewelry case and even his orbship! A rare ship that would be his mark of honor and glory for dealing with me.

"Grandar," I warned, "a greedy Precian is a dead Precian."

"I'll take everything from you! Your ship, your money, even your name! You'll spend the rest of your days rotting in the raq mines. We'll make sure to break your binding first, just to break your hope of escaping. Everything will be mine! Even the empire itself!" The Precian's joy at his success made him start running his mouth.

Out of the corner of my eye, I noticed several guards with their manipulators pointed at me. I would surely be restrained at the slightest movement so I didn't rock the boat. There was no need.

"Your grace, we have received a request to exit hyperspace! It is a customs inspection!"

"Wonderful!" Grandar smirked. "Activate the EM field around the orbship. Ensure that Surgeon cannot contact it. Place the pirate under guard and notify the authorities that I have a dangerous criminal on board! An enemy of the Precian Empire! Tell them that I have personally detained and neutralized him!"

At these words, the guards wrenched my hands behind my back and Grandar himself snapped the handcuffs on my wrists so that everything corresponded to what he just said. The cuffs came as an unpleasant surprise, since now I couldn't use any devices. I'll need to get a pair of these for myself. They could come in handy.

"Docking request received."

A CHECK FOR A BILLION

"Permission granted. Take Surgeon to the brig! Don't let him out of your sight for a second! He must not be allowed to die before his binding is adjusted!"

For the second time in two days I found myself imprisoned. This time was different however. Back on the cruiser it had all played out by chance, whereas now it was of my own free will.

When my cell door opened again, I encountered Grandar in the company of the third adviser — and there was not a trace of his former joy on his face. He stared at me in perplexity, trying to fathom where he had miscalculated and how bad everything was for him. Now it was my turn to triumph over Grandar's greed.

"Release him!" the adviser ordered, and the guards of the former imperial favorite rushed to perform the order with the same zeal with which they had recently dragged me to the brig. Getting in each other's way, the meatheads almost broke my hand as they removed the handcuffs.

"On behalf of the Precian Empire, I thank Surgeon for his help in exposing Grandar," the adviser proclaimed. With each word, the proud Precian's shoulders slumped lower and lower. Grandar hunched over and began looking around desperately in search of an escape.

Mission accomplished: Double Agent. Reward: Unlimited access to Belket, official permission to receive the third list of Hansa upgrades, −15% discount on Hansa equipment.

"This belongs to me!" The adviser slipped his hand into Grandar's pocket and retrieved his jewelry case. Nodding in satisfaction, he ordered the guards: "Take him away!"

The same guards who had only recently groveled before Grandar moved towards him menacingly and at this point, their former leader lost his last nerve:

"No! You wouldn't dare! The Emperor will have you all flayed alive! What did this pirate tell you?! It is all lies! I have been framed! The case was planted on me! I demand a fair trial!"

"You shall have your trial!" grinned the adviser, pointing to the far end of the corridor. There, surrounded by a dozen warriors, stood Narlin along with Grandar's former servant. The adviser had brought them along. Grandar's face stretched to its limits and he cut himself off mid-sentence. Only when his dazed look reached my face, did he begin to mumble:

"You were supposed to kill him. I ordered you to kill him. I asked only one thing. You were supposed to kill him. I ordered..."

The record broke, the transducer blew, and Grandar went on repeating the same thing even as he was dragged off to meet his destiny.

"Do you not feel sorry for him?" asked the adviser and turned to the guard: "Bring Nurse here!"

"Why would I feel sorry for him? Let the traitor suffer his just comeuppance. He tried to deceive me and turn me over to the authorities. I turned him over first. It's all fair and square."

"It amuses me to hear a pirate speak this way. Welcome to the Precian Empire, Pirate Nurse. Now I remember you as well."

"Good afternoon, adviser," my wife smiled radiantly. The emperor's soldiers had by now completely captured the cruiser, allowing Eunice to join us.

A CHECK FOR A BILLION

"I won't beat around the bush. You have succeeded in your mission and the Precian Empire and I are prepared to work with you again. I know why you decided to treat with Grandar. Do not interrupt, it is my turn to speak. It is true that the emperor allowed Oleander's supporters to download information from his son's ship and send it to you. But I must disappoint you. That which you seek is not on any of those planets. Don't look so surprised — what kind of adviser would I be if I didn't know what was going on in my government? On behalf of those who organized the search for the check, I officially notify you that the prize's location has been changed. Of course, you can check the remaining three planets, but you will not find anything there. Assume that I am saving you some time."

"What do you mean it's changed? On what basis?!" My wife flared up. "That would be a violation of the terms of our agreement!"

"Do not get excited, Eunice. We continue to strictly adhere to our agreement. All our actions are consistent with the contract, you can check if you wish. Moreover, as a sign of goodwill, we will let you know where the check is. This way you won't have to waste time looking for it."

"Let me take a guess," I said on a hunch. Since we were no longer speaking with the adviser, but with one of the admins, there was no need to stand on ceremony. "The check is on the Zatrathi homeworld. The same staging point of the invasion that everyone is looking for."

"You have deprived me of my moment of glory and the pleasure of seeing your surprise," smiled the 'adviser.' "That is all correct. A check for one billion credits is waiting for you in the hall

86

of the planetary spirit on the Zatrathi homeworld. I now bid you farewell and transfer control over this NPC back to its rightful AI. Have fun and may your search be a fruitful one!"

CHAPTER FIVE

OW ABOUT: 'HONEY, YOU TAKE EVERYTHING TOO MUCH TO HEART'...?

Boom! A grenade blasted the nearest cliff to smithereens.

No, not like that. Smacks of cheap melodrama, I might even draw her aggro.

Maybe: 'Don't be so upset, darling. The doctors say that the baby should be surrounded by beauty and tranquility.'

There was a low uterine roar and then a loud explosion. One of the drums of fine dust, which had remained in our hold after the operation with the cruise liner, went shooting into the air in perfect silence. At the peak of its trajectory, the drum burst into a cloud of dust which whirled and dispersed, shimmering with the cooler hues of the color spectrum. There's that beauty and tranquility for you.

"Cap'n, say something to her! I don't have anything left!" The snake popped out of *Warlock*'s hull.

"Bring out the drones," I sighed, looking at my wife. Until

---

she blows off all the steam, I'd rather not risk letting her back on the orbship.

"Not the drones!" the engineer dug in. "At this rate we'll be left destitute. Why did you have to marry her anyway? Or even if you did, why bring her on board with us? She's a maniac!"

"Why, why…Because a man must take responsibility for his acts," I sighed. "All right, come on and bring out the drones. Otherwise I will sic her on you in the ship. Then you'll have to deal with her yourself."

"No, no, no. I read you loud and clear," the snake ducked back into the ship, casting a wary look at Eunice in the process. "You can figure things out here on your own. I'm going to run and uh…oh I've got so many chores…There's the welding and the oil pressure! But you can't have my drones!"

The hatch closed behind her. I looked in her wake and grinned. Here was that crucial moment when the mother-in-law makes up her mind about the young bride.

"Honey, have you calmed down a little?"

"I was never not calm," my wife replied, looking around the carnage. She had let off her steam thoroughly — I was even envious. What was the big deal anyway? After my conversation with the adviser, I'd be happy to join her in this improvised training session too. However, as the snake correctly pointed out, there aren't enough planets and property for the two of us. So I could only express my solidarity with my wife's outrage quietly and to myself.

We were on the third of the remaining planets. Eunice insisted we verify the admin's words, but our efforts gained us nothing apart from disappointment and loss of time.

A CHECK FOR A BILLION

"Excellent." I tried to speak calmly and avoid argument. "Now let's think about what we'll do next."

"We should stop dealing with these assholes in general. They change the rules on the go!"

Eunice's blasters came to life and a lengthy burst of plasma slammed into the mountain range, shearing off one of the peaks. I sighed again. I knew I had to be patient because I had already read a lot of clever books about pregnancy and knew that it often had an adverse effect not only on a woman's mood, but also on her brain activity. And this was even if she was a hardened veteran. Hormones, you see. Suddenly Eunice relented, turned to me and, burying her face in my shoulder, burst into tears. Well, here we are. Honestly, she's like a child who was promised a toy and then didn't get it. Although… If we recall that this particular toy is worth a billion real credits, then I guess I want to bury my face in my shoulder and cry too. We had thought that we would have the check today!

"We need to find the Zatrathi planet," I began to think aloud, voicing platitudes and absentmindedly stroking my wife's marine armor.

"Easy for you to say! You've seen it!" she complained in her turn. "That thing playfully smashed a whole fleet!"

"That wasn't it. You are confusing the Zatrathi Queen with the Zatrathi homeworld," I corrected. "We need to find the planet and then we need to figure out how to get on it."

"So we'll catch a brainworm and beat the coordinates out of it. Too bad you turned the last one over to the Precians! Now we won't get my check because of you!"

Her moods were changing with blinding speed. A second

ago Eunice had been sobbing about how bad everything was and now she'd found someone to blame for it all. I think my patience had reached its limit.

"Sit down!" I snapped, and the girl, who hadn't expected this kind of tone, plunked down on the nearest stone in bewilderment. "What are you? A professional gamer or a pregnant woman?"

Eunice blushed and opened her mouth to get more air before answering this question.

"I..."

After this important pronoun, I hurried to interrupt her:

"There you go! So remember it! Let's get down to business! One more time. How can we locate that planet?"

"We need its coordinates," my wife repeated in a completely calm tone. Though I didn't dare show it, I was delighted that my tactic worked.

"Agreed, and yet Zatrathi ships don't contain them. Brainiac downloaded the data from the flying fortress and there wasn't so much as a hint of them. Whether or not it will be possible to 'beat' them out of a brainworm is a question in and of itself. They could easily have some mental defense."

"This isn't Runlustia. There's no mental defense in Galactogon," Eunice reminded me and asked me to show her all the missions I had in my log. I sat down next to her and we began to pore over each item on the list, generating ideas as we went.

"The only thread is the Zatrathi repair bases," Eunice concluded. "They should have a ship repair schedule. After all, the new ones launch only from the homeworld, correct?"

A CHECK FOR A BILLION

"That's what I've gathered from the info I have, yes."

"Consequently, there should be at least some connection between the homeworld and the repair planets. If we find one, we'll be able to unwind the rest of the riddle."

"I agree. So, we know for sure that the Fighting Breed goons found one such repair base. I have its coordinates. We can go check it out."

"We can't go there without support," Eunice said reasonably.

"I will discuss this issue with Vargen...Hold on, there is another option! The Zatrathi are the Uldans' progeny. This is a confirmed fact. What if we follow that to its logical conclusion? Lumara passed me the coordinates of one planet. That's the first thing. I also have the coded coordinates of the Uldan base. That's the other thing. All we have to do is find a way to the Corsican and get the Uldan coordinate converter from him. There are two planets with Uldan storage facilities, after all. Of course they are sure to be defended now, but if we want it badly enough we should be able to get on at least one of them."

This last realization was the most unpleasant one. After the Zatrathi had seen their destroyed facility for training ship captains, they had garrisoned each 'nebula planet' with three flying fortresses each. Vargen and I had audaciously flown by to assess our potential profits and we had barely managed to get away with our hides intact. It was a good thing we had used my new orbship. The Zatrathi couldn't keep up in terms of speed and quickly fell behind, allowing us to enter hyperspace. Still, it was clear that our access to other Zatrathi training facilities was closed to us. We had naturally shared this info with Ash, but three flying fortresses require a giant raid of twenty to thirty cruisers, some of which would have to have Yamato cannons on them. This weapon in general had become incredibly important all of a sudden. Thus, Kiddo — who had demonstrated her skill at using her Yamato cannon — was suddenly in high demand. Everyone remembered about her existence and wanted to be her friend.

"The Corsican is a good option." Eunice's mood changed again, now to the pensively-enigmatic. What I liked most of all was that this did not affect the constructive nature of our conversation, though she did go off on tangents a little more than usual. "What you say makes a lot of sense…If I were the contest organizers, I would think as follows: It is known that you have the coordinates of a certain planet. So I would have cleared it right away. Consequently, there is no point in searching there. It's empty. Well, maybe some little trifle but no more. So I don't buy that option. The repair base is also an obvious approach, but you still need to find it, and then capture it. It's difficult and unpredictable. That will make it a good backup plan. As for the Corsican — that's a different conversation altogether. Players can't just go find that NPC and offer to work with him. They need to gain rapport with him first. That's it, Lex! We need to meet with the Corsican! That's priority number one! Let's go!"

Eunice jumped up, as if she had seen the light at the end of the tunnel. But when I failed to follow her, she froze and fixed me with an inquisitive look.

"Not so fast. Before we meet the Corsican, I need to reach pirate rank three. Otherwise he won't even talk to us. And to do that, I need to finish Hilvar's mission and find the video recording. That's mission number one then."

"So what's the problem?"

"The problem is that the planet we need is in the former Delvian Empire. And I have a nagging suspicion that we can only try to get onto it once. If the Zatrathi found that system, which I have no doubt they did, they will not give us a second chance, as badly as we may need it. They'll post a flying fortress in the system and that will be that. And this means that we will have to pull off the mission at first go and with good fire support!"

"Vargen again?" Eunice guessed.

"In the flesh. But first, I want to see his people in action. So at the immediate moment we are not going to deal with the Uldan planet, the Zatrathi repair base, or even the Corsican."

"I don't understand...What do you have in mind?" Eunice asked impatiently as I paused at the culmination of my deductive chain. Instead of answering, I checked the time. It was nine in the morning. Vargen was supposed to wake up and enter the game. I got out my PDA and dialed his number.

"Greetings to you, oh great leader of Liberium!"

"Yeah, yeah, hope you're well too, Surgeon. Get on with it," Vargen muttered in displeasure. "Just give me a second to take a seat. Your calls never end well. All right. What is it?"

"Here's the deal: Fighting Breed have three B-class cruisers on their base in the Galvar system. Those boys owe me, and I want to relieve them of any unnecessary worries. In short, I need fire support."

"I was hoping that time would make you more tolerant of

other people's mistakes," grinned Vargen. "Will Aalor with his assault team suffice?"

"Yes, I'll have my people with me too, so we should be able to manage. When can I expect them?"

"Closer to lunchtime. He's busy at the moment. Who are your people? We don't work with just anyone," Vargen warned.

"I'll tell you that later," I avoided answering for the moment. "We'll meet on Belket. By the way, do you need anything from Hansa's third list? I can offer a 15% discount. Minus two percent commission. Think about it."

"I'll think about it. Just make sure to get back to me about my question, Surgeon." Really, the head of Liberium was too principled for being the leader of such a large guild. Hanging up, I encountered Eunice's surprised look. She also wanted to know who 'our people' were.

Indicating with a gesture that everything would be clarified in short order, I dialed another number on my PDA.

"Marina, how are you?" As soon as I uttered the name, Eunice grimaced. I don't know what caused her dislike for Kiddo, but my wife always reacted like this whenever my pirate partner was mentioned.

"I'm listening. Just hurry up."

"I miss Graykill. I can't live without him. Will you let me hire him and his band of thirty marines for about six to seven hours today?"

"How much?"

"We can figure that out face-to-face, partner. I'll be waiting for them on Belket around lunchtime."

A CHECK FOR A BILLION

"Okay," Kiddo replied and hung up.

"Do you have to involve her?"

Marina's curt tone did nothing to reassure Eunice. To the contrary, she now seemed like a boiling kettle to me. I would have to remove the lid before it blew off on its own. Slowly, stressing every word, I said:

"We can only trust family. No one else. I don't trust either Vargen or Kiddo. And yet her marines will be our insurance in case Aalor decides to betray us. I've seen what Graykill is capable of. Trust me, he will be invaluable. Come on. We'll fly to Belket early and go check out their market. We might find something interesting."

Now that the plan was taking shape, my wife's face brightened a little. The last sentence seemed to cheer her up too. It turned out that Eunice loved markets. Small markets, big markets, pop-up markets, crafts markets, black markets or slave markets. It didn't matter what they were as long as there were merchants, wares and fellow shoppers. And not only did I learn that Eunice loved markets, I also learned what she did in them. For she went there not for the objects, but for the sensations. She liked the bustle, the ambience of commerce; she examined shop windows for lengthy periods, compared the goods and consulted with the talkative vendors. But the worst thing was that she loved to bargain! She haggled until she was in a stupor, hoarse, and red-eyed. Eunice would lose all control, knocking out the maximum possible discount from one victim after another and when an exhausted opponent, sprinkling ashes on his head and bemoaning his ruin, would finally give in and agree to her price, my wife would proclaim that she'd changed her mind and just walk away…I don't know why. This aspect of Eunice's personality remained a mystery to me.

For me, shopping has always been about exchanging money for something specific. I came, I saw, I purchased. Even now I had a specific objective — I wanted to acquire the handcuffs I had worn on Grandar's ship. According to Stan, the Rialto Bracelets were available to players, though they were not popular. On some planets, however, they were outright banned, and Belket was one such planet.

We figured out where to buy contraband and headed out. Brainiac called me when the market was looming on the horizon.

"Attention, Captain! I have detected two individuals tailing you. You picked them up the moment you left the dock." By way of proof, Brainiac showed me the footage from my armor suit's rearview camera. It was evident that the two Precians were professionals. If it weren't for Brainiac, I would never have guessed that we were being followed. Diving into the crowd of idle customers, I tried to lose them. In vain. Every time I changed direction, the Precians hustled to get ahead of us and a couple of minutes later they would invariably come drifting through the crowd in front of us. Realizing that they knew the market better than we did, I simply went about my business until I spied an inconspicuous tent at the far corner of the market. If there were any prohibited items to buy around here, this would be the place. Eunice and I had agreed that she could get on with her bartering hobby once we had done everything we needed to do.

The shop was empty. At first glance, the assortment of goods did not suggest any smuggled items. Conventional booster units for armor suits, extra armor plates and other cheap stuff. The catalogs, which lay scattered on the counter, offered some rare but unmarketable goods to order. Eunice took one catalog, flipped through it, and, chuckling, delved into the study of some object. No one seemed in a rush to sell anything to the store's only visitors. The owner or the sales clerk was sorting something at the far counter without paying any attention to us. Peeking out of the tent, I checked for our pursuers and cursed to myself. What the hell was all this crap? We were constantly being harassed as of late and it wasn't even clear why. Out in space it was that battlesphere — here it was a couple of suspicious individuals of Precian nationality. Pure espionage and intrigue.

"Is the gentleman looking for something specific or just browsing?" the vendor squeaked from his place at the counter. I moved closer so as not to speak loudly. Two beady eyes examined me with interest from the store's half-gloom, which was diluted by streetlight from the dusty window. An ordinary Precian — though with a very attentive and inquisitive look. I wondered how to broach the subject of the handcuffs without scaring him away.

"The gentleman has not yet decided," I replied, trying to flash him what I hoped was a meaningful glance. "My friend, do you have an emergency exit?"

"No." Pursing his lips in displeasure, the Precian angrily waved his hand. "Master Dow has nothing to hide from his customers! I always use the same entrance as they!"

I nodded silently. It's too bad. An emergency exit would come in handy. Next I tried unvarnished flattery.

"Yes, I was told that you are a reliable Precian and that I

should come see you if I had any special requests."

"Is that so?" Master Dow asked and turned to me completely, indicating that he was ready to hear me out. "What led you to me then?"

"I am looking for something special," I muttered softly. "Something a bit risqué, you could say…"

"Aaah," the vendor cooed understandingly and cast a passing glance at Eunice. "I think we understand each other."

A catalog appeared from under the counter as if from a magician's hat. It was soiled from heavy use. Glad to see everything work out so quickly, I snatched it up and started flipping through it. My joy was premature.

"What is this?!" It was a stupid question on my part, but I couldn't hold it back when I saw the wares on offer.

"What you asked for…" said the salesman, puzzled, retreating a couple of steps from me just in case. "Something risqué…"

"I was looking for a pair of Rialto Bracelets — not this!" I tossed the catalog of toys onto the counter indignantly.

"Hey now. This is a respectable establishment!" the Precian took offence for some reason, concealing his dirty catalog back under the counter.

I smiled to myself. But of course! Judging by the inventory I had just seen, this place was as respectable as an ice cream parlor run by an overworked Snow White with seven dwarves smoking cigarettes out back. We had nothing more to do here.

"Lex…" Eunice called me over — when an explosion in the distance interrupted her.

A CHECK FOR A BILLION

The blasters on my shoulders automatically snapped to combat readiness even before I turned and ran to the exit, assessing the situation. All the market's guards soared into the air and quickly zoomed off somewhere outside the market. Another series of explosions thundered. It sounded like some kind of attack was underway.

In a split second, the market grew empty. The vendors piled their goods into their shops and fled for their precious lives. The place had become a thieves' paradise. Come and take whatever you want, only there was no one to do this. The buyers disappeared even before the vendors.

The only ones who remained nonplussed by the thundering explosions were our pursuers. Standing in front of the store with their blasters drawn in plain view, they paid absolutely no attention to the sounds of combat in the distance.

"What are we going to do, Lex?"

I had no answer to this. A third Precian had joined our two tails. He stepped out from behind them and moved toward us at a leisurely pace, demonstrating an astounding confidence in his belief that I would not kill him. A Precian named Vardun. The cybernetic arm and scars all over his body piqued my interest.

"Surgeon?"

I nodded silently.

"We need to take a walk."

"And if I don't feel like taking a walk right this instant?"

"That's understandable," Vardun shrugged, and my armor suit's HUD blinked and went out completely, plunging me into the gloom of an unpowered metal coffin. The EM grenade had done its job.

"Eunice, how are you?" I called my wife on my PDA. No grenade could disable this last-ditch means of communication between the players.

"Nominal. Tell me that you have a plan B," Eunice asked hopefully and I was forced to mumble a sad no. "That's no good. Damn, I don't think I feel well."

"Do you feel claustrophobic?" I grew worried.

"No, just nauseous. These blockheads are carrying me like a log during a storm."

I winced and made a silent decision. It looks like it's time to send Eunice to some resort. She doesn't need to be hanging out with me in Galactogon. As soon as we locate that check, I'll send her away. There are too many emotions here and too little constructive substance.

The armor suit shook and I fell over backwards as someone outside yelled, "Clear!" We were being carried somewhere and I can't say our kidnappers were careful about their work. The shaking did not last long and we ended up in some kind of cargo compartment. Judging by the sounds, Eunice was placed right next to me. I surmised that we were being flown somewhere by the sensation of light inertia, which I felt lying in my coffin. We called each other a couple of times to make sure everything was in order. Several times I had a bout of claustrophobia but I closed my eyes and meditated. I even got so carried away that I didn't notice that we had stopped. They began to turn me over again and I got ready to come flying out of my suit at a moment's notice. Luckily it wouldn't be my first time. A short discharge ran through my suit and

A CHECK FOR A BILLION

I got ready: Roll, jump to the side, produce a blaster from my inventory and a powercell for my body armor to provide some basic protection. Everything turned out so smoothly that you could think I'd been practicing it. Out of the corner of my eye, I noticed Eunice tumble out of her own armor. She exhaled with relief, but remained lying on the floor, not at all wondering who had kidnapped us.

My tactical helmet, integrated with my bullet-proof vest, illuminated the Precian in the room. He seemed taken aback by my agility. I did not bother to ascertain whether he was friend or foe. One shot — and a loot crate fell to the floor. Whoever our kidnappers were, I did not expect anything good from them and therefore gave no quarter.

After making sure that there was no one else in the room, I threw my armor suit into my inventory and ran over to my wife, not forgetting to cover the door with my blaster.

"Eunice," I called. "Get up."

"What the hell for?" My wife replied languidly. "I'm fine here."

"Understood," I replied, turning the girl onto her back. Her foggy eyes and a scratch on her head suggested that she had a debuff. I changed the powercells in her body armor and its medunit immediately snapped to action, injecting her with restorative drugs. Her eyes cleared and, groaning, Eunice rose to her feet. The first thing my girl did was check her blaster and then put away her armor in her inventory. The expression on her face boded nothing good for whoever had had the imprudence to kidnap us.

I took out my comm and called the orbship.

"Brainiac, are you here?" There were no problems with the

signal.

"Almost!" the computer responded, determining our location. "Whoa! You are at the other end of the city. I'll be right there."

"Greetings, Surgeon," said a familiar voice.

Our host preferred to communicate with me on the speakerphone system and he was right to do so. Were he to show up in person, I'd pop him before he got a word in.

"Put away your weapons," barked the speaker. "Neither you nor your female are in any danger. Exit the room, the doors are not locked. Just don't let my people scare you. I assure you they are more afraid of you as it stands. If you leave them alone, they will sit quietly. Come on, I'm waiting for you."

A loud click let me know that this was the end of our conversation.

"Who is that?" asked Eunice, watching me obediently put away my blaster.

"Eh, an acquaintance. We did some work together."

The door led us to a narrow corridor, the walls of which bristled with flamethrowers, blasters and other weapons. I suppose this was done to pacify any difficult guests. Fortunately we had been warned and moved to the exit calmly. Several times I caught frightened eyes sparkling behind the flamethrowers. For some reason, the Precians chained to the floor hid in the shadows, holding their blasters with trembling hands and trying not to attract attention to themselves. It didn't seem like a good idea to leave scared people with weapons in their hands, so I collected their blasters and handed them to Eunice. By the end of the corridor, my wife was almost collapsing from the load of weaponry, but I couldn't help her. What if we have to fight now and I'd be too tired?

"Dump it all here," I gestured at the free space next to the door. The blasters and flamethrowers tumbled into a heap with a clamor and were followed by Eunice's sigh of relief. I didn't even look at this heap of scrap metal. If you can even manage to sell a D-class blaster, then only over the barrel of a higher-level blaster.

The mastermind of this whole farce was waiting for us on the other side of the door.

"I have only one question: What the hell?!" I was pretty pissed.

"I owe you one," Tryd replied hoarsely and hummed with satisfaction. "Or did you think I would forgive you for abducting me in your tin can? Sit down. We have something to discuss."

Vardun was in the room with Tryd. Leaning against the wall, he seemed relaxed, but his hand resting on his manipulator and attentive gaze suggested that he was ready to interfere in our conversation at any moment.

"Sit down," Tryd said again and pointed me at the second chair.

"You're a vindictive one, Tryd. You could have just called," I said, settling down comfortably. "Or did you forget to ask for my number before you ran away?"

"I did forget," Tryd snorted and first pointed his finger at Eunice and then at the place by the far wall where he wanted her to go. "I need you."

"Two percent, and I am all attention."

"Volta is no more. The Zatrathi found our planet."

"So it's like that?" I asked surprised. "They figured out how to bow to the red sun?"

"They simply blew up both suns. The planet was vaporized along with everything on it. Volta's planetary spirit was destroyed in the process." Tryd said, an expression of melancholy passing across his face.

"Isn't it nice to have a binding to a safe planet, right?" I asked sarcastically. The gist of this conversation was already clear to me. All I had to do was sell myself for the highest price possible.

"Enough!" Tryd growled, distorting his disfigured muzzle even further. "I didn't risk my neck to listen to sarcasm from some snot-nosed scallywag! I need you!"

"Why me? A pirate who's only at his first rank...a scallywag."

"There are no others," Tryd seethed angrily. "Out of Hilvar's current pups, you're the only one who's even mildly competent. The rest are either idiots or cowardly jackals!"

"It won't be easy to sneak onto Zarvalus," I said. "I imagine that..."

"I didn't say anything about Zarvalus, small fry," Tryd cut me off. "Zarvalus encountered the same fate as Volta. Filta has been reunited with our pups. May she rest in peace. I need you for something else."

Tryd trailed off, giving me the opportunity to assess the scale of the Zatrathi conquests. They were destroying one planet after another! This was both impressive and terrifying. It's difficult to fight an enemy you don't understand.

"Then explain to me why you need me. You just called me

small fry again, so…"

"Hilvar said you have a mission on the planet Shurtan. I will go with you."

"You could go with anyone. The coordinates of the planet are no secret. But you said the rest are idiots or cowards. What's the catch then?"

"The catch? Small fry or not, you're perceptive. Shurtan has been taken over by the Zatrathi. They garrisoned a flying fortress in the system and are using the planet's orbit for their repair docks. It's a lucky thing they haven't found our base yet."

"How would you know?"

"Our people made it out alive. Or do you think the pirates would voluntarily abandon such a base? It's been captured by synthoids, Anorxian renegades. Anyway, I need to get to it. As do you, by the way."

"So you want me to sneak past a Zatrathi flying fortress, make my way to the base, clear it of robot renegades and unfurl a red carpet for you?" I did not bother hiding my sarcasm. "You know, I'm even curious what you can offer me as payment for such job? I mean, it all sounds like suicide."

"This." A small object appeared in Tryd's paws. It looked like a thick stranded cable and I bit off whatever caustic gibe I was about to spit at him when I recognized what it was. A long and tedious pause followed. In the silence I considered my chances of snatching the item from the Delvian's paws and busting out of here with Eunice unharmed. Vardun assessed my intentions accurately and pulled out his manipulator, ready to use it at any moment.

"What do you say? Is such a reward worth suicide?"

"You sure do know how to motivate people, Tryd. When do you want to set out?" I asked. Like it or not, this was a prize I needed. And I had already promised the video to Hilvar anyway.

"The earlier, the better. I have nothing to do here on Belket."

"Welcome back to my small but friendly crew, Boatswain Tryd," I said, swallowing. Eunice coughed meaningfully behind me but I didn't have time to explain things to her. Just seeing the object in the Delvian's paw gave me hope. It was none other than the Lora — the long-lost coupler unit of the infamous Vengeance set: a weapon capable of destroying even the Zatrathi Queen.

Perhaps even a weapon capable of ending this war…

CHAPTER SIX

FIGHTING BREED'S HOME SYSTEM — GALVAR — was like a shopping mall a few days before Christmas. Everyone was in a rush, constantly arguing about who cut whom in line to land, demanding the best dock available, cursing the large cruisers obstructing the way and the fighters that got underfoot. In other words, ideal conditions for sneaking into hostile territory undetected.

The Cruiser *Inevitable* hovered in the midst of this chaos, occupying her place according to her status: In the lowest orbit, as close as possible to the central planet. The Precian customs officers did not even bother to inspect her, limiting themselves to an external hull scan and quickly gave us the green light as a show of respect for Liberium.

"We're in position," said Aalor with all the calm of a mummy.

The captain's marked aloofness was caused by a set of circumstances that were rather unpleasant for him. In order to sneak my ship into the system undetected by the Precians or the Breed, *Warlock* had to be hidden in the cruiser's hold, and the two ships' power circuits had to be linked together. Only by fully integrating the orbship could she become a natural part of the cruiser and avoid detection by the prying scanners. Tryd put me on this idea, explaining that this was an old pirate trick, which had served him more than once before. As soon as he heard the plan, however, Aalor categorically refused to take part in it, which led to an awkward and unpleasant conversation between him and Vargen. I didn't hear any of it, since the players spoke over an internal comm channel, but after the dust settled, the face of *Inevitable*'s captain was an impassive mask. *Warlock* received all the necessary permissions to dock and integrate, while I acquired what seemed like a powerful foe. Aalor would never forgive me this public humiliation, although really I had been no more than a trigger for the conflict between Vargen and his subordinate.

"Suppose I'm about to deploy the assault teams," Graykill asked Aalor. "Am I to understand that I shouldn't count on your marines?"

"My people will take *Vehement*," Aalor replied condescendingly. "On their own."

"How nice." Graykill scratched his head thoughtfully. "In that case we'll take *General Gracie* and *General Liddell*. Shall we clear the ships entirely?"

"No, no. You only have to capture the bridge deck." I took out a remote terminal and placed it on the table. "My orbship computer will overwrite the cruisers' mainframes in a minute or two. The main objective is to gain access to the central ship mainframe and hold it for a few minutes while Brainiac does his job."

"Oh! Even better then! Several minutes won't be a problem at all. When are the Breed cruisers scheduled to leave hi-sec space? When will they be outside of the system?"

"You're asking the wrong guy," Aalor replied. "This is Surgeon's show. My job is to smuggle the orbship into the system. Nothing more."

"Why does it matter when the cruisers leave the system?" I tensed a little as everyone craned to stare at me. "What's wrong with just flying up to them while they're parked and capturing them while they sit there?"

"Err…" said Graykill meaningfully and scratched his head again. "Are you serious? You've brought us all here and you have no idea what you're getting into?"

This sounded ominous. If there was any problem with capturing the ships while they sat in dock, Vargen should have warned me. Or did he not have to? He seemed a little too eager to help once I'd explained my campaign to him. He even forced me to cover all the expenses for the preparations and the aftermath.

"What are you talking about? Am I missing something?"

"Why you're missing everything!" Graykill snapped. "Aalor, bring up the system map."

A hologram of the Galvar system appeared between us. It bristled with points and lines, indicating ships and their trajectories. Graykill frowned and asked Aalor to highlight the important objects.

"All right. Listen up because I'm only going to tell you once and only because I owe you. And I hate being in debt. Here is our current position, at this green dot. These red dots there, are

Fighting Breed's cruisers sitting in their docks. This empty space all around them is the guild's official territory. Non-guild ships cannot enter it. The Grand Arbiter will pulverize anything that's not ID'd as friendly. To be honest, I have no idea what you expected. We can't enter the guild's hi-sec space. We cannot get on the ships. And even if by some miracle we succeed in capturing one, it will cease to belong to the Breed and the Arbiter will disable it with its EM battery. Their marines will recover it in five minutes. Hence my earlier question: 'When should we expect them to leave secure space?' Although, no, that's no longer a question. Now I have another one: Surgeon, are you a moron or what?"

T.K.O. — and such a thorough one that I couldn't even argue. This wasn't enough for Aalor, however; wishing to get a kick in while I was down, he threw in his two cents:

"I am required to be in the system for twelve hours. After that, I'll be on my way. Now be so kind as to remove yourself and your belongings from my ship."

"He's right. You didn't hire us for the rest of our lives," Graykill warned.

Confusion. That would be my best characterization of the feeling that washed over me. Stan began crawling the forums but found nothing sensible about base security. At my request, he made a thread on the official forum, but the moderators immediately deleted it. They even slapped me with a warning: Such issues were not subject to public discussion and here are some helpful links to official stores where such information could be purchased.

An incoming call to my PDA was so unexpected that I even

flinched.

"I see you're already in position?" Vargen decided to personally test my readiness — or to mock me. "How's it going?"

"Why didn't you tell me about their defenses?" I asked him straight on.

"And why would I do that?" Liberium's head asked with genuine bewilderment. "You are a friend of our guild, not an officer. I did everything that I promised. Aalor is with you and ready to help you seize the ship. Nothing more."

A pause ensued. I was panicking a bit inside but still managed to ask in a completely normal voice:

"What is this all about? Isn't it a bit petty for the head of such a large guild?"

"No, Surgeon. It's not petty at all. Consider this an expression of my appreciation for our earlier collaboration. I like you. I like you because I like arrogance in general..." Vargen paused and added: "I did you a favor and you got off with a mere bloody nose. Remember your level. Forever. And if you decide to play outside of your league again, maybe you'll remember this lesson and think twice. Got it?"

"Oh sure," I snorted, hearing his motives. "You've really explained yourself there."

"Excellent. Then tell Aalor he can come on back."

"No."

"What do you mean 'no?'"

"I've hired him for the next twelve hours."

Again there was a pause, after which Vargen exhaled noisily into the mic.

"As you like. I hope you won't mind it if I show your raid to some of my friends here? We will assume that this is your finest hour! The leaders of all the top guilds will watch your attempt. We're already making bets about how long you'll last. Want me to put in a wager for you?"

"What're the odds?"

"Eight to one. Ash himself is the bankroll. He's guaranteeing the payoff. And the bettors are all our friends, so there won't be any leaks. Fighting Breed won't know you're coming."

"In that case, bet a billion for me. On me succeeding, obviously."

"Are you sure?" Vargen grunted. "Transfer the money, since you have it to spare. I'll make the wager for you."

"One billion, Vargen. And another thing. I won't need the three cruisers we'll capture, so you can have them at market value in honor of our partnership."

Vargen burst out laughing in response.

"I'll take them, I'll take them," he agreed and disconnected.

My entire body was trembling as if I was freezing cold, even though my armor suit maintained a steady temperature. The medical monitor indicated that everything was nominal, so my state was not caused by any debuffs. The problem were my nerves. I was angry. And not only with Vargen, who had turned me into an object of mockery, but also at myself for allowing it to happen.

On my suit's external camera screen, I could see that Aalor was offering me something. I turned on the external microphones and heard:

"Vargen told me that you placed a bet. Transfer the money

to my account."

Without further ado, I transferred the required amount, causing my PDA to squeak, informing me that my bet had been accepted and fixed.

"General meeting in twenty minutes!" I said, heading to the orbship. I needed to thoroughly assess the situation. I had bet on myself based on nothing but my feelings and my desire to throw a counterpunch at Vargen.

Meanwhile, my mind whirred, frantically searching for a way out of the situation. I had no choice but to spend some real credits on intel about how the guilds arranged their naval bases. It turned out there really was a no-fly zone and special security agreements with the locals delimiting a high-security area around the guild's fleet. You'd have to be a damn fool to try to sneak into such a Fort Knox.

"Lex, what if we try the cruise ploy again? We'll distract the Grand Arbiter and zip over to the cruisers and land our marines. Then, once we've captured the ships, we can distract the Arbiter one more time and get out." Wisely, Eunice did not share her thoughts about my decision — whether by word or hint. Instead, she focused on helping me forward by offering the various options she could think of. I was very grateful to her for this support.

"It won't work. The Arbiter is capable of doing several tasks at once. She controls the entire system and this jumble of ships too."

"Damn...If we could only sink that tub..."

"Not an option. The Precians would flip their lid. And we just barely reestablished relations with them. There is no way to destroy the Arbiter," I said and shook my head. And yet an interesting idea took root in the back of my mind and began to grow, gradually coming to resemble a complete solution.

"Okay, I see." Here, Eunice noticed that I was thinking of something and went on: "We have to sneak into the no-fly zone without anyone knowing about it. What if we somehow obtain 'friendly' status with Fighting Breed?"

'Friendly' status. There was something in this. I nodded. The plan was almost ready.

"And importantly, it's not just the assault team that needs 'Friendly' status but the cruisers too, once Brainiac steals them and they become ours. Damn! Anyway you spin it, everything comes down to that damn Arbiter!"

The Precian cruise cruiser…A friendly status, but only with the Arbiter instead of the guild…That's it!

"Eunice, you're the best!" I couldn't resist and pulled my wife to me, kissing her deeply. "Brainiac, you're our only hope! I need you to retrieve everything you have about the Arbiter from your memory banks — the comm nodes' locations, the hull dimensions, and any other specifications. I need a good place to infiltrate it safely and, most importantly, undetected by the Precians. Our ships will receive 'friendly' status!"

During my short time in Galactogon, I had managed to get onboard an Arbiter twice. Once as a guest of the adviser, another after the Arbiter had fallen on the imperial palace of the Delvians. The time had come to take advantage of the knowledge I had acquired.

Twenty minutes later, a final meeting took place on board

A CHECK FOR A BILLION

Cruiser *Inevitable*. I was in charge.

"We have everything we need." I collected my thoughts, reigning in their chaotic scurrying. "How many marines can we fit into a frigate?"

"If we don't have to land on a planet or jumping into hyperspace, about a hundred."

"Wonderful! We're changing our plans a bit. I'm not going with you. Everything else remains as before. Load up into frigates, wait for my command and fly to your objectives. Send the frigates back as soon as you board the cruisers. They can't be seen loitering around the system. Make your way to the cruisers' bridge decks, connect the remote terminal and give Brainiac a minute to work his magic. The problem of accessing the no-fly zone is my job. I will ensure that you can pass freely. Aalor, can I count on your help?"

My question was met with a cool, steady gaze and his customary silence. Assuming that he wanted me to qualify exactly what kind of help I needed, I explained:

"I need a fighter with a pilot."

"They're all busy," came the immediate response from the captain. "I have none to spare."

"So then I can't count on you. No problem. Graykill, do you know a daring pilot who has access to this system?"

"How daring?"

"About as daring as you were right before you killed those Zatrathi guards back on the flying fortress."

A pleased smile appeared on the marine's face.

"I do know one. Let me just see if he has the access. I

should warn you, his services don't come cheap."

"Well, I didn't find you in the bargain bin either," I muttered, but Graykill did not hear me. He had already made the call.

"He'll be here in ten minutes. His name is Valmont. You can discuss the price with him."

"Got a space in your hangar?" I turned back to Aalor. Checkmate jerkface! Even a mangy sheep's good for a little wool, as they say. Either he has room and he'll have to help, or he doesn't have room and everyone will see his true nature. I don't think that Vargen instructed him to obstruct me. The twitching jowl on the captain's otherwise stony face spoke volumes. At last he replied:

"Hangar two. Portside. I will make the necessary arrangements."

"Spectacular! In that case, start loading up into the frigates and wait for my orders. And oh yeah, be careful with these things. They are fragile and expensive." I placed three remote terminals on the table.

Valmont turned out to be a pretty extravagant character. In a game rated 12+, he still somehow managed to get a cigar. Valmont smoked like a good old fashioned train, flouting all social norms, municipal ordinances and naval regulations. Instead of the customary pilot's jacket, he wore a ragged vest, which revealed his weightlifter's arms. His three-day stubble, which was supposed to be impossible in Galactogon, suggested that Valmont had carefully worked on his avatar's appearance and foregone the default transfer of his real appearance into the game. He generally stood out from everyone around him, like a feral cat on a space station — uncaged and grappling with zero gravity, naturally.

A CHECK FOR A BILLION

"What's up, doc?" He asked, taking a drag and billowing the smoke in my face.

I wasn't about to indulge such a childish provocation, so I stepped around Valmont and went to his fighter. A standard triangular design with three retractable landing gear. The only way I could ride externally was to hug one of the landing struts.

"We have to sneak up to a Grand Arbiter, without starting a fight."

"Each Arbiter is surrounded by a no-fly perimeter that's one click in radius. The flight instruments go haywire as soon as you enter it." This was punctuated by a new column of smoke.

"And that's why I called you. Only this isn't all. You'll need to fly with the landing gear down."

"The hell for?"

"Because I'll be sitting on one of them. Up until you drop me off on the Arbiter's hull."

"Guy, are you a moron or what? You'll be smooshed like a flapjack." Valmont stopped smoking, fixed me with a lengthy, serious look and suddenly added: "Can't fly with the gear down. Crazy turbulence."

"Sounds like you understand the job. How you do it is on you. All I'm interested in is how much you'll charge for such a trick."

"How much?" Valmont grew pensive again. "You compensate me for the loss of a class, if I have to respawn."

"Is that all?" I asked surprised. Graykill had suggested the price would be astronomical.

"If you succeed — yes. If you fail — a hundred million."

Oh! There you have it! A fellow adventurer. Well, this is

great. Another hundred million reasons to pull this thing off. The family budget will be better off for it. We shook hands and the pilot immediately waved his hand calling for one of Aalor's engineers.

"Hey, you! Come here! You look like the type who likes a good puzzle. Of course you do! I can see it in your eyes. Disassemble the front landing gear. And mount a strut under the nose. What are you standing there for? Get jumping! There's no time to waste!"

The player was taken aback but did as ordered. Summoning a brigade of assistants, he began to work on the fighter. The hangar filled with the jarring buzz of circular saws and hydraulic hammers. The only way to dismantle the landing gear was to first amputate it.

"Now you," Valmont returned to me. "I don't know what your deal is, but I like your derring-do. So let's get down to the business. Here's the plan: You'll cling for dear life here. I'll fly you up to the Arbiter. Remember: I get one chance — after that the Arbiter will repel me with its tractor beams. You'll have like three seconds, max. And the turbulence on our approach will be strong enough to knot your guts. Changed your mind, yet?"

"If this were meatspace, maybe." I turned to the pilot. The cigar was still wedged in a corner of his mouth, though at least he wasn't dousing me with its smoke. Behind him, the fighter's landing gear crashed to the hangar deck with a loud clang. The fighter almost slammed its cowl down in its wake, but was caught by a restraint at the last moment.

"Load up, load up. Let's see what kind of dough you're made of."

A CHECK FOR A BILLION

"Soft and fragrant. I got all crusty like this from being in the oven."

The landing gear compartment was very cramped and the engineers were forced to help me. Using all my limbs to secure myself in place, I heard Valmont ask snidely behind me:

"Ready, dead man? Off we go. Flaps in and thrusters to full."

Everything began spinning before my eyes and a lump formed in my throat. I was about to lose my virtual breakfast. The suit responded to my unease, injecting some kind of drug. The stars before my eyes disappeared and were replaced by cosmic darkness. Valmont took off at full throttle hurling us straight at the Arbiter.

"Get ready! We're about to encounter some turbulence," he warned over my PDA a few seconds before the rodeo started in earnest. The fighter surged and ducked 'up and down,' then swung 'right and left,' and punctuated it all with an Immelmann turn. The holds I was clutching trembled violently and gradually began bending from the forces involved.

"Are you alive out there? It's about to get worse!"

Valmont did a barrel roll and my heart sank into my heels. A film descended over my eyes, the chemicals could no longer keep up with the loads I was experiencing — and still the pilot refused to let up. Kicking in the afterburners, he went into a corkscrew.

"Now!" Valmont yelled and I released my grip. My angular momentum was so huge that I shot out away from the fighter like a bullet. Valmont hadn't missed — I flew straight at the Arbiter instead of open space. My suit's screens began to blink madly. The locals' security ship was surrounded by a static EM field that scrambled all my electronics.

"Welp — my goose is cooked! It's all up to you now, Maverick!" said Valmont and a ball of fire appeared behind me. The Precians didn't bother negotiating with the trespassing fighter and simply blasted it to pieces.

I shrank, getting ready for the blow but the EM field vanished near the hull itself. I regained control and immediately engaged reverse thrust, slowing down. However, the distance to the Arbiter was so small that this didn't help much. The crash landing made me go deaf for a moment. A whole bunch of debuffs bloomed before my eyes. Stun, daze, fractures. I was glad of one thing — the magnets had worked as intended, attaching me to the hull. Then again, the suit's system report was disappointing. About half of its functions were failing and the rest were blaring with warnings and alerts. Changing an armor suit in outer space is pure recklessness, so I fell over backwards, merging with the ship. Just in case, the Precians were looking for me.

"Brainiac, where should I go next?"

"I am establishing your current location now. Captain, couldn't you have landed in some other place?" the computer grumbled. "I cannot see you at all."

"What do you mean you can't see me?"

"Exactly that. I am reading your signal but I cannot determine where it is coming from. I'm also not picking up a visual ID. Roll your head around, I'll try to locate you using the stars."

As soon as I raised my head, my heart stopped: I was

staring straight down the barrel of a capital ship beam cannon. One of the Arbiter's turrets — capable of blasting a frigate out of the sky in one shot — was aimed directly at me.

A hundred thoughts flashed through my head. Both good ones and bad ones. But mostly expletive-laden, bad ones. I was staring into the face of death, unable to move a muscle. Perhaps this is what despair feels like — a condition in which there is no longer anything left — no desire to fight, to resist, to come out victorious — a feeling of utter emptiness but for the dull ache of failure.

"Captain, why'd you stop moving? I'm telling you — turn around! I can't figure out where you are!" Brainiac buzzed again in my ear. I swallowed, not taking my eyes off the barrel. The shot had not come. "Captain?"

Slowly, expecting to respawn at any moment, I crawled sideways. The turret did not follow me, remaining in the same position. I moved further still. Finally, I crawled far enough to understand that the gun was inactive.

"Oh! Give me a sec! Let me just figure this out," Brainiac did not know what was happening and went on calculating my location. "I have two pieces of news. Good and bad. I'll start with the good — I've located you. The bad news is that you're on the other side of the Arbiter and I can't see you."

"What do you suggest I do?"

"To your right, about twenty meters away, there is a deflector. Behind it there are some reflectors and…"

"Lex, just climb into that thermal exhaust port over there!" barked Eunice. "The Arbiter has a triple hull. It will take you forever to cut through it. Here, all you have to do is cut off the outer seal — and you'll be inside just like that. Place the pressurizing force field here and then twenty meters further cut your way inside. It'll be a cakewalk after that."

"Brainiac?"

"It is feasible," the ship replied with notes of discontent. "Of course, if you wish to stick to the original plan, then my option…"

"Brainiac, which of the two options is easier and more efficient?"

"Through the thermal exhaust port. Judging by its structure it is used to dump excess gas. The duct should be wide enough for you to fit. It will be easier."

Everything was not as rosy as I had hoped. Cutting the seal was a matter of five seconds. Hot gas was venting out of the duct and my damaged suit began blinking plaintively, its warning lights coming on. The suit's thermoregulation system could not cope, and it grew as hot as if I were in an oven. I grew sweaty and my suit's medunit began to administer various injections trying to put out the overheating debuffs — and still I kept crawling onward waiting for Brainiac to give me further orders. Finally I heard his voice:

"Here!"

Bending over, I pulled the portable forcefield and plasma cutter out of my inventory. As I cut, the powerful stream of gas blew the sparks away from the Arbiter and as soon as the hole was big enough, I tumbled through it, crashing to the floor. By the end, I was acting entirely on autopilot, barely conscious. The suit's medical injections had ended and the heat had done its job. I even lost consciousness for a couple of minutes until the suit cooled off.

A CHECK FOR A BILLION

Brainiac's insistent voice was the only thing that kept me from drifting off into oblivion. Pulling out a spare armor suit from my inventory, I got out of my current stove. As soon as my poor body slipped into the new suit, I felt a sense of relief. The onboard computer even squealed a warning and began resuscitation procedures. It couldn't cope with all my debuffs, but at least I could function normally. Rising to my feet, I sat down a couple of times, getting used to the new armor. It wasn't my legendary suit of course, but it should do for the mission at hand.

Looking at what was left of my main, I sighed heavily. I do not even know how I managed to survive in this pile of tattered metal.

"What's next, Brainiac?"

"You need to go down the corridor, then take a right and walk another twenty meters. There are no network connectors where you are."

"Got it. I'm on it."

The door slid up and I almost butted heads with a Precian redshirt. His astonishment was so sincere that you'd think the technician lost contact with reality, gaping at the armored colossus before him. That is what did him in. I could not allow him to shout or warn his superiors about my presence, so I quickly grabbed the poor fellow with a manipulator and flung him at the ceiling with all my might. The Precian went limp but didn't turn into a crate. Releasing the motionless body, I cocked my blaster, when a crazy thought popped into my head. I had several Jolly Roger tokens in my inventory. Why not test a pet theory I'd concocted? If it works, great — if not, no big loss.

I slipped a token into the unconscious Precian's jacket pocket and then turned him into a shimmering loot crate. I didn't pick it up. Let the locals do it themselves. They have some means of locating where one of their number had died. Let's see how they react to find the Jolly Roger's calling card.

I traveled the rest of the way without incident, following Brainiac's directions. Barricading the last door behind me just in case, I pulled out a remote terminal.

"What is the plan?" asked Brainiac as he hacked the Arbiter's security layer. The locals' ship stood no chance against the advanced Uldan AI.

"Two objectives. The first and most important is that we're about to send three frigates full of marines into Fighting Breed's no-fly zone. The Arbiter has to perceive them as friendlies with all the access that entails."

"Give me a second to locate the relevant permissions. Got it! You may launch the frigates. The Arbiter will now treat them as its own family."

"Graykill, you've got the green light." I immediately called the marine. "Move out!"

"If I lose my armor suit, I will flay you alive and wear your hide into battle," he muttered in reply. "Everyone head out!"

"I see the frigates," reported Brainiac. "Taking control now. Got it! Labeling them friendly now."

"Full speed ahead, boys. Semper Fi and all that...!" I ordered into my comm. The players were tarrying at the very edge of the no-fly zone, expecting the Arbiter to react. The Arbiter did nothing, however, and three glittering lightning bolts zipped toward

---

the Breed's cruisers. Encased in their armors, the marines began to file out of their frigates, dispersing throughout the hulls and burrowing like termites into a tree. Brainiac could monitor Graykill's actions and he relayed the video stream from the marine's suit to me. The marines did not make their own jobs harder; they breached just outside the bridge deck. Their plasma cutters erupted in a shower of sparks and one by one the players slipped into the hull. A smattering of shots, a quick dash to the bridge, the cutting of the door to the bridge and then the bridge's clearance. Everything went so fast that no one understood what was going on. Neither on the planet, nor on the ship itself.

"We're in position!" Graykill reported.

"We're in position! We're in position!" reported the other squads. We had captured the bridge decks, the remote terminals had been connected. Now the marines were busy digging in against any counterattack.

"Do your magic, Brainiac!" As soon as I issued the order, three progress bars appeared before my eyes. One went faster than the others but on the whole all of them grew steadily to 100%.

"Three ships without friendly tags are about to appear in the Galvar system. The Arbiter should not be able to see them."

"Understood. Executing now." For a few moments, the progress bars paused and then began moving again. I watched each percentage with a skipping heart.

Seventy percent.

Fighting Breed's leaders had begun to suspect something. I could see new ships scrambling from the planet; they began to circle the cruisers, making docking requests. There was no reply, however.

Eighty percent.

A frigate joined the fighters. Like everyone else, it circled around the ships, trying to figure out what was going on.

Ninety percent.

Puffing heavily with its engines, a destroyer rose from the planet's surface next. I even began to wonder how they had managed to land it to begin with — I had thought that this vessel type was only space-faring. The destroyer did not rush around chaotically, but stopped in front of the cruiser that had been taken by Aalor's marines. Perhaps, Fighting Breed was still hoping to solve the problem through negotiations. They were too late.

One hundred percent.

You have acquired a new vessel: Cruiser General Gracie. Item class: B-87

You have acquired a new vessel: Cruiser General Liddell. Item class: A-12

You have acquired a new vessel: Cruiser Vehement. Item class: B-66

"Here I am!" announced Brainiac. "I have assigned 'friendly' status to all three cruisers. Calculating hyperjump now. One minute. Oh…the Arbiter has opened fire…"

For a few moments there was silence over the air. My heart sank, I even stopped breathing, waiting for everything to fall apart. The pause dragged on.

"Brainiac, what's going on over there?"

A CHECK FOR A BILLION

"Ah, it's all fine, Captain. Fighting Breed lost their cool and attacked. Then the Grand Arbiter intervened and put them in their place. It wasn't shooting at us. That's it! The cruisers have jumped!"

On my screen, the three giant ships blinked and zipped away into the starfield.

"Okay, Brainiac. Your next assignment is to download everything you can get your digital tentacles on," I smiled, taking off my suit and putting it in inventory. I understood perfectly well that I could not be extracted. Therefore, I had to make the most of my forced respawn. Five minutes later, the Precians had triangulated my location and began trying to break into my room. Pulling out a grenade, I closed my eyes and pulled the pin. I'll have to part with this set of body armor I'm wearing. In exchange, the Jolly Roger insignia stamped on my pauldrons should knock the Precians off my trail. Let them suspect anyone at all, so long as it isn't Surgeon.

There was a bang…

You were killed and will respawn on Blood Island.

Your rapport with the Corsican has grown. Current Rapport: 10,000.

You have impressed the leader of the Brotherhood of the Jolly Roger.

CHAPTER SEVEN

REAK..."

"*Dead man walking...*"

Uh-huh.

"*Run while you can...*"

"*This is your last warning...*"

"*Freak...*"

I see. Neither originality nor creativity.

Having scanned through the messages, I added yet another member of Fighting Breed to my blacklist. Getting a third list from Hansa is like being a member in some special club. In addition to the ecstasy of merely reading the capabilities of their weapons, you can't help but revel in the exclusivity of it all. My new armor suit made my pulse race, pumping endorphins to every bit of my digital body. I preened in front of the mirror for several minutes, observing how well the cloaking field worked. The slightest distortion, a waver in the room's air, indicated that the player Surgeon was in fact preening in front of the mirror. Eh it's too bad I didn't have this thing when I was in my teens.

A CHECK FOR A BILLION

Checking the cloak's effect with a thermal imager and infrared motion sensors, I was pleased to discover that I didn't even show up when accelerating. This piece of gear really was worth the credits I'd spent on it. Especially since I'd earned the money so quickly and easily.

Vargen paid me twenty-two billion GCs for the three Fighting Breed cruisers as well as for the contents of their holds and equipment. He tried to bargain, naturally, but Eunice made it clear that he couldn't win in this deal. I really enjoyed their exchange and mostly just sat back and kept my mouth shut. Vargen couldn't say no because he would lose face in front of his friends in that elite 'league' of his. As a result, the head of Liberium was forced to haggle, complaining that the cruisers were in poor condition and that it was unseemly of me, a friend of his guild, to ask for their nominal market price. At this point, Brainiac kindly played a recording of Vargen saying, 'You are a friend of our guild, not an officer.' The whole thing was a lark, in other words.

I won another eight billion from the bet and one more from Ash personally as a 'gift.' The head of Vanguard called me on my PDA and floated the idea of sharing the data I had obtained from the Arbiter with the public at large. 'The public at large,' naturally, consisted of two or three powerful acquaintances of his. They were interested in the Arbiter's layout, performance characteristics, vulnerabilities and capabilities. Ash understood perfectly well that I would not have left the defensive citadel without getting ahold of this very information. I had no choice but to act like I was happy to share. I'll assume that this is an investment in our future relationship. Having dealt with all my payments and debts, I dumped half of my GCs on two armor suits from Hansa's third tier and was quite satisfied with the results.

"Are you going to preen and pout in front of that mirror for a long time, small fry?" Tryd asked, surly at my delay. "We have no time to spare — it's time to head to Shurtan!"

The pirate had a point. I would need to go meet the Corsican tomorrow and I still wasn't ready. After the last operation, I decided that I would reach out to Vargen or Kiddo (for that matter) only as a last resort because working with partners like that was by far the most difficult thing in Galactogon.

"We've received the reconnaissance data." Eunice turned on one of the screens. Without my noticing, my wife had gradually become an important member of *Warlock*'s crew, taking over the routine and business affairs. Do we need to contract some scouts to explore the system? No problem! Do we need to supply our ship at the lowest price possible? Already done! Even the Hansa engineers were more willing to deal with her than with me.

"A flying fortress, an orbital station, two cruisers in the repair docks and a total of three hundred and twenty smaller ships. Look here. They're preparing two more repair docks at the flying fortress. That means there are more cruisers en route."

"If we jump in there right now, we won't last a minute." I soberly assessed the prospects of a raid onto Shurtan. "We'll need help."

"And fairly elaborate help at that. I've studied the flying fortress's capabilities. The only weapon that can pose a threat to her is Ringold's cannon.

Seeing my puzzled face, Eunice sighed and explained:

A CHECK FOR A BILLION

"A scroll of Black Death in *Runlustia* terms. It's analogous to the Yamato cannon that Kiddo has on *Alexandria*. But Ringold's cannon is no panacea either. It'll only be able to eliminate the flying fortress and maybe any ships that are in the path of its fire. We'll need another five or six cruisers for the remaining enemies."

"I just settled my accounts with Vargen and don't feel like renewing our partnership," I gritted my teeth.

"Vargen alone won't be enough. His ships don't have a Ringold's cannon and he'll ask too much for his services. Of course there's Kiddo, but...Well, basically, we need a reliable group."

"We could bring Gammon and Kiddo instead of just Kiddo. They will work together for sure."

Tryd snorted contemptuously.

"Arr. Pirates today are a meagre, mangy breed. All you scurvy lot know is how to beg for help."

Eunice and I exchanged glances and turned to Tryd, waiting for a hint.

"So what do you suggest?"

"What can an old pirate suggest?! Jump right into the thick of it! Take a risk!"

"Then we will try to solve the problem ourselves," Eunice backed him. I wanted to argue, but she didn't give me a chance. "Wait! Hear me out. Tryd didn't show up for no reason. Right? He's reminding us that we have to get back to the pirate-based gameplay. And before you go to the Corsican!"

"Yes, but this doesn't mean that we have to run headlong into certain death!"

"We have to think, Lex. Tryd is hinting that we should do

this ourselves."

"I don't see any alternative to going in guns blazing." I examined the system map once again, giving in to Eunice's and Tryd's combined onslaught. "Running the gauntlet won't work — neither with speed nor with stealth. There are just too many Zatrathi there!"

"Here it is! The key phrase is 'too many!' What does that mean?"

"That I don't understand hints?" I said. "Come on, out with it."

"There's constant traffic in and out of the planet — frigates, scouts and small transports. The traffic is huge. Some of them stop here on this moon. The Zatrathi harvesters are mining something there. Could be stone for construction, could be sand for hourglasses, who knows. I don't see any resources there. Our job will be to get to the moon, stow away on a transport and reach the planet surface in its hold. There are so many ships in this system that there's no way they inspect the cargo holds. The main obstacle will be surviving the landing."

Hmm…I stared at the jumble of ships. We'd only had cloaks on our armor suits for a few hours and Eunice had already found a use for them. Hold up!

"Let's say we manage to sneak in. What are we going to do with Tryd? He doesn't have a cloak on his suit."

We turned to look at the Delvian.

"I have to get in there," he declared, correctly interpreting our looks. The idea of leaving him on the ship seemed self-evident. "Keep thinking!"

A CHECK FOR A BILLION

"Can the scout you hired figure out what the harvesters are mining?"

Eunice nodded and went to negotiate. The image on the screen changed, zooming in on the quarries that the Zatrathi had set up. I was forced to commend the courage of our scout, who was verging on pure recklessness. The player had crept to the very edge of the quarry, recording the entire mining and transportation operation.

The Zatrathi were quarrying marble. The harvesters were cutting out giant slabs of the stone and loading them on conveyor belts. These ferried the slabs to the transports. We counted seven slabs before the transport shut its hold and made way for the next one in line.

"That's enough," Eunice ordered and the player crawled away to safety.

I looked at the topographic map of the moon again and drew Eunice's attention to a point near the transports' landing zone. It was very well hidden from the larger area by a sizeable boulder.

"Can your scout explore that area? Tell him to look for a cleft or a pit large enough to conceal a slab of marble."

The player was a real pro: Twenty minutes later we found the hideout we needed.

"Now a question for everyone. How can we get to that moon without aggroing the Zatrathi?"

"Only in a scout with its reflectors turned on," both Eunice and Tryd replied simultaneously.

"Brainiac, isn't our orbship an Uldan scout? Do we have reflectors?"

"Unless this system has some active scanners in place, it should be no problem to get to the back of the moon without being noticed. We could even risk it if there are active scanners, as long as they're in the outer orbits and not looking for us specifically. But I would not want to go there. Remember: The Zatrathi know how to disrupt planetary spirit bindings."

"Don't panic. Snake, make a dummy marble slab. Here are the external dimensions — your objective is to make space in the slab to fit one Tryd in an armor suit."

"A Trojan horse?" Eunice's face brightened. My wife understood what I had in mind.

"More like a Trojan slab. Works just like a Trojan horse but, well, it's a slab."

The preparations took us a long time, though the main difficulty was not the equipment. The problem was the marble. It turned out to be impossible to buy it — the stone was utilized so little in-game that no one sold it on Belket. So we had to order it — interstellar express — which meant that the piece of stone came out pretty pricey.

We lost another couple hours on routing a hollow compartment into the slab, and then at last we crossed all our limbs for good luck and headed for the Shurtan system.

"We're in position. I have deployed our reflectors," said Brainiac and *Warlock*'s bridge deck plunged into a deep gloom illuminated only by several screens. Any and all other devices that could betray us had been turned off.

"I don't think they can see us," I remarked a couple of minutes later, never taking my eyes off the passive scan monitor.

A CHECK FOR A BILLION

The Zatrathi did not react to our appearance and went on rushing around their system with the chaotic purposefulness of ants.

"Sit her down here," ordered Tryd and pointed his finger at a point on the map. "We'll go on foot from there."

No one bothered arguing with the pirate, not even Brainiac. We landed on the airless rock without any problems and emerged to the surface about ten kilometers from the quarry. I cast a doubtful look at the hoverboard I had bought for the operation. It was the standard means for conveying players along the surface of a planet, yet I'd never used one before. I am neither a surfer nor a skater. And in general, I had little to no idea how to properly move on this thing. All my attempts to use it inside the ship ended with me running into the walls — to the Delvian's ridicule. This could turn out to be a problem.

"Don't fall now, small fry." Tryd didn't bother hiding his condescension as he tethered my board to his. I climbed up on it, fixed my armor suit into place and picked up an empty container with my manipulator. Tryd looked questioningly at Eunice, who hopped up on her hoverboard with enviable ease and casually bragged:

"I was top of my class in flying this thing."

"Turn on your cloak," grumbled Tryd, tossing a reflecting cape over himself. The pirate did not vanish completely, but one would have to look at him directly to notice him. The hoverboard under me jerked and we rushed forward. A lump formed in my throat, forcing me to swallow. Strange. I was used to flying with high Gs, so I should have been immune to motion sickness, yet the system had different ideas and kept burdening me with various debuffs.

"We're in position." Tryd lowered his hoverboard to the ground and a countdown timer appeared in front of my eyes. Three minutes of disorientation.

"Hilvar won't be happy that one of his scallywags is incapable of raiding on land," the pirate concluded, helping me change the medunit in my suit. I felt relief almost instantly. "You chose the wrong mentor, Surgeon."

"You are the second person to tell me so," I agreed, catching my breath. "I don't remember anything like this before. But what does Hilvar have to do with it?"

"His pirates are all landlubbers. You are more cut out to be a space pirate. That much is clear. That one there," he indicated Eunice, "she's a natural landlubber. Nurse hasn't made her choice yet. You have. Your way lies with the Corsican. Hilvar won't be able to teach you."

This was both unexpected and unpleasant news. When had I strayed from my chosen path? Tryd ignored my question, pointing to the container:

"Let's get down to business now. Help me get in."

We were about a hundred meters from the area where the marble was being loaded on the transports. A tall cliff separated us from the Zatrathi, but even that wasn't enough to muffle the rumble of the extraction and processing operations going on nearby. The earth shook and I had to cut my external microphones to a minimum so as not to go deaf. A recon drone sent out by Brainiac showed that there were no living Zatrathi around us. The process was automated, which fit our plans perfectly.

A CHECK FOR A BILLION

Getting onto the transport turned out to be a cinch. Waiting until the next ship was half full, we threw the dummy slab with Tryd in it onto the conveyor belt. The Zatrathi systems paid no attention to the extra slab and loaded it aboard. Invisible to the surveillance cameras, we followed it into the hold and, after just a couple of minutes, the transport's hull shuddered as its engines turned on. The first part of the plan was executed so perfectly that I wasn't even surprised to hear Brainiac's warning:

"Captain! There's a problem!"

"Have we been detected?" Eunice asked.

"Not exactly. Not yet. Better see for yourself. I'll display it on your screens."

Tryd's litany of expletives was like a triumphal march, a fanfare to which the battle fleet of the Anorxian Empire entered the Shurtan system. My initial hope that they had come in peace was quickly obliterated by the fire that began pouring from the newcomers. One by one, the Zatrathi ships began bursting into fireballs, unable to withstand the onslaught of four Grand Arbiters. The synthoids had approached their raid into the depths of Zatrathi territory methodically, pulling their defensive ships from several planets at once for the purpose.

"Brainiac, what's our ETA to the planet?" I began worrying once I saw the speed with which the Zatrathi forces were being wiped out. The Anorxians were destroying the fighters and frigates scrambling to defend but also the transports and harvesters that came across their path.

"Ten minutes."

"Damn, we won't make it...We need to somehow let the

Anorxians know that we are here!"

"Belay that!" Tryd commanded from inside the slab. "There's no use. These are renegades. They won't talk. They're the same ones that captured our base."

Indeed, the insignia of the robot empire on the Arbiter closest to us had been crudely painted over.

The Zatrathi finally reacted in full force to the attack. Both cruisers disengaged from the flying fortress — and then all my screens went out, plunging me into darkness. My armor suit had shut off.

"Brainiac?!" Lumara's present did its job, allowing me to reconnect with my ship.

"This is really something, Cap'n!" the snake replied instead of the computer. "The Anorxians have detonated a giant EM bomb in the system. An excellent solution! We'll need to speak to Hansa about this device!"

'Sure we will,' I said to myself as I swapped powercells. My new armor suit had been designed with all the latest ergonomic features. It was comfortable, cozy, secure and, most importantly, it was possible to change powercells from the inside. Perfect for dealing with EM traps.

"Eunice?"

"I'll be up in five seconds."

"Brainiac what's the status in the system?"

"The smaller ships are all disabled. Only a flying fortress and two cruisers remain. Ah! Here comes the Zatrathi reply!"

As my screens came back on, I saw a pillar of plasma erupt from the flying fortress's main cannon. It rushed through the

A CHECK FOR A BILLION

vacuum in a direct line to the Arbiter and another sun appeared in the system. The enormous guardian ship, the pride of Galactogon's locals, burst at its seams and vanished.

Despite the inertial dampeners, the blast wave knocked us over and pressed me into the hull. The transport began to spin at an incredible speed, generating artificial gravity, but apart from feeling a bit more sluggish, I had no difficulty coping with the force. Nothing was spinning within our own coordinate system.

"Brainiac, can you pick us up?"

"Me?! No, Captain, I can't risk joining you!"

The Anorxians did not wait for the flying fortress to reload and scrambled their squadrons. The system again plunged into chaos. And even though the Zatrathi maintained control in the midst of this jumble of ships, I couldn't help but start feeling a headache coming on. Perhaps deciding that the chaos wasn't bad enough, the Zatrathi scrambled their reinforcements too. From *Warlock*'s perspective, the system turned into one big bright point.

"Eunice, cut the bulkhead to the bridge!" I ordered, since the girl was closer the bridge deck than me. "Brainiac, can we pilot this tub?"

"I will need to analyze the control systems," the computer answered vaguely, unwilling to promise anything definite.

"I don't understand, small fry, is anyone going to pull me out of this coffin?" Tryd's terrible roar reminded us of our passenger. I had figured that the EM blast would disable his cybernetics, but the pirate was tougher than that. Activating my blasters, I punched a hole in the transport's hull and began to push the slabs out into space, at last freeing the slab with the Delvian. In the process, I took one peek at what was going on out in space and immediately regretted it. We were spinning incredibly fast.

"Ready!" The sparks ceased and Eunice knocked out the bulkhead to the bridge with a kick. Reaching the pilot's console, my wife said: "Nothing! All systems are down!"

"What do they teach young pirates these days?" grumbled Tryd, climbing out of his slab. "Clear this deck, scallywag. The last thing we need are stones flying at us as we try to land. Nurse, get away from there! There is only room for one."

Eunice climbed back to me in the hold, obediently giving way to the pirate. He began to yank out the panel, wires and all, trying to get to the power plant.

"Orbship computer, are you tracking our flight path? Where are we falling?"

"Erm…I don't understand the question."

"You're just as stupid as your captain. I am asking you where we are headed — are we leaving the system or heading for its center?"

"A second, please." Brainiac was obviously offended. "The explosion has accelerated you in the direction of the sun. You should pass the planet Shurtan at a distance…"

"Be quiet," Tryd cut him off. "How much elo do you have on you?"

"Forty powercells," I replied, consulting with Eunice.

"Not enough…Okay, I'll use my own. Give me half of what you have! Look alive, we have very little time!"

"Tryd, why do you think the Anorxians are here so deep in Zatrathi territory?" Eunice wondered as she helped the pirate collect the elo. She had managed to burrow her way to the transport's reactor and was now almost up to her waist in the hole she had made in the control console.

"They've come to liberate the base," muttered the fox in response, interrupting his litany of curses in all the languages he knew.

"Why?" Eunice continued to pry, but he did not answer. It was perfectly clear that the Anorxians needed the base exactly for the same reason that the Delvian needed it.

"Tryd what are the Anorxians looking for at the base?" I repeated the question. "I'd rather not get involved in someone else's business."

Suddenly the dashboard began to blink — the old fox had restored our power. Grunting, he climbed out and saw two silhouettes frozen in the opening.

"Tryd?!"

"What?!" snapped the pirate, slumping into the only seat on board. "They're renegades! They've freed themselves of the main Anorxian CPU and Motherboard so if they get hurt, the Anorxians will only be happy."

"Tryd, what do you need at that base?" I wasn't about to give up and activated my blasters. "I'll blast you here and now if you don't start talking. What the hell do you need that planet for?"

The Delvian's muzzle twisted with anger and with one abrupt dash he appeared beside me. Our eyes locked.

"I'll tear you in half with my bare paws, you barnacle!" the pirate growled, as the ship shook violently around us.

"The Anorxians have noticed that your power has been

restored," announced Brainiac. "You have three fighters on your tail."

Tryd refused to look away. I wasn't about to give up myself and I was really getting close to killing the pirate if he refused to answer. I can always get the Lora some other way. Even if I had to deal with the Corsican to do it. Maybe this NPC could read my mind because he finally growled:

"Arr! They need Prince Northbridge! A chipset that we stole many years ago from the Anorxian Motherboard!"

I stepped back, uncocking my blasters. It was odd that Tryd was so worked up over some device.

"*Stan what is the Northbridge and what does it have to do with the Anorxians?*"

There was no reply. I looked with surprise from Tryd — who had gone back to the pilot's seat and was now disengaging the autopilot — to my PDA. My signal was fine and I had a connection.

"*Stan, can you hear me?*"

Silence. Our transport shuddered from another hit, which left a neat round hole in our hull.

"Hold on to your skivvies, mollusks. These be rough waters!"

We grabbed onto the handrails. I kept trying to reach Stan, but my smart home did not reply and a few moments later, I had more important problems to deal with. Everything turned upside down.

Tryd banked sharply entering Shurtan's gravity well. The pirate had been right about the marble slabs — if we hadn't dumped them, we would have been crushed at this point. We clung to our handholds as tightly as we could, activating our suits' magnets to help. Once again a lump formed in my throat and the pirate's laughter sounded in my headphones. He was shouting some kind of battle cry:

"*Merkata da Kula!*"

The constant change of direction mixed with weightlessness started getting to me. Another restorative injection dispelled the 'nausea' debuff. I closed my eyes, trying to calm down. If I was powerless to do anything at the moment, I needed to focus on surviving.

"We're about to take a hit! Brace for impact!" Tryd warned and a few seconds later the transport ceased to exist. The terrible blow almost tore my hands off. The lower part of the ship sheared off as if cut by a knife. The floor collapsed after it and we were left dangling, hanging on by our hands. Mountains and black smoke rushed under our feet, mingled with sparks from our burning ship.

"On the count of three!" Tryd peeked out from a hole in the partition, eyeing up the scene. "One! Two! Jump!"

The pirate dived down through clouds of smoke. I didn't need to be invited twice — unclenching my hands, I flew behind Tryd. Some part of the ship collided with my leg. It didn't hurt me, but it did send me spinning like a propeller, completely disorienting me.

"Brainiac, take control of my armor suit! Set me down next to Tryd!"

"Me too!" I heard Eunice add.

"Executing!" replied our savior instantly. I stopped spinning and my speed began dropping until Eunice and I settled quite

---

calmly next to the pirate.

"And these slugs call themselves pirates," remarked Tryd scornfully, watching us fall to the surface beside him.

Several Anorxian fighters screamed by overhead, chasing the smoking transport. The robots had not noticed our jump. A loud explosion sounded somewhere in the distance. The transport had been destroyed.

"What are you standing there for?" Tryd checked his map and a grimace crept over his muzzle. Pulling out another hoverboard, he tossed me the end of a towline: "The base is 1500 clicks from here. We have to get moving. Our time is running out!"

At this moment, something flashed over our heads, and a Zatrathi cruiser began to fall onto the planet. It was falling far away from us, so it was safe to enjoy the spectacle. The Anorxians were going all out. It seems that they really needed this Northbridge thingy. After making another call to Stan, I began to grow anxious. Once again there had been no answer. Perched on my hoverboard, holding the towing rope, I prepared for the long journey — when my PDA came alive with an incoming call. I picked it up as quickly as I could:

"*Good afternoon, Mr. Panzer. My name is Martin Sherper, Senior Detective. Sorry to bother you in the hospital and interrupt your gameplay, but I do have to speak with you. Should I wait for you in a special location or will we be able to talk right now?*"

"*Now's good. Has something happened?*"

"*Yes. I have some bad news. Three hours ago, your house was blown up. Unfortunately, there are several casualties from the explosion.*"

CHAPTER EIGHT

I T ALL HAPPENED IN BROAD DAYLIGHT. Three men in camouflage and black balaclavas flew up to my house on speeders, placed small devices all around its perimeter and blew my barely rebuilt home into a huge pit. The police even had to turn to the military for help because they could not independently identify the type of explosives used. Eyewitnesses noted that there was neither a blast wave, nor a roar, nor any damage to the neighboring properties. Simply, in the blink of an eye, a large fireball destroyed the structure of wood and drywall. The casualties were a couple of technicians who were just then completing the installation of a video surveillance system. Upon being turned on, all that the cameras had time to record was the appearance of the terrorists and their operation. The whole process took about five minutes and then the recording, which was streamed to the third-party servers of the security company, ended. In a strange coincidence, all nearby cameras on our streets and the surrounding blocks had been turned off for a half hour. Both the police and the military were inclined to think that this was the work of professionals from the special forces. All they could do was guess where and when I had come across their radar, given that I had been in the hospital for quite a while. One of their theories was that this was somehow related to Constantine, but I did not believe this.

"*No, that is unlikely,*" I said. "*I suspect the Fighting Breed guild from Galactogon. We have been competing in-game recently and I have received threats from them. These guys are either ex- or active military. It would not be difficult for them to carry this out. You should investigate their leader as well as their accounts.*"

"*Did they know your name? Your address?*"

"*No! They could not have known either my name or my address, but they found it out very quickly. Look for any connection between the Breed members and Galactogon's customer relations department or even developers.*"

"*Perhaps. But then they should have known that you were not at home. Your connection's IP address to the game has been the same all month.*"

"*In that case,*" I suggested, "*they wanted to get me back for seizing their property in-game. Something like an eye for an eye. I would guess that the casualties were an unforeseen accident.*"

"*Thank you for the information. We will follow up on it.*"

I didn't want to go so far as to accuse someone of murder, even after my recent episode with Constantine. Eunice, however, was more direct both with her words and her conclusions. Upon learning what had happened, she joined the conference call and

---

began demanding the detective get a search warrant immediately. Even though she had no evidence, she wanted to appeal to the World Progamers' Association for its support against the Galactogon corporation. After a tense conversation, Detective Sherper asked for 24 hours to deal with the situation before my overzealous wife began acting on her suspicions. Both of us were still trembling from the shock. What if we had been at home? I don't even want to imagine that. Dantoon — or whoever was behind this — had crossed all possible boundaries. Personally, I was pretty certain that this had been Fighting Breed's doing — revenge for the lost ships and reputation. The only question was whether they were merely trying to scare us or actually kill us.

"Here," said Tryd and stopped suddenly. He jumped to the ground. Instead of 1,500 kilometers, we had covered like fifty, if that. The mountains ended, parting onto a green idyll: a thin band of grassland spoiled only by several downed fighters and some ugly Zatrathi buildings with tall spires. Beyond it, the sea glittered away into the horizon.

While Eunice and I got off our hoverboards, the pirate circled a boulder and, straining, rolled it aside.

"Watch out!" he yelled as a blast of dust washed over us to the rumble of falling debris. We jumped away from the entrance and waited until the rockslide subsided and the dust settled. The stone revealed a passageway stretching deep down into the hillside. Tryd disappeared into it so quickly that only the echo of his footfalls suggested that someone was inside.

"What are you waiting for? My death?" the Delvian grumbled in my headset. "Don't hold your breath! Now come on and climb on down."

We obediently crawled in after him. The passage was so narrow and low that I had to take off my armor suit and crouch to make it through. The light vanished after a dozen meters and we had to continue by feel alone. As I reached out for the next step, I encountered something metallic. At the same moment, a medgun touched the back of my head, a quiet buzzing sound sounded in my ear, and my body ceased to obey me. An equine dose of tranquilizer saddled me with the 'Torpor' debuff for two minutes. I still had my senses, which allowed me to feel how someone stepped on my back, twisted my arms back and put handcuffs on. As I wheezed with indignation, my legs were also bound. After that, my assailant joined the two pairs of handcuffs, forcing me to arch backward. And all this took place in total darkness and silence. The debuff meant that I couldn't warn Eunice. She had been crawling behind me and by the sound of it, she had suffered the same fate.

A switch clicked and we beheld our attacker.

"That's better, small fry," Tryd chuckled and dragged us into a small room with normal ceilings and a door. "You'll feel better soon and then we'll have our chat…"

Tryd calmly walked over to the door, raised his paw to the scanner and it blinked green. A click — and perennial dust rained from the open door.

"Look at that. It still works," Tryd said with surprise and tried to stifle his sneeze. For the NPCs, dust was not simply a particle effect like it was for players. "Don't glare at me like that, small fry. There's a bonnie bounty on your head. A hundred million for bringing you in alive and in one piece. And fifty for your location. As a fellow pirate, I hope you'll understand."

I was about to curse, but stopped short. Something doesn't add up. Of course Tryd was capable of betraying me. He doesn't owe me anything, and yet a betrayal like this would have made much more sense on the moon, long before our descent to this planet. Doing it here, waiting this long, seemed like a contradiction. And why would someone as wealthy as Tryd was — and so utterly unconcerned with this same wealth — go to such lengths over a mere hundred million?

"Drop the act, Tryd! I don't believe for a second that you've lured us across the entire galaxy to this foxhole just to betray us!"

The old fox came up to me and spat at the dust before me.

"What do I care what you believe? A spare coin never hurts."

"You overgrown rat," Eunice, who didn't know the pirate as well as I did, reacted more violently — and it seems like Tryd had been waiting for just this. He broke into a croaking laughter, reveling in our helplessness. It was like our feelings of betrayal were nourishing the prate, making him stronger. Finally, he took out a comm unit and made a call:

"I heard that you're interested in two pirates named Surgeon and Nurse. My name is Tryd. I have them here with me. Yes, I'll turn on the video," the Delvian panned his PDA, recording us on the floor. As he did so, I kicked out at him, barely missing. "Yar, take a look at this rabid one. If you still want him, then I am ready to send you his coordinates and leave him all wrapped up for you until you get here. A mere two hundred million. One half up front and a hundred more on pick-up...I don't care what you

---

promised! I caught them and I'll name the price! Want them? Then get your checkbook out. I'll send you the account number now and our coordinates once you've paid."

Satisfied with the results of the negotiations, the pirate grabbed us by the chains and dragged us to the open door. Tryd waited until the green beam of the scanner passed over us and, heaving, dumped us into a trolley. The weak illumination allowed me to see the railway tracks receding into the darkness, several automatic beam cannons and flame throwers, as well as an old self-propelled trundle rusted from time but still called 'trolley' by will of the devs.

Climbing on top of us and utterly unconcerned with our discomfort, the Delvian said with satisfaction:

"Travel with me some more until your buyer appears. It'll be safer that way."

My doubts wouldn't leave me alone. Who knows — what if I had been mistaken about the state of Tryd's finances and he really did need Fighting Breed's millions? Although, on the other hand, how would Fighting Breed even make it to this planet through the epic space battle going on above?

Meanwhile, the pirate touched the control console and a forcefield appeared above the trolley, protecting us from the headwind. Bursting into motion, the shaking carriage rushed into the darkness.

We passed five automatic checkpoints. Each time, the trolley would stop abruptly, the green scanner-beams would traverse it from top to bottom and the laser turrets, ready to burn us to ashes, would turn away. With each checkpoint, the scanning took longer and longer, and Tryd seemed to grow more dour. He kept glancing at his wrist. As I understood, the result of the scan and the permission to pass were displayed there. We never made it to the sixth checkpoint. It was already beginning to grow light in the distance when the pirate pulled the brake lever and the trolley ground to a halt with a shower of sparks.

"From here on, we're going on foot." With these words, Tryd bent down and quickly released our cuffs.

As soon as I was free, I surged forward, throwing my best right hook at the pirate. Yet with an elusive feint, the Delvian ducked aside, spun and came back with a flying roundhouse. The stone wall greeted me with undisguised delight and was disappointed by our brief acquaintance. My trusty body armor blocked all the damage. I rolled to the side, dodging the pirate's arm reaching for my side. I think there was something in it, but then Eunice joined me. She came flying out of the trolley like a torpedo. My wife did not leave things to chance, having first put on her armor suit, and now slammed into Tryd with her full, armored mass, looking to overrun and crush the traitor. Yet again the fox proved to be faster. Not only did he find the time to dodge but he went into a combat roll and clapped something metallic to the girl's suit. There was a loud bang and the suit went dead. An EM grenade! That sly little bastard! My desire to get my own armor out of my inventory instantly evaporated. I jumped back into the darkness and pressed myself against the wall, trying to keep an eye on the fox. A blaster appeared in my hands and I moved it from side to side, getting ready to shoot at anything that moved.

"Looking for me, are you, small fry?" the pirate hissed right into my ear. I jumped back, tripped over the rails and began to fall. Instead of breaking my fall, my hands decided to fire the blasters. The tunnel shimmered as the blue plasma bolts from my blasters flew along its length. It was a pity that there was no one in that direction.

"Where is he?" Eunice clambered out of her armor suit and helped me up. We fired in the different directions at the same time, illuminating the tunnel yet again, but there was no sign of Tryd. As soon as the darkness returned, the pirate's voice sounded right next to us again!

"Have you had your fill, mollusks? Shall we go on or do you want to blow off more steam?"

"Why don't you just go to hell?!" My wife's emotions went off the charts. Breathing hard, she tried to regain some semblance of calm, but even I could feel her anger radiating from her body.

"Maybe I will, darlin', as long as you come with me for company. Drop your pea-shooters. You'll hurt yourself and I need you alive. On the double, I said!"

A sharp pain struck my leg. Tryd zipped past, slitting my leg with a knife. "You bitch!" roared Eunice and lit up the tunnel with another burst of blaster fire. Tryd had gotten her too.

"I'll give you a minute. After that, I will smear you across these walls and open the base on my own."

"What about your client?" I asked, peering for the pirate in the dark.

"I'll tell him that he should've been here sooner," said Tryd.

"So I was right?" I put my blaster away and signaled to Eunice to do the same.

A CHECK FOR A BILLION

"Right, wrong…Get into your armor suits. They will come in useful up ahead. We'll figure out all the moral stuff later." Tryd appeared right in front of my face. I could even feel his hot breath but the darkness kept me from making out his eyes. "I've deactivated the suit lock."

This was addressed to Eunice, since her armor again flashed its initialization lights. I did not argue. Tryd had dealt with us quite easily when we didn't have protection. Let's see what he can do against two well-equipped players covering each other's backs. He won't be able to hide from my spatial scanner, that's for sure.

And yet, as soon as I climbed into my armor, I heard another resounding clang.

"I've attached a suit lock to your armor, small fry. If you screw around, I'll cut off your electronics. Is everything clear to everyone or should I explain it again?"

I could finally see the pirate. Mmm…yeah. We had been searching for him down below, while he, like a spider, had been crawling up on the ceiling, clinging to the various wires and pipes up there. It was at this point that I recalled that Tryd had served as a marine for the Corsican for twenty years and later fought the Delvian underworld on his own. The pirate's combat experience was insurmountable. We were little more than kindergarteners for him. After making sure that we were going to behave, Tryd pointed down the tunnel.

"The main base is twenty kilometers ahead. But we won't make it. The Anorxians have begun to attack the security systems. There were problems at the second checkpoint already. That means the first one has been compromised. We need to go around."

"Three pirates armed to the teeth can't cope with a pair of cannons?" I asked with surprise — to which Tryd merely grinned:

"This base was built to last centuries. What you see here is just the tip of the iceberg. Even a heavy mech won't make it down there. The only ones who survive have permission to enter."

He paused and then added unexpectedly:

"Or their prisoners. The security system annihilates everything else. All right. Move out! There is a second passage over here."

Tryd left us alone and calmly headed to the next checkpoint.

"Brainiac, what is going on up there — in orbit?"

"The Anorxians have only one Arbiter left. The Zatrathi have lost three cruisers and half of the flying fortress. The remaining forces are in a tug of war. I think the Zatrathi will win. The Arbiters have failed twice already. Some players tried to sneak by in scouts, but the Anorxians and the Zatrathi wiped them out."

"You old pirate snout. You could have warned us!" grumbled Eunice angrily. "Half that money is ours!"

"A third!" came Tryd's reply. "I had no chance to warn you. You wouldn't have played along and they wouldn't have taken the bait, honey. I half expected Surgeon to figure it out. If he had, sure, I'd have given you half."

My wallet beeped, notifying me that I had received the promised credits. Tryd had shared his loot with us. It was a good move — he had duped Fighting Breed into paying money to get to us. Of course, it remained unclear why they would set themselves up like this after blowing up my house. Moreover, not only had they lost their credits, but their ships had also gone to respawn. Now our kidnapping made sense. Tryd let us go as soon as he learned that the scouts had been destroyed.

We went on and about a kilometer later overtook the pirate, standing still next to a wall. With my suit's sensors, I could see much more of the checkpoint. The beam cannons directed in our direction were props. They could not shoot. But the minefields, the cannons secreted in the walls and the plates that could generate EM fields were quite real and effective. And all this was noticeable from afar. What awaited us once we got close, was a bigger question.

"This way." Tryd had also put on his armor suit and began to smash the walls with his armor-clad fists. "Help me!"

Eunice and I began to help clear the rubble, helping the pirate burrow deeper into the wall The stone crumbled and the falling dust made it difficult for the scanners to work, yet the Delvian went on digging until at long last the rubble caved in instead of falling out. Using his legs to help himself, Tryd widened the passage further.

"Ancient burrows. They existed even before the base was built. Follow me!"

From the passage came a heavy, drawn-out moan, turning into the ghost of a whisper. I couldn't be sure that it was a voice instead of an echo, but I still got goose bumps all down my spine. Seeing Tryd ready his blaster did not reassure me.

"Onwards! Are you pirates or timid sheep? Have you soiled

your trousers?"

With these words, the Delvian disappeared into the passage. Eunice and I exchanged glances and followed him. My spatial scanner rendered a 3D model of the area we were in, and my wife exclaimed in surprise. There was no doubt that the wide passageway, about four meters in diameter, had not been made by hand. Resembling the intestine of some petrified animal, the tunnel looped in on itself, branching into several off-shoots. A stone labyrinth filled with strange rustling and moans. I wanted to filter out this noise, but Tryd warned:

"Don't turn off your microphones, you need to stay on your guard. The vermin can appear at any time."

It didn't sound like the NPC was joking. If a marine vet like Tryd was concerned over some rats, we should probably be concerned too. I asked for the sake of curiosity:

"Vermin? Like rats? Moles? What do they eat down here?"

"Rocks. Metal. Each other. These aren't ordinary vermin, small fry. Get a move on!"

Tryd set off, setting a good pace for an old fox and deftly jumping along the ledges. The Delvian constantly turned into corridors, orienting himself perfectly in this maze. After twenty minutes of this, I realized that we would not be able to find our way back. Our only chance would be Brainiac's omnipresent memory. At the next fork in the path, Tryd stopped, took off his helmet and took a deep breath, jerking his nose ridiculously. First he sniffed one corridor, then another. This did not seem enough for the pirate. He leaned down to the floor and began sniffing the stones, even licking one — then spitting and cursing softly. Rising to his feet, he checked his blaster and its powercells and declared:

"Bad news, scallywags. There are no more robots in this base. There's a new boss running the show. I can't go any further."

"Are you talking about the vermin again?" I guessed, but Eunice corrected me:

"Or rather whatever creature gave birth to them. Why haven't the pirates destroyed it?"

"Because they couldn't," Tryd snapped. "The vermin mother is immortal! When they first stumbled across her, it took an orbital bombardment to drive her deep into the earth. We spent many years hauling victims from all over Galactogon over here to appease her, to feed her. Just to get her to stay below and not eat us. We called her the Scourge — few are those who have seen her and lived to tell the tale. Five years ago, the Anorxians captured the base and, as you can see, the Scourge made a meal of them. All the corridors are filled with the robot's internal lubrication and the air stinks of burned silicon. A slaughter took place here. A slaughter of synthoids. I think the Scourge is somewhere deep inside the base, waiting for new victims."

Tryd fell silent, breathing hard after such a long speech.

Once more, a haunting howling flooded the tunnel we were in. There was no doubt that this was no wind. I knew it was some living creature because I could discern a slurred mutter buried deep in the sound:

'*Pain. So much pain. Only pain.*'

When I looked at the Delvian again, his appearance made me start: The fur on the nape of his neck had stood up and his lone eye was twitching. His jowls jerked. His tail curled up around his groin and stomach. He put his blaster up to his lower jaw as if he was about to blow his brains out and he began to backtrack from us, step by step backing away from the fork in the path.

"What is the danger of encountering the Scourge? Rebirth? Are you a terrible pirate or a cowardly jackal?!" I didn't like the way Tryd was acting one bit, so I tried to bring him to his senses. It worked. The Delvian started, exhaled a couple of times noisily, putting his nerves in order, and replied:

"You humans might be reborn. Somewhere here — in these warrens. But I would not be so lucky. The Scourge can break your binding to your planetary spirit and then she kills you slowly, relishing your pain and agony. Rumor has it that some spent weeks being digested before they died. The monster knows how to keep her food alive even as she feeds on it."

"Then uh where did the vermin come from?" Eunice frowned. "Why would the Scourge allow competition in her territory?"

"The vermin aren't competitors — they are the Scourge's spawn, her hands and eyes." Tryd had fully recovered his senses by now. "They are but smaller scourges, temporarily detached from the main body. We need to leave. I have nothing to do down here."

"Oh come off it!" I wasn't about to give up so easily. "Let's give it a try. You're here because of the Northbridge, right? Where do we find it?"

"You have made your choice, small fry. I said my piece, but you have to try. Both of these passages lead to the base. The Anorxian prince is housed in the third warehouse. If you bring it to me, I will give you the Lora."

A CHECK FOR A BILLION

New mission available: A Prince fit for a Pirate's Soul. Mission description: Recover Prince Northbridge from the pirate base and give it to Tryd. Rewards for completion: Lora Coupler Unit. Penalty for failure: None. Deadline: 3 days. Do you wish to accept this mission?

Before I could take the assignment, Tryd pulled the trigger and turned himself into the main character from Mayne Reid's *Headless Horseman*. His body did not even have time to fall — it flickered and turned into a loot crate. To my disappointment, the pirate hadn't bequeathed us anything of value — a paltry ten powercells.

"Remember how you said that he 'didn't show up for no reason?'" I turned to Eunice. "Well, he showed up to bring us to this hellhole and then he bailed."

"But bringing us here was the whole point of his mission," Eunice disagreed. "Now I am even more confident that we are on the right track…What is *that*?"

An ominous knocking sounded behind us — from the direction we had come from. It was as if a thousand metal hammers were hammering the stone walls, pulverizing them bit by bit. My spatial scanner had a range of a hundred meters and pretty soon we could make out the new enemy. I guess if you squinted really hard, you could indeed call these creatures 'vermin,' although I preferred a different name: cacodemons, of the *Doom* variety. Each creatures was little more than an enormous mouth full of voracious, moving teeth. Their single tiny eye remained shut — in the warrens' pitch black darkness, the cacodemons simply had no use for them.

Despite their tiny limbs, they moved rather quickly. In the few seconds that I had been watching them, they had traveled a dozen meters already.

"We got a fight on our hands!"

It took two seconds to activate our blasters, another second to take aim and one more to send four blue plasma bolts in the direction of the nearest cacodemon. Another couple seconds passed until the dust cleared and we could see the result. The vermin had traveled another thirty meters in our direction and suffered no damage whatsoever.

"Run!" I yelled. Turning abruptly, I grabbed Eunice by the hand and we rushed away. Our four legendary blasters hadn't so much as inflicted a scratch on the toothy creature. To the contrary, the cacodemon opened its mouth and swallowed the shots with pleasure. Then it grew a bit larger. Meanwhile, its fellow vermin ran alongside, jumping up and down, trying to snatch a lethal plasma clump for themselves. It was their gluttony, their constant getting in each other's way that gave us the opportunity to escape.

We were flying as fast as we could but the space scanner remained inexorable. The tide of cacodemons was approaching too fast. Realizing that there would be no more food in the form of plasma, they rushed after us. We turned a corner and found ourselves in a dead end. I lost my breath but then Eunice shouted happily:

"A door! I think we're going to make it, Lex!"

Two grenades appeared in my hands. I set the fuse to two seconds and tossed them at the vermin. I wasn't even hoping to hurt them. Tryd's behavior had already made it clear that no weapons could threaten the vermin. I had another target in mind — the passage. A powerful blast wave overwhelmed our inertia dampeners and we were thrown facedown onto the floor. Yet instead of subsiding, the roar of collapsing debris was replaced by an even more unpleasant roar, similar to the sound of a dentist's drill.

Jumping to my feet, I took out another grenade and threw it after the other two, causing the cave-in to grow larger. There was no doubt that the cacodemons would burrow through eventually. The only question was how long it would take them.

"It's locked!" Eunice reached the door first, but the red indicator stopped her. "We need help, Brainiac!"

"Figaro here, Figaro there," the computer grumbled as an interface probe emerged from my wife's armor suit. "All right…I'll need a minute to lockpick it."

"We don't have a minute! Open it now!"

"Don't yell at me!" the computer snapped. "I'm already going as fast as I can. If you want me to go faster, buy me an upgrade from Hansa. One minute!"

Cryptic symbols began to scroll down the small screen of the door panel. Brainiac concentrated on the task at hand but we did not have time. The debris behind us began to fall inward, as if a hollow was forming beneath them. The cacodemons were gnawing at the blocks with the same ease as they absorbed blaster bolts. Damn! How had the pirates dealt with these voracious vermin? I threw a couple more grenades — to little effect. The tunnel's walls were reinforced and didn't collapse as easily.

"Forty seconds! Lex, think of something! We have to get

inside!"

Think of something? Why that's easy. I just won't have time to do it. Thirty meters from us, one of the huge stones moved, collapsed inward and disappeared. It seemed to me that the cacodemon that devoured it even grinned with satisfaction. It froze, trying to digest the block, which stopped the movement of the cacodemons coming up behind it. They jumped and clumped unhappily, unable to pass. Finally, the cacodemon in front began to shrink. What do they have in their stomachs that allows them to digest rocks so quickly?

"Thirty seconds!"

Eunice's cry jolted me and the manipulators appeared in my hands. There was only twenty meters between the nearest creature and me when I aimed both arms at it and then sharply spread my arms akimbo. One manipulator was aimed on the right corner of its maw, the second on the left. My actions were quite logical. If the cacodemons cannot crawl over each other, I'll just make this one as large as a puffer fish. Like I said, quite logical. The last thing I imagined was what would actually work.

"Twenty seconds! Just a little more, Lex!"

With one swift movement I spread the manipulators apart tearing the cacodemon in two and flooding the floor with its entrails. The small stones still covering the floor dissolved in the blink of an eye. The floor itself held out a little longer. A huge hole began forming, growing larger with every second. But even this was not the most surprising thing. The cacodemons that were behind the one I'd torn apart fell on the remnants like vultures, forgetting all about us. Unfortunately for them, this free meal would be their last.

A CHECK FOR A BILLION

Whatever these creatures had as bile in their stomachs began to calmly dissolve not just the rocks, but also the seemingly-invulnerable monsters. Smoking holes appeared in the front rank of vermin and the ones behind immediately attacked them, smoking and dying in turn.

Achievement unlocked: Unparalleled power! Your ZPEF Manipulator has reached level 100. Item class changed. Current class: Legendary. +20% to all stats. Durability and Energy fully restored. +2 integration slots available. Maximum lifting weight increased to 5000 kg. This manipulator now ignores all EM protection.

Two small suns blazed in my hands for a couple of moments — a visual effect to go with the new levels. I clearly remembered that before the slaughter, my manipulators had been at level A-3, so the XP gained from killing the cacodemon must have been immense.

A click sounded behind me and the door slid upward with a creak.

"Ready!" Eunice said with delight, but then from the darkness of the base came the familiar moan and whisper.

"*At last, the food has arrived. Come to me, my meal. I await you!*"

A shiver ran down my spine, but I still took a step inside — Scourge or not, the Corsican won't deal with a pirate of the first rank.

CHAPTER NINE

"AP'N, WE CANNOT ACCESS THE SYSTEM," the snake reported, giving up on the third network jack we had tried. After the first failure, the ship computer said that the jack was damaged. After the second, he claimed that the contacts inside the wall had rusted and come apart. After the third, Brainiac had to admit his impotence.

"Are you going to complain about needing an upgrade again?" I asked suspiciously. There was indeed a ship mainframe upgrade in Hansa's third list of upgrades, and Brainiac had hinted several times that it would be a good idea to spend twenty billion GC on my favorite AI.

"No, Captain. It's serious over here. Something or someone is interfering with us. Every time we bypass some security system, a new one pops up. I don't think that even upgrades would be enough to compete with the local security."

This was unfortunate news. I had been hoping that Brainiac could figure out where the third warehouse was located and even

---

download the video I needed. At this rate, we'll have to go find the Scourge, who seemed very happy at this prospect. The monster would not shut up for a second, repeating the same phrase like a broken record:

"At last, the food has arrived. Come to me, my meal. I await you!"

The dark viscous fluid underfoot made the floor slippery. The armor suit's sensors indicated that this substance was the equivalent of Anorxian blood. Considering how much of it was here, the Scourge had made a feast of the synthoids. At the same time, there was nothing here at all — neither synthoid remains, nor furniture nor even just junk. The rooms were all bare but for the blood of the massacre. We had already traveled through several corridors and areas without discovering anything.

"I watched the video of your raid on the Uldan base. This seems very similar to the boss's second phase," said Eunice. "What if the local monster is already born in this case? And those vermin are her progeny?"

"An interesting theory," Brainiac agreed. "That would explain why I can't hack the system. The Uldans knew what they were doing when it came to network security."

"Let's check," I agreed. "Brainiac, turn on the loudspeaker and make an announcement in Uldan. Say: 'We come in peace. We require assistance.'"

The guttural speech of the Uldans blared over the jarring and frankly unnerving whisper of the Scourge. At first, Brainiac kept the volume down but by the third repetition, he turned it to 11 and I scrambled to turn off my external microphones. The broadcast ended and the pirate base plunged into silence. The whisper went silent too.

"Is this good or bad?" Eunice inquired and then the space around us shook with a thundering response. The walls trembled, cracks shot to the ceiling, and chips of stone rained on us. The Scourge herself had deigned to answer:

"*Who are you?*"

"I am a friend of Warlock, the guardian of the planet Blood Island. I am the captain of an orbship."

"*Warlock... Yes, I knew him. He was a good scout. He had potential. It sounds like he found his planet. Good for him. Is he no more?*"

"Yes, Warlock gave me the orbship and went to his rest."

"*I want to know the details. I await you. Follow the light.*"

The walls of the base vibrated, we heard the hum of a dynamo starting up and the corridor directly ahead of us lit up. The light radiated from the walls themselves instead of the lamps — as these had been eaten too.

"Stunning technology." The snake made me stop near one of the walls and remotely, with the help of a drill that she extended from my suit, took a sample from the wall in front of me. As soon as I brought the little piece of rock up to the wall, it began to glow — when I removed it, it stopped. At the same time, the luminous object did not heat up or deform in any way. It simply emitted photons in all directions without visible loss of mass or energy. If there were magic in Galactogon, this phenomena was it.

The owner of the base did not rush us. A creature that had lived more than a dozen millennia could afford to be patient.

A CHECK FOR A BILLION

Though, as we passed through the rooms, the light dimmed behind us.

"You don't suppose we're being led to a slaughter?" Eunice asked with undisguised skepticism as soon as we descended to a lower level. There was so much synthoid fluid here that at times we were forced to wade in it up to our ankles.

"I haven't the slightest doubt. Here, take this just in case." I offered Eunice an unpinned grenade. My wife refused, however, holding up her clenched fist.

"I have my own. Look Lex, I don't like any of this. How is it that this monster hounded the pirates for who knows how long and yet it's willing to be quite reasonable and talk to us as soon as we just ask politely in Uldan?"

"I have a theory about that," I admitted honestly. "And the further we go, the more certain I am that it does want to talk. Brainiac, what's going on in the system?"

"The fighting is over, the Anorxians have been defeated. The Zatrathi reinforced with another flying fortress and are now busy making repairs. They've even begun to quarry the marble again."

"Could you scan the planet? I need to know how many bases there are here."

"Captain, that is an unrealistic request. It's too far away."

"Okay, another task then. Watch the recording of our encounter with the vermin. What can you tell me about the falling stones?"

"They are heterogeneous in structure. It is as if a thin stone lining has been applied over the walls, three to four centimeters thick. It resembles marble quite a lot. The structure is very similar."

"Wonderful! Keep working. Over and out."

"And what is all that supposed to mean?" Eunice stared at me with interest.

"That the pirates did find a way to resist the Scourge. As did the Zatrathi. Let's go. I think our meeting will be an interesting one."

I was not mistaken. We descended two more levels and found ourselves in a huge conference hall. Or rather, I decided that this large auditorium would be suitable for the pirates' negotiations. Now, however, the entire space was occupied by a single being coiled into rings.

"Snake, this isn't like your aunt or something?" I asked just in case.

The Scourge turned out to be a snake — an Uldan engineer to be precise, and judging by her size, one that served aboard a large cruiser. It had none of the Zatrathi spikes that the Vraxis queen was covered in. This one was a vanilla Uldan, without any Vraxis genes mixed in.

"But this…Why this is…" Brainiac's shocked voice sounded in my headphones, he cut himself off and then suddenly, in a solemn tone, intoned: "Kneel before Lady Mercaloun! She is the senior officer in charge!"

The snake lifted her head, staring at us with four unblinking eyes. I swallowed, regarding the size of the creature. Mercaloun's head alone was larger than my three-meter-tall armor suit. If she so much as placed her head on top of us, she would crush us without any difficulty. And then there was the rest of her — the long serpentine torso which filled almost the entire room. What is this colossus even doing here?

"*You are right, orbship, I am the commander here. I smell the spirit of Warlock in this human. So, he went to the ether freely after all. Very well. I wish to hear the details before I devour you.*"

The snake spoke to us without opening her mouth. The very walls themselves generated the sound as if they were speaker membranes. At the same time, I suddenly realized that Mercaloun had demonstrated her ability to listen in on a closed comm channel between me and my ship. I need to take into account that she is listening in whenever I speak with Brainiac...

The sound of hammers filled the corridor, and with it came the cacodemons cutting off our retreat.

Attention! Due to your current location, your homeworld binding has been changed. Your current respawn point is: Planet Shurtan — Lady Mercaloun's Dominion.

The trap has sprung. My wrist twitched with the desire to release a grenade and go to rebirth. Even if we respawn somewhere underground, at least we won't be here with this thing anymore. However, Eunice, who was standing nearby, reacted faster, putting her hand on top of mine.

"Don't jump the gun. Remember, this is a game. We can always come to some agreement."

Having made sure that I would not blow myself up, Eunice turned to the snake.

"Lady Mercaloun, we can offer you a deal. You need food,

so let us deliver it to you! Those who lived here before, the synthoids, coped well with this."

"*Coped?!*"

With an elusive movement, Mercaloun surged forward, stopping right in front of Eunice. To give credit where it's due, my wife did not even start, although her heartbeat sensors went berserk, spiking to 150 BPM.

"*They locked me away in the depths, cutting me off with their detestable marble! The pitiful scraps that they tossed me — you cannot call that food! Do you know what eternal hunger is, human? Do you know the torment of your own stomach digesting itself? What could you offer me when you have nothing but the flesh you carry on your bones?*"

"If you go on sitting here, the food will run out for good. I have seen the Zatrathi operation to transport marble to this planet with my own eyes. They are planning on marbling the entire planet, forever imprisoning you in the prison of your own hunger. What will you eat when there is nothing but marble around you? Yourself?"

Eunice was not going to give up. Of course, she knew how to misrepresent the facts, but her theory lined up even if she didn't know that it was easier for the Zatrathi to destroy the planet or the sun than to fiddle with such a small trifle as covering the surface of the planet with marble.

"*The Zatrathi? What is that?*"

The question was unexpected, but Eunice quickly got her bearings:

"Brainiac, project holograms of a Zatrathi warrior and an engineer," she ordered the ship computer, and Mercaloun was forced to back up in order to get a better look at the projections.

"*These are the deliverables of Project 2373. These creatures were created to clear planets of the Vraxis — but they turned out poorly. I was told that the project had been canceled and all the samples were liquidated.*"

"You have been deceived. Not only did your experiment survive, but…"

"*This matter no longer concerns me, human. I want to eat!*"

The cacodemons surged forward with the clear intention of devouring us, but Eunice reacted first:

"There is a flying fortress in orbit around this planet. You should see its size. Show her, Brainiac! Give us your spawn and we will bring that ship down! You will have more food than you can eat in a year!"

The cacodemons stopped as Mercaloun shut all four of her eyes. The snake meditated, considering the offer. Finally, the eyes opened and the walls vibrated with the answer:

"*I do not feel anything. The marble blocks my signal.*"

At this point, Brainiac came to his senses and displayed a hologram of the Shurtan system. The flying fortress had drifted over and docked with the orbital station, which had been severely damaged by the Anorxian assault. The projection shifted to the moon and the immense marble quarry. Just then a fully loaded transport took off and, tracked through its short journey by Brainiac, reached the planet's surface.

"*They cannot hurt me. Even if it has managed to survive by some stroke of luck, the experiment has no right to harm its creators. We were the ones who designed them.*"

"Brainiac, show her the brainworm and the recordings of the planets being destroyed." I joined Eunice, sensing a note of doubt in Mercaloun's voice. The ancient serpent or whatever she was, did not comprehend her true position.

New images appeared in the projection. Seeing the brainworm on the Uldan's head, Mercaloun snapped her eyes wide open and Eunice and I all but collapsed to our knees. I cannot describe the feelings surging within me at this moment. It just seemed to me that it would be the right thing to do — the only thing to do. It was a state of pure obedience.

"*What is that?! Who is that?!*"

"Servants of the one who is called the Queen. The one who leads the horde seeking to destroy Galactogon. The one who can destroy even you. Maybe not directly. But she can easily cover everything with marble. Therefore, I will return to my proposal, oh Great One. Do you want us to deliver food for you?"

"*My spawn cannot go out into the sunlight. It will destroy them. I myself cannot leave the planet. I am the Spirit — it was the only way I was able to survive for so long. Food. I need food. I will eat you only once. Quickly. Then we shall talk.*"

"No! Or you will get no help!" Eunice snapped as the cacodemons tried to approach again. In the meantime, I pulled two reserve armor suits from my inventory:

"You are fettered here, but not your children. Maybe they cannot step into the sunlight. No problem. What would you say if they go to space in armor suits? There is no sunlight inside spaceships. There is food there. Tell me, what do you like to eat? Only the living?"

A CHECK FOR A BILLION

"*My spawn can digest any matter except marble. Marble is poison. How big is your armor suit?*"

For the first time in our conversation, a note of curiosity sounded in Mercaloun's voice. Without displaying any aggression, three of the cacodemons approached to us. I opened the armor suit, and the cacodemons hopped inside and instantly devoured everything within, turning the suit into a useless case. Despite my immense disappointment at seeing a legendary suit subjected to such treatment, I managed to maintain a perfectly normal expression. Another trio came up next. And then another. When I slammed the armor shut, there were fifteen toothed balls in there compressed to an implausibly tiny size. The next wave of vermin came up. Fifteen at once. Damn! I had to watch another suit get ruined as they crammed themselves in.

"*You have received my spawn. They will obey your orders. What's next? How will you get into space?*"

What a smart talking snake. I had to improvise:

"We know for sure that the transports land on this planet. We need to get inside one of them and steal it. Nothing complicated. The only thing we need to find out is where they land."

"*I don't sense anyone. The planet is empty.*"

"That just means that the Zatrathi have masked their landing zone with marble," I said confidently. "We need some mode of transportation to get around the planet quickly. Can you arrange it?"

"*How fast? Would five hundred kilometers per minute suffice or do you need something faster?*"

I coughed and sputtered. Five hundred kilometers per

minute? The inertia alone would crush us and our suits wouldn't be of any help.

"That will be enough," Eunice quickly replied. "We also need a map of these warrens to figure out where the ships are."

"*You have two hours. Either you bring me food, or you will become food. Get in and hurry. My spawn know where the exits tunnels are located.*"

New mission available: A Meal Fit for a Lady. Description: capture the Zatrathi flying fortress and bring it down to the planet Shurtan. Reward: Hidden. Penalty for failing the quest: Two-month binding to the planet Shurtan.

Deadline: 2 hours.

Another fifteen cacodemons stepped forward. They began to clamber over each other, merging their bodies and transforming into one terrible whole. A minute later, the transformation was complete, revealing a disfigured rhino. It was as if a child had tried to draw the rhino in my orbship — except the child was using crayons and had no knack for drawing at all.

The rhino's sides split open revealing four seats. We got in and the rhino rushed forward at a blistering pace, deftly jumping any obstacles and miraculously avoiding both walls and dead ends. Despite the fact that the thoughtful cacodemons had left us portholes to enjoy the view, all our attention was focused on not smashing our heads against the interior. We were being rattled so hard that you'd think that Mercaloun had ordered them to shake the souls out of us. After an eternal thirty seconds the running stopped.

A CHECK FOR A BILLION

I rolled out, collapsing onto Eunice. Our trip hadn't brought her much joy either. The rhino raised its paw, pointing upward. My spatial scanner immediately identified a passage in the ceiling ascending straight up.

"Brainiac, we're taking off!" I ordered, taking the two armor suits full of cacodemons. My thrusters roared to life, struggling to overcome gravity. The toothy monsters sure did weigh a lot.

A deep shaft led us into an empty cavity. I scuffed the floor with my toe — it was marble. All around, everything was covered with marble, protecting the inhabitants of the planet from those who lived below its surface. Sunlight penetrated one of the far edges of the natural cave. Brainiac immediately directed us that way — away from the 'generous' Mercaloun. The walls, the ceiling, the floor — everything was clad in marble. The vermin sat quietly in their armor suits and did not object even when we emerged into the sunlight. The armor protected them. We took off from the ground and, as stupid as it sounds, once we were outside in fresh air, we tore off our helmets and breathed deeply. Shurtan's frosty air tickled the skin, reinvigorating our minds.

Brainiac took over our suit's autopilots, while Eunice and I reveled in our newfound liberty. Even if it was temporary and still under threat, it was liberty. After a short flight, Brainiac set us down on a stone, which naturally, turned out to be snow-white marble. We activated our cloaks and started scanning around us. A transport was being unloaded about a kilometer away. The Zatrathi were loading the slabs into a slow moving machine, which was evenly laying the slabs all over the surface.

"We have two options," said Eunice, kicking over the can

of cacodemons. "We can open it here, fry these monsters, and use our cloaks to steal aboard the transport. Brainiac will pick us up and we hightail it to Blood Island where we restore our binding to the planetary spirit and treat all this like a bad dream. And who'd blame us? The other option is the heroic and risky one. No one knows what a well-fed Mercaloun will do. It's your quest so it's up to you to decide. I've got your back in either case. We can find some other way to that prize check. We're not short of money at the moment so there's no rush."

My wife had voiced what we had both been thinking and stepped aside. I was staring at the armor suits trying to organize my thoughts. Instead of racing at a gallop, my mind was like an empty prairie with a tumbleweed driven by a silent wind and a lonely cow mooing in the direction of the rolling morsel. I could even hear the ringing of her bell. Who will win the contest between the wind and the cow's laziness?

"It's time, Lex. What's the plan?" Eunice prompted me but I was still waiting for a result. At last, the cow proved more agile. She snatched the tumbleweed mid-tumble and began to chew it slowly. We cannot run away from this mission. It clearly states that if we fail it, we will have to spend the next several months stuck on this planet. Even if we rush off, some abnormal event will happen, and we will be forced to respawn. And I bet we'll lose Brainiac on top of it all too. Furthermore, let's just keep in mind who this Mercaloun is. An Uldan. I'm sure the Precian adviser would flip his dome if he learned that I had run away. In effect, we only had one option:

"Let's risk it. We'll head for the flying fortress."

A CHECK FOR A BILLION

What an immense relief it is to finally make up your mind! No more anxiety, no more endless thinking about the 'what ifs.' The decision has been made and all that matters is the execution. Nothing else.

The planet-wide marbling project was in full swing and to our delight it was fully automated. The giant marbling combines paid no attention to the appearance of two strange armor suits. While I was securing the armor suits in the transport's cargo hold, Eunice cut a hole into the cockpit and hooked up Brainiac.

"This ship has forty-two cycles left before she must returns for maintenance," the orbship computer announced, reading the internal data. "Shall I take the controls?"

"It's not necessary." I pulled out my manipulators and picked up the last of the remaining slabs. There was little space, but it was enough to accelerate the marble and smash it against the hull. This caused an impressive dent in the wall and a red warning light to pop up on the console.

"Ten cycles left!" Brainiac updated his report. "Smash another one against the other side."

By the time the harvester appeared to pick up the marble, the transport was a wreck. The doors slammed shut and the ship's system began running a self-diagnosis. Something squeaked somewhere, some lights blinked red and the autopilot adjusted our course. We had a reservation at one of the flying fortress's repair docks. However, we could barely lift off. I had gone a bit overboard and made some holes in the hull. Now the wind howled inside the cargo hold and the pressure was dropping. I grew worried about the cacodemons. The husk of an armor suit might protect its occupants from sunlight, but what about cosmic vacuum? To make sure, I opened the faceplate and encountered a hungry cacodemon eye. It immediately fixed on all the tasty metal around us and I had to shut the faceplate again to keep its appetite in check.

"And how are we supposed to control these vermin?" Eunice wondered. She did not seem thrilled by our new teammates.

"We're not. We'll just have to assume that...Wait. Something is wrong. Why have we stopped? Brainiac?"

The transport had come to a stop beside the flying fortress.

"Everything is reading nominal over here. I detect no problems. We have passed the scanning procedure."

Scanning procedure?

"Take the controls, Eunice!" I yelled. "Full speed ahead and ram us into the hull."

A stupid oversight on my part! I completely forgot that the NPC ships automatically scan any approaching vessel for the slightest presence of unauthorized living organisms. No matter if it was a Grand Arbiter, an orbital station or whatever else. Why wouldn't the same mechanic apply to the Zatrathi? In this case, the scan had detected 32 unauthorized creatures. And naturally at that point, the Zatrathi grew curious and detained the transport.

We almost made it. The transport rushed for the flying fortress as fast as it could, yet the Zatrathi beat us to the punch. First our electronics went out, then a tractor beam stopped our lunge and moved us aside. You just can't predict a thing in this game!

"Let's go!" I grabbed both cans of cacodemons and with two shots of my blasters knocked out the rear loading ramp, opening a way into space. I guess we'll just have spacewalk the rest of the way. Eunice was occupied with swapping the powercells, making me a little nervous, but a few seconds later we were hanging in space watching our transport get moved a safe distance from the hull of the flying fortress and then turned into a brief, beautiful fireball by three torpedoes. The Zatrathi did not stand on ceremony.

"Lex, tow me to the flying fortress, will you?" asked Eunice, clutching my leg. She was not very fond of maneuvering in space with her suit thrusters.

This time nobody bothered us. Inside the security perimeter, we were tiny dust motes against the backdrop of the immense flying fortress. The fighters which might have noticed us were busy being repaired after the battle with the Anorxians. The stream of transports going in and out of the fortress were all on autopilot, so I calmly opened my throttle and headed for the central part of the vessel. We didn't have the time to mess around with a spire like last time.

Ten minutes of flight, and my suit's magnets tightly clamped us to the hull. Eunice cut a small hole in the surface, we crammed one of the armor suits inside and opened its visor.

"Get to work, boys! Show us what the pirates were so afraid of!"

CHAPTER TEN

FIFTEEN OF THE CACODEMONS HAD GROWN TO SUCH A SIZE that they now obstructed the fortress's corridors with their bodies. Lazily opening their jaws to meet the oncoming waves of Zatrathi, they consumed all the defenders and went on growing. Having reached the ceiling, the creatures crawled along the corridors, like bacteria that had encountered a Petri dish. To my disappointment, the consumed Zatrathi did not leave any loot behind. Mercaloun's spawn devoured everything without leaving any leftovers — even the loot.

"Brainiac, where should we go next?" I connected the orbship to the fortress's network and waited for an answer.

"There is no connection and there is no signal. The vermin have chewed through all the wiring. Captain, do we have to work with these gluttons? There's no profit from them, only losses. Why do they have to eat everything?"

It was easy to understand the computer's complaints. Instead of dealing with the personnel on board, the cacodemons gnawed through the bulwarks, the floor, the ceiling, and even the furniture. Everything their circular jaws could reach. By the time the Zatrathi defenders arrived, Mercaloun's gluttonous spawn had lost their former agility and could no longer move very effectively. But this in no way prevented them from feasting on the plasma from the defenders' blasters, as well as the blasters themselves and finally the defenders too.

"Follow me!" I barked at Eunice, squeezing into one of the unobstructed corridors. There were no Zatrathi here, which, undoubtedly, was a bad sign. In theory, all of the enemy combat units would be fighting the invaders and an empty passage meant that there was either a dead end or some non-essential ship system ahead. Either way, it would surely not be the ship's bridge.

Attention! You have lost a party member. 29 Mercaloun spawn remaining.

A couple minutes later, we received some unpleasant news. Then some more. And still more. The Zatrathi had found a way to deal with our raiding party. The creatures that the pirates and the Anorxians had spent centuries fighting to no avail were defeated within ten minutes by Galactogon's main foe. The last swollen cacodemon managed to hold out for another three minutes, giving us time to get away. We ran as fast as we could. If Brainiac can't connect to the network, then the Zatrathi on board had lost contact with this part of the ship too. It stood to reason that they couldn't track our movements. Rounding a corner, we stumbled onto a dead end. The corridor had ended.

I kicked in the nearest door and we found ourselves in an industrial facility. Everything here was automated. Dozens of long robotic arms deftly manipulated and maneuvered huge vats and tanks, constantly stirring them, swapping them, and pouring the mysterious contents into smaller containers. A pair of smaller, nimble units picked up the containers and put them on a conveyor belt which whisked the cooked 'food' to the upper decks. There was no doubt about it — we had found our way into the ship's kitchen. Six open ovens brought the temperature here to such heights that my suit activated its integrated AC.

"Brainiac, translate this inscription," Eunice asked, indicating a series of odd characters on the side of a container. The computer did as requested, but I didn't really see the point of knowing that one of the containers contained 'galinurium' and the other 'betar-carnitine partina.'

"What are they for?" the girl followed up, poking around the container with odd curiosity.

"One solution provides calories — the other, minerals to grow muscle fibers."

"Oh! How fascinating!" Eunice hummed and, grabbing a container of energy drink, carried it to a large cauldron. She dumped the contents inside, raising a large cloud of dust. The automated assembly line did not react to this change in the formula and went on with its manufacturing process. After a few dozen seconds, the first batch of energetically saturated 'shlocage' went up the conveyor belt.

"Why'd you do that?" I asked, since Eunice hadn't explained anything.

A CHECK FOR A BILLION

"Well, you never know…maybe it'll like poison them or something," came her reply.

"Or they'll go into hyper berserker mode," I proposed an alternative. "And then they'll tear us to shreds."

"No they won't," waved the girl. "The overall volume of food is very small, which means that there are not that many Zatrathi up there. They'll get their required calories and get done eating faster. Then they'll rush off to do their duties. The mess will clear, and the next round of diners won't have arrived yet. That'll be our chance. Just wait a bit!"

Saying this, Eunice hopped up on the conveyor and activated her stealth cloak. A minute later she reported:

"Eh…It didn't exactly go as I expected…but it'll do. You can come up now. It's clear."

I tossed the remaining suit full of cacodemons onto the conveyor and joined my wife. The mess hall was like set from a horror movie. Zatrathi warriors crawled over the floor trying to tear apart their own throats. Others were vomiting without interruption, literally turning themselves inside out in the process. After a bit of suffering, they froze and died, freeing the system resources allocated to them.

"The worst part is we got no XP from that at all." Eunice was entirely unconcerned by our enemies' suffering. Pulling out her blaster, she shot a few of the Zatrathi who had not eaten enough of the poisoned food. "Not even from these guys. Come on! There is nothing to do here."

I did a double take at my wife. I didn't know she could be this cold-blooded. And yet, she was right too — it was time to go.

GALACTOGON BOOK THREE

We had just over an hour left to complete Mercaloun's mission. Looking around for anything that could be of help, I noticed an automated food cart. Deftly skirting the corpses along its route, it went on delivering food to the tables. Having made its final delivery, the cart stopped, awaiting the next wave of diners.

I smashed its CPU unit with my fist and brushed off the leftover food. After making sure that the cart had lost its automated control and could still roll tolerably well, I loaded the armor suit full of cacodemons onto it and the disguised it with some Zatrathi armor that was lying around. Turning on my stealth cloak, I pushed the cart out of the mess, keeping to the right wall as close as possible. Eunice followed behind me. Hardly had we walked a few meters, when we encountered a squad of Zatrathi on their way to the mess hall. There were about a dozen of them, clumped in a dense group, so that it was clear that one of us would have to make way. Still pushing the food cart, I mentally prepared for a fight. The Zatrathi approached. I squinted at the cart a bit doubtfully. I wish I knew how these things ordinarily behaved in this situation. Maybe they were programmed to cling to the wall and stand still whenever it encountered a living creature? For that matter, were they even allowed to leave the mess? Suddenly, I started from Eunice's hand clapping me on my shoulder. She was ready too. We continued calmly on our way, neither accelerating, nor slowing down. Here came the moment of truth...

A meter before the collision, the Zatrathi reacted to the oncoming obstacle. Two of the warriors directly in my path deftly stepped aside, letting us pass. They paid no attention to the strange armor suit we were transporting. The Zatrathis' full attention was

A CHECK FOR A BILLION

focused on the door to the mess hall. The starving soldiers wanted to eat. Minor details like impolite food carts did not concern them.

Turning the corner, I exhaled loudly. I had been holding my breath the entire time, terrified that they would hear me breathe. Stopping the cart, I turned to Eunice. I wanted to understand how she passed this test.

"*Strasder woo premintal shlocage cartoo!*" The guttural exclamation came like a bolt from the blue. Slowly, trying not to make any sudden movements or disturb the air around me, I turned. Eunice was about to pounce, but I grabbed her hand in time. A Zatrathi warrior had emerged from a nearby door and stopped next to the cart. We blocked his passage, and the Zatrathi stared at this unexpected obstacle with evident displeasure.

"He said: 'A pox on these experimental food carts!'" Brainiac translated the Zatrathi's speech.

Making sure Eunice wouldn't move, I let go of her and slowly pushed the cart away from the doorway. The path was now clear, but the warrior was in no hurry to go about his business. All four of his upper limbs began to move, inspecting the junk on top of the cart. He picked up a piece of armor, clicked his mandibles, and carefully placed it on the floor. Then he picked up the next one.

"He is surprised." Brainiac could understand the reason for the warrior's confusion. "As I understand it, this armor belongs to his squad members. This is the commander of the Zatrathi you just poisoned."

"Got it!" Eunice had remained patient for as long as she could. Seeing the Zatrathi get closer to our armor suit of monsters, her patience snapped. Pulling out her blaster, she came out of stealth. The Zatrathi's mug expressed surprise and then puzzlement. He generally seemed like a puzzled type. I couldn't stop my wife in time. But I did manage to send the Zatrathi back through the doorway with a kick. Eunice's blaster bolt struck the wall with a shower of sparks.

"This way!" I cried, rushing after the enemy. "Get the cart in here!"

My kick had some spite to it — the Zatrathi slammed into the opposite wall and slumped to the floor. This cabin was a small one — three square meters at most — and furnished in a Spartan manner. A vertical contraption that vaguely resembled a bed, a table with a monitor that almost looked fit for a human, a small chair and a rack with a disassembled armor suit. Nothing more. Neither personal belongings, nor plunder fit for a pirate.

"Let's finish him off!" Eunice took aim but I stepped between the blaster and the unconscious Zatrathi. "What're you doing? What's wrong with you?"

"Chill! This is a prisoner. We need to talk to him."

"We don't have time for that!" Eunice dug in — but I dug in too.

"I will deal with him myself. You go and plug Brainiac into the socket. We need him to take over the ship's network and figure out where we need to go."

Eunice put the blaster away and got to work. Naturally, we were equal in our partnership, but as she had already pointed out, this was my mission and therefore I called the shots here.

While the Zatrathi was out, I disassembled the 'bed,' fashioned a few durable bands from the resultant material and tied up the prisoner. Using my manipulators, I lifted him into the air and forced his limbs into different directions. There was an unpleasant crunch, then a long moan, and the warrior regained consciousness.

"Brainiac — translate: 'You are my prisoner. If you cooperate, you will remain alive.'"

My suit's speaker echoed the message in the guttural Zatrathi tongue. Good thing Brainiac had been to the orbital station. There was no one else in all of Galactogon who knew how to communicate with the Zatrathi.

"Who are you? What do you want from me?" The prisoner asked without betraying the slightest emotion. Perhaps our sudden appearance had blown his fuse and his brain was no longer capable of processing what he was feeling...

"Where is the captain of this flying fortress? Can you show us the way?"

"The captain?" asked the forever-puzzled warrior — puzzling me in turn. I tried to explain.

"The senior officer. The Uldan with the brainworm."

"Brainworm?" Clearly, we were lost in translation. "Only the Queen reigns over us!"

I had no idea what the proper name of the creature that controlled the Uldan butterfly was. Then it hit me suddenly:

"There is a room on this ship with a multicolored door. I need to see the one who is inside."

"You seek the Regal Relay? The conduit of Her Will?"

Why look at that! Helpful info about our old friend the brainworm. They are not independent beings, but relays of the queen's will.

"Yes! The very one. How can this be arranged?"

"The Regal Guard won't permit it. You must have authorization. Neither the junior nor the senior officers have it," the Zatrathi said quite frankly, forcing me to think. Why is this prisoner so helpful anyway? Why would he want to cooperate?

"If I let you go, will you attack me?"

"No. Why should I attack you? Are you an enemy?" For a moment, the Zatrathi regained his emotional faculties and surprise sounded in his voice. Now I really was stumped. I slowly lowered the warrior to the floor. He leaned against the wall, lowered his bound paws and went limp in a rather uncomfortable position. Like a doll. Just as I had set him down. At this point the question that occurred to me was so stupid that I couldn't resist asking it:

"Why did the Zatrathi attack Galactogon?"

"We are fulfilling the purpose for which we were created. We are cleansing the galaxy of the Vraxis."

"*Ask him where their homeworld is!*" Behind my back, Eunice was closely following the interrogation. I had Brainiac translate the question, but the Zatrathi just shook his head.

"I am a simple warrior. My job is to command my company, doing as my Queen commands. I don't know where the planet you are talking about is located."

I readied my manipulators to restrain the prisoner if he tried anything and deactivated my helmet. The Zatrathi did not even twitch as if he already knew that he was speaking to a human.

"*Brainiac, why is he not aggressive? Why doesn't he think we're enemies?*"

This was no trivial question. Back at the orbital station the

A CHECK FOR A BILLION

Zatrathi had fought tooth and nail. Later, on the flying fortress, they did all they could to kill me and the rhino. The ships of Fighting Breed that had come to pick us up on Shurtan had been shot down immediately — but for some reason this one Zatrathi was friendly. He just stood there, blinked his eyes, twiddled his mandibles and answered all my questions. Where's the catch?

"We are ready!" Eunice announced happily. "Brainiac has calculated a route to the brainworm — it's only twelve kilometers. Wrap it up here and let's go. What'd you take your helmet off for?"

The helmet! Every time I had encountered the Zatrathi warriors, they had been wearing their helmets. In effect, this was my first chance to see the Uldans' creation without their customary armor.

"Cover me. I want to check something," I told Eunice and took off my armor suit. The prisoner remained still. I even came right up to him and untied his limbs. The Zatrathi was about two heads taller than me, yet even now, having the opportunity to attack, he showed no aggression. He massaged his stiff paws and sat down calmly on the floor, his legs crossed beneath him.

"Let's go, Lex!" Eunice reminded me impatiently, but I just raised my hand in a calming gesture. Leaving the warrior alone, I walked over to his armor. The helmet was larger than mine, but quite recognizable. Turning it over in my hands, I couldn't think of anything better than to put it on.

"*You are great! You are mighty! You are unique! You are all my children! All the others are enemies! The Vraxis are all around us! They must be destroyed! You are great! You are mighty...*"

The red glow inside the helmet filled my head with the weight of lead. My thoughts became confused — disjointed. I looked up and saw a Vraxis swinging its sharp limbs next to me. My hand reached for the blaster — to kill the revolting insectoid. Alas — the monster was faster! The creature dodged and was out of reach! Bells clanged in my head, my legs buckled and the red glow faded into darkness.

"And what did you mean by that?" An ache in my shoulder brought me back to my senses. My armor suit's medunit was diligently healing my debuffs. The Zatrathi helmet was lying nearby, the Vraxis was gone, and I was splayed out on the floor looking up at my wife. Understanding perfectly well that my question might be a stupid one, I still ventured:

"Mean by what? What happened?"

"You don't remember anything?" Eunice frowned and came closer. "Hold still. Let me look at you."

She fixed me with her penetrating gaze, searching my eyes for something known only to her. At last, evidently not finding anything, she sighed.

"Everything seems normal."

"I remember a little. As soon as I put the helmet on, it began to brainwash me. 'The Vraxis are enemies, they must be destroyed, we're the strongest and the best' and all that. Then I saw a giant bug and rushed at it — and then darkness."

"A giant bug?! Oh, thanks! That was me, you idiot. You started from me like from a leper. And immediately reached for your blaster…"

Eunice didn't finish, staring at the Zatrathi helmet.

A CHECK FOR A BILLION

"Brainiac? Can you connect to it?"

"About time you asked," said the computer impatiently and an interface plug extended from Eunice's armor suit to the helmet. "Let's see what we have here. The memory, the CPU, the transmission module. Narf!"

Brainiac fell silent and at the same time the warrior's armor suit began to melt like a wax candle under a heat gun.

"Cap'n, we didn't mean to..." said the snake.

"Report! What was that?"

"The helmet contained a controller that was very much like a remote terminal. Only with a smaller operational radius. It was constantly broadcasting a recording about how great the Zatrathi are and how the Vraxis must be annihilated. Furthermore, the helmet's optics were set up in a very particular manner. They render all creatures who don't have special friendly tags as Vraxis and transmit the picture and audio directly into the wearer's brain, so there's no need for translation. We traced the remote channel upstream and then were cut off — someone sent a self-destruct command. That's why the armor self-destructed."

"To keep us from finding the man behind the curtain, running this entire show," I made the obvious conclusion. Suddenly, I went further and added: "The Zatrathi aren't the aggressors in this war. They are victims just like us. The victims of the one who knows how to create the brainworms. The Queen. Eunice, we have to take this warrior with us!"

New title: Devil's Advocate. You are the first player to figure out that the Zatrathi are an enslaved race. Find the evidence that

---

will vindicate the Zatrathi before all of Galactogon.

An icon in the form of ancient scales appeared above my wife's head. Checking her avatar's properties, I saw that she had received the same rank as me.

"This is odd," said our Zatrathi 'evidence.' "My armor has returned to our mother without me…yet I am still here."

"Has this happened before?" I latched onto the warrior's confusion.

"Yes, the higher the rank, the more often the mother returns us to her. We become stronger every time we're reborn. Well, nothing to be done. I will request new armor from the officers. It doesn't do to go rushing into battle naked."

"Maybe you had better take a nap, right now," I said. "Brainiac, knock him out!"

An injection of sleeping solution and the Zatrathi's compound eyes turned dull gray.

"No way!" Eunice objected. "How are we supposed to haul him out of here? He'll die without armor."

"Let's figure that out later. First we have to kill the brainworm. Brainiac, we're going to head to the bridge. Help us avoid any detection along the way. If the Queen orders the fortress to self-destruct, we won't be able to complete Mercaloun's mission. You'll have to block the signal somehow."

"Orders received. We will need a little time to figure out how to do this," the snake replied in a serious tone. "We have some of the data from the other flying fortress. Maybe we can find the source of the self-destruct signal it received. Then perhaps we could divert it somehow."

"Spare me the details, I need a result." I climbed back into my suit, picked up the pieces of the Zatrathi's armor scattered across the floor and loaded them back onto the food cart. All I had to do was figure out what to do with the warrior, but here my wife came to the rescue:

"We can put him in here." Eunice unscrewed the food cart's side panel and pulled out the motor. This cleared a large cavity into which we then stuffed the Zatrathi with some difficulty. Replacing the cover, Eunice opened the door and checked the corridor.

"It's clear. Move out!"

Our journey to the fortress's command center could be characterized by one word: 'lucky.' First of all, we were lucky that the flying fortress had a very rapid moving walkway, which meant that we didn't have to sprint at breakneck speed, attracting attention to ourselves. Second of all, we were lucky in that the majority of the enemy's manpower was busy mopping up Mercaloun's spawn. We were just passing by the place where the cacodemons had gnawed their way through the bulkheads between decks. Looking inside, I saw a huge melted hole. The cacodemon blood was worse than acid and had already burned a hole through several decks. The Zatrathi were busy hectically patching the ensuing leaks and had no time for a cart loaded with junk. Given the emergency situation on board the ship, their coordination was spotty at best.

As a result, a mere thirty minutes later we found ourselves

outside the brainworm's chamber.

"You managed to kill those without any fire support?" You could tell from Eunice's voice that the Zatrathi Regal Guard had made an impression on her. Four barrel-shaped bodies stood at the rainbow-colored door, guarding the chamber of the brainworm. Or, now that we knew its proper name — the Regal Relay.

"I had a good partner," I replied, opening the dummy armor suit and unleashing Mercaloun's starving spawn. "Lunchtime! Eat those fat ones first — then everything else."

The creatures with the circular jaws blinked their eyes obediently and surged towards their meal. The guards immediately opened fire — but what can four mortals accomplish against an immortal hunger? The cacodemons did not even notice their attempts at resistance, almost instantly tearing the Regal Guards into their constituent components. Swelling up to enormous sizes, the cacodemons settled down to digest their meals. Our time had come. Pushing the cart ahead of me, I blasted the rainbow door without worrying about my stealth. A nasty general alarm resounded throughout the flying fortress. There was no doubt that the brainworm knew about our arrival. The Relay even tried to resist, trying to jump on top of us while brandishing his blaster like a club. But Eunice zapped him in mid-leap, turning him into a loot crate. Undistracted by all this, I pulled out the remote terminal and connected it to the ship. Braniac won't be able to protect us through the armor suit's interface — he needs a bit more bandwidth. We had a minute to save ourselves. This was how much I figured it would take for 'mom' to react to her relay complaining about the arrogant humans who were invading his chamber.

A CHECK FOR A BILLION

"Got it!" It took Brainiac thirty seconds to cope with the greatest threat. "Self-destruct has been disabled. There's no longer any danger of you exploding!"

"Welcome news. Now start the engines and fly this tub straight into that planet. We're going to ram 'er!"

"Captain, there's one problem. I lack the system resources to manage a network this large. I can do the little stuff, but flying the entire flying fortress..."

This news was so unpleasant that I even grew upset. Our entire plan was based on my assumption that Brainiac would be able to pilot the flying fortress. I had miscalculated.

"Thirty minutes!" Eunice reminded me. One of the screens displayed the silhouettes of Zatrathi warriors fighting our cacodemons. Finally I got a chance to see the method they found of killing them. Or rather, the method of just letting them die. The reckless monsters never stopped eating until they simply burst to pieces. Their stomach acid flooded the floor, reached the neighboring cacodemon and I received another notification about a fallen party member. Sigh. Victims of their own gluttony.

"Is there anything you can do?" I asked hopefully, but Brainiac was implacable.

"With this ship no. There is so much data onboard that my cores are starting to overheat."

"What do you mean 'with this ship?'" Eunice took exception to the Brainiac's wording.

"Well...I could connect to the orbital station that the flying fortress is docked to. Ninety percent of its functionality is disabled from the Anorxian attack, which means there should be enough resources."

"We won't have time to get over there," my wife objected, but here Brainiac had a solution:

"You don't have to go anywhere. The vessels are currently linked, I can pilot it from here."

Here was a chance! We could hope to triumph again!

"What's still functional on the orbital station?"

"Some maneuvering thrusters and a few cannons. The functionality is extremely limited."

"Rotate the damaged station around so that the fortress is between it and the planet! Hurry!" I ordered, unable to hide my excitement. An NPC would never think of this — it was time to show the advantage of the human mind over the programmer's creation.

"Eunice, cover the entrance! Our support's about to run out! Don't let anyone in here! It should work!" I ordered, receiving a notification about another dead glutton. Eunice silently rushed for the door, activating her shoulder blasters.

"Done." Brainiac broadcast an external image to one of the screens. The orbital station and flying fortress orbited the planet in tandem, linked like a dancing couple.

"Fire the station's thrusters. Set its throttle to full!"

"Cap'n — what you're doing — it isn't very safe." The snake didn't like my idea, but I snapped:

"Execute! Push the fortress with the orbital station!"

"Roger that. You're the one in charge," the engineer sighed and added: "Hold on. Three seconds to contact. Two. One. Contact!"

The connective passages between the two vessels

collapsed as the orbital station slammed into the fortress. The ensuing crash sent me flying across the room — with the rail I had been holding onto still in my hand. The flying fortress began to vibrate, shake and, judging by my screens slowly slip out of its orbit. Meter by painful meter.

"Thrust to full, I said!"

"Cap'n these vessels won't be able to withstand reentry."

"They won't burn up entirely! There's too much metal here. Full throttle!"

"Roger full throttle, Cap'n, sir!"

Jets of light erupted from the myriad thrusters that dotted the orbital station. A terrible shaking from the acceleration joined the shaking from the collision. At the same time, the force of gravity began to grow, pulling us tighter to the floor and making us fight for every step.

"We have entered the atmosphere. Altitude is fifty kilometers. I am picking up hull damage. Attention, the power cables have melted. We have lost contact with the orbital station!"

I barely lifted my head off the floor, looking for the cart. It was lying on its side, on the opposite side of the bridge. Turning on my thrusters, I pushed myself along the floor to the objective.

"Altitude is twenty kilometers. Estimated time to contact is twenty seconds. I strongly recommend abandoning ship."

"Eunice, take off your armor suit!" I yelled, crashing into the cart and grabbing it like a prized possession. The force of gravity had reached 3Gs. A little more and I would be at my limit, so I needed to hurry. I yanked the poor warrior out of the cart. The acceleration had almost flattened him into a cake, but the Zatrathi was still alive.

"Altitude is five kilometers. Time to contact is six seconds."

I ejected out of my armor suit and groaned. Without the assistance of my suit's servomotors, I could barely move a finger.

"Four seconds!"

Straining my tendons as hard as I could, I just barely reached the Zatrathi. A system dialog appeared asking me to confirm that I wanted to put my armor suit on the alien.

"Two!"

The suit initialized and its medunit began automatic resuscitation procedures. Circles appeared before my eyes. I felt like I was swimming in an invisible liquid, but I was still holding on. I didn't have the time to pass out!

"Contact!"

I had only one nanosecond for my one attempt. The armor suit with the Zatrathi disappeared into my inventory as everything around me vanished in a fiery whirlwind. There was a short pang of pain and then darkness. I was free to pass out.

CHAPTER ELEVEN

WHEN THE DARKNESS CLEARED, returning me to Galactogon, the first thing I saw was a rebuke from the system:

You cannot store a living creature with a developed intellect in your inventory. Zatrathi Officer ?!?!?!?! has been removed from your inventory.

A drawn-out groan sounded beside me. Respawning in Galactogon came with its own special discomfort and this was Eunice's first death as far as I recalled. My head was spinning, yet when I sat up, I couldn't help but whoop triumphantly: The Zatrathi warrior had been ejected from my inventory and now lay beside me whole and unharmed. The only thing he had lost was his name, but this was a mere trifle compared to the alternative. How critical can a single nanosecond be sometimes!

"What are you whooping about?" Eunice grumbled, rubbing her temples.

"Put on your armor suit. It will remove your debuffs," I advised and donned my own golden spacesuit. The medunit immediately set to work, eliminating the warning icons dancing around my status screen. Placing my hand on the motionless Zatrathi, I ordered Brainiac to reanimate him. A few dozen injections and the pale gray body regained its customary colors. The Zatrathi's breathing evened out, his eyelids stopped twitching, and his body regained the tranquil repose of sleep.

The next thing I heard were a myriad tiny hammers and our respawn point filled with cacodemons. They flashed their fangs menacingly, but did not attack us. Just in case, I pulled the Zatrathi a little closer to me. What if they decide to eat him? Having verified that we weren't aggressive, the vermin began to transform, turning into a transport rhino once again. I had to give them their due — this time the weird monster rhino had seats for three. I guess they had examined my Zatrathi and deemed him worthy of meeting Mercaloun.

Five minutes later we appeared before the snake, who was busy eating without a second's pause. An endless conveyor of food in the form of blackish gruel was being delivered straight into the mouth of the Great Uldan. Once her mouth was full, Mercaloun rolled the contents over her tongue, savoring and enjoying each drop with evident pleasure. Three of the snake's four eyes were closed, while the last one kept a close watch on us, albeit without any sign of menace.

"You made it in time. The flying fortress and orbital station will last me a long time. You have earned your lives and you have earned a reward as well. Order your ship to fly over here, I would like to make some modifications to it."

The snake never actually stopped eating as she spoke, communicating with us through the walls' vibrations.

Mission accomplished: A Meal Fit for a Lady. Reward: +4 orbship upgrades; comm link to Lady Mercaloun; access to Planet Shurtan; +5 Mercaloun spawn integrated into the orbship.

Your rapport with Lady Mercaloun has grown. Current Rapport: 10,0000

"I'm already en route, Captain." Brainiac had anticipated my orders. "Send me the coordinates of the landing zone. There is such a mess taking place in the system right now that no one should notice me."

"Fly here, Orbship. My spawn will meet you. Surgeon, I want to hear the story of Warlock and the reason why you came to this planet."

It took me half an hour to satisfy Mercaloun's curiosity. The snake was interested in everything, starting from where I met Brainiac and ending with how I recruited my crew members. After that I was forced to tell her about the pirates and my missions to find the video and the warehouse on the pirate base. By this time, Brainiac had reached the planet and fallen into the short paws of Mercaloun's spawn. I didn't know what they were doing to my ship

— but the periodic exclamations of joy from my crew indicated that everything was going well. All of Eunice's attempts to discover what was going on were met with a polite request not to disturb the work and assurances that the surprise would be a pleasant one. I finished my story and looked expectantly at Mercaloun, hoping that she would grant me full access to the base. And yet, the Uldan's response were disappointing to say the least:

"You are too late. A week ago, I transformed everything that was here into energy. Objects, walls, living and nonliving creatures. There is nothing left."

How can I describe the utter disappointment that I felt? I don't think I could. We can only describe what fills us. Hate or love, for example. My disappointment, however, was a complete emptiness. A spiritual vacuum that bred apathy and sapped my will to go on. There is little that can resist such emptiness.

My hands dropped, a heaviness settled on my chest, and I just looked at Mercaloun mindlessly, not understanding what to do next. Was it worth going on a suicide mission just to find out that everything was in vain? The snake did not look away and suddenly declared:

"I can help with the video, however. I absorbed the recording and it has remained in my memory. I am able to recover a small excerpt. Do you know the date and camera ID you need?"

A glimmer of hope tingled among the vacuum of disappointment. Here it is — my best bet at getting anything out of this situation.

The camera posed a problem indeed — Hilvar hadn't said anything about which of them had recorded the episode he needed.

A CHECK FOR A BILLION

However, I did know the exact date and time, and Mercaloun agreed to suffer a little to recover the records of all twenty cameras from her memory. A few minutes later, a beautiful crystal appeared on the floor before me, shimmering with all the shades of green.

"This is a one-time memory medium. It contains all the recordings you need. You need only to break the crystal to view them. Everyone who is present will be able to see the footage too. Now go, for I must rest. Recovering memory saps a lot of energy from me. My children will take you to the ship. The upgrades I promised you have been installed by now."

Mission updated: In Search of Cause. You have acquired the video recording. Deliver the recording to Hilvar or the Corsican.

I was surprised to see the modified description. I guess Hilvar isn't the only one who wants to know what happened between him and the Corsican. The mangled pirate king was interested in the data as well! I could leverage this, but first I had to settle my business on Planet Shurtan. While the cacodemons were morphing into a rhino, I made the call.

"I've been waiting for your call a long time. Did the Scourge scour your stupid face?" Tryd gibed instead of a greeting. His voice was filled with open mockery. "Don't worry. I can get you out. The price will be your ship."

I took a calming breath, restraining myself from telling the pirate off. This bastard had lured me here specifically to extort the orbship from me! Having managed my outrage, I thought of a calm reply, though even then — a bystander would have thought that I was speaking each word with difficulty, all but spitting it at the fox:

"There's no need to project your own cowardice onto others. I'm done with the base. It is clear! The Scourge cleaned everything she could reach. There's no Northbridge here. No Anorxian prince."

I could hear fangs gnash on the other end.

"I am the coward?! Why, I'll twist you until you look like a ram's horn! The signal..." the pirate began, but he cut himself off. "Keep looking. Prince Northbridge is intact. If you want the Lora, you'll get me that synthoid! The warehouse is on the second level."

The short beeps that followed indicated our conversation had ended. But the most important thing had been spoken — Mercaloun hadn't devoured everything. She had listened in on our conversation and as soon as I put away my PDA, I encountered all four of her eyes staring at me with interest:

"I scanned the various signal frequencies in the area and found the signal your friend mentioned. The transmitter is one level above us. Follow the light. It shall guide you."

The walls began to glow again, illuminating the path. I loaded my sleeping Zatrathi into the rhino and we moved out. A few minutes later we encountered a marble wall.

"Step aside," Eunice told Mercaloun's minions and pulled out a plasma cutter. The layer of marble splintered and crumbled, flying in all directions in contravention of logic and earthly physics. In theory, the stone should have melted. I wasn't the only one to notice this inconsistency. My wife did too. She halted her work and knelt down. She pulled out a drill and bored a small hole right above the floor. Her drill bit seemed to encounter a hollow several times

---

and then abruptly sank a meter into the wall. Eunice removed the camera from her armor suit, attached it as a tip to the drill, and stuck it into the hole again.

"Brainiac?"

"There is a door here. Hang on. Step back a little. Wow! Check it out, Captain!"

My screen displayed a hollow between the ordinary door and the stonework — it was filled with activated elo and small pellets of raq. I had seen this kind of application before. Graykill had used shrapnel like this to deal with the two Zatrathi Guards. I naturally had a hefty respect for the cacodemons, but their bodies were unlikely to withstand a direct hit from such a mine. And anyway, the marble lining isolated this area from the vermin. The pirates had approached the task of base security very seriously.

"Keep going," Brainiac said and Eunice extended the camera deeper. "Hah! There are more surprises here!"

The door behind the marble layer was also mined with more raq shrapnel, only it was aimed in the other direction, toward the warehouse. Inside the warehouse itself we could make out the object of our raid: Shielded by several layers of metal mesh, a 1×1×1 meter cube rested on a small pedestal in the middle of the warehouse. The nearby shelves were packed with chests, bars of precious metal, weapons, and other equipment. A space pirates' treasure vault. All we had to do was figure out what the local equivalent of 'Speak friend and enter' was — and we would be in the money. The signal that Tryd had mentioned and which Mercaloun had detected was being transmitted by one of the detonators. Once a minute, a short burst of data would emanate into space, indicating that everything was all right. There wasn't anything else here, except for a shimmering loot crate. Whoever had created this room, had barricaded the door from the inside and then gone to his rebirth. There were no other doors, nor ventilation shafts. It was an ideal long-term storage chamber.

Eunice poked her finger at her PDA, gesturing me to call Tryd again. We wouldn't be able to slip through these traps without outside help. But I was against it. The fox wasn't really on our side here. And the time had come to decide who I wanted to be: a pirate seeking to plunder lost treasure, or a blind sheep incapable of independent thought who looked to someone else for help.

"Snake, make us ten strong pickaxes from raq and prepare the droids. I will send the transport over now. By the way, I'm sending you the Zatrathi we captured onboard. Take him to the medcapsule and keep him in suspended animation. He is our loot. And he's worth a doozy. All clear?"

Mercaloun continued monitoring our progress through her spawn, but she did not interfere. I barely had time to sit down to wait for the rhino when Brainiac announced:

"We have received the Zatrathi warrior on board."

The cacodemon rhino had reached *Warlock* and was waiting to pick up the droids. Suddenly, Brainiac streamed an interesting spectacle to my screen — our own rhino marine had begun circling around the new arrival with evident interest, snorting with agitation and shaking his rump demonstratively. The snake decided to adopt the role of nature documentary narrator:

"Our marine has found himself a mate! Cap'n, what would you say to the chance of expanding our *Warlock* family? Some cryptosaur pups? If you agree to it, the cryptosaur will transform into a female."

WHAT?! My rhinoceros, the alpha male, the crazy marine will become a female?! Never!

"Abort!"

"Come on, Cap'n! The little cryptosaur pups will grow to full size at a cost of a few tons of raq. This will greatly increase our combat power."

"Damn, couldn't we accomplish this without breeding those two?" I asked, my confidence wavering.

"No, Cap'n. That's not how it works."

I merely grunted in response. I should know…

"Snake, how long does a cryptosaur pregnancy last anyway?" I mumbled.

My greed had begun to grapple with my deep reluctance to have to look at my marine and think '*Et tu, Brute?*

"One lunar month. The litter is typically between three to five pups."

I didn't say anything.

"Come on, Cap'n. Be a mensch!" the snake pleaded. "We can sell the ones we don't need. And we'll keep one for ourselves."

"Enough!" I had to put an end to this dispute decisively. "Mercaloun, can you transform your cryptosaur into a female? Like give him some extra bits and curves…or whatever a female rhino has… My marine is a male and that's the way he's going to stay!"

"This is an amusing request, human," the Lady cackled in reply. *"I too would like to see what comes of their tryst."*

The mating ritual on my screen changed dramatically. My

marine had just been showing off his rump when, prompted by an invisible tweak from Mercaloun, he proudly stuck out his chest and began circling his mate like a pompous peacock. The newly-made female growled something in response, my cryptosaur reared up and…ripples distorted the image.

"Let's not forget that we're rated strictly 12 and up," the engineer reminded and added in her ordinary voice: "The pickaxes are ready. They're about to be delivered to you."

"If any cryptosaur pups are born, you will get one. I promise."

I didn't want to continue this discussion further. I'm accustomed to thinking of marines as men and the only thing I'm open to is celebrating my marine's future paternity. The droids arrived three minutes later and immediately began demolishing the wall. Only not the one that led to the door and was booby-trapped with explosives. I shifted to the right and ordered my metal workers to dig a new passage. After a couple meters, I adjusted the direction of the digging, heading now for the warehouse wall. Eunice went on cutting the spacers, retaining beams and other structural elements without any further comments. There was no need to worry about the base's structural integrity. Mercaloun's children would follow in our wake and eat everything inside the warehouse anyway, walls included.

"Ready!" A large piece of metal plate collapsed in our direction. The droids dragged it away from the aisle and immediately the unpleasant buzz of circular saws filled my ears. The cacodemons had grown hungry during the wait. Having no great faith in my own dexterity, I sent the droids to scout the

---

warehouse first. Brainiac guided them expertly and pretty soon they were hauling out everything they could. Bars of platinum, locked chests and some peculiar wooden figurines. The droids dragged all kinds of loot away from the potential epicenter of the explosion. I had no doubt that there was another booby-trap under the cube. The pirates were sure to mine the pedestal, so it was better to extract anything of value first. Some of the items had pretty singular seals on them, indicating their owner's identity. I suppose Hilvar will be pleased to see his belongings again.

"Everyone move aside!" Once there was nothing but the cube in the warehouse, I ordered the droids to deliver the loot to the ship. Securing all my things in my inventory, I asked Eunice to shine a light for me and began crawling through the hole we had made. The warehouse itself was filled with an intense cold which made me instantly regret coming in here all but naked. And yet, I did not rush to lay my hands on the cube, first taking a moment to examine it carefully from all sides — while hopping from foot to foot to warm myself up. Brainiac removed the lattice, but found no fixtures. It does not hurt to check one more time to be sure, however.

Finding nothing, I reached out my hand. It was numb and shaking from the cold, but I acted slowly and deliberately, prepared to pull back at the first sign of danger. My fingers had almost touched the cube's surface without encountering any resistance — when I jerked my hand away. Something didn't add up. I didn't like how easy this all was.

"Lex, what's taking you?" Eunice asked impatiently, but I just waved her away and went on examining the pedestal.

Should I lift the cube up with my manipulators? No, this solution seemed too obvious. There could still be some undetected trap that would incinerate everything. I need to find some other way. Something that no reasonable creature would attempt. The pirates would set up their security system to foil anyone — anyone but a complete fool! After all, a complete fool would never make it this far to begin with…

"Lex?" Eunice was surprised when I backtracked to the far wall and, getting a running start, sprinted straight at the pedestal. Coiling, I sent myself flying almost horizontally. The leap was accurate enough for me to crash into the cube. Something cracked, both inside the pedestal and inside me. As I had predicted there were additional fixtures here which Brainiac had not detected, yet they could not resist the inertia of my body mass. The cube, which practically stopped my flight, rocked and flew off the pedestal — straight into my inventory. There was a short pang and I was sent to respawn yet again.

You cannot store a living creature with a developed intellect in your inventory. Exiled Anorxian Prince I-455-772 has been removed from your inventory.

I was lying on the floor in complete darkness, laughing. Not even laughing — I was cackling maniacally. I could feel the debuffs that came with respawning, but I could not get into my armor to remove them. I needed help. The Debility debuff afflicted any player who died more than once within an hour. It could only be removed by another player — or by a half hour of inactivity. At least, I ignored all damage from players, creatures and items for the duration of the debuff. I suppose someone could drop a granite slab on me and as soon as the debuff expired, I would die again, but this was farfetched. The main thing was that I had invulnerability from any aggressive creatures that might wander into the respawn area.

"Stop laughing!" said my wife's dissatisfied voice. "Can you move?"

"Did it get you too?" I almost choked with laughter, imagining the cost of restoring the class her armor suit had lost. I suppose Tryd will never get his cube until he compensates us for the repairs.

"You bet! That conflagration you set off back there was enough to wipe out a dozen pirate bases. I believe even Mercaloun got hit."

"As long as the planet is whole, its planetary spirit will remain unharmed. But you are right, Nurse. The explosion completely destroyed the base. I will have to relocate to another lair."

I felt a prick in my shoulder and the Debility debuff disappeared. I jumped to my feet and immediately donned my armor suit. A couple of injections and I was fine. Mercaloun's minions were already hovering over Eunice. Some sharp-looking implements flashed in the cacodemon's paws and her debuff vanished without a trace. Eunice got up and pulled her armor suit out of her inventory — causing my eyes to go wide.

"It's a bit too valuable an item to risk so wantonly," the girl explained, interpreting my astonishment correctly. "When you crawled inside, I decided to play it safe and took it off. Try and warn me next time you decide to do something insane. Restoring an armor class will hurt our family budget."

"So what happened there anyway?" I decided to change topics, accepting her criticism.

"Give me a second, I'll bring up the video. Here, look. I think I'll call it 'Surgeon's Surgery.'"

Eunice shared the video with me. My leap really had been an epic one. As soon as the cube rocked, an energy grid fell from above, cutting me into three neat pieces. The explosive at the door detonated, blasting pellets of raq in all directions, while a fiery hell opened up beneath Eunice's feet. The camera managed to record only one millisecond before the girl followed me to rebirth and as a result, the last frame of the video displayed nothing but fire. Even my scant knowledge of the sapper business was enough to understand that the blast wave had not come from the warehouse, but from beneath its floor.

"I didn't know that you were recording," I said, surprised.

"Yeah. Initially, I wanted to make a let's play series for the marine class but then I realized there wouldn't be much interest in it. There are lots of marines in Galactogon, but not so many pirates. I already published the first episode. I'm editing the second one and shooting the third. The warehouse explosion should make for a good ending!"

"Ep-episodes? W-what episodes?" I stuttered from surprise.

"Why are you all tense suddenly?" Eunice failed to understand my reaction. "Yeah, I'm making a video series about being a space pirate. I'm even shooting it from two angles at once.

A CHECK FOR A BILLION

You're the one who granted me access to your camera, remember?"

"You never said you'd use it to make videos. You just said you wanted to see yourself from a 3rd person POV," I seethed. It's not that I was opposed to video recording in general. I just didn't like that she had never told me about it.

"Lex, I..." Eunice hesitated and came closer to me, putting her hand on my chest. "I wanted it to be a surprise when you saw the result. Don't be angry. I studied video editing and cinematography. A couple of my short films even won first place in amateur contests. And that was all with material from Runlustia where nothing epic ever happened. Imagine the kind of interest we can generate with advertisers when they see material like this!"

The smile crept onto my face of its own volition. That little devil! She knew exactly what buttons to push! Advertisers really would be interested in this material, and if we packaged it in some slick format, they'd perhaps even go into a frenzy for it.

"Whether or not we'll find that check remains unclear, but either way, half of the rights to the video will be ours. They're our Plan B."

The cacodemon rhino snorted loudly next to us. We were being delicately reminded that our adventures on this planet had ended and it was time to move on. Picking up the cube, I hopped into the rhino and a few minutes later we were standing before my updated ship.

The first thing that caught my eye was that the hull's color had changed. Whereas the orbship used to be a cascading silver, *Warlock* now proudly sparkled all in gold. Nothing had changed to the touch, however — it was all the same cold metal.

"Cool, huh?" The snake's head popped out of the orbship. The hull functionality that allowed the crew to form passages at will had remained unchanged. "Load up and get ready for blast off. We need to test this baby's combat maneuvers!"

The snake's excitement was alarming. The only other time I saw her like this, it was after we'd gotten our paws on the third list of Hansa upgrades.

"Brainiac, give me a report on the upgrades!" I ordered, getting comfy in my chair and handing the Anorxian prince over to the engineer for safekeeping.

"Cap'n, could we do a performance test first? Pleeeaaase?" the snake begged. Eunice and I exchanged glances, perplexed by such childish impatience from the engineer.

"All right. Let's take off. Brainiac, take control. Let's see what you're all so raving mad about."

The launch went smoothly without any jerks or shaking whatsoever. Brainiac made a few orbits around Shurtan, demonstrating our improved inertia dampeners. And he did all this still within the planetary atmosphere, without popping out to space. The sensors read a significant increase in the hull's surface temperature, but everything went just fine. After we'd had our fun, *Warlock* shot straight up, leaving the stratosphere.

"Our hyperdrive is being disrupted. We are being locked on by an EM cannon. Twelve torpedoes have been launched at us. Their speed is 50% our maximum. What is our destination, Captain?"

There was no panic in Brainiac's voice — just unvarnished

bravado. Having already lost a flying fortress and an orbital station, the Zatrathi rallied four more of the enormous vessels to the system, so as to nip any further trouble in the bud. Itching for a fight, the reinforcements were happy to see someone they could beat up on and the first thing they did was make sure we wouldn't be able to slip away. As a result, Brainiac's question came as a surprise, yet I replied coolly:

"I'm supposed to meet the Corsican in the Silmar system in a few hours. Let's go there."

"Roger. Calculating hyperjump now," Brainiac reported officiously and deftly dodged the torpedoes. The Zatrathi fighters and frigates, who had begun to circle around us did not last long. *Warlock* now had some new cannons to match her engines, and the gunner was blasting single stroke fours at the enemy bandits with terrifying accuracy.

"EM blast detected!" reported the engineer. I looked at my screens — but the customary flicker of light never came. We never even noticed the hit.

"Hyperjump calculation complete," said Brainiac. "Captain, please confirm jump activation."

"I confirm." I was slowly beginning to understand what Mercaloun had given me and what it would mean to an ordinary player like me. I mean, this was as good as cheating...

"Entering hyperspace!" the ship computer announced proudly and the stars turned to white lines. "Estimated flight time: twenty minutes."

A pause ensued. Brainiac was giving me the opportunity to process what had happened — but couldn't contain his excitement that long:

"Captain, they upgraded my CPU! The disruptor beams can still pull us out of hyperspace, but they can't keep us from jumping into it! Let's go take over a flying fortress, what do you say? I'm sure that I'll be able to hack one now!"

A list of upgrades scrolled across my screen. When Mercaloun was being generous, she didn't mess about. In addition to the upgrades mentioned in the mission description, she'd upgraded almost every aspect of the orbship. The overall performance characteristics had only increased by 10–15%, but that was enough to turn the orbship into a destroyer in terms of combat potential. The new hull, the new computer system, the new reactor and the new cannons were something else. We were so absorbed in studying every upgraded detail that we barely noticed the time fly by. As soon as we emerged from hyperspace, several 'flycatchers' locked onto us. The pirates were much more on the ball than the Zatrathi. The Silmar system was packed with orbital stations. Brainiac reported a dozen of them, located around various planets in the system. On top of this there were five Grand Arbiters here, keeping the peace and looking out for the pirates' interests. Where did they get this firepower? A scanner beam ran along our hull and the dispatcher's voice roared in the bridge's speakers:

"Orbship *Warlock*, follow corridor 2-2-1. Dock five. The Corsican is expecting you."

Access to the Silmar system granted.

Only now did it occur to me that before coming here, we

should have headed back to Blood Island to restore our planetary binding. After all, who knew how our meeting with the head of the Jolly Roger would turn out?

CHAPTER TWELVE

T HE CORSICAN'S RESIDENCE WAS SO 'IMPRESSIVE' that it was hard not to roll your eyes. No simplicity or modesty here — only magnificence multiplied by vanity. Everything reeked of luxury: marble statues, three-meter-long tapestries, ornamental plants, vintage fountains, mirrored ceilings, a white piano, fur carpets (large enough to house a tribe of mice) and a huge crystal chandelier in the shape of an imperial crown above it all. This place seemed more like a deluxe showroom than the home of the most powerful pirate in Galactogon. Although who am I to judge the Corsican? Maybe this tasteless, frilly interior concealed some deeper sacral meaning, which was simply beyond my comprehension.

In deference to our host, I entered the Corsican's conference room alone and without my armor suit. Eunice had

A CHECK FOR A BILLION

remained on *Warlock* at my request. I didn't have much faith in the pirates, so someone back home who could respond if things went sour was useful. The sumptuous surroundings pressed on my mind, which was accustomed to visual modesty. The walls draped in red velvet, the immense table which occupied most of the room, and the pompous armchairs, all made me want to snort like a bull, bow my head and charge the pirates who had assembled in the room. Instead I scuffed the floor with my foot and stopped unexpectedly.

Fresh out of respawn after I'd blown him up on that cruiser, the head of the Jolly Roger met me in a guise I did not expect. All his scars and mangled features were gone. The Delvian was now a handsome prince, sitting at the head of the table, conferring in hushed tones with his secretary who had bowed down to him — without any chest speakers or other devices.

Arcana, the Precian, sat on the Corsican's right. She was his assistant, deputy and who-knows-who-else. The only NPC woman who had earned her right to speak at the pirate council. And I mention her being an NPC because there was another woman at the table. The captain of Cruiser *Alexandria* — Kiddo. Marina was conferring with Anton, and looked up only for a moment in order to nod me a greeting. I did not know the other three pirates, but when I saw none other than Tryd — may he rot in his foxhole — sitting a few places over from where I stood, I could barely keep myself from pouncing on him. The pirate looked at me with undisguised malice, and I could tell that his glance boded nothing well for me. But even Tryd wasn't the most curious attendee of this council. Hilvar sat to the Corsican's left — chatting with his adviser, defiantly turning away from his former boss.

All eight pirate captains, all eight gentlemen of fortune, all eight endowed with the power to vote on the council were seated in a semicircle of chairs that resembled thrones. Meanwhile, the only seat allotted to me was a tiny wooden stool before them, either as a reminder or an emphasis of my novice status. Having appreciated the jest, I ignored the stool and remained standing.

"You made us wait," said the Corsican in a velvet baritone. His voice was not as deep as Oleander's but it did indicate clearly that he was a high-born Delvian.

I checked the quest timer — the three days that the Corsican had given me after the cruiser blast had not yet expired. I suppose I could object to this accusation, but the fact that Kiddo was here already told me that I had arrived fortuitously to a meeting that was not just for me. Marina was no 'local' and could not instantly teleport from one point of the galaxy to another.

"No one gave me an exact time. You gave me three days and they haven't expired yet. I'm here on a personal matter. Well, and I'd like to tour the pirate capital. Since you granted me access, I figured I'd make use of the opportunity. Anyway, no one told me that you were waiting for me. Before you make a complaint, you should deal with your subordinates. Galactogon is my witness."

A snow-white aura erupted around me confirming that I had told the truth.

"Tryd? Explain yourself," demanded the Corsican, and the eyes of all those present turned to the mutilated Delvian.

"I don't have to," the pirate growled. No wonder he'd given me such an ugly look. I imagine my appearance wasn't part of his

---

plans. "The scallywag is here, so we can get on with it."

The Corsican fixed Tryd with a stare, but the marine merely stared back. Two strong-willed individuals had met, and neither one would back down. It did not escape me that both Delvians began reaching for their belts. Regulations are regulations, but weapons aren't armor. Pirates don't surrender their weapons under any circumstances.

"Calm down, Tryd," Hilvar decided to defuse the tension, ordering his subordinate to back down. Although, I guess I wasn't really sure that Tryd was his subordinate anymore. An ordinary rank-and-file pirate wouldn't be sitting at this table as an equal. "Surgeon, our base on Shurtan was seized by the Scourge. What do you know about this?"

"Everything," I replied quite simply, defusing the standoff between Tryd and the Corsican. Everyone's attention again switched to me. "What exactly are you interested in, and how would you like to pay for the information?"

"You're forgetting yourself, you mangy cur." Of those assembled, Tryd was the most unrestrained. "You were asked a question — answer it!"

"Oh but of course, master, right this instant," I snapped. It was childish but also well-suited to stoking the tension. "If you're not willing to pay me, all I'll offer is that the base is gone. It's been destroyed."

This caused a hubbub of outrage to erupt among the pirate council. The pirates jumped up from their seats and, flailing their hands, began shouting at each other, arguing and gesticulating in my direction. I didn't understand anything because for some reason

---

everyone had switched to their respective languages and I didn't have a link for Brainiac to translate for me. Having decided that everyone had yelled their fill, I heaped more fuel on the fire:

"I imagine this belongs to you."

With these words, I pulled out one of the wooden figurines I had found in the third warehouse and tossed them onto the table before Hilvar. He picked it up as the entire assembly watched in perfect silence. Seeing the piece of wood, everyone seemed to forget about me entirely.

"This is Realdean oak," the Pyrrhenian managed, nervously twitching his little wings. His gray skin flushed darker. I had no idea whether this was a good or bad sign. "Where did you get this?"

"At the base," I replied enigmatically and asked: "I still haven't understood — what am I going to get for telling you what happened to it?"

"Pirate rank three," Hilvar ventured.

"Pff!" I snorted. "You promised me rank three for the video. I got that too, so your offer is redundant."

"There was no way you could get the recording! The Scourge devoured the base!" Tryd even lunged at me, but the bodyguards standing behind him restrained him. What is wrong with this fox anyway? Is he playing some scripted role here?

"What do you want?" The Corsican turned out to be the most civil member of the council, asking me what they should have asked to begin with, instead of going on with this stupid play.

"I want the Lora. I will tell you what happened at the base in exchange for the coupler unit from the Vengeance."

A CHECK FOR A BILLION

"Isn't that in your possession, Tryd?" The head of the Jolly Roger addressed the still-restrained fox.

"He can't have it! He screwed up," the Delvian growled with rancor. "We had a deal: He delivers the prince, and I give him the Lora. No Anorxian prince — no Lora! I've said my piece!"

In the ensuing silence, Hilvar's pensive voice sounded somehow unkind:

"The Realdean oak was in the same warehouse as the cube. I placed it there myself. And after that, I sealed the vault. How did you get the oak, Surgeon?"

I shrugged, feigning complete disinterest in what was happening.

"What did you tell him about the third rank, you blabbermouth?" the Corsican turned on Hilvar. "Has your tongue been sweeping the floor in front of your brain again?"

"Watch how you talk to me," hissed Hilvar, his skin now fading to a light gray. A curious discovery! I guess when Pyrrhenians get mad they grow pale. Go figure. "Surgeon's got the evidence to prove that you're the blabbermouth! Roll that video! Let's see what you have to say for your rotten deeds!"

I had to compete that mission anyway, so I obediently took out the memory crystal and tossed it onto the table. It never had a chance to land — one of the bodyguards decided that this was some kind of bomb and blasted it mid-air with a well-aimed shot. For a moment, my heart sank into my heels — but then a 3D hologram of the recording from one of the cameras appeared right in the center of the table. It showed an empty room.

The seconds ticked, yet nothing happened. This at first

---

caused puzzled whispers among the council and then gradually the pirates began to openly laugh at Hilvar and me.

"What is this?" The Pyrrhenian frowned and my Rapport with him immediately plummeted by ten thousand points. I began to explain myself as fast as I could:

"You didn't say which camera you needed. There were twenty in that base and I pulled the recordings from all of them. They'll cycle in series, so we just have to wait."

My Rapport increased by five thousand. Hilvar believed me but not completely.

"Each recording will be three minutes long?" scolded one of the pirates I didn't know, when the picture changed to the next camera. We saw a corridor along with a patrolling guard.

"Uh-huh. When I got the recordings, I didn't have a chance to edit them so you'll just have to be patient," I replied, entirely unembarrassed.

Another change of scene and an empty chair appeared in the center of the recording. The Corsican instantly leaned forward, narrowing his eyes. He was obviously familiar with the chair. After two minutes of inactivity, Hilvar fell heavily into it. His barrel-shaped torso swayed, but remained in place. The Pyrrhenian's head nodded and swayed as if he'd had too much to drink. Leaning against the table, the pirate raised his head. Because of the location of the camera, it was difficult to see his face, but we could hear his slurred voice quite clearly:

"Didn't expect this, did you, you stupid chunks of silicon? You bits 'n' bytes, *hic!* We have your prince! Haw, haw — *hic!* — haw! I will re-solder him personally for ya with plenty of flux! You're a damn fool, you Motherboard! You really thought we needed your empire's help? Well you just let old — *hic!* — Hilvar show you where you can shove your charity!"

Hilvar stood up, turned and bent over, wishing to demonstrate where on his anatomy he was referring to — but then lost his balance and collapsed. Here the recording ended, cutting to another, empty room.

The silence among the council was broken only by inarticulate grunts as Hilvar tried to master his breathing. Unable to catch his breath, he finally croaked softly: "It can't be. That's not me. I don't remember that," and he went limp in his chair. No one uttered a word, neither as support nor as censure. The Corsican was the first to break the silence.

"The Motherboard ended all relations with us after this recording. Five years!" The aristocrat's fist came crashing down on the table with surprising force. "For five years I sacrificed everything to eke out an alliance with the Anorxians and you ruined everything in minutes by running your tongue!"

"But I...I don't..." Hilvar interrupted, pleading, but the Delvian refused to listen.

"Shut up! I let you live only on the strength of your past merits!"

He was about to add something else, but just then the camera cycled again. Three creatures appeared on the screen: Tryd, Arcana and Hilvar. Hilvar was lying on the floor unconscious.

"Don't do it!" Tryd stepped in front of Arcana, but it took her a lazy swipe to brush him aside and send the fox flying off to the far wall. The pirate queen was holding a manipulator.

"I've calculated everything! Try and stop me — and I'll feed you to the Scourge! You know damn well that the Corsican will believe me over you!" With her second manipulator Arcana lifted Hilvar into the air. Three assistants ran up and collected the body. "Take him to the conference room!"

Arcana departed with the rest of the pirates, releasing Tryd. The pirate slumped down to the floor and remained seated, his paws clapped over his ears and his knees tucked to his body. He stayed that way for two minutes until the image changed again to the corridor along which Hilvar was being dragged. Arcana and her assistants had already disappeared from the camera's view when her voice sounded:

"Is the recording ready?"

"Yes milady."

"Wonderful! It's time to get rid of this freak! Intercept the broadcast!"

Once again we saw the room in which Hilvar had been speaking initially. Only now it was a different camera recording. We could clearly see how the pirates dragged in Hilvar and, using their manipulators, turned him into a puppet. I have to say they did it quite professionally. One held the body, the other worked his hands, and the third controlled his head. Arcana launched the voice recording herself. The entire performance was done so smoothly that it was evident that it had been rehearsed a dozen times at least.

The camera changed again, to the cafeteria. Then the repair docks, the engineering bay, the central warehouse from various angles, then endless doors and corridors…Until the video

A CHECK FOR A BILLION

recordings of all twenty cameras had played out, not a single pirate of those present so much as twitched. Everyone was silently digesting what they had seen. When the last three minute clip ended, Mercaloun's gift melted into the air with a soft pop.

"You jealous bitch," said the Corsican in an icy voice, causing just about everyone to shudder. My self-defense instinct went off and I backpedaled, looking for cover in case the council descended into a firefight.

"It's your own fault!" responded Arcana, trying to get up — only to be restrained by the Corsican's bodyguards, hovering over her. "You granted him too much power. He had become your equal! Sooner or later he would have rebelled! Why didn't you feed him to the Scourge like everyone else? Why did you merely exile him? I had calculated everything!"

"Surgeon, let me have one of your Zatrathi grenades," said the Corsican in the same icy voice. I did as he asked, tossing the weapon straight into the hands of the head of the Jolly Roger.

"You wouldn't dare! I was always beside you!" screamed Arcana. The bodyguards lost no time and handcuffed her. The Precian struggled like a fish, but it was all in vain. The Corsican stood up, walked up to the wall and kicked aside a beautiful, carved nightstand. Under it was a grate, which the pirate pulled aside. The Corsican's eyes glowed aggro red. His upper lip trembled in anger, exposing his sharp fangs. With a gesture the pirate ordered the guards to throw Arcana into the pit. The Precian began begging for mercy but the Corsican was deaf to her pleas. The former favorite flew into the dungeon, and the pirate tossed the grenade in after her. There was the bang of an explosion, and the face of the

Delvian turned into an impenetrable mask, smoothing out all emotion. There was no doubt that Arcana had been intimately close to the head of the pirates, but he could not do otherwise. It was either this or the risk of losing his authority. Such a betrayal could not be forgiven.

"Now you," the Corsican's gaze alighted on Tryd.

"I was faithful to her in life. I won't betray her now that she's gone," the pirate met his boss's gaze. The guards clapped their hands on the shoulders of the mangled fox, but as they did so his mouth erupted with foam. Clutching his throat, the Delvian managed to wheeze: "You're too late, Corsican. We'll meet again!"

The body convulsed, and after a couple of moments, a loot crate was all that remained of Tryd. The cunning veteran had managed escape the line of fire without losing anything. The Corsican's gaze shifted heavily to me. He did not look pleased.

"What happened at the base?" Each word came out like it was cast with lead.

Confronted by the Corsican, I wanted to fall to my knees and spill everything I knew. Even stuff I didn't know, reinforcing my story with loot, money and the orbship. Resisting took a lot of energy, so I responded slowly, carefully choosing my words.

"I need the Lora."

Three words. But they cost me quite a bit of effort, as if I had run ten kilometers at a good pace. Sweat stung my eyes, a stream of it flowed down my back, my legs wavered under me, and I wanted to slump into my chair and admit my defeat — yet I held on. Until the last — until I had red spots in my eyes and a dozen debuffs. I held on, for I understood very well that my fate as a pirate was about to be decided.

Your rapport with the Corsican has grown. Current Rapport: 20000

Your rapport with Hilvar has grown. Current Rapport: 20000.

Mission accomplished: In Search of Cause. You have been promoted to pirate rank three.

You have received permanent access to the Silmar system, the rank of lieutenant of the Jolly Roger Brotherhood, and the right to represent the Brotherhood's interests at a pirate assembly.

Mission accomplished: Pirate University. Speak with Tryd.

"Very well. Now you are one of us. You may sit down." The Corsican gestured at Tryd's former seat. Kiddo did not take her eyes off the shimmering crate, obviously intent on pocketing what the fox had dropped, but I beat her to it.

Several powercells, a set of clothes no one needed and an envelope with a promising inscription: 'For Surgeon.' This came as a surprise. As soon as I picked it up, the envelope identified me and hissed like a discharged cracker. I quickly dumped its contents into my inventory, without getting a chance to examine them.

"I do not have the Lora, so you won't get what you want." The impassive mask suited the Corsican well. He looked like an Egyptian pharaoh, who had descended to speak with his slaves. Majestic and untouchable. "I will however explain to you why it is important for us to understand what happened to the base. The

Anorxians are the only Galactogon empire with which we had a partnership. We supplied the synthoids with technology, they provided us with repairs. Everyone was happy. Many years ago, their Motherboard suffered a general page fault, a grave error — and this led to the birth of Prince Northbridge: a device that contained an unregistered code. The Motherhood already had a son you see, and the new prince was a headache for the synthoids. Then Anorxian renegades kidnapped the prince in an attempt to overthrow their old ruler. We intercepted the ship and recovered the prince, but we did not have time to return him to his Motherboard. The rebels constantly harassed us. Then there was a rift with the Motherboard because of what Hilvar had said...well...because of Arcana's betrayal, I should say. The base was captured, and you just said that it was destroyed. I want to know what happened and how I should respond to it. I need... *We* need to re-establish relations with the Anorxians. Without their help, the pirates will not last long."

Articulate and plausible. A direct appeal to my nobility, a reference to the interests of the Brotherhood, the recognition of personal desires. Not so much a speech as a guide for suppressing my player's instinct in favor of the NPCs' interests.

"We could discuss another form of compensation," I agreed. "I need the Uldan coordinate converter. I know that you have such a device. I'll be happy to tell you what I know in exchange for a chance to use it."

A crack appeared in the Delvian's mask. The head of the pirates bared his fangs, demonstrating that even mighty beings like him are subject to emotions. I ignored these clear signs of aggression and added:

"Want to know who the Scourge really is and how she manages to disrupt planetary bindings? Do you want to get items from the third warehouse? That piece of wood was not the only item I extracted from there."

"The prince?" Hilvar leaned forward, unable to conceal his excitement.

"There were too many explosives on the cube, so my drones left it on the pedestal," I replied, without actually lying. Frequently an incomplete truth is more dangerous than a bald-faced lie.

"So the prince is dead?" The Pyrrhenian frowned, leaning back in his chair. I was forced to maintain their interest.

"I don't know that. But I do know for sure that the Scourge never touched the Anorxian. Grant me access to the coordinate converter and I will tell you everything."

"The converter is on my homeplanet," the Corsican replied after a long pause. "I won't let anyone there. Ask for a different reward, human!"

The Delvian's expression boded nothing good. I was about to open my mouth to ply my line when Kiddo reminded us of her presence:

"Perhaps I can offer a way out. Surgeon does not have to travel to your planet, boss. He needs the device — merely give him the opportunity to use it. Remotely. Let your servants be his hands and eyes. Let them do everything and share the result with Surgeon. You need only guarantee that you will not use the data obtained. Furnish him with a secure comm channel and the problem will be solved. Everyone will get what they want, and the location of your homeworld will remain a secret."

The pirates began to whisper among each other, periodically glancing at Kiddo. I had to admit that the solution seemed reasonable enough.

"A word!" The Corsican re-donned his mask of stoicism. "What happened with the base?"

"Words cannot convey everything. I would have to show you," I said, taking out a memory cube with the video Eunice had recorded. The footage included everything from our deal with Tryd, to the flying fortress, the gratitude of Mercaloun and the retrieval of the items from the base's warehouse. Eunice hadn't finished editing her episode yet, which was just as well as I needed the full, raw footage. I needed the Lora, and I knew what I could exchange for it. It was not in my interest to hand over the prince to the pirates at the moment.

"When the explosion took place, we were loading the items onto our ship. Mercaloun said that the base was no longer there and that she would seek a new lair. She did not have time to gobble up the warehouse and it's not like she needed that anyway. She has enough food for many years now."

"The prince is alive," announced Hilvar categorically. "The cube cannot be destroyed by a mere explosion. I designed it myself! If the Scourge did not devour it, then it can be recovered and we can forge our alliance with the Anorxian Empire anew."

At this point an active quarrel broke out among the council. The pirates were discussing various options for how to reach Shurtan and recover the prince. I had to cool their expectations a

A CHECK FOR A BILLION

bit:

"As we were leaving, four Zatrathi flying fortresses arrived to reinforce the Shurtan system. Keep this in mind as you make your plans."

The silence indicated that I had been heard. Everyone understood the combat power of the Zatrathi ships. Finally, having waited out the long pause, the Corsican turned to Hilvar, placed a Jolly Roger token on the table and slid it over to the Pyrrhenian.

"I was wrong."

Hilvar did not take his eyes off the token, considering his response. At last, he replied:

"You owe me a case of Walden Whiskey and an evening to drink it with me. We have much to discuss…boss."

With these words, the Pyrrhenian picked up the token and an icon of a grinning skull appeared over his head. The Brotherhood of the pirates had been reunited. The rest of the meeting was a matter of routine. Some guild had declared war on the Brotherhood, the profits from the mining planets had to be divided, the membership numbers had to be extrapolated, ships had to be repaired and other details had to be dealt with — to the point that I started dozing off. I signed up to be a pirate, not an office manager — this stuff was not interesting to me.

When everyone began to disperse, Kiddo took me aside and said:

"I want you to know: I have very good connections in the Anorxian Empire. The Motherboard and the CPU itself will be very grateful for anyone who recovers their child. But you won't be able to see them without my help. The Anorxians don't like pirates, to put it mildly."

"So you're an exception?" I grunted. "You're mistaken, Marina. I don't have the prince."

"Alex, I know you much too well." Kiddo placed her hand on my chest and leaned forward, maintaining eye contact. "You would never leave without him, partner. Tell me, you didn't happen to record the video of the explosion itself? Or did you record it after all and merely kept it from the boss?"

"This conversation is not for Galactogon," I replied, seeing that the Corsican's bodyguard was waiting for me. My teleconference with the Corsican's servants was scheduled in half an hour and the bodyguard was waiting to escort me there. The only thing I couldn't be sure of was whether the escort was supposed to be a form of courtesy, a form of security or simply an extra pair of ears.

"Anytime you like, darling!" Marina followed my eyes and read the situation accurately. "I will be waiting." The girl went about her business, leaving me alone. Making sure that no one else had any complaints or requests for me, I took out Tryd's envelope. It opened on its own, ejecting a small piece of paper with a self-destruct system. Carefully deactivating it, I unfolded the note:

"If you are reading this, small fry, then everything went as planned. That Arcana bitch is dead! She deserved no less. Do not even think of giving up the prince! This pirate rabble has no idea what to do with him. I'll be waiting for you on Belket, at the location we met last time. You have one day to see me. I have a mission for you and the reward really is the Lora this time. Tryd.

CHAPTER THIRTEEN

P IRACY CAN BE A LUCRATIVE BUSINESS. Assuming, of course, you are ready to wager everything on a single card and win! I had run a great risk and bet everything: Brainiac, *Warlock*, my planetary binding, my career as a pirate and thus basically my whole game avatar. And the digital Ying and Yang — the RNG duality of 0 XOR 1 — had favored me, giving me confidence in the accuracy of my decisions. Even if it was temporary, I still reveled in my triumph. These are the moments that gamers like me live for — these are the reasons we immerse ourselves so deeply into virtual worlds and forge new paths through the obstacles we find there! For this feeling of glory and this joy of victory!

The pirates gathered around the orbship in the hopes of reclaiming any belongings that we had recovered from the base on

---

Shurtan. The only problem was that Eunice was in no hurry to part with the items. Considering how quickly her reputation was growing among the pirates, my wife was doing the right thing. In the end, it got to the point that the newly-reappointed deputy of the Jolly Roger — Hilvar, that is — swore loudly, hovered over to Eunice, hugged her like a sister and handed her a token of a Brotherhood lieutenant. For her bargaining skill alone, the pirates recognized my wife's right to be one of them.

Several hours later, I was staring with open glee at several dozen Rialto Bracelets in my inventory. A pirate's dream come true. Now I can rob not only the locals but other players too. I had a burning desire to test the handcuffs out in the privacy of our homeworld, but reason prevailed. Business first, then entertainment. The Corsican's servants helped me decode the message from the base and now Brainiac had the right Uldan coordinates. The only snag was that the Corsican instantly spoiled my suspense about what was located at those coordinates.

"Oh I know where that is. You're wasting your time. That place is death trap and nothing more."

This was bad news, but also accurate. The Uldan coordinates pointed to one of the few black holes in Galactogon. Unlike the real thing, black holes in VR had many limitations. For example, player ships could never actually reach their event horizons. The high gradient of gravitational forces would rip them apart long before. Meanwhile, the locals had no problems reaching the horizon and even the singularity, turning their ships into long thin lines that were no longer subject to ordinary physical laws. Then again, no one had ever returned from a flight like that — not even by respawning. The Corsican bombarded me with terminology like a physics PhD who had cornered one of his underperforming students. By the end of his lecture, I actually understood the workings of a black hole less than ever.

"Will I survive?"

"No," answered the Corsican. "No one has managed to live yet — even your orbship won't save you. This is me telling you this — the Corsican himself! I took over the Jolly Roger after the last guy was dumb enough to stick himself into a similar black hole! But if you want to chance it, go right ahead! You've been warned."

Now completely befuddled, I returned to *Warlock*. By this point, Eunice had bartered off everything we'd found at the warehouse, thereby improving not so much our gaming account, as our supplies. The pirates hauled anything that could serve our orbship or armor suits for barter — as well as all kinds of odd and incomprehensible devices and equipment. The new pirate lady gladly flipped our dead weight for these items. And yet Eunice would have been a bad player if she accepted all their curiosities indiscriminately. Thus, the engineer had final say over whether to accept a trade or not.

"I need Eine. Set up a meeting with him," Eunice asked, reviewing our new acquisitions.

"Why Eine?" I asked with surprise, skeptically looking over our new 'riches.' "I doubt you'll find anything truly rare or valuable here."

"Well, don't tell me, hubby," Eunice snickered and poked at the first thing her eyes encountered. "This, for example, will allow our armor to survive up to three EM grenades. I don't recall Hansa ever boasting about such a capability."

"Are you sure?" I asked. "Sounds too good to be true."

Instead of answering, Eunice whistled the engineer over and handed her the device. The snake coiled around the girl, installing the device on her armor suit 'on the fly.'

"Fancy an upgrade, Cap'n? It's a pity to see you waddling around in the old garb." The snake's wry face turned in my direction. "It's not such a pleasant procedure what with your scrawny little body still inside the armor suit, but it will come in handy. This device integrates with the body instead of the suit."

"Sure thing — unless you smother my wife with all your experiments," I mumbled, watching Eunice's vital signs on my screen. Her respiration and pulse increased, as did her blood pressure, but she patiently waited for the snake to finish the procedure. I turned on the camera inside the armor suit and started. "What are you doing to her?!"

There was something to worry about. Eunice's face had flushed red, she was biting her lip, and only the perspiration on her forehead indicated the pain that my girl was suffering.

"I am implanting three capacitors with inactive elo into her arm. When she is hit by an EM blast, her body will activate them in sequence and they will reset the armor suit."

"And what will happen to her if she is hit by an EM blast when she's not wearing her armor suit?" I asked just in case.

"Erm…I don't know…I guess it might tear her apart…Say Cap'n, I believe I haven't thought this through. Give me a couple of days, and I'll figure out how to discharge the capacitors when there's no armor suit."

A CHECK FOR A BILLION

"The hell are you talking about, you dumb piece of scrap?" Now Eunice grew alarmed as well. "Why didn't you tell me anything earlier?!"

I could understand her anger. And I couldn't help but rejoice inwardly that the implant procedure would be postponed. Considering that women have a higher pain threshold than men, I doubt I'd have been able to last as long as Eunice without uttering so much as a whimper.

"You never asked." The engineer's three eyes flapped in bewilderment.

"Take this junk out of me now!" my wife pressed.

"She's right, snake," I added. "Abort the procedure, take out the implants, iron out the bugs and we can try again later."

"Well, you see, the thing is..." stammered the snake. "Cap'n, it's impossible to remove the capacitors now...they're already in her. For good. They'll even be there if she suffers rebirth."

"Why you thick headed garden hose!" Eunice lost what remained of her temper and tried to kick the snake. Bemoaning her misunderstood genius, the snake once again wrapped herself around the girl and removed the inactive powercells. The capacitors remained in my wife's forearm, but a random EM burst would no longer turn Eunice into a loot crate.

"You really thought that the pirates would give you something of value?" I asked the upset girl, as soon as the snake went off on her other business.

"It's fine. Eine will take everything off our hands anyway," Eunice avoided answering my question directly. "The items are unique, so the German will surely bite. Meanwhile, check these out!"

My wife poured a whole heap of precious stones onto the table. Topaz, emeralds, sapphires and even diamonds. They were beautiful, faceted, and the size of walnuts. I watched Eunice roll the stones in her palms, and their shine was beautifully reflected in her eyes. Of course, I didn't say out loud that gems are absolutely useless to us now, though I did mentally calculate how many potential credits Eunice has sunk into these pointless stones. The problem was that players had no use for gems in Galactogon and so never bought them. There were locals that might be interested, but they were so wealthy that we didn't know any. This would be another issue to deal with later.

"Brainiac, let's go home. We need to restore our homeworld binding." I sighed and changed topics, turning to Eunice. "You will get your chance to go toe to toe with Eine, but in a little bit."

Frankly, I really wanted to watch Eunice and Eine haggle. I'd even have to make sure and microwave some popcorn for the occasion.

An hour later, having made a short stop on Blood Island and unloaded our cargo holds — including the Anorxian prince and the still-slumbering Zatrathi warrior — we found ourselves on board our ship, staring at one of the most mysterious objects not only of Galactogon but the entire universe, whether meatspace or virtual. A black hole in all its glory. Brainiac adjusted his jump coordinates to ensure that we emerged some distance from the indicated point. And yet even at this considerable distance, the force of gravity was incredible. We had to constantly maintain 30% thrust, just to remain in one spot!

"It's both beautiful and terrible. The blood in my veins is ice cold," Eunice said, spellbound and unable to look away from the view before us.

The absolutely black center was surrounded by rings of burning plasma and rocks that glowed red. As we watched, one of the asteroids was pulled into the hole — thinning out to a thread that then looped around the black hole like around a spindle. The flattened stone slowed down, then at some point stopped and disappeared. The asteroid had crossed the event horizon.

"Cap'n, we're not alone here." Brainiac's warning interrupted the solemn sight. "The Zatrathi are here!"

Four cruisers, each one looking like some deadly virion, emerged from the other side of the black hole. The ships moved slowly in medium orbit, paying no attention to us. I wasn't going to get involved in a battle with four enemies at once. It would be far too risky. After making sure that the Zatrathi really were disinterested in us, I opened the throttle and put some burning plasma between us.

"They are studying the black hole," the engineer concluded after analyzing the cruisers' behavior. "They seem to be sending drones into it, which transmit a signal until they are pulled inside. We have managed to intercept the signal. It contains ordinary telemetry: pressure, temperature, energy flow. Cap'n, why are they interested in this?"

A question with an asterisk. I could only shrug. Who knows what these aliens have in mind?

Suddenly Eunice leaned forward and ordered:

"Brainiac, send the following message on the open channel. Send it in both Uldan and Zatrathi: 'Explain the purpose of your visit. Otherwise, I will attack!'"

"What are you doing?! What do you mean you'll attack them?" I turned to my wife. She had sufficient permissions for the ship computer to obediently execute her order.

"Lex, they're closer to the black hole than we are. The gravitational forces are so immense there that any equipment they have must be going nuts. What if their brainwashing helmets don't work so well out here?"

I opened my mouth to answer, but a Zatrathi voice interrupted me:

"Our cruisers are not controlled by the queen. I repeat our cruisers are not subject to the queen's influence. Please do not attack. We are studying the interference with the queen's signal. Please do not attack. The Zatrathi are not enemies of Galactogon."

Checkmate, Pirate Surgeon. What are you going to say now? Hah! I always have an option for such a case:

"To confirm your peaceful mission, send us the coordinates of the Zatrathi homeplanet."

"We do not know them. The Regal Relay we have onboard is hibernating."

I was already rubbing my hands in anticipation of this chance to dig around a Zatrathi ship, when my plans were rudely interrupted.

"I am picking up a hyperdrive disruptor beam. Captain, we have guests — and mean ones this time!"

The Zatrathi flying fortress appeared so far away that I

A CHECK FOR A BILLION

couldn't tell it from the surrounding stars. The Zatrathi aboard the cruisers also began to worry. This was evident from how their ships began to hastily turn around and hide themselves behind the black hole. Brainiac didn't think much of their plan:

"There's another flying fortress there. And likely more. I am counting nine enemy ships. They are arranged in a sphere formation. We are surrounded. I am detecting 1,500 torpedo launches. Their speed is 50% of our max and growing. Their target…they are not aimed at us. They are attacking their own ships! What are your orders, Captain?"

"Human! Save the child! It is clean and has no binding. The queen wants to destroy it! You know that we are innocent."

Title enhanced: Devil's Advocate. You have a chance to obtain evidence that the Zatrathi are an enslaved race. If you accept the child, the Zatrathi that have arrived will attack you. If you ignore the offer, their flying fortresses will depart without causing you harm. In that case, you will lose the title of Devil's Advocate.

Those bastards!

"Lex, remember the check!" Eunice reminded me just in case, as if I wasn't thinking of it already.

"What's the torpedoes' time to contact?" I wanted to delay my decision as much as possible, yet Brainiac didn't offer much solace:

"Sixty seconds!"

"The title gives us nothing. In fact, it might even harm us," Eunice went on plying her line. She has already made her decision.

I looked over at the Zatrathi cruisers one more time. If I only knew why we had been brought here. If there was something here, then the black hole would have crushed it long ago. And anyway, I didn't believe for a second that the Zatrathi were here by coincidence. There were simply too many coincidences occurring at one point in space and time. Without a doubt, the enemy was here to force us into a decision: Find the prize check or participate in the scenario. But was this even a choice? What if there really was no choice at all? What if this 'child,' whatever it was, is the only being who knew the coordinates of the Zatrathi homeworld?

"Thirty seconds until contact," Brainiac pushed me to make up my mind.

"Lex, have you considered it thoroughly?" Eunice asked me in an icy tone as I placed my hand on the orbship's projection.

"There is nothing to think about, Eunice. This is just a test. Brainiac, transmit the following message: 'I am ready to accept the child. Where shall we rendezvous?'"

"Thank you, human! Take it and save it. The fate of the Zatrathi race lies in your hands."

One of the cruisers catapulted a fighter in my direction — mere seconds before fifteen hundred deadly missiles turned the renegades' cruisers into empty husks. The Zatrathi did not even try to take evasive maneuvers. The black hole greedily welcomed the new mass.

"Catch it, Brainiac," I ordered. Our tractor beam easily locked onto the fighter and pulled it toward us. The flying fortresses meanwhile had not yet aggroed us. They were waiting. I grew anxious once again. All I had to do was launch this fighter into the

A CHECK FOR A BILLION

---

black hole and they would leave us alone. Then I would get a chance to study this location at my leisure. What if I'm wrong? What if this is a test to see what we're willing to do for a billion real credits? Are we prepared to oppose all of Galactogon? If the empires discover that we refused to help the Zatrathi renegades, the pirates will be our only refuge. No one will ever work with us. I shook my head, driving away these thoughts. This is a weakness, unworthy of a professional gamer. The coincidences are no accident and the renegades were here to help us with our quest. I had no doubt about that.

"Bring it in!" My own voice sounded like a stranger's to me. The gunner lasered off the awkward spires and the fighter's fuselage was pulled into our cargo bay.

"Warning! I am detecting two thousand torpedoes inbound. Their speed is 50% of our max. They are locking onto us. Sixty seconds until impact."

"Brainiac, set course for Belket," I ordered, watching the emptied fighter tumble away from us into space.

"Captain, we can't leave. We need to be further away from the black hole's gravity well. It is interfering with our hyperdrive. Attention! The flying fortresses are firing their main cannons at us! Taking evasive maneuvers!"

Three flying fortresses at once erupted with enormous blasts of plasma — we were positioned between them, basically in the palms of their hands. This is the last thing I needed! Avoiding both torpedoes and the capital ship cannons is risky business. Sooner or later, our agility would fail us. The orbship meanwhile zoomed to portside and down, yet it was like the Zatrathi were waiting for just this. Their other ships opened fire, forcing us to repeat the maneuver and think only about how to survive. There wasn't even a thought of escape.

"Two and a half thousand torpedoes detected. Captain, the flying fortresses are coming closer. They are tightening the noose! Plasma beams incoming! Taking evasive maneuvers!"

To avoid the fate of the destroyed cruisers, the flying fortresses drove hundreds of fighters ahead of them. We dodged another salvo of fire and encountered a terrible sight: The fighters stopped as they came close to the black hole — it was as if they had stumbled upon an invisible barrier. The flying fortress following immediately behind them lit up with its point defense cannons — but this wasn't meant for us. The Zatrathi captain had ruthlessly ordered the destruction of the fighters, whose pilots had slipped out of the queen's mind control. Now having established the precise boundary of the black hole's effect on the mind-control helmets, the Zatrathi fortresses stopped, peppering us with torpedoes and plasma from a distance. Dodging it all grew harder, and Brainiac sounded as if he was on the verge of tears. All his attention was focused on finding some gap to slip between the deadly fire, all the while grappling with the black hole's monstrous gravity.

"Fly us closer to the event horizon. Let the black hole deal with the torpedoes," I suggested. "How is the child? What is it even?"

"Cap'n, I'm not sure I could explain that to you quickly enough." The snake's head popped out in the bridge deck. "I think I had better just show you. Here. This is 'the child.'"

A small transparent container, resembling a fishbowl,

appeared in the engineer's hands. Instead of water, it was filled with a pinkish liquid — and instead of a fish, it contained a brainworm. The brainworm was busy using its tiny appendages to stuff itself full of pieces of stuff that floated in the liquid. The 'child' turned out to be a Relay that had no binding to the Zatrathi queen.

"There's countdown timer here," the snake pointed to a control panel attached to the bottom of the fishbowl. "I guess maybe when it expires, this thing will hatch."

"I don't imagine this thing came with a manual, did it?" I asked, knowing the answer perfectly well. If we didn't find a host for this 'child' before the timer ran out, it would no doubt die. And the only host fit for this brainworm was a live Uldan, who were pretty scarce in the galaxy these days. This was a conundrum to put it mildly...

Warlock began to shake and I directed my attention back to the screens.

"Captain, we won't last long out here," Brainiac warned. "We have enough fuel for two hours, no more."

The black hole was close enough to touch. Our engines burned at eighty percent throttle just to keep us from further falling into the cosmic abyss, and Brainiac was using the remaining twenty percent of power to maintain our trajectory. On the other hand, the torpedoes were no longer a problem. The missiles' electronics could not withstand the effects of the anomaly, causing them to initiate self-destruct. As a result, the space around us was lighting up with beautiful balls of fire. Only the immense plasma charged fired from the fortresses' main cannons threatened us, but our twenty percent of available throttle was enough to avoid their

---

trajectories.

I turned on a 3D map of the sector and traced a line between two flying fortresses with my finger:

"Brainiac, as soon as they shoot another round, fly us at full speed along this line. It's time for us to get out of here."

"Wait! Lex, we can't leave!" Eunice objected. "We need to solve the mystery of the coordinates."

"There is no mystery here," I snapped. "There's only that damn black hole!"

"In that case, the time has come to take a risk. Brainiac — fly along this course."

Eunice drew a short line that plunged us straight into the center of the black hole.

"Captain?" the ship computer asked anxiously. "Is she serious? Let's just blow ourselves up. For one, it won't hurt as much."

I encountered my wife's determined look.

"We'll be crushed," I reasoned.

"You don't know that. No one has flown here before. What if the black hole is the key? Why is everyone so afraid of it?"

"Because it's certain death. Without the possibility of rebirth. Are you ready to risk everything?" I reiterated what everyone else seemed to know.

"Meeting Mercaloun was also certain death. Flying at a flying fortress is death squared. Why should it be different here?"

"We will lose the brainworm."

"Or acquire something that no one has ever seen before. I will record everything on video. Look, I can't explain my hunch, Lex,

A CHECK FOR A BILLION

but we need to go in there. Otherwise we will regret it for the rest of our lives!"

"Uh-huh. We'll regret everything, including the prize check we'll lose forever!"

What a day! Why does everyone keep trying to put me on the spot and forcing me to make decision after decision? First it was between the prize check and the brainworm, now it's between escape and certain death. Perhaps my first choice was wrong; I'll admit that I acted slightly recklessly. I liked the title of Devil's Advocate a little too much and I wanted to see the quest chain to its end. But what Eunice was proposing now was entirely beyond logic. 'I can't explain my hunch, but...' What an argument!

"Brainiac, do as I ordered," I decided. Eunice sniffed indignantly, but I had more important business to deal with. The flying fortress fired again, forcing my ship to strain and move away from the line of fire. The orbship completed the maneuver and pulled away from the black hole.

"Captain, we do not have enough time!"

Even without this warning, it was clear that my plan would end in failure. Instead of darting away like a bullet, leaving the flying fortress behind, the orbship crawled away from the black hole at a snail's pace, fighting for every new percentage of thrust. We had only fifteen seconds between the main cannon salvos, and during this time we were able to reach an orbit that gave us thirty percent of thrust to maneuver. Everything else went to fighting the monstrous gravity. Shrapnel from the torpedoes exploding ahead of us, began to pepper our hull — if I could represent the orbits around the black hole in terms of our available thrust, then the torpedoes were exploding where we would have forty percent. The Zatrathi did not spare the deadly missiles, sending them at us one after another. At the speed we had, it was almost impossible to slip away from them.

"Brainiac, hang on. Let's wait for the next shot!"

"Roger. Taking evasive maneuvers. Captain, we have thirty minutes of fuel left. My initial calculation was incorrect, we have wasted too much elo. I propose we self-destruct."

Three clumps of plasma zoomed past us. The further we moved from the black hole, the more accurately the Zatrathi fire got. Even if we could slip through the blizzard of torpedoes, our lives wouldn't get any easier.

"That flying fortress is lying in wait for us." Eunice pointed to the vessel straight above us. It had moved in an arc closer to our potential point of escape, but hadn't used its main cannon yet. The bastard was waiting for a clear shot. What kind of advanced AI had the corporation assigned to these Zatrathi? It was almost impossible to use the same trick on them twice.

I stared at my screens without seeing a way out. Anywhere I looked, the possibility of escaping seemed closed to us. The enemy did not conserve their resources, seemingly deciding to deal with the annoying pirate once and for all. And they still had their regular beam cannons in reserve, since we were still out of range of those. As soon as we got closer, we'd have to deal with a wall of plasma.

My reflections on the meaning of life were unceremoniously cut short. The orbship jerked sharply, shuddered, all our screens went out, and we began whirling in a frenzied dance.

A CHECK FOR A BILLION

To make matters worse, the ship's inertial dampeners shut off too, allowing us to experience firsthand what astronauts encounter during their training. The armor suits fought valiantly to maintain our health, but it was a losing battle.

An eternity of three infinite seconds passed before *Warlock* came back to life.

"We've been hit, Captain!" screamed Captain Obvious. "Our hull has been breached! Orbship functionality has been reduced by seventy percent! Our shields our down! We are running on backup systems! I strongly recommend you begin self-destruct procedures! Ten seconds until the next shot!"

I glanced at Eunice. My wife turned away, demonstrating that she had already said her piece and all further decisions were to be made by me alone. And I alone would be responsible for them.

"What's up with the brainworm?"

"I placed it in the medcapsule where it will be easier for it to deal with the inertia. Cap'n, we have five seconds! Remember that being hit by Zatrathi fire could disrupt our planetary binding in addition to killing us!"

God damn it all! What was that Eunice had said about her hunch?

"Turn her around, Brainiac! Head for the black hole. Full thrust! Do it now!"

"Copy. Heading for the black hole at full thrust, Captain." The orbship burst forward, away from the cluster of incoming torpedoes. A flash erupted behind us as a clump of plasma flew into the place we had just been and powerlessly licked the void. I would never have thought that the computer's AI could be so emotional. The typically snide voice had now given way to humility and an acceptance of the hard facts before us. We began to shake and the closer we flew to the event horizon, the stronger the shaking became. Brainiac tried to say something, but it did not work out very well:

"So long…thanks…all the…Captain…farewell…"

With a sinking heart, I watched the utterly black disc fill our screens. Gradually, they began to go out. The orbship's electronics could not cope with the chaos of physical laws reigning around us. The extinguished screens began to drift away from me and they were followed by my own legs stretching to infinity. The shaking ceased and gave way to a transformation. *Warlock*, my crew, my wife and me turned into a thin string, winding around the black hole like a thread around a spool. Something blinked and the surrounding space turned into a completely black nothingness.

Only a few lines of system text before my eyes kept me from losing my mind. I clung to them as a drowning man at a straw, reading and repeating them again and again:

You have crossed the event horizon of a black hole.
Access check: Success.
Loading data…

CHAPTER
FOURTEEN

I SNAPPED MY SPARE POWERCELLS INTO PLACE, reviving my armor suit. The ventilation turned on, blowing a fresh breeze across my face. I felt some relief, despite the utter darkness around us. With a movement of my eyes, I activated the space scanner and waited for a three-dimensional projection of *Warlock*'s bridge deck to appear.

A bit of good news — my ship was still there, instead of some fading line across a broken screen. I could make out the pilot's chair and some items. I looked down — my legs also looked the way they were supposed to. But the best news of all were the normal pressure and atmosphere readings on board.

As for the bad news — that would be the engineer's head hanging limp right out of the wall. Her mouth was frozen open in a sleepy yawn with her long tongue dangling out of it to the floor like a fire hose. Next to it, Eunice was slumped motionless in her chair.

I turned on the searchlight, dispersing the darkness, and the captain's cabin acquired some new, not at all joyful colors. The screens remained out. Brainiac didn't say anything. But the most horrible thing was that all three of the engineer's eyes were open and staring at me. The snake neither blinked nor moved — she just hung out of the wall and stared. The blank look on her face gave me the chills.

"Are we alive?" Eunice's voice, echoing through the orbship, snapped me out of my hypnotic trance. Only now it occurred to me that I couldn't hear the customary stamping of the rhino, nor some rudiment that the gunner was typically tapping out somewhere down below. My wife got up from her chair, grunting like an old woman, and stretched her sore muscles. Naturally, I couldn't actually hear the cracking of her joints in the game, but my vivid imagination supplied the illusory sounds as I watched her stretch. Some unconscious part of my brain compelled me to repeat her actions, and I realized why Eunice had grunted. If it weren't for the armor suit, I would not even have been able to stand up. My body had grown stiff and cold.

"We survived, but not everyone did," I pointed my spotlight at the broken snake. Eunice approached her, looking into the snake's wide-open eyes.

"Can you move?"

There was no reply.

"You can't. Okay. Can you move your pupils? Excellent! Up and down means yes. Right and left means no. Okay?"

A pause, after which the engineer's pupils jumped up and

immediately dropped.

"Is there a way to recover you?"

'Yes.'

"Do you need energy?"

'No.'

"What do you need?"

The snake rolled her eyes in response.

"Oh, hang on…Do I have to do something to you?"

'No.'

"No?!" Eunice echoed.

'No.'

"Is it something with the ship?"

'Yes.'

The conversation with the engineer was long, tedious and somewhat reminiscent of a cavewoman interrogating an alien about the principle behind spaceflight. We simply didn't know what to ask or even what words to use. Any way you spin it, Eunice and I weren't engineers. You know it's bad when you never knew anything and forgot even that much.

After a countless number of maddening 'No's,' we were about to give up, when the perfect solution popped into my head. 'Yes' and 'no': zero and one. What is that if not binary code, damn it?! All that we had to do was make up an alphabet and teach it to the snake!

"I saw you have a diamond. Give it to me, please," I turned to Eunice, taking a spare armor suit from my inventory. Its flat, smooth breastplate was perfect for my purposes.

"Why?" asked my weary wife, handing over the diamond.

Instead of answering, I began to scratch the common alphabet on the surface, complementing it with a variant of Morse code. Once upon a time, back in my first days in Galactogon, knowing this code had helped me a lot. Now was a good time to resort to it once more. I dragged the suit over to the snake.

"Do you understand what is written here?"

'Yes.'

"Take a pause of five seconds between each letter. Tell us what to do."

Things got more fun after that, though no more productive. The snake began by telling me what she thought about all this.

'Werent you told to activate the self destruct many question marks.'

"Uh-huh," I replied, appreciating how the engineer had solved my omission of any punctuation marks in my ad hoc code.

'Why didnt you listen question mark exclamation mark.'

"If this is all you're going to talk about then I think we had better wrap up this séance. Many exclamation marks!"

In response, the snake rolled her eyes furiously. However, she continued in a more constructive fashion, periodically reminding me that 'We should have self destructed exclamation mark.'

"Got it!" Eunice unscrewed a panel and pulled out the backup control unit. Without Brainiac, the orbship could no longer open holes in its hull at will. In order to access the engineering deck, we first had to make a door. The options were to cut our way through with a plasma cutter or use the backup terminal. The engineer preferred the second option.

A CHECK FOR A BILLION

The next and indeed the last step of the plan was to start the reactor. It wasn't enough to merely swap out the elo. The inner core has been extinguished and we had to start the system manually. That was not easy. We had to get the starter running in order to trigger the chain reaction. We tried running in circles, pushing the starter lever both individually and together, but we just couldn't build up enough speed. I don't know how much longer we would have kept running like this until I remembered that I could use my thrusters to spin in place. Taking off, I hovered horizontally, grabbed the lever and began to accelerate as fast as I could. My head began spinning after a couple of passes, but shutting my eyes, I continued to increase the speed.

"Greetings, Captain!" The sound of Brainiac's voice was so welcome that I momentarily lost my concentration and released the lever from my hands. Physics is a terrible thing, especially that part of it that is responsible for centripetal acceleration. I shot off like a cannonball tearing through everything in my trajectory. A thought flashed through my head that I was a goner, but the ship computer reacted in time. A hole appeared in the hull and I shot straight out into space. Or rather, what I had imagined would be space.

The place I now found myself in, however, was more reminiscent of a soufflé than ordinary deep dark space. The only difference being that generally soufflé is opaque, whereas the 'soufflé' around me now was transparent enough that I could see a little ways ahead of me.

The viscous medium slowed me down and allowed me to remain near the orbship. I tried to move. It turned out to be hard, the 'soufflé' resisted, but I insisted. Turning on my thrusters, I made my way back to my ship at a turtle's pace. As soon as I reached the hull, the engineer's hands popped out and pulled me aboard.

"Were you planning on going far, Cap'n? What's the rush? Let's have some tea before you go! Why so English and so brusque?" grumbled the snake, looking me over from head to toe. "We kept yelling and yelling, but you didn't say anything. What was that?"

Her tone was full of nothing but concern, as if she had forgotten all about her recent paralysis.

"I don't know. You saw yourself what it looks like out there. I guess signals can't pass through it because I couldn't hear you."

"Clearly this is an enigma," came the pensive reply. "Come quickly."

"Is there any news?"

"You bet! Hurry — you have to see this for yourself!"

The milky infinity turned out to be indeed infinite, yet with a quite definite center in the form of a luminous cube. A countless number of ships had gathered around it. There were scouts, fighters, cruisers, and even a couple Zatrathi ships of the typical virion design and the size of destroyers. All of the ships seemed lifeless. They did not move, they had no power, and they did not attempt to contact us. We were all like flies stuck in the web of some abstract spider.

"Brainiac, can we move?" I asked the most pressing question of the moment.

"Analyzing systems now." Brainiac's voice sounded steely and mechanical, as if his personality AI had been turned off. "The answer is yes. However, speed will be minimal. The elo reserves are running out. More than half has been spent on reactivating vital systems. There is enough elo to reach the indicated destroyer. There is a probability of replenishing elo. The alternative is self-destruction."

"We always have time to blow ourselves up. Head for the destroyer. Have you determined what the white substance around us is?"

There was a long pause. I even began to think that I would not get an answer, but the computer was simply systematizing its data.

"The surrounding atmosphere consists of high density helium, an inert gas. No other substances were detected in the samples. The cause of the viscosity is not determined. Helium does not have this characteristic. The space scanner does not work in this environment. Signals are likewise blocked."

The orbship jerked, forcing Eunice and me to wobble.

"To save energy, all non-essential systems have been deactivated," Brainiac explained.

"Well done," I praised him for his initiative. We didn't need inertial dampeners to fly. Now I was sure that Brainiac had deactivated his own personality AI in order to save some system resources.

"What is the status of the marine and the gunner?"

"They are in anabiosis. Estimated time of arrival to the destroyer is ten minutes. I am disabling the screens."

Brainiac was very serious about economizing any available power. Every piece of elo that could be used by the reactor had been counted and carefully moved to the right place. I took stock of my own elo reserves — it was a good thing Eunice had replenished them before leaving. Offering the ship a few extra powercells, I could not avoid the snake's tight hug. The engineer was moved. We could not offer much, of course, but it was still enough for ten minutes' flight.

However, the friction from the helium atmosphere grew with each passing meter. We were crawling, not flying. Once a couple of minutes were left until we docked with the destroyer, Eunice got up and ran full check of her armor suit. I got up to do the same.

"No, I'll go there alone."

"Oh sure. I'll just sit here while you go scout out a strange ship with who knows who on board," I said ironically, checking over my armor. How could I possibly accept her proposal? "I'm curious myself. Plus, you're not good at flying these things. Have you forgotten?"

"But I am well-versed in ships. This is not an offer, Lex. You are the captain, we can't risk you. Especially now. If something happens, you have to give the order to self-destruct. We'll see each other on Blood Island. Brainiac, can you fly us as close as possible to the airlock?"

"Affirmative. ETA is two minutes," the ship responded.

"And if we don't see each other on Blood Island?" I asked, doubtfully.

"Then we will see each other in the clinic in meatspace," Eunice smiled encouragingly and kissed me on the lips. "Everything will be fine."

"Be careful out there," I gave in, acknowledging the girl's

A CHECK FOR A BILLION

point. "Brainiac, send five drones with Nurse."

"I will try. I won't be long." Eunice touched my shoulder and ran off with quick steps, as if afraid that I would change my mind. Her vital signs had spiked slightly. I wonder if she knows that I have full access to her armor suit or not?

"I'm out!" my wife reported a minute later and her screen turned gray. I was worried, but Brainiac quickly established visual contact. The ship's concept of 'as close as possible' was thirty meters. With bated breath, I watched Eunice force her way through the dense gas to the cherished goal. A cable tied to her connected her to the droids. However, the tin cans shut down immediately upon stepping out into the 'soufflé,' losing all of their energy.

"Cap'n, something's amiss," said the engineer. The snake's head was next to me, watching the only active screen.

I could see that something was wrong myself, but I couldn't tell exactly what. Eunice and the droids almost reached the destroyer when odd currents of turbulence began to appear to her right and then to her left. It was as if someone or something was moving nearby.

"They are under attack!" Brainiac boomed and at the same moment a black beam painted the droid squad. We saw its source immediately — a frigate-sized creature that looked like a woodlouse. A kind of cosmic arthropod or something, charged with monitoring the 'soufflé's' temperature no doubt.

The black ray triggered a transformation. The droids began to crumple into themselves, as if they had fallen into a field of tremendous pressure. First they turned into one dense piece of metal, but then they continued to shrink and condense: to the size of basketballs, then tennis balls, golf balls and at last nothing at all. The black ray did not stop there, however, and continued to bear down on the now empty point of milky haze. The 'soufflé' circling around it began to curl in whirlwinds, rushing to this point. First slowly but then faster and faster with every passing second. The orbship jerked and slowly began stretching towards the destroyer. And the destroyer, in turn, began stretching toward us.

"I detect the formation of an artificial black hole!" Brainiac boomed again, underscoring the gravity of what was happening with emergency lighting. "There is a 100% chance that Nurse and *Warlock* will be sucked into it!"

On my screen, Eunice latched onto the destroyer's airlock with a death grip, hanging from it horizontally.

"She'll be crushed!" the engineer predicted. "And we'll be next!"

"Brainiac, open fire!" I ordered, making my decision. "Aim at the source of the black ray!"

"Roger, open fire!" The computer reacted instantly. Without the orangutan, it fell to the snake to operate our beam cannons, but she managed just fine. Four ragged lines of red-hot plasma pierced the woodlouse. If the insect was surprised, we didn't notice. The creature was blown open, staining the white helium with specks of green. The artificial black hole burst immediately after, scattering the crushed droids in different directions.

"Captain, the ship is in need of repairs," Brainiac assessed the damage. The armor, designed to take a hit from six torpedoes, survived, but my wife's armor suit didn't. It drifted near the damaged airlock utterly empty. Its owner was nowhere to be seen.

A CHECK FOR A BILLION

"Lex, respawn works fine." The call to my PDA was like music to my ears. I sighed with relief. Eunice had already been reborn on Blood Island. "Did Brainiac figure out what it was?"

"Uh-huh. An artificial black hole. The locals are having fun. Some sort of woodlouse blew up you and the droids with a black beam.

"Don't forget to grab my suit. No point throwing away twelve billion," said my wife. "I have more news. The first is that the comms don't work in the white fog, even among players. I tried to call you, but it didn't go through. The second bit of news is that that destroyer has living creatures onboard. I knocked and heard a knocking in reply. The third bit is this: Don't be afraid. If anything happens just blow up the ship."

"Attention! Collision alert!" Brainiac warned a few seconds before the collision. The artificial black hole had accelerated us and even the subsequent explosion did not slow us down. The hull shook, activating my suit's inertial dampeners. A nasty screeching sound of metal scraping against metal followed. Several screens on the bridge went out again and after a moment, Brainiac reported:

"Docking procedure successful! Hull damage is 40%. We have 30 minutes of idle power remaining. Access to the airlock granted."

"I can hear you're having a party over there," Eunice said from the other end of the line. "Watch it, Panzer: If you die before you manage to record something interesting, I'll kill you again! Got it? Now go on and kick some ass! And do consider why the Uldans would send you into that...that hole!"

"I've recovered Nurse's armor suit, Cap'n." The engineer

waved what remained of the once-expensive armor and on that joyful note my wife hung up. I tossed the scrap metal into my inventory: In our current situation, the cargo hold was not to be trusted.

"Prepare the droids. Do we have enough elo to activate the marine?"

"No, Cap'n..." the snake sighed. "He's not what you would call energy efficient."

"Understood. Move out!"

After some discussion, we decided that five droids would be enough for our sortie. The engineer depowered the rest, removing their powercells.

The destroyer's airlock was severely deformed. And not only by the black hole's explosion and subsequent collision. We were forced to literally cut our way through to the hatch. A jumble of pipes and plating obstructed our way, and it was entirely unclear where it had all appeared from. While we were at it, I managed to repurpose the plating, welding it over the holes to keep the gas out. The 'soufflé' really did block all transmissions. As soon as I stepped out into it, Brainiac's voice went mute — to resume as soon as I stepped back out. The droids did not work out so well, and I was forced to send them back. Two of them touched the strange helium condensate and shut down. All of their power had been drained from them — siphoned off to feed the hungry, wandering woodlice. I was sure that the specimen we encountered was not the only one among the local fauna.

It took me fifteen minutes to break through to the destroyer — exactly half the time we had left according to Brainiac. Reaching the airlock, I knocked with my fist, warning that I was about to open the door. For a couple of seconds there was nothing — and then someone knocked back from within. Eunice was right. Someone was in there.

A fresh droid dragged a cable from the orbship and I hooked Brainiac into the control port. I had to use this chance before *Warlock* went completely dead. Brainiac began hacking the password, but the inhabitant of the destroyer responded faster. The door jerked, air rushed noisily into the airlock and I thanked my stars that I had patched the holes. For facing me on the other side of the door, sat a giant green toad — without any armor suit or anything. If there were still vacuum here, the poor fellow would have been torn to pieces.

"That's a Bufondian," said Brainiac. "An empire of the Voldan Alliance. They are amphibians who can survive without air for a long time."

I had already encountered a specimen like this back on the Zatrathi orbital station. The Bufondian prince had kept to himself, seemingly not wishing to be noticed. However, I had not had a chance to interact directly with these amphibians and therefore did not know their habits or etiquette.

"I come in peace!" I said in the common tongue and held up a Vulcan salute. "I need powercells or elo."

The Bufondian reacted oddly. It began to jump like a dog that had met its master, clapping its front paws and opening its mouth. With its last leap, it jumped up on me. My first instinct was to knock the amphibian away with my fist, but I noticed in time that neither Brainiac nor my armor suit had signaled any danger. The

---

Bufondian embraced me like a child embracing a parent who had returned from a long business trip. The toad even tried to lick my faceplate, but I swiped away the indecently long tongue and assured the creature that I was happy staying friends.

When the frog had convinced itself that I was real, it erupted in a long and indistinct croaking. Brainiac provided a very brief translation:

"Ribbit, thanks its savior."

"Is that all?" I asked doubtfully. "It's been croaking for so long, you'd think this toad is running for president!"

"Ribbit is very pleased at the appearance of the gallant knight with a brave heart in this not at all friendly system. Ribbit admires the courage of the valorous captain who through untold perils managed…"

"Right. I see. Let's get to the point then."

"Ask away, Captain. Time is running out," reminded my ship computer.

"How many creatures are there aboard this ship?" I commenced the interrogation.

"You speak our tongue?!" The toad pressed even closer to me once as Brainiac provided the translation. "There is no one else here! Everyone has died. I have been here alone for five years now. You have saved me and from now on I belong to you. Do you wish me to spawn tadpoles for you, my liege?"

The discovery of the gender of the frog currently hanging off of me stumped me. Trying to disengage as gingerly as I could, I asked the most important question:

"Is there any elo on board this destroyer?"

A CHECK FOR A BILLION

"There is plenty of it! The entire hold is full of elo! Only I do not know what to do with it. I was taught to serve the pilot and not to bother with clever words. From now on, I will serve my new master! All my dances will be for you!"

Oh goddamnit! I wish Stan were here to explain to me what the hell is up with these Bufondians. I felt that I was walking on the very edge — open my mouth in the wrong place and that's it — now I have a frog slave to deal with.

"Eunice, what do you know about the Bufondians?"

"Show me," my wife demanded and I had to turn on the video. The girl spent a long time instructing me on how to position the camera for a better view, but when the amphibian began to praise my imaginary virtues again and assure us of the good genes of her tadpoles, Eunice lost it. She began to giggle. At first, just a little, then stronger and stronger until she began to snort and clapped her hands over her face.

"Well, now I know a lot more about them than before you called," Eunice managed through her tears. "If you believe in fairy tales, then I do not envy you. Put some lipstick on her."

I was uncomfortable. I had hoped for some solid advice.

"Is that all you have? Then go deal with our house. We were supposed to get a response yesterday. I need Stan. Bye."

While I was talking to Eunice, Ribbit had already gone from threats to deeds. First, she smeared my entire helmet with snot-like drool and smacking contentedly, slid down to my chest.

Overcoming the suction, I tore the toad from myself. In a pathetic attempt at protest, she kicked her legs and stuck out her tongue like some kind of dangerous weapon. I gave her a couple shakes.

"I need the elo! Where is it?"

Ribbit looked at me with her immense moist eyes. I shook her one more time. Not so much because I felt it was necessary, but because I felt like it.

"Where's the elo?"

"In the second cargo bay, my lord. I will show you."

Glory to the developers! Having regained her freedom, Ribbit rushed in long leaps deep into the destroyer, eager to please her new master. I ran alongside, ordering the surviving droids to follow me. Ten minutes to the cargo bay, a minute to fill all the powercells and ten minutes back.

I did not make it in time. Brainiac had already gone into hibernation.

Warlock's reactor had consumed the last bit of elo and stalled. Suppressing my urge to immediately launch the ship, I unloaded the loot and went for the next batch. I need to get enough elo to activate Brainiac and the marine. Hauling the elo should be done by those meant for the job, not by me.

"Captain!" Brainiac greeted me and started the transportation process. In four trips, I was able to get enough elo, not only for the rhino, but also for the snake. The engineer immediately began resuscitating the orbship's damaged systems. Of course, if we self-destructed, the ship would respawn restored anyway, but letting the crew rest was not in my rules. If there's work to be done, let them do it.

I left the most important thing for myself — to figure out what happened to the Bufondians. Ribbit refused to leave my side,

---

following everywhere, but she also answered all my questions about the fate of the previous owner in the same way: He had died and could not prevent her from serving me.

When I reached the captain's bridge, I froze for a while — there was no door. On top of this, like the orbship, the destroyer had been depowered. Brainiac directed me to insert a powercell into a receptacle, powering only the computer, but the powercell was drained almost instantly. The next powercell suffered the same fate. And the next one. After idiotically wasting five powercells, it became clear that something was wrong here.

"Brainiac?"

"Analyzing now," the ship computer replied. "But first tell me, captain, why do you wish to reactivate the destroyer?"

"Hmm…I suppose I don't need it at all."

"In that case, I recommend we extract the data drive and transfer it to the orbship. Decrypting it should take some time anyway."

Ribbit jumped away and screamed in fright when I began breaking through the control panel. Ripping it up by the root and tearing off braids of wires, I got to the central processor. The engineer snorted with contempt when she saw such antiquity. Calling the destroyer a museum piece, she pointed to the data drive — a small box, wrapped in wires and a soft insulator so that no vibration would harm the ship's brain.

"What is my master doing?" The toad continued to jump after me, even after my bit of vandalism.

"I'm pillaging. I'm a pirate, you see," I did my best to dispel any illusions of my heroism in her mind — but I only managed to make things worse. Ribbit hopped onto me again, hugging me.

"Sovereign! You are a great warrior! I shall spawn you an army of children and you will conquer Galactogon! You will become strong and mighty and everyone shall tremble in terror before you!"

The toad tailed me everywhere, even aboard *Warlock*. Giving the engineer the data drives, I sat down in my captain's chair, wishing to distract myself for even a minute. I was sick and tired of hearing the same thing.

"Psst. Cap'n," the engineer silently called to me. "Look here. Brainiac can show you what really happened to that destroyer's crew."

A video appeared on one of the internal screens. It turned out the crew had been ordinary Qualians. They had locked themselves in the captain's cabin — the last ten survivors of the huge ship. They were aiming their blasters at the door. The view changed to a different camera. My friend Ribbit was clawing her way inside, leaving deep grooves in the door. Eventually, the door couldn't hold any longer. Everything went bright from the blaster fire — but the plasma did not cause Ribbit any harm. The toad pushed through the torn metal and attacked the Qualians, devouring each one in two or three bites.

Just then, I heard someone say in the common tongue:

"Did the master find out about Ribbit's little weakness? It is a pity…Ribbit will have to wait for another master."

The toad opened her maw — filled with a terrible darkness — and leaped at me.

You just can't trust giant toads these days.

CHAPTER

FIFTEEN

THE MANIPULATORS APPEARED IN MY HANDS, and I aimed them at the flying toad. Just in time. At the very last moment. I moved more by reflex than consciously. The suddenly suspended Bufondian replied by shooting out her tongue and coiling it around my throat. It's a good thing I had an armor suit between me and the slobbering monster. The toad couldn't crush the suit's metal.

"Cap'n, I don't have a shot! She's too close to you!" fretted the engineer.

"Hold your fire. Ask Brainiac — can a Bufondian survive in open space?" I asked. The spike of adrenaline had passed and I was regaining my composure. It's only the unknown, the unresolved, that is frightening — when the enemy is in front of you, everything becomes easier. Here it is, the enemy. Now I must destroy it.

"No better than any other sentient creature. She'll have ten to fifteen seconds and then she'll suffocate."

"Make me a door then," I ordered and taking Ribbit with me, I left the orbship. Brainiac was in such a hurry to get rid of the dangerous passenger that the hole appeared almost under my feet.

Once we were out in the viscous 'soufflé,' the fake concubine began tearing with her paws at her own throat as if she wanted to rip herself open. Her tongue finally released me, yet it never got a chance to return to its mouth as ice instantly covered it. Ribbit's eyes bulged, filling with a cloudy liquid. It seemed like she was about to explode. To avoid getting any of her entrails on my suit, I kicked the Bufondian away from myself. The green mass jerked convulsively one more time and stopped. And that was that.

Turning to the ship, I reached it in a couple breast strokes — only to discover that Brainiac was in no rush to let me back aboard. The hull remained impenetrable. I raised my fist to knock and almost managed to do it when two beam cannons popped out of the hull and fired off two salvos of plasma almost at me. The deadly plasma passed inches from my suit, singing it.

"You thought you could kill me so easily?!" I heard a familiar voice right in my head. Trying to stay clear of any further plasma, which could instantly kill me, I turned around. Ribbit was alive and well exactly where I'd left her. Brainiac was hosing her down with plasma without any effect, even opening up from the turret. But it seemed to me that the Bufondian was perfectly happy with this turn of events. Puffing out her belly with pleasure, she moved in time with the shots, carefully collecting them with her body. It was like she was mocking our attempts to finish her off. I started to worry, seeing that Ribbit was only growing more powerful.

Backpedaling to the orbship, I knocked on the hull. The engineer replied immediately.

"Tell Brainiac to hold fire," I said, without turning my back to the toad. "Get one of those vermin from Shurtan ready. I may need it."

"Understood, Cap'n," came the reply and the hull became whole again.

"Who are you?" I asked mentally, but then, after a little thought, I repeated the question out loud through my microphone.

"Me?" echoed the strange creature, grinning. "I am the concubine, whose job it is to entertain her master. I please him with dances, song and carnal pleasures. I give birth to an army of his children that will conquer Galactogon in his name. Isn't that what you wanted?"

"No, you wanted that, not me."

"Well, as you wish. In that case you can call me master," the toad all but burped the last word. I wasn't even sure whether I had heard it in my mind or if my eardrums were somehow picking up her voice. What I was sure of was that her mouth was moving.

"What do you need?"

"To begin with, food," said the Bufondian, reminding me of Mercaloun. "Why did you stop shooting? That won't be enough to feed my pets.

The creature locked its front paws together, brought them to her lips and blew. The strange jetties I had seen earlier rippled across the 'soufflé' and a giant woodlouse crawled up to the toad and nuzzled her. Ribbit petted it on the head, and lightning flashed across the louse's skin, transferring the stored energy to the pet. This strange creature absorbed energy not for herself, but to feed the woodlice!

"If you need food so bad, why didn't you consume the elo?" I knocked on *Warlock*'s hull giving Brainiac the signal. I needed to buy some time.

"Do not confuse food and absorbed energy, human. Order your ship to shoot some more. I need to feed all my pets," Ribbit ordered, ending the transfer of energy to the woodlouse.

The woodlouse licked her owner's paw in parting and vanished among the jetties. At that moment, the hull behind me opened again, and someone gave me a gentle nudge. Just in time. I still hoped to solve the standoff with the toad peacefully, yet as they say, hope for the best, but keep a cacodemon at the ready.

"And anyway, we're wasting time. Your ship won't shoot. Isn't that so?" The toad licked her mouth and moved toward me. I gently stepped aside, sending forward one of Mercaloun's minions.

"Gobble at will and report back!"

Two toothy creatures floated towards each other, seeking to resolve a simply question: 'What will happen when an unstoppable glutton meets an insatiable object?'

But as soon as they reached each other, something went awry. Bumping muzzle against muzzle, the Bufondian and the cacodemon froze. Eye to eye, maw to maw. Neither attacked nor retreated. Then the Bufondian stepped aside and my little monster went on his way, poking around and sniffing. I got the impression that the cacodemon hadn't even seen Ribbit and didn't understand what had impeded him. Finding nothing worth eating, the toothy furball turned around and returned to the ship. I even felt sorry for him. All this fuss and no food to show for it.

"Hmm…This changes things quite a bit," Ribbit said in a completely different tone of voice and followed after the cacodemon. "Let's go. You'll have to tell me how you came by one of Mercaloun's minions. And, more importantly, why it obeys your commands."

The Bufondian entered the orbship like it was her own house. Utterly befuddled and putting my jaw back into its place, I followed after her. I was sure I had more questions for her than she had for me. The only person who didn't take well to the sudden alien invasion was Brainiac. The ship computer turned on all the alerts available to him: A red strobe blinded my eyes, a howling siren blocked my ears and some kind of mist began seeping from the ventilation ducts.

"Attention! Unauthorized access detected! Battle stations! Battle stations! Attention! Danger! Danger!"

"Don't panic!" I ordered, as soon as my comms began to function again. "Where is our guest?"

"Cap'n! What guest? That thing passed through our defenses like they weren't even there! Get it out of *Warlock*! Brainiac's about to lose his mind," the snake cried out.

"Enough!" I snapped, not recognizing my own voice. My frustration with my bumbling crew had overflowed its limits. "How dare you yell at me? It's embarrassing! Have you forgotten about your rank? You're my subordinate! I asked you, where is my guest?"

The engineer opened her mouth in amazement. I had never spoken this way to my crew before. The entire ship went silent. The lights blinked two more times before they too went out.

Blinking her eyes, the engineer answered me in an even voice.

"I have not forgotten my rank, Captain. The guest is in the cabin. In your chair."

I nodded and made my way to the deck in silence. The snake followed me with an odd look, but I did not feel any remorse. Merely a slight surprise. Why had I just lost my cool like that? I don't remember ever acting this way before.

Puzzled, I reached the bridge deck and took the free seat. Ribbit turned to face me in the captain's chair and smiled as warmly as a toad could smile.

"So how did you come by Mercaloun's spawn?"

"First tell me who you are."

"A Bufondian?" the toad teased playfully. I shook my head and the next moment, none other than Kiddo appeared before me in my chair.

"A human?" The pirate asked.

As soon as I saw Kiddo in my seat, I blew my top.

"What the hell?! Get out of here!" I grabbed Marina by her shoulders and threw her out of the chair. Odd, I just reacted to someone occupying my customary place. What's happening? First I flip out on my crew and now I utterly loathe the sight of Kiddo.

"Oops, I guess not?" Marina burst into mirthful laughter. "You're hard to please, but I will try again."

Now I was staring at Tryd and all I felt was a deep thirst for vengeance. For his constant mockery, for all his betrayals. The hate smoldered deep inside me, but I had also comprehended what was going on.

"Enough," I asked. "Let's just talk."

What I was seeing was a mere illusion, some kind of magic. And this is supposed to be a sci-fi game that observes the laws of physics.

"All right," my guest agreed simply. "Does this appearance suit you?"

"How about some Delvian I don't know?" I sighed. The creature complied with my request, turning into a cute fox. "Yes, that's better. Thank you."

Ribbit grinned and suddenly suggested:

"Ask away. If the question's interesting, I'll answer it."

I was not at all deceived by her generous tone. More than likely, she just wants me to calm down after her impressive demonstration. She wants to talk. And that means that she…or it…needs something from me that it can't force through violence.

"Can you take any shape or form?" I chose to begin with a neutral question to give myself time to consider the situation.

"My customary appearance is merely that race that I have consumed the most. At the moment, it's up in the air between the Vraxis and the Bufondians."

I recalled our initial encounter and could not resist asking:

"Why did you pretend to be a concubine?"

"I'm bored," the Delvian shrugged and nodded at the screen with the cube and the ships. "I've eaten almost everyone here. Sometimes I want to have some fun."

This remark again reminded me of Mercaloun.

"So you are like a local guardian? And you need food. Or…do you want to get out of here?!"

For a mere moment, a shadow of surprise slipped across the fox's face, but I managed to notice it. The tension within me eased. I was sure now that this thing wouldn't eat me. At least not right this instant, so I decided to consolidate my progress.

"Can I help you with that?"

"How?"

"Well, like taking you to some place that's full of delicious Zatra…uh…specimens resulting from Project #2373."

"Oh really?"

A pause ensued. The guest stared at me, evidently thinking of how to best continue. A couple of times her eyes glossed over — a sign that the AI was downloading data. At long last, Ribbit replied:

"How did you come by Mercaloun's spawn?"

"Is that to say that seeing my orbship doesn't surprise you?"

"You are a pirate. Surely you stole it. The spawn is much more interesting. They obey only that old crone. Is she really still out there, darkening the skies with her coils?"

"Something like that, but more underground. Mercaloun became a planetary spirit. I did her a favor, and she thanked me in kind."

It didn't take me much time to retell what had happened. Skipping the minutiae, I talked about the catering services I had provided and the bonuses I received in return. The guest did not interrupt, nor ask questions. I did not like that. What if Ribbit is like some old enemy of Mercaloun and will attack me for helping a nemesis?

"But I'm not here because of her. I got the coordinates to this place from another source."

"Which one?" The guest leaned forward with interest.

I began explaining about Warlock, Zalva's moon, the inscription on the wall, the destruction of the base and how I decoded the coordinates.

"I am stunned. It worked," laughed the fox, putting his paw in front of him. Long black claws grew out of it. So that's what scraped the coordinates into the wall! The threads were beginning to weave themselves into one whole. Too bad there were no hints about where the Zatrathi homeplanet could be.

"Why did you leave that inscription?"

"That was a long time ago. It doesn't matter anymore. So you came here seeking treasure then, pirate?"

"I was hoping I could find help here," I tried to steer our conversation to the right direction. "I need the homeworld of the creatures that were created as a result of Project #2373."

"They never had a homeworld," the creature said dismissively. "When it became clear that the experiment was a failure, all the specimens were loaded onto a ship and sent to be recycled."

"*Brainiac, what is this thing? How does it know such details?*"

To my surprise, Brainiac responded in his ordinary voice. I guess he had turned on his personality matrix.

"Captain, I have no idea! We are all in shock over here! We are just trying to keep quiet and not interfere…especially after your outburst."

"What does it matter who I am? You are focused on solving the wrong puzzle."

Pause. The fox looked at me with undisguised mockery, relishing my surprise. Braniac went silent, silenced all the systems, and extinguished the screens. The ship went into hibernation in order to prevent the creature from rummaging around the computer's mind.

"You're wasting your time, computer," said the fox. "I've already learned everything I needed to know. For example, the coordinates of your planet. When I get out of here, I'll be sure to drop in."

"Can you help us?" I asked in a quivering voice. It is difficult to talk to someone who seems like a crazed deity. "The war must be ended."

"Ha ha ha," the fox laughed deeply. "The war! The war!"

The creature went on laughing for a while, slapping his knee periodically.

"Surgeon, would you call a race of cockroaches, a war? No? Neither would I."

"Then help me win the roach race."

"Very well. I am pleased that you are not arguing with me about your place in Galactogon," snickered the monster and began to think. "I will help you find the planet, and you will get me out of here."

"So I am right?"

A CHECK FOR A BILLION

"Right, wrong — what's the difference? Is it a deal or not?"

"The orbship doesn't have enough power to escape the event horizon." I wanted to sound the depths of this creature's powers.

"We'll figure that out," the guest answered enigmatically. "Do you accept? I will give you a thread. If you untangle it, it will lead you to your planet. In exchange, you get me out of here."

The deal sounded too good to be true. This was exactly what Ribbit was after, from the moment he had stepped on my ship. Too bad I had no other options. Either I agree to the terms or this bastard will take my orbship from me. I can be sure of that. Ribbit was already examining the ship like he owned it. By the way, is Ribbit even his name?

"I'd like to know your true name."

"That will not benefit you in the slightest."

"I insist. I want to know who I'm making a deal with."

The guest did not think for too long. Cocking back her head, he addressed Brainiac:

"Orbship computer: I prohibit you or your crew from telling Surgeon who I am. My name is Belmarad."

No one said anything, yet the fox frowned anyway:

"Whom did you just send that message to?" he roared. "I will wipe all your data banks and turn the lot of you into scrap metal!"

"Why don't you formulate your orders more accurately, Belmarad!" replied Brainiac and my back bristled with the foreboding of misfortune. I'd never heard so much hatred in Brainiac's voice. Meanwhile, the mysterious Belmarad immediately switched from anger to mercy.

"No matter. It is the captain who decides — not whomever you just spoke to — and the time has come, Captain…"

This sounded ominous enough for me to dial Eunice on my PDA — to no avail. The signal was blocked.

You may not contact other players in the given scenario. Would you like to contact Galactogon customer support?

"This is my system, Surgeon. You play by my rules here. Do you agree to our deal?"

Belmarad reclined with a relaxed look on his face, but I had no doubt that he was dissimilating. He was too dangerous to be allowed out into the common world. It was bad enough out there with the Zatrathi.

When I realized that I was thinking like a player who has lost touch with reality, I straightened up and tried to clear my head. Who cares what happens with this stupid game, as long as I get my check? Why burn it all down to the ground for all I care!

"Deal! I'll get you out of this prison."

"Captain…" Brainiac groaned and trailed off. Pleased, Belmarad rubbed his paws together.

"Are you really so tired of the Zatrathi?" The creature ignored my bait about the prison.

"Tired's not the word for it. They destroyed the Delvian Empire. All of Galactogon is next."

"Who are the Delvians?" asked Belmarad. At first I frowned, but then I realized that this ancient creature had been here for a very long time. The current in-game empires had probably arisen after his imprisonment.

"The Delvians are a race of fox-like creatures, the same ones whose appearance you're currently using. Didn't you know?"

"You think that I ask every meal I eat what it's called? If they're foxes, good for them. In my day, they were displayed in cages and there wasn't even the whiff of sentience about them! This place was built to ensure that the food comes to me. Otherwise, I will grow disgruntled and come out. I've eaten all kinds, all races. Mmm…Fluffy ones, smooth ones, gray ones, blue ones. Even living pieces of metal. Can you believe it? I was downright shocked when some robots popped in here…"

The incoming call to my PDA came as a surprise. Belmarad froze in mid-sentence. NPCs only do that when a call is really important. It was from an unknown caller.

"Speaking!"

"Good afternoon, Mr. Panzer. This is Galactogon customer support. Your partner asked us to inform you that she respawned perfectly sound and sane. In particular, she asked us to emphasize that there were no problems with the child and there is no need to worry. She also requested that you contact her as soon as possible as there is important information about penalties related to your home. You may answer her if you wish. She can hear you. However, you are only allowed to discuss real-life matters."

"Thanks, honey! I really was worried," I replied, mulling over the situation as I spoke. For some reason, Eunice had deemed it necessary to contact me right after Brainiac had sent off the message to her. Or is this a coincidence and there really were some kind of fines related to our house? "I am very glad that you respawned without any problems. I got your message about the penalties and I understand. Wait there. I will be back soon!"

The PDA disconnected and Belmarad immediately resumed, ending his sentence. Only I was no longer listening. Brainiac had managed to warn Eunice that I was going to pull this terrible creature out of here and my wife was trying to warn me. The content of the call was complete nonsense, besides the part about the 'penalty.' There is no way that has anything to do with our IRL house. I'm willing to bet that Eunice meant our 'in-game house' — the orbship or even Blood Island. But in any case, the call was a warning. I cannot permit this 'guest' to leave this place!

"Belmarad, I have another request," I interrupted the creature. He had already launched into a long rant about how the grass used to be greener and the sky used to be bluer in the good old days. "Since we're going to be working together, I'd like you to use your true appearance, please. I'd like to see you without all your masks."

The Uldan — and there was no doubt that my guest was precisely this — began to consider my request. He fixed his eyes on me, his AI building the right behavioral algorithm, until finally he said:

"I suppose that will be acceptable."

His form changed once more. The fox vanished and in its place, one of the winged progenitors of Galactogon appeared before me. I could still clearly remember the only living Uldan I had met. And this creature too resembled Warlock — as an ape resembles a human. Yet though both have two legs and two arms and one head, the difference between them is fundamental. In the same way, as far as I was concerned, Warlock and Belmarad could have belonged to two different races, if you could even say that about Uldans.

Belmarad radiated darkness, the air around him seemed heavy and filled with negativity. Black mist swirled around his wings, his long claws terrified with their sharpness and his grin or scowl was more frightening still. It was like a scene from a horror movie or a cheap thriller when a new character appears and everyone in the cinema knows that that's the crazed serial killer. Worse than that, for some reason, the Uldan decided to start playing his hallucinatory tricks again.

A deep sadness welled up from within me. The melancholy filled me from head to toe. I began to ruminate on my inescapable loneliness, my fundamental worthlessness. Eunice faded to a fleeting dream and the orbship's crew seemed to me nothing more than some mercenary strangers.

"Cap'n, what's wrong with you?" the engineer's voice reached me from afar. Here she is — the traitor. I always knew that they were all just biding their time to betray me! How painful and humiliating it all is!

"Captain! Cap'n, dear Surgeon, wake up," the calling grew closer and more insistent. With surprise, I felt moisture on my cheeks. "Cap'n...wha...what are you doing?! Don't cry..."

Cry?! Who is crying? Jolted, I momentarily forgot about the overwhelming self-pity I felt. What in the living hell?!

The obsession subsided, leaving behind only an echo of resentment against my companions. In its wake, I realized that the source of the pain was this Uldan's aura.

"Brainiac, how are you?"

"Everything is nominal, Captain," replied the computer. *"All systems are functioning one hundred percent! Blood Island has plenty of raq in case we need repairs."*

"I would not make any rash moves if I were you." Belmarad intervened again.

The computer was openly hinting that it was time we blew ourselves up. Immediately! Functionality would drop to thirty percent, but that didn't matter. There was enough raq to go around. The only problem was that I doubted that Belmarad would allow me to push the self-destruct button. That bastard has tapped into every comm line I have. I'd wager that he can fly the ship and all if he wanted to and Brainiac simply hasn't realized it yet.

"Well what do you think? Don't be angry now! You've done well! You deal with the attack better than an average human. We should work together." The Uldan's voice was full of contentment.

"We'll see about that. But it would be better if you did not do that. At least until we get out of this place. Where do I look for the Zatrathi planet and how do we get out of...here?"

My voice faltered at the end of the sentence. It was easier to resist the Uldan's psychic attack now that I knew the origin of what I felt, and yet it became more difficult to manage my own natural emotions.

"This ship has good engines. We can simply fly away. The guards shouldn't pose any problems."

"The planet!" I insisted. Belmarad attacked me again, demonstrating that just because I understood the problem didn't mean I knew how to solve it.

"First of all, destroy the cube," ordered the Uldan. "You will have to use the main cannon on that cruiser over there. I left its crew alive for this very purpose."

"Not before you tell me where that damn planet is..." Instead of words, however, what came out from my clenched teeth sounded more akin to growling. It took everything to keep myself from grabbing my chair and smashing it on this stubborn butterfly's head. Only my childhood conviction — instilled in me by my parents — that solving one's problems with violence was unworthy of a grown adult, kept me from doing just that. Yet my seat's armrests were creaking from the fierceness of my grip.

"We will have only one and a half minutes before the source is destroyed. The orbship has some decent brains in it, your computer should be able to make all the calculations in time. Set course for Blood Island!"

I jumped up from my seat, driven by the single-minded desire to twist the neck and pluck out the wings of this arrogant asshole. Unfortunately, I couldn't manage so much as a step in his direction. The Uldan took control of my armor suit and sat me back in my seat.

"Psychic influence level four...That's very good. In fact, given it's your first time, I'd say it's superb."

I felt relief and embarrassment simultaneously. Once again I had been manipulated by Belmarad without being able to help it. I was tempted to dial the corporation's tech support but I was afraid that doing so would end with me being teleported away from the ship. Then I'd lose *Warlock* as a penalty for failing the scenario and

I wouldn't be able to do a thing without my ship. No, I need to calm myself, turn off my emotions. Just like Brainiac when he had disabled his personality matrix!

"What about the planet?" My voice sounded almost computer-generated.

"What have you done? Something has changed but I cannot tell what." Belmarad looked me over pensively. Another wave of anger rolled over me, but this time it broke against my stony detachment. I wasn't here. There was only the question I wanted answered — and I asked it again. Then again. And again. I kept repeating it until the Uldan gave up. A metal cylinder about the size of a cat appeared in his hands.

"Here. This is a data drive. The coordinates you need are on it. Don't get excited, Surgeon. I have encountered humans before. A few have ended up in this place. Your kind cannot be trusted. As a result, this data drive is protected with riddles. There are four riddles. I will give you an answer to each one in exchange for four months' faithful service to me! I need to be sure, you see. Catch!"

Belmarad still had control of my suit, so effectively he caught the cylinder himself. All I managed to notice on it was a small screen, some buttons and a comm jack.

"Now let's get down to business. It's time we got out of here."

"Brainiac is the child still alive?"

"Yes, he is fine. The timer is currently at thirty minutes."

"Snake, take it out of its container. The child needs to be returned to its parent."

A CHECK FOR A BILLION

As I assumed, Belmarad cut into our conversation:

"What are you talking about? What child? Why don't I know about it?"

"We will introduce you shortly," I replied aloud and ejected from my armor suit. Moreover, I even took off my body armor. I should not have a single device on me.

The Uldan drew closer to me. He didn't like my behavior. His wings grew darker and the fog they spewed grew denser. A wave of warmth passed over my body, triggering deep-seated, puerile feelings. Belmarad's attack was a probing one and so not overly intense. As a result, my wall of detachment held. It had to hold.

"Who is that?" the Uldan asked with surprise when the snake carefully carried the Relay into the cabin. The brainworm pulsed and writhed its tentacles, groping for food. There were two strokes of luck here. Belmarad's aura did not affect my crew — and he had no idea what he was facing.

"Just another creature. Didn't you say you were hungry?"

"Are you trying to poison me with this vermin, Surgeon?" the Uldan guessed. It looked like his own suspicion even took him aback.

"Why not?" I did not bother denying anything.

"Why I can swallow a red giant if I want to! I am the dark god — Belmarad!"

"Now!" I yelled at the snake.

The manipulators worked like a charm. The terrible monster had given us a mere second, convinced of his own invulnerability and power. That was what did him in. I spread the dark creature's arms in different directions, while the snake slapped the brainworm on the Uldan's head.

"What the…"

These were the last words of the entity known as Belmarad. Able to withstand a direct hit from three cruiser cannons at once and then fall into the center of a black hole, the Uldans' dark overlord was defenseless against the Zatrathi parasite, just as humans are defenseless against hookworms. The winged creature's eyes rolled up and we heard a nasty smacking sound: The brainworm had reached its nest.

"Thank you for not letting me die," came the guttural Uldan speech. The queen had imbued her Relay with only one language. "But I sense a strange emptiness within me. Something very important is missing. Something kindred."

There was a pause, during which the brainworm settled more comfortably into his new home. Having accommodated himself, he asked the most unexpected question of all that I could imagine:

"Tell me, who am I?"

CHAPTER SIXTEEN

I HAVE A SHODDY IMAGINATION. When the brainworm began to question his identity, the best I could think of helping him was to give him a name. It wasn't a very original one: Balthazar. I think I remember a demon that went by that name. Or maybe it was some NPC from my Runlustia years, I can't recall any longer. What's important is that that was enough. The Uldan's face broke into a wide, daffy grin, expressing the brainworm's feelings on the matter. The Relay began ravenously filling in the gaps in his knowledge, eagerly absorbing everything there was to know about Galactogon. It took him just five minutes to devour the contents of the computer we pulled from the destroyer and then he reclined to digest the gleaned information.

I can't say I felt any better, despite the notification telling me that I'd retained the title of Devil's Advocate. Now, in order to receive my due reward — which, by the way, hadn't been mentioned — I would need to deliver the brainworm to any friendly empire. There were three problems, however. The first was that the brainworm had no idea where the Zatrathi homeworld was. The second was that Brainiac refused to divulge who Belmarad was, even after the individual in question had suffered a complete lobotomy. The Uldan's order remained inviolable, explained my computer. And the third were the riddles of the cylinder, which I was free to see even now:

1. *In what year, according to the Varlian calendar, was the cryptix grubbled for the first time?*

2. *How many full cycles of natanix are needed for the dysplasia of cartosis?*

3. *What is Mercaloun's main corpitain of dalir?*

4. *What is the minimum distance of zlapartit for the mardiration of the ulborsa?*

This is how the riddles sounded in Brainiac's translation — and he had no idea what it all meant. The only clue was Mercaloun, but going to see her would be sheer suicide at the moment. We couldn't break through four flying fortresses.

All we could do as a result was wait until the marine completed transporting the elo, the engineer completed her repairs to the hull, and Brainiac calculated a route to the cruiser which supposedly still had living beings onboard. It was time to get out of here.

It wasn't possible to claim the destroyer. The Uldan had short-circuited all its systems, causing the powercells to discharge

A CHECK FOR A BILLION

immediately — transferring their energy to the helium soufflé. Brainiac did manage to figure out how to restore everything, but it would take him 2–3 hours to actually do the work. I didn't feel like a D-class vessel warranted this. Not only would I earn very little for selling it, but I'd have to waste more time looking for the local ship graveyard. Not the best use of our time. The other ships were in a similar state. Everything short-circuited and not a single living soul onboard. A frigate, several fighters and even a now familiar Zatrathi tub. The sabotage had been applied equally everywhere.

"Take a look, Cap'n!"

The cruiser we were headed for stood out not so much as a result of all the holes and patches in its hull — which suggested a storied past — as the white skull painted on her bilge.

"Greetings from hell! Yours truly, the Jolly Roger Brotherhood," I grunted. "I guess that would be the flagship of the former leader — the one who considered himself immortal. I wonder if he made it..?"

The question was a rhetorical one. Three woodlice circled around the cruiser, ready to devour any trespassers. They responded to our appearance with black rays that struck random points in our vicinity. For some reason, the bugs either couldn't crush the orbship herself or weren't allowed to. In any case, I could not afford to be intimate with these creatures who spawned black holes as easily as a magician pulling a bunny out of a top hat. Three accurate shots from *Warlock* and the rainbow cube had three less guards.

I found my way inside the cruiser without any problems. Like all the other ships here, it had no power. The airlock looked quite functional, but then my air analyzers flashed yellow, warning of low oxygen levels, elevated levels of nitrogen, carbon dioxide and hydrogen sulfide. On top of this, paradoxically, the fire hazard warning also flashed on.

"Water…I beg you…some water!" someone grabbed my leg weakly. I looked down, and the space scanner traced the outline of a creature that had withered to all but a skeleton. Mother of God, how did this corpse still have the strength to grab passersby like that? The silhouette looked a bit like a Precian, but you couldn't be sure. He looked like he'd spent a month in an oven. I turned on the searchlight, but the Precian didn't even react to it. There were no eyes on his grimy, scabbed face. Having decided that nothing would happen to him if he waited another half hour, I freed myself and went on my way, now carefully looking where I stepped. I encountered more mummies like the first one all along my way to the bridge deck. The mutilated and haggard pirates lay clinging to their lives with the last of their strength. They breathed rarely, conserving the already scant oxygen. Many more neither moved nor showed any other signs of life. Only the odd breath suggested that they were still living creatures and not just part of the decor.

Somebody had broken down the door to the bridge deck, yet the passage was barricaded. Boxes, pipes, grates and partitions had been welded together to obstruct it. I shone my light at the obstacle and almost jumped. Two glittering blue eyes stared at me from a small crack.

"Who are you?" Brainiac translated from Pyrrhenian. The question came in a hoarse whisper, the speaker having no more strength.

A CHECK FOR A BILLION

"Lieutenant Surgeon of the Jolly Roger Brotherhood. I've come to help my brothers."

Silence.

"Hey, are you alive in there?"

"Shh," someone shushed me. "What's your proof?"

"You know who Tryd is? Hilvar? The Corsican?" I listed the most famous pirates I knew. Surely the old guard would know them.

Those on the other side of the barricade — there were clearly a handful in there — began to confer among each other in whispers. And they were so quiet about it that no matter how Brainiac tried, he could not catch the gist of what they were discussing. All he made out were snatches: 'trap,' 'aid,' 'pirate,' 'food,' 'water.'

"How do we know you're not with her?" the eyes reappeared in their hole. These ones were hazel, however.

"'Cause I'm the one who killed her." There was no doubt who the pirates had in mind. "It's time to get out of here, oh my brothers. Are you with me?"

"There be one and a half thousand souls on this ship," the eyes were replaced by another pair. Bright yellow ones. "Will you take them all?"

"I won't take anyone at all. You'll fly out of here on your own."

"This ship is dead!"

"This ship has been rewired to channel any energy in it to the creatures outside. That can be fixed with a few hours of work, and I have someone for the job. I will enter, and we…"

"Stay where you are!" came the barked response,

accompanied by a guttural gurgle. Given the speaker's already weak voice, the sound effect was horrible. "Just try and touch our barrier and I'll blow this wheelhouse! It's better to die a final death than to be consumed by that creature."

I realized now why the pirates hadn't simply died and respawned — Belmarad had broken their bindings to their planetary spirits, just as Mercaloun had once done to me. That's why they were still here — clinging on. It was pure suffering, but they were clinging on.

"Once again: The monster is dead and I am about to head home. I need the cruiser to do that. I'll get this damn tub started even if you do blow up the wheelhouse. And then I'll get out of here — with or without you!"

The eyes disappeared again and again I could hear whispering. I started a timer but the yellow eyes returned almost immediately:

"Who is the head of the Brotherhood?"

"The Corsican. Hilvar's his second-in-command."

"Why he's worth a bitch's guts!" spat someone behind the barricade and then added some choice curses. It didn't sound like this bit of news was very pleasant to them. "All right. Come in! I'm not about to let that mongrel and his flying barrel run our upstanding organization!"

Where did he have the strength for all this emotion? The yellow-eyed pirate had uttered the last phrase in an almost normal voice. A pair of kicks and the flimsy barricade collapsed, raising clouds of dust.

"Snuff out the lantern, lad! We've lived here without light for three years."

Three years? I calculated the time difference between the black hole and the rest of Galactogon. The Corsican has been running the Brotherhood for thirty years. One year a decade? I'd better hurry up or I might miss the end of the war out there. Although, how do the devs deal with the time difference for the player? I'm no local. You can't just hibernate me for years at a time. Will they blame Belmarad for everything? That it was his presence that stopped time? It would sound plausible enough.

I obediently turned off my light and examined my audience in the 3D rendering provided by my spatial scanner. Ragged, scabby, frail and weak. Five officers, barely able to stand on their feet. The captain — also the former head of the Brotherhood — looked better than the rest. He still sported his uniform at least. It hung like a sack on the Bufondian, yet managed to conceal the toad's emaciated body. That would be the last thing I would want to see.

"What's your name then?" I asked the captain. The toad croaked scornfully in response.

"I can see you're a shabby pirate. In my day, they wouldn't even let you up the front steps. Ignoramus!"

"There was no time to learn. They made me lieutenant just yesterday and today I'm already here. By the way, thirty years have passed out there, in the big world. So if anyone knew about you 'in your day,' well…now they don't. Maybe one or two."

There was a general ruckus. The officers began peppering me with questions, but the captain quickly squashed the din.

"Quiet! Shut yer yapps. To your stations! Look alive! If you get us out of here, lad, I'll make you major! You'll fill me in on the Brotherhood's history. I'm Captain Wit-Verr. Now let's get to work!"

The exhausted, yet unbroken pirates helped as best they could. And this at its core entailed not getting in the way and not making a mess in their trousers when they saw a ten-meter talking snake. With that said, the haler among them arranged themselves in a chain to transport elo. Unfortunately, more than half of the crew had lost their eyes and, even with a great desire to help the common cause, really just could not. As Captain Wit-Verr explained, Belmarad considered eyes a great delicacy and would periodically visit their ship to get a bite of his favorite snack.

"This tub's ready to fly, Cap'n." It took the engineer three hours to figure out the intricacies of the half-fried electronics. During this time, the pirates had devoured my orbship's food supplies. Everything that could be eaten or drunk was eaten and drunk. Even the liquid in the brainworm's fishbowl. Was it nutritional? You bet! No one even thought to complain about the taste.

"Cap'n, I am detecting multiple enemies in the vicinity of our ship. I am afraid that they will attack us as soon as we try to leave."

"How much time will we need to turn around?"

"To shoot? None at all. All the ships are already facing the cube. We can shoot right this instant. It's what will happen after that remains unclear."

I recalled Belmarad's answer about how he would slip through the guards. "We'll figure that out," he said and he really had begun to do this, transferring energy to the woodlice. What if the lack of energy wasn't a result of something the Uldan had done to the ship, but a consequence of the dense helium we were in, absorbing all the energy? But why then doesn't it do the same to the orbship and the armor suits? It was a bit of a stretch, of course, but I thought I had an explanation. The orbship was the brainchild of the Uldans, so there was not much wonder there. As for the armor suits — well, these had players inside of them, and the game was for the players to play. If it had been an NPC in the armor suit, perhaps everything would be different. It was worth checking.

"Captain Wit-Verr!" I called the pirate over. "I need a victim. Is there anyone on your crew who you wouldn't mind losing? I need to test a theory before we try to take off."

Wit-Verr's expression was far from accommodating, so I felt it prudent to explain my theory about the soufflé. The toad bared his sharp fangs, grinning with a vicious grimace.

"I'll cut your throat if you dare stick one of my men overboard. I'll go myself!"

"Come now, Captain! Your job is to command. You can't afford to play the hero."

"We survived all those years only because we stuck together. We shared everything! What kind of captain would I be if I betray one of my crew? I'll go, lad. Full stop!"

The Bufondian's armor suit resembled an assault mech. A two-meter hull on four stumpy legs. The engineer merely groaned when he heard the creaking in its joints. Deprived of normal maintenance, the machine had rusted thoroughly. And yet, Wit-Verr piloted this pile of junk quite expertly, following me to the airlock. Just before stepping out, he said:

"If anything happens to me, lad, make sure to retrieve my

GALACTOGON BOOK THREE

body. I don't want it to be eaten."

And that was it. A simple request for a decent burial. My esteem of Captain Wit-Verr grew significantly. Even granite is known to crack and crumble from time to time, yet not this pirate captain's will.

"We're being attacked! Bring him back!"

The woodlice aggroed as soon as a fully-charged armor suit carrying a 'local' stepped into the dense helium. Three black rays immediately struck the pirate captain, trying to crush him to a tiny point. My gunner opened up with a withering pataflafla of plasma, mercilessly blasting the woodlice, but the rays appeared again and again. The woodlice died, spattering the snow-white soufflé with their green entrails but still more woodlice spawned in their wake. Meanwhile, Wit-Verr's armor lost its energy instantly and I was forced to use my manipulators to haul the captain back onboard. The snake hooked up two wires to the armor suit and the toad flopped out and onto the floor where he lay convulsively inhaling air. Both his front paws had been crushed and his ribs protruded from his jacket. The woodlice had managed to crush the armor suit enough to hurt its pilot.

"I'll see to him." Without further ado, the snake dragged the captain off to the medcapsule. She reported back a few minutes later: "It's not serious. He'll be as good as new in a day. Of course, it wouldn't hurt to have a doctor look at him. Cap'n, he's regaining consciousness. He wishes to speak with you. I'm patching him through."

"What's the result?" The toad's voice had grown husky and gurgling. It sounded like he had suffered some kind of internal

301

---

trauma as well.

"Negative. The creatures immediately attack any device filled with energy. We can't launch the cruiser right now. We'll need to think."

"Think, lad, think! Get us out of here!"

New mission available: Greetings from Beyond the Horizon. Description: Find a way to escape the black hole's guardians and rescue the pirates of Captain Wit-Verr. Reward: Rank of Major in the Brotherhood of the Jolly Roger.

"The orbship won't be able to accommodate one and a half thousand crew members," Brainiac warned immediately, as if reading my thoughts. "The question may as well be written on your face, Cap'n. But it just won't work. We need to find another way."

I glanced at my PDA. This was one of those rare instances when I could use outside advice. The only problem was the notification I'd received earlier:

You may not contact other players in the given scenario. Would you like to contact Galactogon customer support?

I stared blankly at my screens, trying to figure out a way out of our bind. And I knew for sure that there was some solution to the problem, otherwise it wouldn't have been a mission to begin with. Furthermore, the solution must be rather straightforward because the reward sure wasn't much to write home about. So what do we have? As soon as the ship tries to blast off, it will be surrounded by woodlice and turned into a small, high-density particle. *Warlock* won't be able to cope with all our enemies. Clearly the soufflé around us was crawling with woodlice. This means that I have to concoct a situation in which the woodlice leave us alone for a full minute. A diversion? But how? The intuitive solution would be to launch some other ship in another part of the black hole, but the problem was that there was no way to signal in the dense gas. And this meant that the launch couldn't be done remotely, while Wit-Verr would refuse to sacrifice any of his crew. A timer then? It's an option, but I didn't actually have a timer. I conferred with the engineer who shook her head — she wouldn't be able to slap something together quickly enough.

What was it that Belmarad had said? *'The guards shouldn't pose any problems.'*

This phrase refused to leave my head. The dark Uldan had been feeding the local mobs, channeling energy to them. As a result, they left him alone. But neither Brainiac nor I knew how to do this. So what do? How was Belmarad going to negotiate with the woodlice?

I looked at the screens again. An orbship, a cruiser, the destroyer a little ways off, and beyond that only shadows. Hold up! Why is the destroyer so close to the cruiser anyway? In normal space terms, this wasn't just 'close to' but 'in the same spot.' The distance between the ships was so insignificant that even another cruiser would be unable to pass between them without touching one of the ships. About three hundred meters. In the infinite sprawl of a black hole, such an arrangement of ships was really quite an amazing coincidence, one worth considering.

A CHECK FOR A BILLION

"Brainiac, fly us over in that direction!"

At first glance, the destroyer was no different from the other ships. No crew, no energy. And yet my engineer had quickly identified the distinguishing characteristic — the huge deposits of elo that were piled around its reactor. The powercells were interconnected with each other by means of switching connectors, forming a single supply loop.

"Check it out, Cap'n," the engineer pulled a clockwork mechanism out of the jumble of wires. "It's a timer set for thirty minutes. It activates the elo, which supplies the reactor and...And all the energy just gets dumped out. I don't get it..."

I even stopped breathing: Unlike the snake, I did get it! Belmarad had trained the woodlice to absorb free energy. The guardians would be unable to resist and energy whirlpool around the destroyer. They will rush to gobble it all up, giving us the time we needed. The Uldan had planned his escape masterfully, calculating every little detail. If it hadn't been for the brainworm, the dark lord would have certainly made it out to Galactogon and caused a disaster out there.

It took us a lot of time to make our preparations. I had to empty the destroyer's food reserves in order to give some strength to the exhausted pirates. Then the time came to train them, since almost all the officers and their aides had lost their eyes. We were forced to seek out those who could see anything at all and then instruct them in how to operate the cruiser's systems. This required plenty of effort, emotion and patience, and by the end of the training I myself looked like one of the pirates: desiccated and emotionally drained.

"Look alive, you space rats!" Wit-Verr went on issuing orders from his stretcher. The rhino had dragged the captain to the bridge and I helped the crippled toad get settled in a chair, securing him with straps. "What are you bumbling about for like zombies? You're not zombies! You're pirates! It's time to get out of this hellhole! Bartok, why do you keep staring at your screen like a space slug at a space amoeba? Pull yourself together, sailor! Our life depends on you!"

The captain was exaggerating. We weren't about to let any of the trainees near the critical systems, but they wouldn't know that anyway. It was important to raise the crew's morale and Wit-Verr knew how to do this like no other.

"Lad, we're ready! Synch your watch!"

You wouldn't think the toad was afraid by his outward appearance. If I made some mistake and the destroyer fails to draw the woodlice, the cruiser would be doomed. Wit-Verr understood this too but made no effort to share this with his crew. The pirates had to believe that they were going home up until the very last moment.

We had agreed on the precise sequence of actions and thus exactly twenty minutes after checking the clock I started the timer on the destroyer. In forty minutes the moment of truth would come. Either we'd be free or we'd be doomed. The orbship hovered near the cruiser in tedious silence as we waited. Almost a day of preparations had come down to this one minute. And there was no guarantee that we would get it for free.

"Captain, it is time," Brainiac reminded me. The engineer was beside me, nervously jerking her tail from side to side, her eyes fixed on the screens. I felt an anxious weight settle in my stomach. I even bit my lip, trying not to blink, so as not to miss the right moment.

Now!

The destroyer blinked and lit up, sparkling like a Christmas tree inside a Tesla coil and arcing lightning all around it. The soufflé immediately began swirling as the woodlice appeared around the ship and began to absorb the discharges with their bodies. There were no black rays this time. The creatures had come to feed and were in no hurry to rid the black hole of their energy source.

"Fire!"

The pirate cruiser came to life and a thick beam of plasma from its main cannon slammed into the rainbow cube. The next two seconds seemed like an eternity — until suddenly the soufflé disappeared. It was like it had been shut off, and at last I could assess the size and scale of the space prison we were in. It truly was immense. Brainiac counted more than fifty cruisers alone and there were even several Grand Arbiters in here with us. There were also quite a few woodlice. Several hundred had plastered themselves to the destroyer devouring the energy it was discharging — and a few thousand more circulated around the other ships. The plasma beam went out and the central cube began to pulsate. At first slowly, but faster and faster with every second. At the same time it swelled like a sponge.

"We're out Captain. We're back in normal space!" Brainiac cried excitedly. "Calculating hyperjump now! Setting course for Blood Island! I will need forty-five seconds!"

The woodlice caught on that something had gone

drastically wrong, but they could not react to it. They remained stuck in place, twitching in different directions. The sudden absence of the dense gas made them helpless. The destroyer meanwhile continued to shoot sparks into the surrounding space. As the hyperjump timer counted down, I watched comfortably as the surviving guardians exploded one after another.

"We are ready to enter hyperspace!"

"Let's go home!" I ordered and the stars on my screens stretched into lines. Fifteen seconds later, the system announced that the pirates had made it out and entered hyperspace themselves. I did not know where Wit-Verr headed off to, but every self-respecting pirate captain had his own secret hideout.

Mission accomplished: Greetings from Beyond the Horizon. Received rank of Major of the Jolly Roger Brotherhood.

As it turned out, my enjoyment of this fancy new title did not last long. About five seconds in all, actually.

Your rapport with the Corsican has decreased. Current Rapport: -100000

Your rapport with Hilvar has decreased. Current Rapport: -100000

A bounty has been placed on your head. The galaxy's bounty hunters have been notified.

The Brotherhood of the Jolly Roger has been dissolved.

But the worst was still to come. A few seconds after the

messages faded away, Kiddo called me on the PDA:

"Tell me, partner, does your credo happen to be: 'Screw you, I got mine?'"

CHAPTER SEVENTEEN

RBSHIP WARLOCK, FOLLOW CORRIDOR THREE-SEVEN-TWO! You must go through customs inspection!"

"Do it, Brainiac," I ordered, handing over control of the ship to the computer. Here they are, the downsides of the collapse of the pirate fraternity. Previously, a member of the Jolly Roger would have been greeted with flowers and music on one of Belket's first ten docks. Now, however, the Precians regarded this freelancer with deep suspicion, unsure what to expect from him. Even my generally positive rapport with the empire did not help. To put it briefly, over the last few hours, I had lost almost all of my old friends. Kiddo tore up all our contracts and declared war. I could forget about partnering with her. No matter how I tried to explain to the hot-tempered girl that this was just a scenario, and it didn't matter if I had done it or someone else, she refused to listen. Marina had too much invested in the Corsican and she had lost too much upon the Brotherhood's dissolution. She was no longer a General of the legendary Jolly Roger, feared and respected by all — but an ordinary veteran, one of millions.

Following her call, I received news that Hilvar and the Corsican had sent bounty hunters after me. A dozen more pirates — whom I'd never even heard of — hurried to express their condemnation and sent me a 'black mark.' In fact, basically all of Galactogon's shadowy factions were up in arms against me for having rescued Wit-Verr from the black hole. Did I regret it? Not one bit! The cylinder in my inventory assured me that I had acted logically and correctly. And whoever wished to dispute this could do so in open battle.

The orbship docked with the Arbiter and opened its hatch for the customs brigade. This time, the inspection was not limited to superficial scans. The Precians turned my entire ship upside down, looking for contraband. They paid no attention to the Anorxian Prince but they did get pretty worked up when they found the Zatrathi and the Uldan with the brainworm. One of the customs officers immediately scurried away to make a report to the appropriate authorities. I really hope that the adviser will take our bait and meets with us.

Meanwhile an armed cordon and a flock of scientists resembling strange birds because of their white protective overalls and green gloves assembled outside our ship. Outwardly, none of them inspired confidence, so I did not allow them to enter the ship. My rapport with the empire deteriorated slightly, but I was within my rights. A player's property is inviolable and the Zatrathi were now just property.

"Pirate Surgeon, you must come with us," said the head of the cordon.

"He's not going anywhere without me," Eunice offered her two cents and cast the Precian a defiant glance. He grew flustered, unsure of her status and level of access.

"My partner here will conduct all the negotiations for me," I confirmed, delegating all the talking to Eunice.

"Just a minute. I need to verify her information." The Precian stepped aside to make a call. He cast several glances in our direction, nodding to whatever was being said on the other end of the line. Finally the decision was made: "Pirate Nurse has been granted access. Follow me. The both of you."

The apartments of the new viceroy were in no way modest, yet they did manage to balance practicality and wealth. There were no solid oak desks taking up the center of the whole cabinet or throne-like chairs. But at the same time, the multi-level shelves, numerous screens, holographic images of Belket and other high-tech innovations surely cost much more than any mere table. They were convenient, practical, and still quite expensive.

The guards escorted us to our seats but before we could take them, the adviser joined us in the form of a hologram. His chair was no different from ours.

"The better I get to know you, Surgeon, the more I wonder. How is it that an ordinary pirate has had such incredible luck? And yet, instead of becoming a true legend, instead of using your skills to the benefit of all, you decided to waste your talents on...why I don't even know what."

"Does the adviser wish to offer me something?" I decided to take the bull by the horns.

"Citizenship of the Precian Empire," the old man stunned me. "Access to the capital, the title of Baron, land for the construction of personal residence as well as aid in building said residence. A monthly allowance and limited access to 'top secret' information."

"And what is the price of such a generous offer?" I had no doubt that there would be a catch. The bait was too tasty.

"The price corresponds to the offer. You hand over the Zatrathi warrior, the Uldan and the Regal Relay to us. You explain why they are not aggressive and tell us where and how you got them. But even more importantly, you furnish us with the coordinates of all the pirate bases! The alien foe that threatens Galactogon at the moment is too dangerous to allow us to tolerate enemies from within. The pirates are to be destroyed once and for all. Clearly you understand as much, since you yourself have abandoned your Jolly Roger. Right after being named a lieutenant!"

Why look at that! They have spies among the pirates, but low level ones, since they have not yet reported on my new rank and disintegration of the Brotherhood as a whole.

"There is much the adviser is unaware of," Eunice interjected. "Surgeon was promoted to Major."

I was about shush her, but my wife cut me off with a gesture. I had to remember to abide by our agreement about her doing the talking.

"Hmm..." the Precian hummed pensively. "It is true, I did

not have such information. A Major of the Brotherhood…this is quite the news… But ultimately it doesn't matter!"

"Captain Wit-Verr is back," the girl continued. "And the Brotherhood as you know it, no longer exists."

"Are you saying that you shall sail under the banner of the Bufondian?" A note of steel sounded in the adviser's voice.

"We have come here to transfer two Zatrathi to the Precian Empire — without any expectation of compensation." Eunice played our trumps. A bit crude if you ask me, but I did not interfere.

"*Without* expectation of compensation?" the Precian repeated this utterly unusual phrase for me and my crew with unvarnished sarcasm. "Pirate Surgeon — renowned for all of Galactogon for the fact that one must pay him to so much as move from his place — wishes to do something without expectation of compensation?"

"That's right. You take the creatures, we tell you where and how we got them, and then we leave, without you owing us a penny."

A long pause ensued. The adviser froze several times, his eyes glassing over, to call his emperor — then froze again, until his AI figured out how to behave in this unexpected situation. A player was about to give away something extremely valuable to an NPC, something for which the NPCs were already prepared to pay a large sum for. Clearly there was some trick here. Definitely. But where? After all, everything seemed clean and transparent.

"And you depart the planet immediately?" the adviser asked again, glassing over once more.

"Not quite. We still have some business on Belket, but it

has nothing to do with the Zatrathi."

The adviser made a show of thinking, though everything had already been decided.

"Tell me how you got these creatures," he said at last. This was definitely a test because Eunice placed the pre-prepared disk drive on the table.

"It would take a long time. You can have your people check this disk for viruses and then open it. There are two videos on it. One concerns the Zatrathi warrior, the other concerns the Relay. You will understand everything right away."

A servant ran into the office and whisked the drive away. Several minutes later, a colorful half-hour film about the heroic exploits of two pirates began playing on one of the screens.

Your title of Devil's Advocate has been confirmed.

+1000 Rapport with all empires.

Speak to any imperial representative to receive your reward.

Brainiac reported that the Precians had shown up again and this time I granted my permission to hand over the Zatrathi. The time had come to get rid of them. The adviser made sure that the transfer was complete before stepping closer to us and asking in a businesslike tone:

"All right. What do you want? Let's dispense with the pretty talk about charity."

"Before you accompanied Surgeon to Zalva's moon, you promised him complete access to all of the information that the empire has about the Uldans. The time has come to pay that bills. We need everything you have."

"Will you accept Precian citizenship?" The adviser's voice grew thick.

"We are pirates," Eunice refused. "We were pirates and we will remain pirates."

"This is not an answer that suits us." Now the adviser grew defensive.

"In that case, thanks for the reception, we will be on our way." My wife didn't bother arguing and rose from her seat. "Surgeon, we are expected at Hansa. Come on."

"Are you threatening us?" The Precian's question had nothing to do with the given context. Something had gone wrong with his AI.

Eunice merely shrugged, indicating that she was not interested in further conversation. There was much that I wanted to say, but I followed her silently. The door turned out to be locked. My wife raised an eyebrow questioningly, turning back to the Precian.

"Enough, sit back down," he said harshly. "This is no kindergarten. Let us talk like the serious sentients that we are."

"Let's talk." Eunice sat back down without a shadow of embarrassment. "We need data about the Uldans."

"Impossible. We cannot provide such information to the empire's enemies. The pirates are our enemies."

"Even we?"

"Even you. We cooperate as long as it is mutually beneficial to us. As soon as that benefit disappears, nothing will prevent you from striking us in our weakest points. It would be foolish to trust a pirate. Such is the emperor's position and that is my position too."

"There is another way." I felt that it was time for me to speak up and placed the cylinder of riddles before the adviser's hologram. "We need information in order to find the answers to these riddles. If you help us with this, you can keep your knowledge about the Uldans."

A twinkle sparkled in the Precian's eyes as soon as he saw the rare artifact. I had to give Eunice her due — she had anticipated the logic of the conversation almost to a T. Her understanding of the locals' essences — the AI and psychology that underpinned their motives and behavior — turned her into a dangerous negotiator indeed. Servants ran into the office bearing strange devices. The cylinder was measured, scanned and photographed. A copy of the device appeared in front of the adviser and he began conferring with the emperor yet again.

"I know who Mercaloun is, but I don't know what 'corpitain of dalir' means. The same goes for 'the dysplasia of cartosis' and 'the mardiration of the ulborsa.' These words are meaningless to me. I can, however, be of some help with regards to the 'cryptix.' This is one of the techniques to transform gurlan energy into its erotophenic state. Indeed it is odd that your ship computer does not know such an elementary process. The problem is complicated by the need to use the Varlian calendar, since the years are distributed unevenly in it, but…What's this?"

A hand reached into the adviser's projection holding out a piece of paper. The adviser read it and broke into a smile: "The answer to this question is as follows: 7X5Q82G. Try it."

I touched the red line on the cylinder. A virtual keyboard appeared. The adviser repeated the sequence once more, and after entering it, the line lit up in a pleasant light green color. One of the four answers was in.

"I am sorry, but the Precian Empire cannot help you with the answers to the rest of the questions. Surgeon, Nurse — the Precian Empire repeats its offer: Become our subjects and receive lands and titles as a reward for your service. Few humans in Galactogon have been granted such an honor."

"Do we have to quit being pirates?"

"Without any discussion. The commonwealth of the ten remaining empires has decided to exterminate them. Especially in view of the recent return of Captain Wit-Verr. We will do this with or without you — it does not matter."

"Unfortunately, we cannot make this decision right this instant. Give us time."

"A day. The emperor's offer will be valid for twenty-four hours, after which you either quit piracy altogether or become the enemies of all the empires. All the best, Surgeon! I look forward to your wise and informed decision."

The adviser disconnected. The servants who had brought us here coughed helpfully, pointing to the exit, and a countdown timer appeared before my eyes: 23 hours 59 minutes. What could we do in that time? Why just about whatever we needed to!

"Brainiac, get the Prince ready! Eunice, come with me. Hello, Tryd...? Oh shut up and listen for once. I am on Belket, we can meet in thirty minutes...Why I couldn't care less that that's not enough time. If you want that Anorxian, you'll be here on time."

A CHECK FOR A BILLION

"Lex — look out!" As soon as we stepped out of the viceroy's residence, Eunice shoved me aside. Three lines of red plasma pierced my wife, casting her against the wall. We had been forced to remove our armor suits before the meeting and as a result Eunice had been wearing nothing but a bullet-proof vest. Already falling, I saw a huge hole in her chest, after which my wife turned into a shimmering loot crate.

"Hilvar sends his regards!" I managed to hear before a loud bang filled my ears. The shots ceased and shadows began flickering before my eyes — Belket's airborne guards had come to and began doing their jobs. I peeked out from the column I had taken cover behind. There were no enemies in sight. Realizing that they didn't have the time to get me too, they had decided to respawn. The guards circled over the corpses, but could not do anything. Being the target here, no one paid any attention to me. So what if some player was attacked? He should be more careful next time.

"Don't come pick me up," Eunice called me on my PDA. "They'll be waiting for you to do that. I'm sure, Kiddo will disrupt you out of hyperspace. Let's first deal with the Tryd business. Oh and another thing: I know where we can start looking for the solutions to the cylinder's riddles. Mr. Eine!"

That a girl! How did I not think of that myself?

"I'll brainstorm what we can tempt him with," Eunice went on. "Let's hope that he can help us. Take my armor."

She didn't even have to ask. Everything was already safe and sound in my inventory. I put on my own armor suit and requested permission to fly to my ship. I was not about to go trudging back through a crowded street. Nor was I going to start opening the loot crates that my assassins had left in their wake. The pirates were quite capable of planting a bomb in one. Ordering Brainiac to self-destruct if I left Belket without him for some reason, I took off and headed for the docks. No one attacked me — but I felt that this had less to do with there being no more bandits and more with the three escorts flying beside me. The Belket police made sure that pirate Surgeon was flying in the right direction, without deviating from his requested route.

Half an hour later I was sitting in a familiar office, awaiting Tryd's arrival. Getting here had not been difficult — I picked up the Prince from *Warlock* and took the black cube to the market. They were already waiting for me over there — Vardun was standing near the pseudo-smuggler's shop. This time there were no EM grenades, blindfolds or cryptic abductions. The pirate's residence was located in the basement of the market's administration building, hinting pretty openly whom the market actually belonged to. Vardun adopted his habitual pose, leaning against the wall, and left me to myself. Eunice has already passed the customs inspection and was supposed to join me any minute now. Of course the risk of losing our spare ship was a big one to take, but now was the time to do it.

"Please, make yourself at home." The door opened and Tryd let his new guest in ahead of himself.

"Thank you," answered Eunice. She sat down beside me and asked in a whisper: "What'd you agree to?"

I had to explain that there had been no negotiations as of yet. Tryd settled himself across from us and declared:

A CHECK FOR A BILLION

"We're just waiting for someone else to join us. He'll be here any minute now. We must wait."

I'd never seen the fox look so happy before. He radiated joy and happiness. It was as if he'd managed to set up a couple hundred players and make a hefty profit in the process. A short while later, the door opened and another participant joined us. Still dry and weak from his three-year-ordeal, yet now clean and well-dressed, this was the first mate of Captain Wit-Verr — Gloom the Precian.

"It's not so easy to get on Belket these days." The pirate's voice has not yet regained its strength, and he spoke in a hoarse whisper.

"A temporary inconvenience," said Tryd. "Recently, a henchman of the Corsican visited the Qualian trade planet and almost razed it to the ground. Everyone has rushed to tighten security in response. In a year or two, their attention will start to lapse again and everything will become as before."

"If someone does not find a way to repeat the trick again. Anyway, I have little time and energy. Let's get to the point without further delay."

Two badges of the Jolly Roger Brotherhood smacked the table in front of us.

"These are rightfully yours, Major Surgeon and Lieutenant Nurse. Whether you accept them or not is up to you. No one insists. But you do need to make the choice. Here and now."

"The Brotherhood is no more," Eunice objected without taking her eyes off the badges. But Gloom merely grinned:

"The captain started a new one. The old one had

---

compromised itself. The Corsican and Hilvar forgot what the Brotherhood had been created for. They became mired in squabbles, luxury and hatred towards each other."

"We need time."

"You can have a day, even less actually. We need to know exactly who is with us."

A second, red countdown timer appeared next to the Precian adviser's one. Remarkably, both showed exactly the same time remaining.

"Anyone want to explain what's going on? Why did Gloom come to the meeting?"

Tryd glanced at the first mate, and Gloom nodded: "They deserve the truth. They have earned it."

"That remains arguable but I will do as you command." At least Tryd's nasty character remained a reassuring constant in this quickly changing world. "I am Tryd. The former second mate of Captain Wit-Verr. For several reasons, I was not on the ship when the captain set forth to investigate the black hole."

"Speak directly and completely," ordered Gloom, and the fox grimaced with displeasure.

"The captain expelled me. The reasons are not important." Tryd paused and looked at the Pyrrhenian defiantly, who nodded in agreement. "Since I was no longer part of the crew, I didn't fall into the trap. Only the son of the Delvian Emperor himself had the means, influence, opportunity and desire to get rid of Wit-Verr and become the leader of the Brotherhood. Three ships set out to investigate the black hole and only two of them returned. The Corsican and Hilvar."

A CHECK FOR A BILLION

'I know where it is. You're wasting your time. That is a deadly place,' the ex-head of the Jolly Roger had said to me. Galactogon's not such a small place that someone could remember the coordinates of a single location in space. So the Corsican had surely been in the vicinity of the black hole and Tryd's story is likely to be true. But only 'likely' because I'm not about to trust anyone in this game ever again. The pirates have fully justify their name. They are lying, arrogant thieves. Does it really make sense to become one of them? I imagine business would be a bit more reliable with the Precians.

"Before vanishing, Wit-Verr managed to send me a message. An order. I was to do everything I could to get him out of the black hole. This required good relations with the Anorxians. The synthoids were the most advanced in the matter of studying these spatial anomalies. Their empire encompassed three such black holes. I got a job with the Corsican to somehow influence the Brotherhood's politics. In time, I became one of its best and most influential members. I even almost managed to resolve the issue with the Prince, but then pirate Surgeon showed up and everything started going haywire. All my cunning plans went down the drain."

"You were sitting on Daphark, not moving so much as a whisker," I reminded the fox.

"Did it not occur to you why I was on the same planet as that crystal? You were ever a brainless small fry, and so you've remained. I am opposed to promoting him to Major! He is not worthy. Nurse — yes. She is smart, cool-blooded and appropriately ambitious. A true lieutenant. Surgeon — no. That is my opinion."

"Are you trying to dispute the captain's decision?" Gloom

glanced at the fox heavily, but the Delvian refused to be cowed. He could withstand even the look of this creature who had escaped death.

"I am a free pirate until I am accepted back into the fold. You can't bar me from speaking my mind about whatever I wish."

"This is true," Gloom backed down.

A pause followed.

"This is all very interesting and fascinating, of course, but I am not here to listen to your tales. You promised me the Lora in exchange for the Anorxian Prince. Here he is — signed, sealed, delivered."

I placed the cube on the table.

"An ally like this will be useful to us," Gloom responded, but Tryd only snorted:

"It won't do, small fry! I needed the prince to bargain with the Anorxians. Wit-Verr is free, so there's nothing to bargain for now."

"We need the Anorxians, Tryd," Gloom reiterated with urgency.

"If you need him, you can buy him. I don't need him anymore. My job's done. No, small fry, this won't do. If you want to get the Lora, you'll have to do something for me personally!"

"Are you kidding?" Eunice's patience gave out. "You lured us to our slaughter for the Scourge, put us in harm's way, abandoned us like a cheap, two-bit traitor and without so much as dropping us a hint about what to do next and now here you are insisting on your rights?!"

"Bridle your wench, Surgeon. I don't work with her."

A CHECK FOR A BILLION

The hormones won out and a Zatrathi grenade appeared in Eunice's hands — the kind that broke planetary bindings. Vardun almost drew but Tryd gestured for him to remain in place. Looking at my wife with contempt, the Delvian growled:

"You really think that I still haven't thought of a countermeasure to that toy? You are dumb and naïve! I take my words back. You are not worthy of the rank of lieutenant. A female true to form."

That was enough for Eunice to pull the pin and toss the grenade at the fox. The only hitch was that she never had time to. A thin red beam from the ceiling struck the grenade and Tryd deftly caught the harmless device. Spinning it in his paws, he lobbed it back at Eunice.

"No need to litter in my place. You're not at home! And don't come back here again. I won't let you in."

Eunice blushed like a boiled lobster, ready to blow herself up just to destroy the offensive NPC. Our eyes met and the levee broke. Covering her face with her hands, my wife burst into tears, pouring out her pent up emotions. Oh come on! Why do pregnant women go from 'I am positive, mindful and constructive!' to 'Don't you dare give me any of you attitude, pig!' or to 'Oh this poor little helpless bug!' at the speed of light?! Deciding that I would deal with my wife after I had dealt with the Delvian, I asked:

"So what do you want, pirate Tryd?"

"Call me Captain Tryd," the fox leered revoltingly. "Like any captain, I need a ship. A cruiser, but I still haven't decided which one. Either the *Alexandria* or the *Inevitable*. Bring me the access key from either one and you will get the Lora in return. I've said my piece! You can deal with the Prince between yourself. I don't care about him!"

Mission failed: A Prince fit for a Pirate's Soul.

Mission available: The Education of Captain Tryd. Description: Capture either the Cruiser Alexandria or Cruiser Inevitable and give the ship access key to Tryd. Reward for completion: Lora coupler unit.

CHAPTER
EIGHTEEN

*H*i! *RUMOR HAS IT that there are beacons that allow one to track a ship traveling in hyperspace and thus pull it out of hyperspace. And also, that the Belket system is surrounded by about fourteen cruisers. Kiddo isn't in a stingy mood: She could easily pull up more cruisers and picket the entire system in a sphere. And you, of course, haven't received this letter and, if you happen to fly through the sector watched over by our mutual friend, make sure to announce your surprise and outrage loudly on the public channel.*

Your buddy, Gammon.

My old partner found one of the most ancient ways to apprise me of the news: A paper letter delivered by courier. A player courier from another empire. It remained a mystery to me why Gammon hadn't simply called me, preferring this odd form of communication. But since he did not call, I supposed he had a good reason for it.

"She's signed her own death sentence," Eunice murmured loud enough to be sure that I'd heard her. After our meeting with Tryd, my wife needed a punching bag and Kiddo's appearance was just the thing. "Brainiac, where's that damn beacon?"

"Captain, I don't detect anything. Our hull is clean. Maybe this is ruse?"

"No. Remember how carefully the Precians searched us. Kiddo has good relations with them. She could easily have made a deal with their customs officers."

"Yeah...Also, they checked us before departure," my wife added. "They could have placed the beacon inside, not outside."

"What?!" Brainiac realized the deceit that players were capable of. These aren't mere locals following their ordinary AI scripts. "They've planted a bug on my *Warlock*?"

The computer began running a full inspection, but I had no doubt that he wouldn't find anything. The beacon would turn on only once we'd entered hyperspace. No sooner. At the moment it is deactivated and hidden somewhere under some bucket or mop.

"Do you believe him?"

"No more than the rest. We worked together, but it wasn't anything more than that."

"Could this be a setup?"

"Sure. But it also fits Kiddo's M.O. She was pretty angry."

"Do we have serious problems then?" Worry flashed in Eunice's voice.

"What makes you think that?" I asked, surprised. "So they

A CHECK FOR A BILLION

yank us out of hyperspace — so what? We'll just fly away."

Kiddo's approach were reasonable enough — under the assumption that she was dealing with an ordinary ship. Yank us out of hyperspace, fry our electronics with EM cannons, board and capture us and then rewrite *Warlock* to Kiddo's name. An ordinary hyperspace ambush, which could be adapted even to my orbship — before my last upgrades, that is. As I recall, Kiddo only knew of my old ship's capabilities. It'll be fun to see her reaction when she realizes that she has nothing to go up against my current *Warlock*. I wasn't thinking so much about how to avoid her cruisers, as where to go in general. The last thing I wanted was to suggest to the pirate captain now actively after my head what quadrant my planet was located in. Kiddo was easily capable of arranging some dragnet just to hurt me a little more.

"Shall we visit Mercaloun?" Eunice suggested after I shared my reservations with her. "We can make a run for the atmosphere. They won't be able to reach us once we're planetside. We need to solve Belmarad's riddles one way or another."

"Makes sense. Brainiac, set course for Shurtan. Activate recon mode."

We weren't risking anything. I had handed the Prince over to Gloom, who promised to get me a nice bonus from Wit-Verr in return, so there was nothing valuable in our cargo hold. As soon as the stars turned into long light lines, the ship computer announced happily:

"I have located the bug! The beacon has been destroyed! Warning, I am detecting an active hyperspace scan. Our hyperdrive is being disrupted! Exiting hyperspace in three…two…one…Threat

---

detected! We are under attack!"

"Shields are up! I am detecting a hyperdrive disruptor. There are multiple EM cannons tracking us. Fire incoming!"

The captain of Cruiser *Kerbal* didn't waste time on pleasantries. As soon as his fishing rod pulled us out of hyperspace, a powerful EM broadside slammed into our ship. But the lights in the cabin didn't so much as blink — with the orbship's new capabilities, the enemy couldn't do a thing to us.

"Brainiac, set throttle to eighty. Maintain heading for Shur…tan."

I spoke the last syllable in complete silence and darkness. Another EM broadside raked our ship and this time *Warlock* couldn't cope. It took me several seconds to swap out the elo and reset my armor suit, but all my efforts came to naught — the screens barely came on before everything went dark again. The orbship had been hit by another EM wave. Another swapping of the powercells — a reset — and again darkness. I repeated this procedure two more times before I finally understood — we were trapped. *Kerbal's* captain went on frying my ship's electronics with terrifying regularity and accuracy. I decided to wait for the next salvo and eject myself from the armor, but I didn't have time. A message appeared before my eyes:

> *You have been killed by Nurse.*
> *Respawn point: Blood Island.*

Eunice appeared beside me just as the world was beginning to regain its sharpness.

A CHECK FOR A BILLION

"We'll have to re-upgrade to legendary class." Instead of an explanation, she pulled my armor suit out of her inventory. By killing me, she had knocked off a level of my armor and now though it still looked pretty rad on me, it was a mere A-class suit.

"What happened to *Warlock*?"

"She's at the graveyard. I blew her up."

"How?" I asked surprised. "There were only like ten seconds between broadsides!"

Eunice's mysterious smile forced me to think a little.

"You went through with that elo implant in your forearms? You could have been torn apart!"

"But I wasn't torn apart. I felt like it would come in handy. But you know, hubby, you're not asking about the right thing. Why don't you ask why that cruiser was shooting so fast?"

I was curious about that too, but I had no idea what the answer could be.

"This is what Brainiac managed to see before he disconnected..." My wife sent me a screenshot. As we emerged from hyperspace, the computer ran an automatic scan to assess the size and composition of the ambush. A hyperdrive disruptor always pulled the victim out of hyperspace facing its assailant. Right before we lost power, Brainiac had generated a situation report of the space around us — and it was this report that was captured in the screenshot.

As expected, *Kerbal* hung in front of us, precisely where she should have been. And yet, not far away and behind us, was another vessel that had not been involved in pulling us out of our hyperjump. When I saw the name of our second assailant, my chest tightened and I began to breathe quickly. It was none other than Captain Aalor and his Cruiser *Inevitable* in person. The EM cannons of a Legendary-class cruiser would certainly overwhelm our countermeasures.

"What the hell?" I snapped.

"That's the right question all right, but you haven't formulated it properly. The fact that Aalor positioned himself to intercept us means that he knew that we were making a break for Shurtan! The proper question to ask then is: 'How the hell did he know what we decided to do at the very last minute?'"

Eunice sure did know how to ask an unpleasant question. I took out the note supposedly written by Gammon and struggled to keep myself from crumpling and tearing it to pieces. They'd played us like toddlers! The Precian adviser had told them about the riddles and mentioned that one of them concerned Mercaloun. Kiddo knew who she was and where to look for her — and thus it had just been a matter of technique and run-of-the-mill psychology. It's not pleasant to discover that someone saw through you. If it weren't for Eunice's elo implants, Liberium could have captured *Warlock* for good. Would Vargen give her back to me? Not in a million years.

My wife and I walked out to a clearing and lay down on the grass, fixing our eyes on the sky. Our orbship was somewhere out there in a ship graveyard. Our other ship, the fighter, was on Belket. We didn't know how to fly on our own. And we couldn't ask Stan to hire some freelancer. Our current situation could only be described as 'up the creek without a paddle.' I hadn't been here in a long time and I'd even forgotten all about how 'nice' it was here.

A CHECK FOR A BILLION

"Who are we going to call?" asked Eunice. "A player or a local?"

We didn't have a choice — we would have to reveal our homeworld's coordinates to someone. There was no other way to get Brainiac back. The locals were out of the question. I didn't have any contacts besides the pirates and the Precians and recent events had demonstrated that neither of those could be trusted. In the best case scenario, they'd take over the planet and in the worst case, they'd sell us out to Aalor or Kiddo. That left the players, but there were some pitfalls here too. I hadn't the time to make any real friends in the game and everyone else was sure to betray us for a chance at unique loot or just GCs. Judging by her actions, Kiddo was really pretty pissed with me.

But why am I such a ninny anyway? I don't need to look for new friends, I have old ones! I still remembered the number from my Runlustia days, even if it wasn't in my current contacts list.

"Hello, wanderer!" a familiar voice greeted me from my PDA. "Have you already been discharged?"

"Not quite," I ducked the question and got down to business. "Alonso, I need help. Are you in Galactogon?"

The process of recovering the orbship ended up taking quite a while. Alonso's wife showed up with him. As the head of their guild, Lucille flat out refused to let her husband go alone. It was a good thing that they arrived in a simple scout instead of an entire cruiser. Dismissing me with her customary scornful look, she immediately walked over to Eunice. Alonso and I were in for a long and thorough conversation, the general gist of which was 'why the hell hadn't I called earlier?' He had a point and so I had to make sincere excuses, playing the pity card. After that the girls joined us and we all began talking about Constantine.

"He forced us to abandon the contest by threatening our children," Alonso said in a heavy voice, lost in memories. "We submitted an official letter to the corporation stating that we were giving up the search for family reasons. That damn freak! He died the death he deserved. So is this why you're in the hospital?"

After that we began to relax a little. Alonso brought with him a traveling cooking set which included some strong drinks and snacks. While our wives flew off to Belket to get Eunice's fighter, we relived some fond memories of our past over a couple drinks. By the time the girls came back, we were already dozing, drunk to all hell. I think we'd even managed to get into a fight, but I can't remember about what or how it ended. What I do remember is our promise to see each other in meatspace as soon as I got out of the hospital. It had been a long time since I'd felt this kind of warmth and friendship.

A light injection into my forearm brought me back to the game. The 'hangover' debuff hung in front of my eyes for a few moments, forcing me to hear my heartbeat right in my skull, but then it dissipated. Alonso and Lucille had already gone. While I was asleep, Eunice not only came back with the fighter, but even managed to fly to the ship graveyard and recover the orbship.

"Get up, you boozehound," the girl said happily. "I got a call about our home. Can you imagine — the assholes turned themselves in as soon as they heard that there had been casualties. They must've realized that their days were numbered. It really did turn out to be Fighting Breed! Or more precisely that part of the guild that did all the real life fighting. We won't be getting that house back either. They've confiscated the entire lot and offered us a replacement cottage in a new location. I have already approved it. Stan's backup is online so if you want to talk to your smart home, you'll need to contact your doctors."

Ta-da! If only every husband could have a wife like this to help him with his hangover! There's nothing like good news to raise your morale and instill the desire to forge onward.

After a few hours of correspondence, and another hefty payment, a message appeared on my PDA: *"Master, all systems are nominal. My survey of the new house is 83% complete and I have some suggestions for modernization. What are your instructions?"*

Stan was in his element. If there was anything to be improved he'd be sure to do it. Or else toss it in the trash. There was no other option. Having made sure that everything would be taken care of, I returned to the ship. At long last our troubles had ended. Or that's what I wanted to believe.

"Brainiac set course for Shurtan. Recon mode."

This time nobody bothered us. The computer switched off all unnecessary equipment and devices and we soon found ourselves in orbit around one of the outlying planets. Three flying fortresses hung in the system, providing full protection for the repair docks. The train of transports went on ferrying marble down to Shurtan. The hardworking Zatrathi hadn't stopped for a second, following their Queen's orders.

"Our camouflage is working quite well. No one can see…Danger, Captain! We've been spotted! Shields are up!"

"Retreat!" I ordered and the orbship rushed away from the system. The Zatrathi had installed some stationary defenses which immediately began to test the strength of our shields. Meanwhile, the entire Shurtan system came alive with hundreds of small points, rapidly approaching us. Fighters!

"Last time they weren't so quick on the ball. Have the Zatrathi learned how to detect ships with their reflectors up?" asked Eunice.

"The Zatrathi have nothing to do with it," the snake explained. "We remained undetected until that ship there highlighted our location."

A video appeared on the screen. A scout with the name Inevitable-S-332 had been lying in wait for us behind one of the planets. They had anticipated our arrival — and moreover at a particular location. The scout painted the orbship with a beam, revealing both itself and us to the Zatrathi. The stationary defenses dealt with him in a few shots, depriving us of even a chance at revenge. Again that damn Aalor! And again he'd foiled our plans! This was really beginning to look more like a vendetta than a simple contract job for Kiddo.

"Captain, our old friend is here! Warning, external interference detected! Engine power reduced by fifty percent. I am analyzing it now!"

The battlesphere appeared nearby and fired a violet ray in our direction. *Warlock*'s speed fell noticeably, allowing the Zatrathi to close in on us. On top of this, the sensors indicated that the Zatrathi had sent one of their flying fortresses after us. This was really bad. Speed was the only way we could avoid that monstrosity. Is that battlesphere really on the side of the enemy?

"I have identified the malfunction, Cap'n. The acceleration module has been disabled. It will take a minute to repair it."

"What was that beam? Can you protect our ship from further disruptions?"

"I will have to think," the snake replied after a pause, acknowledging her failure.

"Brainiac, head back to Blood Island. There is nothing for us to do here."

The fighters were almost on top of us. The gunner even got a few with some well placed flams before the starfield before us grew long with lines. We flew half of the way in complete silence. The snake repaired the damaged module and began sullenly thinking how to defend against the new weapon. The marine was snoring and the gunner went back to working on his rudiments.

"Do you know where Liberium's base is?" My wife's question shattered the silence on the bridge.

Eunice's eyes flashed with the resolve to fight to the bitter end. Aalor had gotten between us and the check. He needed to be neutralized. Without any further thoughts, I was fully behind my wife's idea. We needed to strike Liberium so forcefully and openly that anyone who wanted to mess with us again would think three times before doing it. Brainiac knew Aalor's base coordinates. He had downloaded them when *Warlock* had been integrated into Aalor's cruiser. There remained the question of who'd we'd take with us, but I already knew who could help. In the end, I still had some cards to play.

"Which cruiser did you choose for me, small fry?" said Tryd

instead of a greeting.

"It'll be *Inevitable,* of course."

"A good choice. I approve. *Alexandria* is off limits. Captain Kiddo can be useful for Wit-Verr. What did you want?"

"An assault team and a skeleton crew to pilot the stolen cruiser. We won't manage on our own."

"Acknowledged. You will get your team. When do you need it?"

"Now."

"Heh. Reasonable. While they're chasing you all over Galactogon, thinking that you're hiding out somewhere, the last thing they'll expect is an attack. You might just be lieutenant material after all. I will notify Wit-Verr. Where do we meet?"

"You're coming with us?"

"Do you really think that I will let you ruin my ship, small fry? Why you'll answer to me for every little dent. You are a pirate, not a hero. So act like one. Jump in, steal it, hand it over to me and you can be on your way! No unnecessary property damage! Planet Barganil in confederate space. I'll be waiting for you there in four hours. I will have my people ready. We'll need fifteen seats."

"It'll be done. Over and out."

Eunice stared at me for a long time before saying with a sigh:

"I don't trust him. In general, I get the feeling that he's being played by a human instead of an AI."

"Just a feeling?" I smirked. "I haven't a doubt. Didn't you hear that the Galactogon corp is constantly hiring people? And not only programmers, but basically anyone intelligent. It's just not

---

realistic to come up with scripts for these characters — they need instant reactions, improvisation. The Precian adviser — he's run by an AI. But Tryd is a human. In fact, I think that the corp dug up a real pirate from somewhere and hired him to play the NPC. No one else could be so true to the real thing. You'd need a genuine pirate!"

"Cap'n, I've figured it out!" The snake's joyful cry echoed across the entire planet. "The violet ray is pionic radiation which interferes with out marchand singulators. That's how it disrupts the acceleration module! It's desynchronization! Elementary!"

The snake's excitement was reassuring but I didn't have much desire to dive into Uldan technical terminology.

"Can you shield all the modules that use singulators?"

"All of them?" the engineer asked, surprised. "They're only in the acceleration module...Although, wait, no there's another couple in the tracing unit...Don't worry, Cap'n, I'll take care of it! Ten minutes! I'll check everything again and close it. They won't get us that way again!"

The snake slithered away to tinker with the ship.

"We need to figure out why that battlesphere attacked us," Eunice broached an unpleasant topic. I had put if off to the very end, since the Uldan's actions suggested to me that they had decided to take my orbship away. And I didn't like that conclusion one bit and so was looking for another logical explanation of what happened. The battlesphere wanted the flying fortress to catch us. Which meant only one thing — the loss of *Warlock*.

"If we eliminate the most likely theory, which, by the way, I do not believe," Eunice continued her thought, "then they wanted to send us to Mercaloun. I doubt we could have made it through by

---

running for it. Is the snake in some kind of danger?"

"Impossible!" said the ship computer. "The great lady said that the Zatrathi could not do anything to her! Her word is unquestionable."

"Maybe the Zatrathi cannot, but I bet the Queen can. Let's head back to Shurtan. Brainiac calculate a hyperjump ASAP! If something will happen, it'll be now. Eunice, I have an assignment for you too. Ask our dear ship computer who Belmarad is. He prohibited Brainiac from telling me, but he didn't say anything about you. I want to know why he had the right to order my computer to do anything at all."

There were no objections to this, and as we flew, Brainiac happily told Eunice the story of the dark Uldan master, who was notable for his cruelty among his race. It got to the point that Belmarad began to conduct his experiments on his own people, for which he was imprisoned. But, since his status meant that he could not be imprisoned in a capsule, the prisoner was sent into a black hole. As for his authority over my ship computer — everything turned out to be so banal that it even hurt. The Uldan had been one of the ship designers and had included his authorization in the computer's very source code. Brainiac could do nothing about this.

The Shurtan system was crawling with Zatrathi as before, albeit the composition of their forces had changed. Two more flying fortresses had joined the three that had been there. We got lucky that our exit point from hyperspace was not far from the marble planet, so we didn't set off any alarms as we passed. The Zatrathi's capacity for learning from their mistakes was frightening. They had spread out across the system, ensuring the maximum level of

A CHECK FOR A BILLION

protection for their shipyards — although questions arose immediately when it came to these. A visual inspection of the system revealed an odd picture — the enemy operations were clearly winding down. The transports were no longer rushing about with their loads of marble, there were no more damaged cruisers undergoing repairs, and the shipyard itself was beginning to drift away from the system. We had been gone for only one hour, but the Zatrathi were already busy relocating. Why?

"Captain, we are receiving a message on the closed Uldan channel," whispered Brainiac in shocked surprise. "I quote: 'You are too late. She can no longer be saved. Flee, you fool!' The transmission source is unknown."

We did not have time to react to this news. A new character entered the scene.

"Lex, what is that thing?" Eunice asked with a hushed voice, staring at her screen like a rabbit at a boa constrictor. From the opposite edge of the system, absorbing one planet after another, an abyss was advancing on us. Its size was terrifying — Shurtan's star, a yellow dwarf, could easily fit inside this colossus and there would probably still be room for one more. The Zatrathi Queen had decided to personally pay her respects to Mercaloun.

The Queen's immense gravitational forces destabilized the star system. Shurtan's sun began to roil and seethe, spewing huge arcs of flame into space. Several of them passed too close to the retreating shipyard, thoroughly melting one of its sides. The rest rushed to the new point of attraction — the Queen — who swallowed them without a trace. The closer the Queen came to the sun, the more erratically the star behaved. From a perfectly round ball, it turned into a burning rugby ball, stretching towards the Zatrathi leader. The consequences for the rest of the star system were catastrophic. Two flying fortresses, the shipyard's escorts, evaporated along with the shipyard itself. Several arcs passed along Shurtan, turning it into a hunk of boiling marble. The planet beside us wasn't spared either. Its orbit changed and it rushed straight toward the sun, as if it too wished to fuel the center of its universe.

"Cap'n, this system has become unstable! We need to leave!"

Our camouflage disappeared, but the Zatrathi paid no attention to our appearance. They were fleeing the system themselves, trying to put as many AUs between them and their own Queen as they could. The main villain of Galactogon was terrifying indeed. It now became clear that the Queen was not just a huge ship of stellar proportions. She was a living being. Her numerous spires were actually tentacles pulling the 'tastiest' parts of planets or ships into her omnivorous maw — a bottomless black abyss, from which even the light did not return. Little eyes were scattered all along the queen's surface — and these were all currently locked on the only nearby dish — the burning and boiling planet Shurtan. Swiping away the approaching sun with a couple tentacles, thereby both incinerating them and changing the star's trajectory away from her, the Queen crept up to Mercaloun's planet. Brainiac was already calculating a jump to Barganil, yet we managed to witness the inglorious end of the great Uldan lady. Shurtan disappeared in the Queen's maw without a trace — and at that point all her myriad eyes snapped in our direction. The tentacles shot for their target —

only to encounter the void. We had jumped into hyperspace.

"Do you have Ash's contact? You need to give him the coordinates of the Queen."

Eunice's voice was firm, but her pulse reading indicated that she was far from calm. The leader of the Zatrathi had just devoured our best hope of getting the prize check.

CHAPTER NINETEEN

THE TWO COUNTDOWN TIMERS in my HUD had ticked off yet another hour, leaving me but four to think everything over. Frankly, I had already made up my mind, though I wasn't in any rush to pull the trigger. As bad as I wanted to see Hansa's fourth tier of upgrades, my path in this game didn't lie with the Precians. What did they threaten me with? The wrath and enmity of all the game's empires? Oh please! There are so many independent planets in Galactogon that they will run themselves ragged trying to find me.

Since I didn't have Ash's number, I was forced to dial Vanguard directly. I managed to get through to one of the leader's deputies, who thanked me laconically for the news about the Queen and hung up. His reaction stunned me actually. It wasn't like I was telling him about a new sale at the nearby store — this was

A CHECK FOR A BILLION

serious business! I'm starting to get the impression that it's better to avoid the powerful in this game entirely. The more ordinary the player, the clearer his intentions.

Looking up from my comm, I decided to dispense with the annoying timers. We had no time for procrastination. I had to draw a line under my dealings with the empires and return to the pirates' camp. The Precians were done with, so the Delvians were next in line.

"Brainiac set course for the Nadin system!"

Since the Delvian heiress had not yet been crowned, the Delvians did not have an official planet. No big deal. All I needed was their temporary refuge and access to Lumara. As soon as *Warlock* appeared in the system, the remnants of the Delvians grew very animated. The dispatchers was in such a hurry to warn me about the planet's restricted access, that they spoke openly over one another, turning the airwaves into a market. Held in the sights of the orbital stations and the Grand Arbiter, I flew up to the planet and broadcast on the open channel:

"As a Devil's Advocate, I demand a meeting with the future Empress of Delvos. I wish to receive my reward from her! Or shall the Delvians refuse me in this?"

The airwaves went silent. I did not observe any players when I was on Nadin, and this pleased me very much. Lately all my relationships with other players haven't been working out.

"Orbship *Warlock*, you have been granted permission to land. Dock one. Follow the escort."

I had no doubt that Lumara would welcome me in the finest way possible. No matter what tone she takes with me, you can't deny that it's only thanks to me that the Delvians even have a hope of reviving their empire.

"Her ladyship awaits you," the head of the welcoming party bowed lowly. Seeing that Eunice was about to come with me, he hastily added: "Her ladyship is expecting Surgeon. On his own. Without any companions."

We didn't bother arguing and about fifteen minutes later I was standing in a kind of makeshift throne room. The grave gaze with which the head fox fixed me boded nothing good.

"Didn't I warn you that you were no longer welcome in the Delvian Empire? Are you trying to end up in the mines? Or have you decided to sacrifice your orbship?!"

"Your Grace, I remember everything, but..." I tried to mollify Lumara as best as I could, simultaneously considering how I could slip away from here whole and without losing anything.

"And yet here you are, demanding your reward!" the future empress interrupted me roughly. "Has your sense of self-preservation failed you?"

This is the second time today that my attempt to have a conversation goes completely wrong. Well, when you don't know what to do next — do something outrageous! What's there to lose?

"No, Lumara, my sense of self-preservation is perfectly fine. It is you, your ladyship, who has forgotten that an imperial crown comes with certain responsibilities. For example, the right of people to receive their due and just rewards unhindered. That's a right every other empire in Galactogon recognizes and respects! Are you now denying it to me on behalf of the Delvian Empire? I am sure the Precian adviser will not approve."

A CHECK FOR A BILLION

The fox scowled, but could find no answer. I was right and all her outrage was a harmless spectacle. She really couldn't do anything to me.

"What do you want? What reward do you want to receive from a ravaged empire? You know very well that we have nothing!"

"You promised to give me everything that the Delvians know about the Uldans. That's why I'm here."

Lumara darkened. We both remembered the conditions under which she had made the promise. I had threatened her with the utter annihilation of her empire. Eh, my sins are grave, but I could not forego such a lever of influence over Lumara either. Since she made the promise, let her fulfill it. Or…help me in some other way, at least.

"I understand that my demand is not well-timed," I said, "and therefore I propose we deal with it another way. I will forget about your debt and my reward if you help me."

"Are we talking about a cylinder with riddles?" the Delvian asked, demonstrating that she was well-informed.

Well, the Precians sure do have a close relationship with the Delvians! Surely this is yet another point against siding with that venal empire. In the ensuing silence, I produced the cylinder from my inventory.

"There are three riddles here. Help me solve them and we can part ways for good. I don't care about the Delvian Empire. And if you can't help with the solutions, then help crack this cylinder open. I need what's inside."

"What *is* inside?" asked Lumara. Confronted with a mysterious toy, she immediately cast aside the mask of the empress and turned into the familiar nerdy tech fox she'd been when I first met her. The same one who would stick her nose into any mysterious piece of technology you placed before her.

"The coordinates of the Zatrathi homeworld. We will be able to end this war once and for all."

"You must give us the cylinder!" exclaimed Lumara but cut herself short when she saw my reaction. I hastily hid the cylinder in my inventory.

"No one will give anything to anyone until I get those coordinates. After that you can do what you like."

"Deal. The Delvian Empire would like to have priority among anyone wishing to buy the coordinates."

"Even if I remain a pirate?"

"Especially if you remain a pirate," Lumara said meaningfully, sending a jolt of relief through my chest. Not all the empires would stop working with me after all. Wishing to consolidate my success, I mentioned casually that I had been in a black hole and was ready to share some data. The fox's widened eyes indicated that she was all ears — at least until my allegiance timers an out.

Losing no time, the Delvian began to fiddle with the cylinder, connecting it to her tablet. As I expected, the empire of bipedal foxes had a lot of information about the Uldans and they were in no hurry to share any of it. Lumara ran program after program, without allowing me to get a good look at her screen for even a moment.

"Oh! I knew that I had seen something like this before. A riddle about the minimal distance of zlapartit. Answer: zero, comma, zero two, three seven, five eight. That's the distance required to start the process of mardirating the active inversion of the ulbrosa. Um…How could I translate this…? Well, it concerns Uldan consumer electronics. A cleaning process using zlapartit particles."

A strange riddle from a dark lord, but I just entered the digits Lumara had told me. It lit up green, indicating that we were one step closer.

"I can't speak to the other riddles." Lumara's hand continued fluttering over her tablet. "I need time. I do not have all the data. We have just begun collecting all the information. The loss of our capital has hurt our databases. And I do not advise you to try and crack the cylinder. That would be quite dangerous."

"I'll wait." I did not refuse such a generous offer, although I realized that there was nothing further to do here right now. The Precians and the Delvians had played their part. That left Eine and…a fourth. But who? Mercaloun had been destroyed despite the battlesphere's attempt to tell me that I needed to see her…So who else could help me?

Time was running out, so I said goodbye to Lumara, assuring her of my cooperation, and hurried to the next meeting. As of late, everything was going so quickly that I was even starting to get worried. I felt like if I let up even for a moment, not only would I be thrown off this merry-go-round for good, but my pursuers could catch up to and deal with us.

Planet Barganil, where Tryd was waiting for me, was reputed to be very accommodating to anyone who cared to spend their credits on it. As long as the wallet was full, its owner remained a cherished guest. But when the money ran out — and it was inevitable that any guest's money would eventually run out — the players were either expelled or sold to slavery. It was, briefly put, a good planet for good pirates.

The dispatcher assigned the orbship a distant dock, tucked away from any prying eyes. The old fox, leading his band of pirates, met me right at the ramp. Tryd rapped on our hull demanding that I open the door. As soon as everyone had settled in the captain's cabin, the Delvian began to introduce us to each other.

"This is Glyr, he is responsible for boarding ops. Badger will take care of the electronics and the alarms. You don't need to know the rest. I will deploy with Glyr and will coordinate our movements from the field. Everyone — a word! This is the Surgeon, our temporary captain. Nurse there is his deputy, don't pay any attention to her. She's a soggy-sorry type of wench."

There was an outburst of laughter, followed by a gnashing of teeth, but Eunice remained silent through it all, inspiring my respect. Were it up to me, none of these forest critters would have ever set paw inside my orbship — but that nasty word 'circumstances' compelled us to endure this rude and motley company. The assault team consisted of ten muscle-bound, scarred space marines. Taciturn, somber and unnaturally calm, as if pumped full of drugs. And as a foil to them, the support team consisted of four sneaky-looking pirates. Despite their various races, they all had rat faces with shifty eyes that cast about for suitable things to steal. In the ten minutes they had been on my ship, they had already tried to get inside the prohibited areas twenty times — receiving a painful zap from the snake each time. Of

A CHECK FOR A BILLION

course this didn't deter them at all, but only spurred their further attempts. For his part, Tryd seemed quite at ease among these brethren.

"Are we going fishing in the base or in the open sea?" Badger had a hoarse low voice, as if someone was rubbing Styrofoam against glass.

"In the base."

The pirates began to grumble and Tryd was forced to raise his voice.

"Quiet! Surgeon has already done this before, and he's about to do it again."

The pirates stopped making noise, and Tryd turned to me.

"You have the most important job, small fry. *Inevitable* is docked in the Barxes system. The alignment is not in our favor. There are three Grand Arbiters and four orbital stations stationed there. They say you can work miracles. It is time to prove it."

"I have friendly status with their guild," I remembered, but Tryd only waved dismissively.

"You'll lose it as soon as we set foot on that cruiser. You have two hours to figure out a way to hack all the systems at once. Either you get the Lora or Aalor does."

Hack all the systems at once? Is that a hint?

"Can you at least tell me anything about the security system?" I tried at random.

"Figure it out yourself. You're no pup. Everyone get ready! Don't forget to congratulate Glyr — his son was born yesterday!"

The pirates piled out of the orbship, slapping the embarrassed mercenary on the shoulders as they went. Various

---

suspicious individuals had begun to circle our ship, their faces hidden inside their cavernous hoods. They looked around, drawing closer and closer. Not wishing to give them a chance to make their move, I released the marine, ensuring a security perimeter clear of any locals around my ship. Meanwhile my timers blinked again, indicating that I had two hours to make my decision. It didn't make much sense to keep putting it off so I called Wit-Verr's deputy:

"Gloom, I accept your offer and I'm ready to join the Brotherhood. I'm on Barganil at the moment. I'll be waiting."

My next move was a search request for Stan. If Tryd is hinting that the security system can be hacked, then someone's already done it. First and foremost, I need to understand the mechanism that coordinates the Grand Arbiter and the orbital stations. It's not like every member of Liberium has to warn everyone when he invites someone to visit.

"I need all available information about the security systems in the Barxes system or similar ones. Even if this info costs money."

"Process understood. Master, what about updating the firmware for the home management system…?"

Ever the perfectionist, Stan began complaining about his available system resources, but I ignored him as per usual. Domestic problems could wait until we returned from the clinic.

"This won't do," Eunice said in frustration, reading the incoming data. The system really did have a centralized security system but it was located in the planetary command center and had tighter physical security than a cash printing machine. As hard as my smart home looked for it, there was no information about the terrestrial complex, even among the paid content.

A CHECK FOR A BILLION

"I get the feeling that you have to hack each ship separately."

"Hold on." I once again revised the scant information. The command center's control tower coordinated all space and ground forces. It was located in an area closed off to players. Unless set otherwise by a scenario, the layout of a command center was standardized for all of Galactogon. Standardized. Everywhere.

"I know how to get into the command center. I'll go alone. Stay on the ship and deliver Tryd to the destination."

"Care to share what you have in mind?" As much as Eunice wanted to know what I was about to do, I couldn't tell her anything. The locals can't read your mind, but they could easily have slipped us some bug that could record what we were saying. Accordingly, I told Eunice only the stuff that no one could influence. And I kept the main trick to myself.

"Cap'n, we have a request for access." How timely did this delegation show up! Gloom did not waste time and immediately flew over to meet me. Locals like him — ones with an AI that acts like an AI — I didn't mind working with at all. None of that initiative. As soon as a player needs something, they're right there on the spot eager to help him out.

You have chosen Jolly Roger 2.0 as your main faction.
Please confirm your selection.

A cute name and a cute dialog. The system wanted to make sure that I had make my choice while in my right mind and could understand the consequences of what I was doing. As soon as I pushed the 'Confirm' button, new notifications appeared:

> *Your rapport with all nine empires has decreased to a state of war.*
>
> *You have lost official access to work with the Hansa Arms Corporation.*

What terrifying words for a player! Everything is terrible! This is the end...beautiful friend...the end! Sell everything ASAP, delete the current avatar, close the account and pray that my karma doesn't transfer to the next one. Then again, when you consider the significance of it all — you realize that things aren't so bad. For example, the Delvians have no empire and who knows when they'll get one. Or if they'll get one. And that wording too...'*official* access.' I love it.

"The captain wants to see you. There's a job for you." The orders started coming in about as soon as the skull and crossbones icon flared to life over my head. The pirates' organizational structure was not remarkable for its complexity. It went ordinary pirate, lieutenant, major, general, deputy and then the head himself. This required strict subordination. Orders descended from above and demanded immediate obedience. Being a major, I had all kinds of cares and duties — but I also had about a thousand subordinates ready to execute any of my orders. At the same time, I in turn, must obey Gloom.

"Do I have time to spare or shall I report at once?"

"No one mentioned any deadlines but I wouldn't advise dragging it out. You are one of us now and you will be treated accordingly. You should forget about having rescued us — we already did. The captain thanks you for the Prince. He is an important prize. What do you need time for?"

"I am in the middle of an operation. It will be difficult to stop it. I have to settle some accounts with an old enemy and then I will appear before the captain."

Gloom gazed at me for a good while, shifting from one foot to the other. Having looked around and making sure that no one except Eunice was nearby, the Pyrrhenian hovered up to me and asked in a whisper:

"Will it get hot?"

"I wouldn't have it any other way."

"Do you have room for one more?"

"I'll make it if I don't."

Gloom began to glow like a star atop a Christmas tree and my rapport with him increased. But this turned out to be a mere trifle compared to the advice the pirate had for me when I let him in on the plan. Just a few extra touches and my plan now shimmered with all new colors, having gone from 'maybe if that happens, I guess I'll do this' to 'in the event of this, we will respond like that.' Like two schoolchildren Eunice and I sat and listened to the wisdom of Wit-Verr's deputy. And with every bit of advice from the Pyrrhenian, I understood that I had made the right decision after all. Paradoxically, with these pirates, I felt like I was completely among my own.

Tryd returned with his gang in exactly two hours. Glancing at the hologram of the Jolly Roger Brotherhood on the chest of my armor suit, he muttered something along the lines of 'At last some certainty around here!' but then immediately encountered Gloom ensconced in the co-pilot's chair. The fox lost it. His upper lip twitched, exposing his fangs, and Tryd whirled sharply in my direction, pointing with his paw to the unexpected guest:

"What is *that thing* doing here? He can't join my team!"

"Don't stick your nose into matters no one asked you about. Gloom is coming with me."

Tryd's scowl grew fiercer, he took a step forward and almost buried his snout in my helmet.

"Watch your words, pup."

"Watch your snout, mongrel." I did not intend on backing down. Having assumed the obligations of an officer of the pirate Brotherhood, I was going to do this job right — right down to insisting on my authority over the mercenary pirate.

"Mongrel?!" the fox flared up. I was starting to think that this time I had gone too far and there was about to be a slaughter here when the Delvian turned to Gloom: "Give it here."

"From now until eternity doth us part?"

"Shut yer gob and give me that damn badge before I change my mind!"

"Welcome to the Brotherhood 2.0, second deputy Tryd." Gloom tossed him the metal disc and the Delvian snatched it out of midair with quick swipe of his paw. The same icon appeared on his chest and over his head, except with extra officer chevrons. Tryd had found a way to pull rank at last, becoming one of my three superiors.

"You'll still answer to me for the 'mongrel' comment," the Delvian threatened and turned back to Gloom.

A CHECK FOR A BILLION

"What is the plan?"

"It hasn't changed. The major and I will land planetside, while you and the lieutenant seize the cruiser. The captain wants to see you, Tryd. As soon as you get that ship."

And not a word about keeping his paws off of me. Why that sly little jerk! The Delvian nodded, confirming that he had heard the order, after which Gloom presented our plan to the rest of the team. Judging by how Tryd's jaw opened further and further, this was one of those cases where we had truly cooked up a miracle. Then again, is there anyone in Galactogon who can boast that he spent two days crawling into every nook and cranny of the standard command center template — besides me?

Half an hour later we were at the far edge of the Barxes system, scouting out the lay of the land as it were. Liberium had spared no expense in the task of securing their interests. The Grand Arbiter and orbital stations were only the beginning. Several destroyers maintained a constant watch, circling from one planet to another. Vargen did not trust the locals and had arranged human security to guard his fleet's harbor. Ten of the cruisers were currently in system, including *Inevitable*. Like I figured, the players needed a rest after a hard day's work and most of them had popped out to meatspace, leaving skeleton crews on board the ships. My hands were itching to call Gammon and offer him a nice piece of business, but I restrained myself. Until proven otherwise, Vargen isn't responsible for his officer's actions. At the moment, only Aalor is guilty, and I intend to punish him.

"Here they are," said Gloom, pointing to the frigate that had popped in not far from us. "Let's go, Surgeon.

The plan had us splitting up. Eunice and the pirates remained on the orbship, and the Pyrrhenian and I headed for Barxes. How Gloom was going to land us on the planet remained a mystery to me, but his confidence reassured me.

"We're going to fly up to the hull and do as follows..." Having made sure that none of Tryd's warriors could hear us, Gloom began explaining how we were going to get on Barxes. This was a secure planet with very tight customs controls. Even my status as a 'friend of the guild' did not allow me to enter Liberium's headquarters without prior permission from a senior officer. However, what Gloom proposed dashed my notions of security systems entirely. And indeed, how had the Pyrrhenian pirate show up on Belket so quickly? Why didn't I consider how he'd done it earlier?

Brainiac jettisoned us both into space, and the frigate patiently waited for us to attach ourselves to its hull — and then abruptly set in motion. Ahead of us, customs was just finishing up an inspection of a transport ship.

We couldn't hear the radio chatter, but Gloom's explanation meant that I roughly knew what was being said. The gist of it was always the same.

Dispatcher: "Frigate X, you are prohibited from entering the Barxes system. Depart immediately or you will be attacked."

Infiltrators: "We request emergency assistance! We have no energy left on board! A bloody battle with the Zatrathi/pirates/space gods has left us in this deplorable state. All our reserves are exhausted and we merely request that you sell us some elo so that we can be on our way."

A CHECK FOR A BILLION

All of this is punctuated by radio noise and interference, as if the transmitter is running on its last bits of juice. While the dispatcher figures out a way to deal with this force majeure situation, the frigate, on the sly, drifts as close as possible to the ship that is undergoing inspection right at that moment. The grim guards threaten the ship with volleys of EM fire, the frigate freezes in fear, and we make our move. Detaching from the hull we set up personal reflectors and drift towards the vessel that's just passed inspection. And that's it. We cut a hole in the hull, tumble inside, quickly patch up the leak behind us and wait for landing. No one's ever going to check the same ship twice.

And no one checked this time either. The price we paid was a rough thrashing as we came in for landing. The transport was carrying inert elo, so the captain didn't bother to be gentle on landing. The cargo hold's doors swung open and robots rushed inside to unload the containers. Nobody paid attention to the two shadows darting out the side exit.

"Over here." I projected the local map and pointed to a site a few kilometers from the spaceport.

"Those are the maintenance facilities. Are you sure?" Gloom squinted doubtfully at my map, looked over at the spaceport and then back again. "That far?"

"That's nothing. The second entrance to the collector is located around here." I poked ten kilometers further ahead. "Just trust me. I know what I'm doing."

"Lead the way then. First time I'll be breaking into a command center from underground."

"Oh, so you've broken into command centers before?"

"Sure. Several times. Our captain loves his capers. Back in the day, we'd mount a raid once every week, sometimes even more. That's why I asked him to oversee you. I haven't been on a job in three years. I sure do miss a good gunfight. But the captain is busy with the new Brotherhood and hasn't the time to go a-raiding."

It took us a long time to reach the location we needed. We couldn't use our hoverboards and so we were forced to jog the distance. During the marathon, I had to swap powercells twice. In this mode, the armor suit guzzled a lot of power.

"Here!" An empty hangar stood over the entrance to the collector. Time had not been kind to its doors and the magnetic lock no longer actually kept the place locked so much as shut. Besides that, a rusty old chain wrapped around the handles was the only other form of security. In effect, it looked like the two doors were propping each other shut and barely coping with the task of keeping the passage closed.

It wasn't difficult to get inside. We simply cut a hole in the wall nearby. If you ask me, such a careless attitude to the condition of one's property stressed me out and made me suspicious and even a little paranoid. I couldn't help feel a jolt of pride for my foresight once we were inside. Gloom climbed in behind me, looked around skeptically and wanted to say something, but then faltered, noticing what the hangar's doors looked like on the inside. All he managed was a meaningful grunt. I think those outwardly-dilapidated doors could withstand a direct blow from an assault mech. The fragility and disrepair of the hangar's facade was an illusion. On the inside, the doors were reinforced, armored, wired with an alarm and booby-trapped with enough explosives to bring down the entire hangar. Liberium had tried to convince any trespasser that this hangar was entirely uninteresting, yet they also set up a nice security system to deal with any doubters. Gloom took out a gadget that puffed green smoke into the hangar and immediately several red laser beams appeared — the security system wasn't just on the doors but everywhere around us too.

"Follow me." Feeling himself in his element, Gloom now took charge. I didn't argue — I didn't have much experience for terrestrial ops. Billowing green smoke ahead of himself, the Pyrrhenian led me to the center of the hangar. Here we discovered a spiral staircase going down. The passage was locked with a lock and chain, but, now understanding the security principles used in this place, we acted differently. Without touching the red lines, we flew over the grid of lasers, dropping directly into the stairwell from above. At the same time, Gloom categorically forbade me from stepping on the steps. He didn't like something about them. Holding onto the railing we hovered down on our suits' thrusters, honing our fine maneuvering skills. Having gone around once in the spiral, I discovered that the pirate had been right to be cautious — every fifth step was booby-trapped with explosives.

After several more turns, we found ourselves at the bottom of the stairwell. Here I was stumped — there were neither passages, nor gratings, nor secret levers. Gloom hovered a few centimeters over the floor, scanning the space. Suddenly he said, "Follow me" and turned off his jetpack.

A moment — and Wit-Verr's deputy disappeared into the floor, falling through it, like a hologram. I didn't have to be told twice and plunged like a stone after him. The floor really turned out to be false. The spiral staircase ended, turning into an ordinary escape ladder, but anyone who didn't know this and set foot on the false floor would go plummeting ten meters into a giant shredding machine. I managed to activate my engines a meter above the terrible maw, capable of shredding even my armor to bits.

"That way!" The ladder ended in the grate to the collector. At long last, I was in my element. There hadn't been any lasers, holograms or shredders in the command center template I had explored. Nor were there shafts as deep as this one. But there was a spillway — the same one as here, which we now entered. The greenish slush probably smelled bad, but my armor suit spared me the local odors. Gloom stuck his blaster into the slush, pulled it out and, making sure that this wasn't acid, dived in headlong. I had to suppress my feeling of revulsion before following the pirate. It's not every day that you have to wade chest-deep through who-knows-what. We traveled the rest of the way in complete silence. I did not want to speak. A single thought tormented me — is this stuff going to wash out of my gear?

"We're in position," said Gloom in a whisper and looked around the corner. The pump room was empty. There were bags of some kind of loose material leaned against the far wall, and following the traces on the floor, it became clear that it was a powder that was being dumped down the drain. It was the same stuff that gave the sludge its rich green color — the sludge that leaked out of the pipes in the wall was actually quite gray.

"You're quite a sight." The pirate clicked his tongue and produced from his inventory the last item that I expected to see in

A CHECK FOR A BILLION

Galactogon. I don't know where Gloom found a pressure washer, but I sure was grateful for it. The green sludge dried very quickly, leaving thick, hard-to-erase stains. "Stand still!"

A powerful blast of water passed down my armor suit from top to bottom, rinsing off the crud. My stealth cloak helped here — as soon as I became completely transparent, the wash was done. The Pyrrhenian handed me the washer and we repeated the operation. Only with a different target.

"Our boys will know what to do with this." Gloom returned the pressure washer to his inventory and picked up one of the bags of green additive. After a little thought, I copied him. What if this is something valuable that I don't know about? The snake might figure it out.

A single door led us into a narrow corridor filled with pipes. The maintenance floor, the lowest floor in the base. The reactor that powered the entire command center was housed here, as well as several warehouses, a sewage system and an elevator shaft leading upward. There were no stairs.

"Engineers! Take the one on the right!" Gloom whispered, merging with the corridor's shadows. The two engineers were arguing quite loudly, waving their hands and constantly insisting that the other was wrong. The gist of their dispute became clear after a couple sentences. These two old friends were falling out over a woman. A short sprint, a shot in the forearm and their two bodies slumped to the floor. It doesn't do to kill bystanders — if they're bound to the planetary spirit and you're still around when they respawn, it'll be the same as triggering the alarm. Let them sleep on their quarrel for a couple hours.

Having dragged the bodies into the back room, Gloom examined the elevator with interest.

"Going up?"

"No." Here was the trick in the entire plan that I had kept secret so zealously. Getting into a command center is only half the battle. The second part is much more important and difficult. And there was no point in going up to the main control room. Instead, I pointed to the hall with the reactor: "That way."

My remote terminal had quickly become one of my favorite items in Galactogon. After my manipulators of course. The reactor was on the same circuit as the control unit, and I wasn't about to fight my way through waves of defenders.

"Are you planning on breaking it from here?"

"No, not break it," I corrected. "That trick's been tried before and I imagine there's some decent defense for it. Hacking the Arbiter management system won't work. Especially so when it comes to the orbital stations. We need to find some other way."

Having made sure that Brainiac had entered the network, I pressed a few buttons, turning off the power to the control room's speakers and spoke into the microphone:

"Cruiser *Inevitable*, this is ground control. Prepare for inspection. You have been randomly selected for a complete ship scan. We would like to make sure that you have no prohibited items on board. Please follow course 3-5-2."

"Ground control, this is *Inevitable*. The captain is not on board. We request that you delay the scanning procedure."

"Cruiser *Inevitable*, refusal to comply is a violation of a direct order from the planetary customs agency. You are hereby

A CHECK FOR A BILLION

issued a yellow-level citation. I repeat — follow course 3-5-2 and prepare your ship for inspection. If you refuse again, your citation will be escalated to level red and you will be attacked!"

"Did you rehearse that in your spare time?" Gloom grunted as soon as I finished transmitting. As I figured, no one dared argue with the locals. *Inevitable* requested permission to redeploy and set into motion. Course 3-5-2 would lead them beyond Liberium's hi-sec space into the general system. A change in the cruiser's ownership here would be noticed but not punished by the Arbiter.

"Cruiser *Inevitable*, prepare to be boarded by customs agents. Airlock one."

"Ground, we are ready to receive the inspection team. We would like to formally notify you that a complaint has been filed about your actions. We consider this to be a violation of our space-lease agreement!"

"Your complaint has been received. The customs ship has been highlighted! Time to docking — ten seconds." I turned off the transmitter and dialed my wife: "Eunice, head for *Inevitable*'s first airlock. The bridge is right around the corner from there. You have two minutes!"

"Got it! Wish us luck!" came the reply.

I changed the orbship's transponder, turning it into a frigate, and, as I expected, the command center around us resounded with the shriek of a siren. The locals had updated their IT firmware making it impossible to infiltrate them without being detected. We were instantly identified and disconnected. The fatal mistake was that they left us alive.

My shoulder-mounted blasters snapped out, locked and

loaded, and a burst of plasma blasted the reactor to pieces — depowering the command center. There were backup systems somewhere on the second level, but it would take time for them to be turned on, for the power to be restored fully and for the transmitters to contact the Arbiter or the orbital stations. That should buy us enough time.

"We're in position! Tryd's inside. Badger's in the ship's network. He's deactivated their self-destruct systems. We have contact! Brainiac's been hooked up!"

"Commencing hacking procedure. Time to completion: 45 seconds."

The loading bar on one of the screens was moving so slowly that I wanted to push it. The emergency lighting came on around us — the spaceport personnel seemed to be responding pretty quickly. They had already supplied power to our sector. The elevator buzzed to life — an assault group was coming down our way. That or some engineers to examine the power plant. A pair of shots ruined the elevator doors, ensuring that we were safe from that approach.

"The vessel's security key has been cracked. Captain, whom shall I designate as the cruiser's owner?"

"Tryd. Eunice, get out of there! It's about to get hot!"

Liberium's other cruisers had realized that something strange was going on. They released a swarm of fighters that surrounded *Inevitable* but were powerless to influence the takeover happening onboard. The new captain ordered the computer to calculate a hyperjump. Forty seconds! Why that's even faster than Brainiac can do it!

A CHECK FOR A BILLION

"We're ready, Lex! We're entering hyperspace, headed home!"

Mission accomplished: The Education of Captain Tryd. You have given Tryd the Cruiser Inevitable without a single scratch on her hull. Your reward: Lora coupler unit. Speak to Tryd.

You have lost friendship status with the Liberium guild.

Gloom saluted, tucked his armor suit in his inventory, took out the cheapest blaster he had and blew his head off with it. Our job was done.

The pirate had taught me a lot during this raid and now taught one more lesson — you should always carry an extra couple blasters you don't mind losing. I did as Gloom did and as soon as the game rendered Blood Island around me, my PDA buzzed with a call from Tryd.

"Small fry, I have a stowaway on board. Calls himself Aalor. He says he wants to talk with you. Anyway, you'll get the Lora right after you deal with him. We can meet on board Wit-Verr's ship. This is Captain Tryd — over and out!"

CHAPTER TWENTY

AVE YOU EVER WONDERED HOW IT FEELS TO BE THE ENEMY OF AN ENTIRE GALAXY? If you have, you should ask me. I would be happy to share my experience. Do you imagine it's a feeling of terror? Or perhaps a kind of euphoria? Not at all! When my next batch of messages came in, I felt a surprise that verged on bewilderment. The intermittent threats were lost among the thousands of offers to cooperate. Countless players wanted to share their schemes and scams with me, yet the general gist of all the letters came down to one thing — my ultimate annihilation.

The Precians did not disappoint — all of Galactogon was now buzzing with various missions for capturing, killing the dread pirate Surgeon as well as locating his planet. I got a mission too: *Mea Culpa*. Just in case I decided that playing as the galactic villain

A CHECK FOR A BILLION

wasn't my cup of tea, the devs had given me a way out. All I had to do was betray my accomplices and reveal their whereabouts.

And yet, there were some positive moments in my situation as well. For example, my encounter with Aalor. The Liberium officer didn't kill himself, hoping against hope that his cruiser's capture was like some ill-conceived birthday surprise. You see, it so happened that he was celebrating his 30th birthday that day, and he figured that Vargen and I were in cahoots and merely playing a prank on him. After all, it just wasn't possible for me to show up in the middle of Liberium's home base, much less steal a ship from it. It was a rare pleasure indeed to look my enemy in the eyes and watch them grow wider and more desperate as I offered to call his boss to prove to him that his beloved ship was really mine. When he did realize the hard truth, there followed an ornate hodgepodge of abuse, threats, flattery, wheedling and finally appeals to my better nature. I did not understand why Tryd insisted that I meet with Aalor. When I got tired of hearing the same thing for the hundredth time, I took out a blaster and shot the *Inevitable*'s former captain, solving the problem of his presence. My new boss nodded in satisfaction and handed me the Lora. At least this business was done with.

Achievement unlocked: Doom Child. You have assembled the Vengeance. You are now a threat to all of Galactogon. You are feared: -10% discount on all goods.
Your rapport with all empires has decreased.

In other words, nothing changed. No one loved me

anyway. Tryd immediately lost any and all interest in my person — something I can't say I was sorry about — and went off to work on his new cruiser. And Wit-Virr, whom I reported to as ordered, did not react at all, immediately issuing me a new quest:

"One of our main bases is located in the Praline system, Confederate space. We haven't been able to establish a connection to it. We need to understand what happened to it and bring it back to an operational state. You have four days. Your reward will be the contents of the base's third warehouse. Everything in there is yours. Now jump to it, pirate!"

New mission available: A Praline Pirate. Recover the Brotherhood's home base. Reward: Contents of third warehouse.

I liked the Bufondian's approach. Want a reward? Go and get it. If you fail — no reward for you. That's all, love. Before heading off, I decided to take a break and take care of some of my own affairs. For example, to find the answer to the third riddle of the cylinder.

"Guten Tag, Herr Eine — do you have a minute? I need your help."

The German and I met in the middle of nowhere. The collector did not wish to compromise himself by revealing his close relationship with a terrible pirate, so we avoided all planets and met each other in empty space.

After the obnoxious rigmarole of exchanging pleasantries, discussing the space weather, the various imperial political happenings and all the other dumb trivia, Eine finally got down to

A CHECK FOR A BILLION

business:

"I have Knowledge about ze Cylinder. Moreover, I have ze Answer to one of ze Questions. I vould like to know vhat I vill receive for my Help?"

"Isn't our mutually beneficial relationship sufficient on its own?" I made a show of being surprised, but then nodded to Eunice. She immediately laid out our offering on the table. Everything we'd gotten from the pirates and couldn't find a use for. Eine twirled a couple items in his hands, but almost immediately tossed them back onto the table.

"Zese are not unique Objects. I understand zat ze Cylinder is an important Issue for Herr Panzer. I vould like ze Orbship. You give me your Ship and I tell you ze Answer to ze Riddle."

There was an unpleasant pause. I was sure that Eine was telling the truth — that he had the answer, but I wasn't about to hand over *Warlock* to him...What a pain is this guy! A virtual ship and crew or a billion real credits? I wasn't ready for such a question, since the billion was still hypothetical.

"I see zat my Proposal has caused your Displeasure. A Compromise is possible to conclude the Contract. Herr Alexis vill remain Captain of ze Orbship, but as a hired Captain. I vill become ze Owner of ze Orbship."

"I have a counter offer," replied Eunice. "Brainiac, put it on the screen."

An image of a planet surrounded by Uldan orbital stations appeared on the screen. We were finally making use of Lumara's present — the last trump card I'd acquired before my wife's return. No one makes me presents like this anymore. To the contrary,

---

everyone just tries to take them away.

"We will take you with us on our raid and offer you everything we can find on this planet. With the exception of information — that will be shared among everyone."

Eine began to ponder. Shutting his eyes, he leaned back in his chair and folded his arms across his chest. Another pause followed, but this time it was impossible to call it unpleasant. The word 'tedious' fit much better.

"You have many curious Possessions, Herr Alexis. I accept your Offer. In addition to ze Planet, you must also give me zese Items here — zen, I vill give you ze Answer to your Riddle."

The cunning collector was trying to eke out an extra bonus after all. Eunice tried to barter with him, but the German remained unshakeable. Understanding perfectly well that we needed his knowledge, the collector firmly stood his ground. We were forced to agree to his demands.

Eine swept the items from the table and into his inventory, read out a sequence of numbers and digits, and the third riddle's light lit up green. All that remained was Mercaloun's riddle.

"Brainiac, set course for the system with all the orbital stations. We need to figure out what it is!"

Eine, naturally, came along with us, ordering his pilot to return to his base on his own. Now that's one place I definitely wouldn't mind seeing. A secret planet full of rare items. What could be more valuable for a pirate?

"Exiting hyperspace now. Scanning in progress. Warning! It's our old friend again!"

When he saw the battlesphere flying beside us, the

A CHECK FOR A BILLION

German plastered his face to the screen, his eyes lit up and he bit his lower lip in unconcealed ecstasy. What an odd bunch these collectors.

"Captain, we have received a message: 'Your access to this system must be confirmed!' They are contacting us using Uldan frequencies. There are no responses to my return requests."

The orbital stations remained motionless, but the instruments showed that they maintained a lock on us. A single shot would be enough to send us to respawn.

We exchanged glances. No one had any idea what 'access' in this case meant or where we could get it. No one — but me.

"Brainiac, I'm taking the controls. Everyone buckle up. When I give the go-ahead, everyone man your battle stations."

To emphasize that I was serious, I fastened my armor suit to the seat, becoming effectively a part of the ship. Further clicks sounded around me. Eunice and Eine obediently performed my orders.

I cracked my neck a couple of times. An old habit I'd acquired back in meatspace. Joints don't crack here in the game, yet as far as my physical body was concerned, such stretches always helped loosen my tendons before some important task. Clenching and releasing my fists several times, also more from psychological stress than physiological, I placed my open palm on the orbship's 3D model. Manual pilot mode had been activated.

"Gunner — fire at will. Snake — tend to our shields. Don't let them finish us off. Don't waste any torpedoes. They're useless in this fight. Here we go!"

I abruptly changed course, rushing for the battlesphere. Our taciturn orangutan responded instantly — our blaster cannons came to life, rhythmically pouring deadly plasma at the enemy. If the Uldan was surprised, he didn't show it. Three EM shots hit exactly on target, along with a dozen plasma bolts — without any effect. The battlesphere blinked and reappeared on our starboard. I banked *Warlock* hard, up and to the left. Out of the corner of my eye, I could see the point of space where we had just been turn into a ball of fire that instantly collapsed on itself. The battlesphere wasn't playing around — he had attacked us for real that time. Turn left. Down. Speed a hundred, turn right and abrupt stop. Another fireball bloomed right in front of our prow. If we had kept going, we would've been in the middle of that. Now, right. Down. Use the small moon to screen us and assess the situation.

The battlesphere didn't fall behind, jumping randomly through the system and mercilessly firing all its guns. Our shields coped with the EM and beam cannons, and I managed to dodge the torpedoes. For now, at any rate. The orbital stations watched our waltz indifferently. From the perspective of these colossi, we were doing everything correctly. I was proving my right to land on the planet by fighting an enemy much stronger than us.

Down. To the left. Now reverse thrust! Accelerate to one hundred and bank left. The battlesphere appeared starboard again, forcing me to fly down and to the left, increasing the distance between us. The enemy continued absorbing our cannons' fire without any effect. However, I had realized something, and the realization could be helpful. The battlesphere wasn't as 'unpredictable' as it seemed.

A CHECK FOR A BILLION

I made another sharp bank, seeking to test my hunch — the battlesphere keeps appearing on the flank facing the sun and flies right at us raking us with plasma and torpedoes. As soon as I pull any chaotic maneuver, the enemy teleports and repeats this trick. And there are exactly twenty seconds between the jumps. Enough time to figure out some strategy.

"Brainiac — when I give the order, I want you to launch three cacodemons at this point there. Tell them to eat the enemy ship's most vital systems first. On the count of three! One. Two. Three! Now!"

One nice thing about dealing with the locals was that they never asked too many questions. If the captain orders you to launch three furry toothy creatures into space…you just do it. No one even wondered why I was about to throw away three of the five presents Mercaloun had bestowed on us. Then again all these questions could be saved for later, if there even would be a 'later.' I cut sharply to the right away from the sun, forcing the battlesphere into a blunder. Further evidence that the ship was being piloted by an AI instead of a human. Our opponent vanished and reappeared exactly where I expected him — portside this time. A handful of clicks from my cacodemons. Rushing in pursuit, the battlesphere rammed them with its prow as if they were the ordinary space debris that one encountered all over Galactogon. No captain would pay attention to such trifles, especially in the middle of a dogfight.

Only the cacodemons weren't space debris. And they weren't interested in being scattered. Latching onto the hull like magnets, Mercaloun's minions began to perform their main function: eating whatever was in front of them. Three small holes appeared in the battlesphere and my heart stopped in my chest. Here was the moment of truth. For a few minutes nothing happened, and we continued weaving about as before, but then the enemy ship began to lose speed. This happened so abruptly that you'd think an engine had failed. I doubled back and went on the attack.

The battlesphere wasn't about to give up. A dozen deadly torpedoes rushed in my direction. The enemy's cannons poured plasma without stopping, turning three of our own beam cannons into melted pieces of raq. EM blasts struck my torpedo autoloader. The Uldan knew where to shoot. We had certainly slowed him down, but a direct confrontation still cost me too dearly — I had lost almost all my weapons.

But 'almost all' isn't the same as 'all!'

"Brainiac, we have to survive!" I shouted through the adrenaline, squeezing the maximum out of the ship and adjusting our course. Let's see how the locals respond to this! The gunner did his utmost, resorting to a straightforward single stroke roll for once, but what remained of our blaster cannons wasn't enough — four torpedoes got through our point defenses. Hansa's armor plating held on, however — we took a direct hit.

"Everyone brace for impact!"

"Collision imminent!" warbled Brainiac. "Collision immi — "

The impact of the two ships slamming into each other was so powerful that our chairs' fixtures failed and three bodies clad in armor suits splayed out over the screens, crushing them as if they were apple pie.

"Brainiac, deploy the marine!" I croaked as my medunit

struggled to cope with the debuffs. The rhino's roar could be heard on the other side of Galactogon. He could not move. A terse report from the computer confirmed my hunch:

"Request invalid."

"Recall the minions. I want a damage report ASAP."

I basically no longer had a ship. The hull was crumpled and the engineer would not be able to repair it. Respawning was our only option. The engineer herself, like the gunner, had lost her functionality, becoming a fixed part of the interior. In effect, the two had already gone off to respawn and were only waiting for the ship to do the same. Only the rhino had survived, but there wasn't much use from him. There was half of him left — the other half having been flattened to a pancake.

I heard a groan beside me — Eunice was coming to her senses. Eine lay motionless on the floor. Only the fact that he had not yet become a loot crate suggested that the German was still on this plane of existence. But we could deal with him later.

"Follow me, Eunice!" I croaked, scraping myself off the wall. My armor suit was damaged, but I did not dare change it in the current conditions. All the oxygen had leaked out of *Warlock*. The lower portion of my armor didn't work, so I had to crawl on my hands. Brainiac — who had lost his voice — formed a passage, allowing me to climb into the battlesphere. Three satiated cacodemons passed me, headed in the other direction. The nibblers weren't ecstatic about having to head back when there was still so much free food around, but an order was an order.

The enemy ship was ten times larger than mine, but this hadn't helped him. The orbship's hull had been stronger. We had smashed our way almost to the center of the battlesphere, crushing the reactor and engineering bay in the process. As soon as the air sensors flashed green, I changed my armor suit and grimaced in displeasure — my medunit continued its recovery procedures, pumping me full of drugs to remove debuffs as soon as possible. I was faced with a dilemma — should I go back after Eunice, or forge onward to the bridge deck? Thankfully, a hoarse wheeze in the intercom answered this question. Wheezing is good. Wheezing is a sign of life. If she's alive then she can reach a safe area on her own...

Pushing aside the fallen panels, I made my way onto the bridge. My blasters were ready to show the local captain how serious I was, only there was no one to show anything to. A shimmering crate lay in the captain's chair. The Uldan had not survived the impact.

With trembling hands, I touched the crate. Only six items, but all of them legendries: an armor suit covered in arabesques, a blaster, a mysterious device that resembled a disk, a perfect metal sphere, a perfect metal cube and a key. A thick, solid copper key to a pirate's treasure chest. I remember seeing one like it before in an ancient movie.

Access granted to the Emir system.

I didn't bother celebrating my newest acquisition. There wasn't any time. My gut told me that I had a few minutes left to spare. It wasn't clear until what, but I knew to hurry as fast as I could.

A CHECK FOR A BILLION

"Brainiac, buddy, I need you to make an effort." I pulled out the remote terminal and connected it to the battlesphere's mainframe. "Crack her!"

"Insufficient system resources...Memory defragmentation underway...Decryption process initialized...Insufficient system resources...Resource reallocation underway...Insufficient system resources..."

I felt *Warlock*'s computer strain as hard as it could, trying to complete the task, but the damage was too serious. The AI needed help.

"Can you use my PDA?"

"Negative. Your device uses a different architecture."

"What about the droids' CPUs?"

"Already connected to the core-stack. There are not enough resources. "

"The marine?"

A long pause.

"Using the cryptosaur's system resources will require partitioning his drives and hard-resetting him."

"Do it!"

The rhino's roar bellowed in my headphones. The marine saluted me before dying.

"Hacking under way. Time remaining: 120 seconds."

Two minutes. I took up a defensive position in case anyone came. A battlesphere's capabilities weren't much different than an orbship's. It stood to reason that there would be an engineer, a gunner and a marine onboard as well. The local 'Brainiac' is no doubt already arranging a welcoming party for me.

I was not mistaken.

Exactly a minute later the wall of the bridge deck dissolved, revealing the battlesphere's gunner. Mangled and broken, with only two hands left, he would have posed a serious threat to any other player but me. Had it been anyone else, it would've gone differently. The orangutan aimed his blasters, but I simply tore them away with his arms attached. A legendary pair of manipulators is no joke! I didn't stop there either — zoning out the orangutan with a few precise volleys, I took aim and fired at his center mass. He collapsed to the floor and froze. Thankfully no one from PETA was around to see it. Then again, this was no time for robotic simian rights in space!

You have acquired an unclassified ship. The closest category is an upgraded destroyer. Item class: Legendary. For a detailed description of the ship's properties, see its logbook.

You are the first player to own this ship and may name it as you wish. Current name: N/A.

This vessel is damaged, current functionality: 15%.

There is no planetary binding. If this vessel is destroyed, it will respawn at the nearest ship graveyard.

The battlesphere's crew is inactive.

Exhausted, I collapsed in my new captain's chair. That's it. The deed is done! I have access to the system and Eine will definitely get his planet. I knew exactly what I'd do with the battlesphere — I had wanted to pull off this trick for a long time, but had no suitable vessel. The main thing was to remember to call

A CHECK FOR A BILLION

Hansa: They had promised me quite a bit for a chance to root around inside the innards of a battlesphere. All that remained was to blow this thing to Kingdom Come and take a relaxing break.

"How are you, Eunice?" I asked into the microphone when she answered my call. I hadn't the strength to go back to her. The debuffs kept popping up and my suit's medunit did not have time to cope with them. Apparently, the crash had turned me into a piece of meat, and I was kept alive entirely by my suit's constant ministrations.

"I'm pretty damn bad," the girl snapped.

"If you're angry, then you're alive. What shall we name the battlesphere?"

A pause.

"You…captured…her?"

"Uh-huh. Eunice, I'm tired and I'd like to respawn as soon as possible. I need a name. Will you suggest one or are you okay flying on the *Nebuchadnezzar*?"

"I don't understand…"

"Honey, I'm giving you the battlesphere!" I said. "After all, I wouldn't trade Brainiac for any other AI!"

"*Captain…I am touched…We are touched…All of us…Thank you!*"

"Spare me the waterworks, Brainiac. Save your energy. Eunice, I need a name!"

"*Lexus*! I want the name to be *Lexus*!" my wife blurted out.

"I get your hint, but you should know that I never like to give the same present twice," I laughed and entered the new name. "Brainiac, update *Lexus'* maps and download her specifications. I want to understand how she manages to jump so deftly. We need that capability too."

"Affirmative."

A loading bar appeared before my eyes. As I had figured, the battlesphere turned out to be a powerful but ancient ship with the typical Uldan crew complement. The coordinate grid was very different from what we were used to — just as it was when I first got my *Warlock.* The sync procedure was supposed to fix that.

"What about Eine?" I suddenly remembered our passenger.

"He's alive, but unconscious. His debuffs will last another half hour. I don't know when he'll come to. It is surprising that he is still in the game."

"All right, let him rest. Maybe he'll be more talkative next time."

The update had reached almost one hundred percent when a new system notification knocked the air out my lungs. Eunice's scream, the annoying calls to my PDA, Brainiac's report that the update was complete and that we were ready to self-destruct — I heard none of it. I just sat there and stared at the message. Self-destruction was the last thing I needed right now.

You have lost ownership of Blood Island. Current owner: [~Liberium~] Aalor.

CHAPTER TWENTY-ONE

THE DIFFERENCE BETWEEN BEING A PROFESSIONAL and an amateur is knowing when it's time to ignore one's emotions. Want to make a living playing games? Then remember that the virtual world is there for work, not for pleasure. No attachments. No desire for virtual objects or possessions. Otherwise, your problems will be countless.

I didn't know myself when I'd stopped being a professional. Blood Island was my home. Brainiac and *Warlock*'s crew were my family. Now the enemy had invaded my home and taken it from me. Neither my anger, nor my desire to find the insolent bastard and tear him to pieces as quickly as possible interfered with my consideration of an even more important issue: Who the hell had given him our coordinates? On his own, Aalor could have looked for my planet until the second coming of Space Jesus to no avail.

There were only two options. The first was that a tracking beacon had been planted on *Warlock* or in Eunice's fighter during our stay on Belket. The second was that Alonso and Lucille had ratted us out. I preferred the first option a lot more, even though it left me without an object to take my anger out on. Making an effort, I rid myself of any notion that my friends might have betrayed me.

"Lex, Eine called. He is conscious again, but he cannot move. He only has enough medicine to last him thirty minutes, then he'll respawn. The German requests that we do anything we can to keep him with us."

Eunice had been immobilized as well, yet she still managed to get through to me. I took a few deep breaths, soothing my burning nerves. I had to come to my senses and think. As if hearing my prayers, a message from Aalor appeared on my PDA:

"You can go ahead and delete your character. Take your losses and count your winnings!"

Kids are childish when they hold a grudge, but adults are much worse, especially when it comes to gloating after they've had their revenge. And Aalor had something to gloat about. In addition to my planet, he had captured my A-class fighter and all my reserves of raq, elo and every other resource I'd been hoarding. Even the inventory I didn't want to carry around in my ship's holds was now his. At the same time, Aalor hadn't been too lazy to call and then send a message when I didn't pick up. I mean, is this middle school or what? But I did feel better. I'm not the only 'professional' around here. An officer of '~Liberium~' wants to start a war? So let's have us a war then.

"Hello, Herr Eine! Yes, I was out, just like you. We will need a transport to deliver us to the shipyard. Could you arrange it? Coordinates? I'm sending them as we speak."

Respawning was now out of the question, but that doesn't mean I'm ready to give up and just go with the flow or whatever. The German called his subordinates and then called me back:

"Herr Alexis, we have a Lot of Problems. Ze rescue Party vill take forty Minutes of Flight. I vill not survive such a long Time. You must come up vit a different Solution. I have ordered a Transport to come for us as a backup Plan."

Yes, indeed, the problem is that transports were rather slow, especially the ones big enough to accommodate us in their holds. I looked at my screens in confusion, unsure of what to do next. We were at an empty location at the very edge of the system with absolutely nothing interesting around us. There was not a single soul nearby, only six Uldan orbital stations, which remained indifferent to the battlesphere's destruction.

"Brainiac," I ordered out of sheer helplessness, "transmit the following in Uldan: 'Mayday! We require assistance. We are in need of urgent repairs! Our ships are damaged and have no planetary bindings. We will not be able to reach the repair docks on our own. We do have access to this system!'"

"Response received: Repair is available at a cost of six million tons of raq."

I almost choked when I heard this reply. Our way out was right there under our noses and here I was reinventing the wheel! The price was steep, but I wasn't in a position to bargain.

"Ask them whether we can pay them the credit equivalent at the current exchange rate? And if not, tell them that we can deliver the raq within twelve hours while repairs are still in progress."

"They do accept payment in GC. A transport has been dispatched to recover us."

Glory be to all the devs! They didn't bother nerding out and cooking up some special payment system for the Uldans. The hull shuddered and I heard a metal screeching.

"We have received an invoice for GC 300,000,000."

"Pay it and let's go get patched up!"

I don't even want to think about how the orbital stations have access to Galactogon's banking system. Let's just assume it's a feature. The shaking stopped and was replaced by a low roar and tremor. Suddenly, a spherical droid appeared on one of the battlesphere's screens and asked in the common tongue:

"Your clarification is required. What is to be done with the ships? Shall they be split up or repaired as a single vessel in their current, integrated form?"

Now this was curious. The Uldans had never let on that they spoke the common tongue before. Coupled with their access to the banking system, it's clear that someone had been working with these orbital stations.

"I'd like the ships split up."

"You have paid the repair price for only one ship. Your payment does not include the separation and recovery of the second vessel."

"Send me the invoice and I'll pay it. I have three wounded casualties on board. We need medical assistance."

"Medical care is not covered by the pay…"

A CHECK FOR A BILLION

"Hold up! Let me just ask a simple question: Can I deposit a billion credits to an escrow account so that you can simply withdraw whatever you need each time, without asking me any questions?"

"That is acceptable. We have issued the invoice."

I heard the sharp squeal of a circular saw spinning up and the battlesphere's bridge deck filled with sparks. The repairs had begun without any further ado. As soon as the hole in the hull was big enough, a giant mechanical arm entered the cabin, pulled me out and took off my armor suit, which was basically junk by this point. I managed to catch a glimpse of Eunice and Eine being extracted from the orbship in a similar way. After that, we were moved to the medbay. The medcapsule's lid closed shut and an alert appeared before my eyes:

Your condition is critical. Time until full recovery: 3 hours. Would you like to watch a movie?

Engrossed in a clever comedy, the time flew by and I even rued having to return to a gameworld full of troubles and tribulations — one that on top of everything now also had a crazed, vengeful Aalor running about it. When I did come out, Eunice and Eine were already waiting for me. Whole, healthy and extremely curious about their new surroundings.

"Welcome to the automated Uldan orbital station," the spherical droid greeted us again, hovering at eye level. "We will need another 24 hours to repair your ships. We recommend you relax in our humanoid reception suite. It is designed for your race."

GALACTOGON BOOK THREE

"Can we walk around the station?" asked Eunice, probing how much of a leash we were really on.

"Your access level is insufficient for walking around the station," said the orb in an utterly neutral tone and then added: "Violators will be terminated."

"We would like to visit the planet," Eine tried another angle.

"Your request is acceptable. Would you like to use the surface shuttle?"

Why of course we would! Less than ten minutes later we stepped out on the surface. The orbital station allocated us a special transport, assuring us that we could return whenever we liked. Now that's service! Though it did cost a penny or two, but that's a different issue.

New planet discovered: Zubrail.

You are not allowed to claim this planet or assign it a second name. This planet is reserved for game scenarios.

Achievement unlocked: Explorer (Rank II)

A portion of the resources mined on this planet will belong to you (current value: 9%, distributed in equal shares among players Eine, Nurse and Surgeon)

The landing dock of our new mysterious planet was in the middle of a dense forest. As soon as we left the circular platform, an Uldan glided down from the thick canopy.

"You're not welcome here! Go away!" The winged creature first addressed us in his guttural Uldan tongue, but when we failed to understand anything, he switched to the common one and repeated his message. "This planet is off-limits for visitors. You don't have permission to be here."

The lower branches around us shook, parting to reveal five rhino marines. The branches higher up set in motion as well, as the orange silhouettes of orangutan gunners flashed among the leafage.

"Forgive us for the disturbance…We need help," Eunice said in a pleading tone, but the Uldan refused to hear her out:

"That does not concern us. Get out!"

His haughty glance left me in no doubt that the winged creature harbored some kind of grudge against us. Although I would be offended too, if he had taken my orbship from me. Asking for forgiveness seemed useless, so I just pulled out the cylinder and held it out in front of me.

"We will go, but first hear us out! This is a gift from Belmarad. It contains something that will allow us to rid Galactogon of the Zatrathi forever. It's not we who need help, but the entire galaxy!"

Sounded a bit dramatic, but it did the trick: The winged creature flinched at the name of the dark lord.

"You're lying! Belmarad is locked away in a secure prison! No one can escape from there! Neither Belmarad, nor anyone else!"

"Your secure prison no longer exists. The Precians currently have the body of Belmarad. Your dark lord succumbed to an ordinary parasite. The same kind that's enslaved hundreds of thousands of your brothers. I call them brainworms — they call themselves Relays. They are the ones who relay Her will."

The Uldan flinched again. Even though I hadn't mentioned any names, he understood exactly who I was talking about.

"What does it contain?" The ancient asked, nodding at the cylinder uncertainly.

"The coordinates of their homeworld. If we manage to get to it, we can destroy it. Then the Zatrathi will stop being reborn."

"You don't have anything that can kill a planetary spirit!"

"How about the Vengeance?" I whipped out the Lira, Lora, Lara as I spoke these words.

"You think you can kill a spirit with that pea shooter?" The Uldan smiled scornfully. "Why that's just a Vraxis toy. The bugs thought they could harm us with it! It is true, the Vengeance can annihilate a planet, but the spirit will remain intact. The ship graveyard will remain untouched. The rebirth point will remain untouched too. Nothing will change! Why should I help you? Get off my planet! You don't have permission to be here!"

I realized that the Uldan wasn't lying and that the Vengeance really couldn't hurt the Zatrathi. Destroy a ship or two — yes. Something more important — nope. No wonder the Precian adviser had hinted that they wanted to use the Vengeance for their own purposes. In their fight against the Qualians, not the Zatrathi.

Oh! The Qualians!

"I know where I can find a weapon that will destroy a planetary spirit! How about the KRIEG?" The butterfly's face didn't change at all, yet Eine, standing beside me, started with surprise. "A weapon that is capable of annihilating everything within a radius of two hyperminutes. It leaves nothing behind. It is a forbidden

A CHECK FOR A BILLION

---

weapon created by my contemporaries."

"Show me this 'KRIEG' of yours and I will give you the answer to the last riddle of Belmarad. Now get out! If you leave the shuttle dock again, you shall be destroyed," barked the Uldan and spreading his wings, flew away.

New mission available: One Last Shot. Description: Get the KRIEG and show it to the Uldan on planet Zubrail. Reward: The answer to the fourth riddle of Belmarad's cylinder.

"My ship and crew need a binding to Zubrail!" I yelled in his wake. "Give us a chance to stay!"

"You dare ask me for favors after you captured my ship?!" The Uldan did an about-face in midflight and swooped down on me. His rainbow wings grew dark and he began to resemble Belmarad.

"Twenty million per person," I refused to be cowed. "Ten for the ship. You do business with other empires, which means you need cash. I'm ready to pay it."

"Twenty and ten?!" The Uldan darkened even more. Thin sparks of electricity began to discharge between his wings. My armor suit's sensors began to warn me of a hazardous EM field in the area. "You dare offer me pennies?"

"Fine. Two hundred and one hundred!" I raised my bid.

"Four hundred per person, six hundred per ship! Right this instant!" the Uldan announced.

I cringed but didn't dare argue. The planet was protected by Uldan orbital stations and so was perfect for a lone player. Especially considering that the number two guild in the game was after me.

"We accept your price!" Eunice understood the gravity of the situation and beat me to the punch. I suppose she was worried that I might get too greedy and refuse. The sum was immense of course, but we would lose even more without the binding.

Your current binding has been updated to Planet Zubrail. Your vessels will bind automatically upon repair.

"You don't even realize what a fool you are! Instead of ramming other people's ships..." the Uldan turned on me but then cut himself short. It was unseemly of this ancient creature to indulge his anger. Having measured us with an unhappy look, he again made to leave, but this time Eine stopped him, rudely shoving his tablet under the Uldan's nose:

"I vould like to make an Offer to his vinged Excellency. I believe zat zis Object vill interest you."

"Where did you get that?" the Uldan asked with open alarm, almost snatching the tablet from the German's hands.

"I vould prefer to discuss zis in private." Eine cast us a sidelong glance. "I am but a Guest on ze Orbship *Varlock.* I am not a Crew Member of Herr Surgeon."

"Please follow me. Welcome to Zubrail, Human Eine." The Uldan amiably pointed the German towards a path that appeared at his command.

"Herr Alexis, I consider our Terms fully discharged and our Obligations to each other fully satisfied. It vas a Pleasure to spend Time vit you in Galactogon."

A CHECK FOR A BILLION

Eine followed the butterfly, while Eunice and I turned back to the shuttle dock. The marines and the gunners didn't back off, scrupulously making sure that we did not wander off our path back.

"At least we have a binding again," Eunice said by way of encouragement, pretending that she didn't care about Eine's business with the butterfly. This only deepened my disappointment with our bargaining failure.

"And two ships," I agreed, and then switched to the subject I'd been avoiding. "Here's what I think...There'll be an ambush waiting for us on Blood Island."

"Do you have a plan of attack?"

"I wouldn't quite call it attack," I sighed, "so much as an elaborate suicide."

"I don't know what you mean, but I have your back." Eunice called the shuttle and turned to me. "We didn't start this war! It is time to show that those who turn up their noses, first and foremost, show everyone around them just how full of snot they are."

We returned to the orbital station, finally finding ourselves alone. No matter how raw our feelings were, everything dissolved as soon as we were in each other's arms again. We did not waste the next 24 hours idly. And we weren't the only ones who were busy either...

"Herr Alexis, I vould like to ask for your Help. You vill do me a small Favor, no?" As soon as our ships appeared outside the orbital station, Eine was ready to go. When I realized what had happened, my eyebrows shot up to my hairline and stayed there for some time. The cunning German, having managed to encounter a real living Uldan, had somehow gotten an orbship from him. A sparkling orb hung some distance from mine, waiting for its map updates. Eine's ship had the same problem as Eunice's battlesphere.

Still, my surprise didn't prevent me from bargaining:

"I don't mind helping, but I'd like a favor in exchange. Where should I look for the KRIEG?"

The German fell silent for a moment.

"Herr Alexis, you must understand zat zis is not my Secret to reveal."

"Herr Eine, you know perfectly well why I need the KRIEG. Can you guarantee that the Zatrathi Queen will never set her sights on your own planet? Everything that you have accumulated during your time in Galactogon will disappear. The Delvians thought their capital was safe. Where are the Delvians now?"

A displeased wheezing in the microphone indicated to me that I had found a sore spot in the collector's heart and was even now rubbing salt into it. The German had already considered this possibility. Eine replied slowly, as if weighing every word:

"It is true zat under critical Circumstances I may reveal certain Secrets concerning others. The Qualians are not in favor in Galactogon. I vill give you ze coordinates and vit zem ze Opportunity to find ze Answers. Get ready to vrite zem down."

How the collector had obtained top secret Qualian information was yet another mystery about this odd character. Everyone chooses his own way of playing the game. If Eine is a fan of rare items and information, then who can blame him? The important thing is that he is prepared to pay for what he wants.

Eunice busied herself with studying her new ship and

agreed to help the German as a way to work on her own skills. Meanwhile, I hurried to my favorite captain's chair.

"Brainiac, give me a systems report."

Unfortunately, the Uldan repair base hadn't added anything in the course of repairs. Pedantic, like any other computer program, it restored the orbship exactly as it had been. The only bonus was access to the station's parts store. Which we'd have to pay for, of course. Brainiac had already analyzed the available upgrades and made a list of about 150 items marked 'required yesterday.' The cost of several hundred billion did not bother him at all. According to the computer, if I gave him what he asked for, our ship's class equivalent would grow from the current destroyer to a cruiser. We could then become Galactogon's assassins — capable of killing any single target, aside from the Queen, on our own. The Queen had truly scared Brainiac straight.

"Lex, I'm ready!" It took Eunice five hours to get used to her battlesphere. We tore around the system, practicing offensive and defensive maneuvers. Her ship did not have reflectors, but this was more than compensated by its other capabilities.

"Set course for Blood Island."

I had no doubt that several cruisers were waiting for me there. Two, maybe three. I was counting on the fact that more than a day had passed since I'd lost the planet and the players guarding it were losing focus. Aalor wouldn't risk signing out to reality to take a break. He would be there, personally leading the cruisers if only to prove his right to the title of leader and top player.

His only problem was that he was up against more than one little orbship.

"Emerging from hyperspace in three…Two…One. Two large targets identified. Multiple EM cannons tracking us. Our hyperdrive is being disrupted. Two hundred torpedoes detected. Their speed is 70% of ours. These are ordinary torpedoes."

If the Liberium players were taken aback when they saw two ships instead of one, they didn't let on. They attacked as soon as we appeared. They had been waiting. Getting ready. Making plans.

Well, it was time to strike back!

"I'm going in!" yelled Eunice and disappeared from my screen — only to reappear on the flank of one of the cruisers. A broadside of thirty torpedoes, and the battlesphere vanished again and reappeared next to another ship. *Lexus* repeated the maneuver while her gunner opened up against the incoming fighters.

It was my turn to make a move. Encountering the torpedoes was not in my plans for this evening. Shooting at the quickest fighters, I rushed away from the system, leaving Eunice alone with the cruisers.

"What the hell is this?! You goddamn hacker!" Some player's indignant voice came on the public comms as soon as the battlesphere jumped back to the first cruiser, only on its other side. Another broadside of thirty torpedoes followed by a jump back to the second cruiser. *Lexus* only had about three hundred torpedoes onboard, yet its torpedo manufacturing system could pop a new one out once every minute. Eunice only had to make sure to feed in the raq — and she had plenty of that in her holds.

I put enough distance between me and the torpedoes to be

safe, while my gunner kept the enemy fighters at bay with single dragadiddles. Having finished with the cruisers, Eunice returned to me. Sixty torpedoes weren't enough to destroy the giant vessels, but they did suffice to wreck the ships' engines.

"This is Pirate Surgeon speaking," I said over the public channel. "You have invaded my system. You can now pay me an inconvenience fee and be on your way. In exchange, you'll be able to keep your cruisers at their current level. Otherwise, I will be happy to continue my attack and send your tubs to the nearest graveyard, where they belong. I will give you a minute to make your decision!"

Instead of answering, the cruiser *Render* began to drift forward. She was using only two of her four engines, but she moved ahead confidently and with the clear intention of punishing us. I had no doubt whatsoever who her captain was. What's going on in Aalor's head anyway? None of this has anything to do with logic and common sense. He was clearly in the thrall of his emotions...

Suddenly, another interesting idea occurred to me. I realized that Blood Island was lost to me forever. A planet whose coordinates have been made public can never serve as a reliable base. And that meant that I could take a risk. It was a childish idea and Eunice was unlikely to approve of it, but heck, he started it first!

"All you know is how to hide behind your crew, Captain Aalor. Let's see how you fight without their help! I — Major Surgeon of Jolly Roger 2.0 — challenge you to a duel. One on one! A fight until our deaths. There was a fighter on Blood Island. If you don't mind I'll use it for myself. You can take one of your own. Everyone else can wait and watch. If I win, you go on your way and return to me everything you took from me. If you win — I'll let you have Blood Island once and for all and we forget all about this."

How I love nobility! It was a pretty speech uttered in a solemn voice and even with a hint of anguish, as if I could barely restrain myself from the turmoil inside of me...But basically, unlike Aalor, I wasn't risking a thing. He could not refuse. Because the price of refusing — above all else — was a loss of reputation. A loss to his very name. Now, if I were in his place, I'd let myself get killed just so I could start preparing for the next battle. But Aalor won't do that. I'd be willing to wager my orbship on that.

"Clear the system," came the reply. "Go ahead and pick up that fighter. No one will stop you."

If words could burn, my ears would already be charred. Aalor's voice was quiet, but full of cold determination. Were there any daisies growing within hearing distance of it, I bet they'd wilt in a second.

No one interfered with my landing. An entire defensive line had been set up on the planet's surface, and now these players — some scornfully, some with curiosity — watched me pass among them. Once I was in my fighter, I set up a connection with Brainiac.

"If I die, head for Zubrail. We'll meet there. Do you understand?"

"Captain, maybe we can take this guy together?"

"This is my fight. Do not interfere. Eunice, that goes for you too."

"I haven't even said anything," my wife objected. "Everyone gets to go crazy in his own way. I don't need to involve myself in how you want to do it. I will make sure everything is fair. Hope you

A CHECK FOR A BILLION

fry him, hun!"

Eunice's faith in my abilities was inspiring, but only to a point. I hadn't had much of a chance to fly a fighter in my gaming career, so I was basically betting that Aalor was a mediocre pilot — more so than me. 'Cause if he really knew how to handle his little interceptor, I'd be toast.

Two small ships stopped opposite each other. We could have started at any moment, yet we waited. The one who blinked first now would lose — even if he won the dogfight later.

"Captaaaain!" droned Brainiac, tearing me away from my staredown.

Eunice was a bit more informative:

"Lex, run! As quickly as you can! The Queen is here!"

I slowly turned my head to the right, where, a black shape was slowly but surely eclipsing the countless stars.

"Attention everyone — that's the Zatrathi Queen! Get out of here!" I screamed into the common channel, already turning my ship and opening the throttle all the way. The duel can wait. "Brainiac, jump to Zubrail! That's an order!"

"You're not going anywhere!" came Aalor's cry. His fighter was already on my tail, firing from all its cannons. The Blood Island system began to unravel — the Queen had already devoured the outermost planet and as a result, even the blasters' fire was now being pulled along unexpected trajectories. Instead of flying in a straight line, the plasma skewed in the direction of the Queen's bottomless maw.

"Cut it out, Aalor! We'll deal with it later!" I dodged the shots reflexively and my fighter did as ordered, banking sloppily. Like molasses! Yeah — Brainiac wasn't around to correct my mistakes.

"No — we'll deal with it now!" Liberium's officer didn't have anything to lose. Even though both cruisers had already turned tail and were steaming away as fast as they could, it was clear that they were doomed. If they didn't jump to hyperspace now, they would be lost.

Meanwhile, my right engine flared up — Aalor had adjusted his aim to account for the gravitational deflection. It was beginning to dawn on me that not only was my opponent one of the best cruiser captains around, but he was also a pretty competent fighter pilot. My attempts to juke him off my tail did no good — Aalor remained on my heels like a shadow.

"Eunice, get him off me!"

"Nah, hubby! You got yourself into this mess. You can get yourself out of it. I'm just the referee. Your ship is safe."

Well at least that's something. The Queen reached the second planet and the sun began to warp, dousing Blood Island with its flames. A rather unpleasant rebirth for the ground troops down there. Aalor hit my reactor and my speed dropped by half. I slammed the throttle to zero, braking and forcing Aalor to overshoot. This maneuver cost me the other engine and ten holes in the left wing. In fact, I couldn't fly anywhere anymore — all I could do was rotate in place. But hey, at least I could still pew pew to my heart's content!

"You missed, you oaf!" Aalor snapped when my two bursts of plasma flew so far from his ship that even I was taken aback. I can't say I've ever seen plasma behave so unpredictably before. "What, is this game too hard when you have to deal with an actual

A CHECK FOR A BILLION

---

player instead of some NPC? I'll take you for everything you got! Your planet, your ship, your name! You'll end up the butt of a joke and the whole galaxy will be doing the laughing!"

Aalor's fighter turned and came to a stop in front of me. My nemesis had understood that I was helpless and decided to revel in his victory. Instead of immediately sending me to respawn, he decided to work on his own self-esteem a little. First he shot off my right wing. Then the left. Then the rear stabilizers. I took advantage of the oxygen in my fighter to quickly swap my armor suit for a cheap spare. I wasn't about to make Aalor a present of my nice one.

Meanwhile, the Queen had reached the cruisers. They never did get a chance to enter hyperspace. One of the tentacles grabbed both vessels and dragged them to its maw, which was large enough to fit several planets, let alone a couple of ships. Having changed my suit, I realized that a myriad eyes were suddenly looking at me and felt goose bumps run down my back. The ravenous space leviathan had noticed us — the two metal fleas — and grown inquisitive. Something told me that the Queen had decided that even two dust motes like us might be tastier than an empty planet.

Aalor stopped shooting and burst into another tirade against me. I wasn't sure who this speech was for, since all the players had already either escaped or died. Even Eunice had retreated, leaving the two of us alone with the Queen. A tentacle shot out in our direction and I fired my reverse thrusters, pulling back. It didn't go so well. Aalor even began to laugh at my floundering as if the Queen's sudden interference in our duel did not concern him.

He was still cackling when the tentacle came whipping back and pierced his fighter, impaling it on one of its myriad spires. I didn't get off cleanly either. No matter how hard I tried to escape, the Queen was faster. Surviving miraculously, I flipped the fighter vertically at the last moment, turning my cockpit away from the tentacle. My pilot's seat had come undone and as I flipped I went flying into the hull. I was saved by the fact that the hull had already cracked. A caustic fog of dissolved raq began seeping in — it seems that the Queen's tentacles were covered with a volatile acid. I unfastened my suit and zoomed upward like Superman. Or, rather, like Iron Man. He's the one who likes flying around space in a tin can. Aalor was nowhere to be found.

The tentacle that had destroyed him returned just as quickly, aiming for its new target. The Queen had swallowed its fancy appetizer and was now heading for the main dish — Blood Island.

I remained hanging amid the asteroids and stars, watching the Queen. An unpleasant feeling of nausea was growing somewhere deep inside me. Gradually, it enveloped and penetrated into every nook and cranny of my consciousness, causing my gag reflex to go off and my throat to spasm. The Zatrathi Queen was horrible not only because of her appearance, which you'd get used to sooner or later — but rather because of her inevitability. The Queen was an unstoppable destructive force. There was nothing in Galactogon that could oppose her. Sooner or later she would reach even the most distant star system and the game's lore would come to an end.

A CHECK FOR A BILLION

Although, why do I say that there's nothing to oppose her? I've got one such item in my inventory. I spent a long time thinking about whom I should call. Vargen and Ash were out of the question. I wasn't about to do either one of those jerks a favor. Kiddo — more of a no than a yes. First I'd need to figure out what our relationship had become after I'd rescued Wit-Verr. Gammon didn't have the skills I needed. Eine? He was useful naturally, but not in this line of work. Ah! I know who can help me!

"Valmont, hello! Wanna become the hero of all of Galactogon?"

A true pilot, a real ace — not some delinquent orbship pirate. He arrived fifteen minutes later, giving me the time to examine in detail what happens when the Abyss enters a system. Planets were consumed first, then large asteroids. When nothing remains and the system's star goes crazy from the presence of an extraneous massive body, the Abyss turns its attention to the dessert.

I was wrong — the players' ships were no delicacy for the Abyss. They were more of a snack. It was stars that were the creature's main treat and dish. The Queen even closed her eyes in pleasure as the deformed sun disappeared in her mouth, illuminating the insides for a few moments. I'm willing to bet Eunice will give me a kiss for getting that on video.

Having finished her meal, the Queen froze. Her tentacles gathered under her body, her eyes closed, and she began to slowly drift away, digesting her food. That was when the scout popped up next to me.

"God — damn! What the hell is that? Is the corp's art

department hiring acidheads again?"

Valmont's reaction was understandable, but he was wasting time. My time. The Queen's eyes opened, and she stared at the new food with interest. I jetted over to the scout's airlock and dived inside. As soon as the doors were closed, inertia ruthlessly pressed me into the bulkhead. The scout began to accelerate out of the system at full thrust.

"Well shit! Are you sick in the head, Surgeon? Wasn't there some easier way to kill yourself?"

I crawled over to the captain's cabin and collapsed into an empty chair. Valmont had arrived alone. The Queen reached for us with a tentacle, but the experienced pilot had no trouble avoiding it. There was no chase — I guess we didn't seem very tasty.

"Why didn't you tell me I'd get your Star Hero medal posthumously? I never signed up to be a kamikaze..."

"Turn around. See her? That's the Queen. She's got two dozen tentacles, every one of them long and quick..."

"Yeah, I noticed. Wish my ex had some like that," the pilot laughed, distracting me.

"Ugh. Skip the personal details. Focus. Your job here is to dodge the tentacles and land me on her body. Preferably in the ship."

"Oh, so it's like a kink of yours," Valmont quipped and suddenly added quite seriously: "Tell me again how helping you pull off this elaborate suicide will make me the hero of the galaxy?"

"Because if you and I do it right, the Queen will die," I said simply. "I have no idea whether she has a binding or not, I don't know whether she'll respawn or what, but I do know that we'll be

---

the first ones to gank the Zatrathi Queen…That's gotta be worth something, don't you think?"

"Okay, but you're going to need more than a dingy blaster. You got some kind of doomsday device you want to tell me about?"

I nodded and pointed to the Queen. She had stirred again, apparently done digesting my star system and was now about to set off for a new goal.

"You'll need some time, right?" Valmont asked thoughtfully and took out a cigar: "Want one?"

"Why not?" I didn't smoke in reality, but this was one of those occasions. "A couple of seconds should do. The doomsday device is easy to set off. The important thing is to get to her torso."

Valmont helped me light the cigar and I took the first puff of my life. Nothing happened. No coughing, no irritation, and most of all and most depressingly — no buzz.

"Well, it's not real tobacco obviously — but it'll help you relax. And by the way, if you take a drag like that in meatspace, you'll cough up your lungs. This ain't a cigarette, cowboy. Now hang on. Turbulence incoming. This scout ain't so quick, but we should make it. This is the last time I help out a lunatic."

The scout came around and headed for the Queen. Something strange was happening to her. She had splayed her tentacles, as if to embrace something, and we saw several discharges of electricity slip along their lengths.

"Look, she's getting ready to jump!" Valmont concluded. "What a monster! She can jump into hyperspace and everything!"

"Hurry up! We have to make it! The tentacles are occupied!"

"Well get your doomsday device ready! We're about to come along her spine like on a roller coaster!"

The Lara crystal, the Lora coupler unit and the Lira pedestal appeared in my lap. The engineer had placed the crystal in an insulating case, which allowed me to carry the Lara on me. The pilot glanced over at my doomsday device, without ceasing to maneuver between the spires that dotted the Queen. The way we were spinning and whirling, I knew I had made the right decision. Valmont was the only pilot in the galaxy who could fly in these conditions.

"Doesn't look very scary. Is it some kind of doomsday trophy? Wait…don't answer that! We're almost there! On the count of three! One! Two! Now!"

The scout's hull jerked, there was a metallic screeching and showers of sparks and utter chaos erupted all around us. But that wasn't the worst part. I did not take into account the size of the Queen's mass — and I paid dearly for it as her gravity crushed me into my seat. The Queen's gravitational force was enormous. My armor suit's servomotors whirred and whined trying to cope with the strain. Sparks began to shoot out of my own body as my screens began to blink from the load of the energy vortices. My medunit couldn't keep up with my injuries and a veil of haze descended over my vision. Well, this had all the hallmarks of a true heroic deed! Overcoming everything, I had to do the impossible.

Am I a hero? But of course! Galactogon told me as much as soon as I managed to bring my hands together and push the button that freed the crystal from its casing…

A CHECK FOR A BILLION

You have activated the Vengeance!

The Vengeance Set has been destroyed. You have accomplished what none of Galactogon's scientists could. You have destroyed the ancient Vraxis super weapon which could turn any battle in their favor. Your rapport with all factions has decreased.

Further down, in small print came something like a footnote:

Achievement unlocked: Hero of Galactogon. You have sent the Zatrathi Queen to rebirth. The Zatrathi must retreat and Galactogon has received a month-long respite from hostilities. Use it to the utmost to prepare for the invasion's second wave. Relations with all empires have changed. Everyone despises you, yet respects your achievements. Your access to the Hansa Arms Corporation has been restored.

Contact any empire for a reward from the hands of the emperor.

Your rapport with Jolly Roger 2.0 has grown. Speak to Captain Wit-Verr.

CHAPTER TWENTY-TWO

"C'MON! REALLY? IS THERE REALLY NOTHING?"

Brainiac scanned the space around us once again and confirmed the unpleasant news: 'Empty.' Only half an hour had passed since the Queen's demise. Either someone managed to grab the loot crate or she never dropped one to begin with.

"Lex, get over here!" Eunice called me. "There's like a giant pajama party in space going down over here!"

She was out in the region that had once been the edge of my star system. I flew up closer. A small forcefield sphere was hanging in the middle of nowhere. It was full of players dressed in nothing but white pajamas. There were so many of them that they were like bugs fumbling in a jar. Periodically someone would get shoved or kicked hard enough to fly out of the sphere. It took only

A CHECK FOR A BILLION

a couple of seconds for the player to become a corpse in the open vacuum of space. The odd thing was that the bodies left no loot crates behind.

"Brainiac, catch me one!" I ordered.

The players were flying out all the time, so this was no difficult task. Brainiac brought a random player onboard and quickly placed him into the medcapsule to nurse him to health. While I was waiting for our guest to recover, I watched about five hundred players kick the bucket.

"Th-thank you!" said the engineer from *Render*. "Th-that's my th-third rebirth. It ju-just keeps happening again and a-again."

The Zatrathi Queen had once again played a nasty trick on the players. Not only had she gobbled up all their gear and equipment without a trace, she'd also destroyed Blood Island's planetary spirit. However, the respawn point had remained and was now regurgitating the combined crews of two cruisers. Obviously the respawn location couldn't accommodate all the victims in the area and they were now simply cycling: They'd respawn in the center of the sphere, gradually be pushed out to its outer periphery and then be cast out to respawn again in the center of this infernal bubble. Gustavo, the engineer, had made three such journeys before I rescued him. On the other hand, the players who had been on Blood Island and had been incinerated by its sun, were now safe at home.

The worst part was that these prisoners couldn't even call anyone. The mass of bodies was so dense that no one could reach for their PDA. I looked at the respawn point. There was little space on my orbship, yet the battlesphere could easily accommodate several hundred passengers. I'm no altruist of course, but sometimes it's worth abandoning the ordinary pirate principles.

"No way!" Eunice cut me off, upon hearing my idea. "I'm not about to save those who came here for one purpose — to kill you and take your ship."

"They're just ordinary players, Eunice. They were simply doing as Aalor had ordered them."

"Oh sure — make sure to spill a tear for them too. That'll move me! What a bunch for you to pity. Lex — they knew perfectly well what they were doing and where they were going! No, I don't want to help them. They have a guild, let it help them. If they can't call home, let them call tech support and complain. This does not concern us."

"Eunice..."

"Eunice what? I've been Eunice for thirty years! If you want to help them — go ahead! Don't count on me! But, before you hang up — tell me: If you were in that situation, would someone from Liberium help you?"

My wife disconnected, leaving me on my own. She was right of course. No one would lift a finger for me. In fact, they'd probably take a selfie and share it around for the lulz.

There was just this one thing that kept me from washing my hands of the situation. It wasn't my conscience. Or the promise of a reward. Or even just wanting to show off in front of everyone, showing them what a good guy I was. No...

There's simply what's right and what's wrong.

These players were in trouble and there was no one else to help them right now. They could not even sign out of the game,

A CHECK FOR A BILLION

since you couldn't do so while inside a respawn area and the desperate few seconds of tumbling through space before dying made it very difficult to navigate the UI's menus. The players would naturally make the corporation pay for allowing such a bug, but that would come later.

"Vargen, this is Surgeon. Your men need help. Here are their coordinates."

My orbship managed to accommodate 150 players. I would have never imagined what survivors are capable of. As soon as they had caught their breath, they huddled up next to their mates and accepted more rescues onto their shoulders — effectively returning to the same hellish situation they'd just escaped from in order to save more of their fellows. I could not provide everyone with medical care and many had to bear serious injuries and a myriad debuffs. But everyone tried to survive. The lack of binding meant that if they left the game before they reached a planetary spirit, they would respawn here all over again.

Bit by bit, the number of people inside the respawn bubble decreased and the players stopped jostling each other. Half an hour later, five cruisers descended on us all at once. Vargen did not trust me. Brainiac warned us that the cruisers had locked on, but they did not open fire. Once Liberium saw the situation, they began to evacuate the trapped players.

Meanwhile, I received a request for a video conference. I found myself staring at a screen with a battered Aalor, Vargen and a couple of sullen players around them, who I figured were the cruisers' captain.

"Surgeon, you bastard, I curse the day you showed up in

Galactogon! Three cruisers in three days!"

"Well, I'd love to take credit for all three, but I'm only responsible for *Inevitable*. You can talk to Aalor about the other two. He's the one who led them to the Queen's maw."

"You destroyed our engines!" one of the gloomy captains objected emotionally. "We could not escape! That's why we lost the ships! It is your fault!"

"I guess if you say that a few more times, maybe someone will believe you? I returned to my home system. I was attacked. Not a single one of you jerks has said word one about why. If you're looking for someone to blame, I have a mirror to sell you!"

"Are you looking for more trouble than you're already in?" Vargen threatened darkly.

"Do you still have something I can steal? Although I can see for myself — five cruisers. Pretty decent loot, I agree."

"I will destroy you," Aalor growled, but Vargen stopped him with a gesture.

"I don't need a war. There are too many preparations to be made for the second invasion to waste forces on you. I'm calling an end to your vendetta. If you want to say something to each other, exit to meatspace and have at it. In here, you obey my orders!"

"Oh really? Is there something I don't know? While I was out here saving your people here, did someone mistakenly appoint me Liberium officer?" I could not restrain my sarcasm. "Well, I didn't sign up for that. You were right when you told me I was out of your league, Vargen. I'm happy here in the minors, I don't want to play with you and your friends."

Vargen allowed himself to show emotion. This was evident

---

by how tightly he gripped the edge of the table. Only, I wasn't much affected by these theatrics.

"I'll be waiting for you to compensate me for the planet you stole from me. After that, I hope that Liberium can forget about my existence for good. Just as I will forget all about your lame-ass guild in return. Have a good one!"

The orbship vanished from Liberium's radar screens and the table cracked. Vargen had managed to break it after all. I liked his reaction and disconnected from the conference call. Brainiac had already calculated the hyperjump and was merely waiting for the go-ahead. Now my enemies can puzzle over how I managed to enter hyperspace despite their cruisers' hyperdrive disruptors. Hopefully simple fear of the unknown will get them to leave me alone.

The flight time was quite long — about an hour — so I allowed myself the pleasure of taking a nap. I certainly haven't been getting much of those lately.

I spent a long time rolling around thinking about how to get the KRIEG. Jumping to the coordinates Eine had given me and hoping for the best seemed the most obvious plan and therefore also the worst. I had to act outside the box, to keep the devs from setting up new obstacles. I therefore set course directly for the Qualian capital in the Marloon system. The three-eyed gray-skinned outcasts of Galactogon still remained an empire, and I, as the system had told me, had the right to receive a reward from whatever emperor I wished. There was no fine print stating that this couldn't be an ally of the Zatrathi.

Brainiac woke me up at the border to Qualian space — the

orbship was unexpectedly yanked out of hyperspace. Not everyone had abandoned the Qualians after the rest of Galactogon declared war against them. Plenty of players liked the idea of fighting for the underdog, even though the underdog was obviously a jerk. And the Qualians in turn understood the importance of these mercenaries — supplying them with new weapons, armor, and ships. In turn, the players had gone beyond merely defending Qualian territory — they began to expand it, invading and capturing the various frontier systems. Through their efforts, the empire had become something like a tumor, a disease animated by a virus called 'humans.'

As we emerged from hyperspace, I banked *Warlock* gracefully, dodging the incoming fire, opened the throttle to 80% and headed deeper into Qualian space, ordering Brainiac to calculate a new jump. I guess the game's forums will have a new topic to discuss today: 'How much longer will this game be so imba?!' And of course the majority of those threads would be full of Liberium tears and Qualian salt. For my part, I simply ignored our assailants' initial threats and demands, then (when they failed to catch me) their warnings to stay out of their territory and finally, simply re-entered hyperspace without a care for all their disruptor beams. It's like they were role-playing space border patrol.

As soon as we emerged out of hyperspace, I had Brainiac transmit my message over the public comms: "I have earned a reward! I wish to receive it from the Qualian emperor."

Nobody was expecting me and so we had only a couple of seconds until the Grand Arbiter destroyed us. I needed to get the Qualians' attention before that happened.

The Grand Arbiter locked onto us. It did not fire, however.

A CHECK FOR A BILLION

We'd made it in time.

The Qualians crawled all over the orbship trying to find some pretext to turn me away. Some bomb, some smuggled contraband, anything...Alas, to customs' chagrin, there was nothing. A group of Qualian G-men showed up next. Their thin ties, suitcases and mirrored glasses made them seem like serious people — very serious in fact, judging by how the customs officers parted before them. They wanted to know how I had passed the border patrols. I had nothing to hide, so I calmly threw the players under the bus. I mean, there's a war going on fellas: You need to take your role-playing more seriously. Satisfied, the security agents signed my pass and I was allowed to pass onto the third level of checks before my meeting with the emperor: psychologists. 'Who, where, why, who gave you the permits, what do I believe and what kind of problems have I had since childhood?' We agreed that I had some form of PTSD, needed psychological help, but was otherwise okay to meet the leader of their empire.

Warlock remained in orbit, ready to blow up at any moment. I didn't worry. Lumara's gift would help me contact the ship even from inside a maximum security prison cell with signal jammers around it. Once I had landed on Marloon, the Qualians demanded that I remove my armor suit and placed me in Rialto Bracelets. The Qualians were well aware of who I was and weren't taking any chances. For my part, I assumed that they'd wrap me in a chain just to make sure.

I was also forced to go through the unpleasant wardrobe changing procedure. Nobody uncuffed me beforehand, so I had to stand around awkwardly as slaves dressed me. You'd think that getting dressed by slave girls would be a pleasant procedure, but when they all have three eyes and a suction cup on each finger, well, pleasure ain't the word.

Having stoically suffered these indignities, I finally found myself at my destination — the throne room of the Qualian Emperor.

In the empty throne room of the Qualian imperial palace.

And I mean empty — there was no one here. Not even on the throne.

"You wished to receive your reward from me," a mechanical voice resounded through the hall forcing me to look around in search of a speaker. "What is the reward you desire, traitor?"

I guess the emperor still remembered my escape from their training center. Initially, my character had spawned in the Qualian Empire — this was why I could still understand the Qualian language without Brainiac's translation. But I did not like this situation. What's up with all this hide and seek? Where's the personal audience? This wasn't the deal!

"How do I know that you are *really* Quisling IV, Emperor of the Qualians?" I asked dubiously. "I have been granted the right to meet the emperor personally, not speak to some secretary over the intercom."

A pause.

"Does the Qualian Empire refuse to honor its obligations?" I pressed — and a system notification appeared:

The emperor offers you a non-disclosure agreement

A CHECK FOR A BILLION

(everything that happens in the throne room, remains in the throne room).

Accept / Decline

Another pause. One of my own making this time. The Qualians had caught me off guard.

An NDA meant that even if I saw something, I could not relate it to another local. In fact, an NPC would simply ignore what I said. Even if I pop out to meatspace, tell another player what I learned, then they tell another player and that player pops into Galactogon and tells the secret to an NPC — they'd still not hear it. Hence the 'non-disclosure' part.

However, these are all details. I mentally pushed the Accept button, impatiently shifting from one foot to the other. What are the secrets of the Qualian court?

Part of the wall behind the throne slid up, admitting the emperor. He walked directly towards me — and with each step my jaw dropped lower and lower. A cheap description, I agree, but it's hard to come up with a better words to characterize my reaction. The creature that entered the throne room was not a Qualian. Or, more precisely, it had once been a Qualian but in some other life. The turban on the Emperor's head could not conceal the brainworm stuck to his skull, while his eyes, emitting a dark mist, were filled with the Abyss. I shivered, recognizing the familiar look within them.

It was the same look that filled each of the Queen's countless eyes.

"You wished to see me, traitor!"

Everything trembled inside of me. The creature's voice

resonated with the world around us, forcing every cell within me to dance. A rustle of shifting stones swept across the hall. The voice of the enslaved emperor affected not only me, but even the monolithic walls.

This meeting was shaping up to become a catastrophic failure. I had come prepared with a definite strategy for how to get the KRIEG from the Qualians. That strategy had just folded like a house of cards. Here it is, the reason for forcing the NDA on me. Qualians, in effect, were no longer an empire of their own. They served the Queen. Hmm…Why this could be a good chance to have a chat with her! Improvisation is all I had — and besides, the Queen shouldn't have any idea what the KRIEG is and how it's best served and eaten. Did I have something that could interest her? You bet!

"And a good day to you, Queen of the Zatrathi!" I bowed. "Glad to see your majesty in fine health! Pirate Surgeon wishes to express his regard."

"You destroyed me!" Plaster rained from the ceiling.

"You invaded my house without warning. I did not have time to make the place look nice for you and took offense. The next time you decide to swallow a star system, consider whether it belongs to someone who could harm you."

"You dare impose conditions on me?!" One of the columns cracked and I couldn't help but glance at the walls doubtfully. Getting buried by rubble is not a good way to end negotiations and I felt like there was progress to be made here. I mean, she is talking to me, isn't she? That's a start! I need to make good use of it.

"I'm not here to impose anything on anyone. I am here to

A CHECK FOR A BILLION

trade with you. After all, don't you need some strong partners? We pirates can come in handy. All of Galactogon is afraid of us. You and I could be beneficial to each other. But, if you're interested, stop shaking the walls. You're making me nervous."

An Anorxian came flying out of the wall. There was also a brainworm attached to its synthoid casing. I could make it out quite clearly. It was very different from the Uldan version. This one was more like a dried mushroom. Dark, gnarled and ugly.

"What kind of partnership are you talking about? What could you offer me, pirate?"

Now I understood where the metal voice came from. The Queen was speaking through the Anorxian's voicebox. The emperor climbed onto the throne and 'hibernated,' hanging his head on his chest. What does it matter which transmitter speaks when the speaker on the other end of the line is one and the same?

"I ran into a Relay who broke contact with you near a black hole. The Zatrathi there called him 'the child.'"

"He is dead. He was sucked into the black hole, from where nothing can return, not even me!"

"I am sorry to disappoint you, but not only did he survive, but he even got out and is now in the Precians' possession. I suppose you know who they are and what their relationship with the Qualians is like. I could deliver the renegade Relay to you. Not a bad offer, right? What do you say, Majesty?"

"You have a day!"

"Uh, no — I don't work like that. That is, I don't take orders from you. But I will work with you. And so — what will the pirates get if I bring you the renegade?"

"You dare impose conditions?!"

"You're repeating yourself," I said calmly. "And in that case, I'll repeat myself too. I'm not here to impose anything on anyone. I'm here to make a deal. You heard my offer. I want to know what you can offer me in return? Or shall I help the Precians develop the Relay further?"

This last part I made up on the fly, at random, and yet the Anorxian suddenly fizzed and popped. Smoke billowed from the synthoid and it keeled over, turning into a loot crate. The brainworm lasted a little longer. I wasn't sure how to react — not sure of what had just happened. Is it me or did the Queen just burn down her own robot? Why? Was my bit of improvisation on the mark?!

"I cannot permit you to do that!" Another Anorxian came bumbling into the throne room. "You cannot grow a Relay that has no binding to me!"

Orly? Well this is interesting. The Queen must have been a brainwom herself back in the day. This begs a reasonable question: Where did the brainworm come from? Belmarad didn't recognize one when he saw it, which means that they're not an Uldan creation.

I turned back to the Queen: "Can...cannot...your problems are not my business. I have enough of my own. Are we going to work together? If yes, then here is my offer: I will deliver the renegade to you and in exchange you promise to respect a star system of mine. That is, not one of your warriors may enter it. You can trade in it, build warehouses, but, please, no warriors. Hell, you can burn the rest of Galactogon to cinders, as long as you leave my system alone."

A CHECK FOR A BILLION

"Your demand is impossible, human." The Queen refused as I expected. Her rationale, however, wasn't what I thought it would be. "There must be at least one flying fortress in the system. It will provide protection from enemies and supervise my own forces to ensure they do not violate our agreement. That is the only way I can guarantee my side of the deal."

"Oh, that will suit me just fine. Although, why only one? You can garrison three or four if you like…"

"Are you afraid of something?"

"I'm a pirate! I have many enemies, and four fortresses will allow me to rest easy when I'm not around. Plus I'll be able to get in touch with you whenever I like — if, say, I come across some fat system for you. Isn't your diet primarily yellow dwarfs, or will red giants do as well?"

"I am still not powerful enough to eat the larger stars," the Queen replied. "I have a list of one hundred systems. That will suffice for six months. Yes, you might come in handy, pirate! Gather information for me. But first bring me the renegade! I must know how it escaped my control!"

New mission available: Return of the Prodigal Child. Warning! If you successfully complete this mission, you will automatically join the Zatrathi faction.

Oh no! This is like threatening a porcupine with your bare ass! At the moment, I'd trade away every point of Rapport I still had just to get my hands on that KRIEG!

"That's a good start!" I exclaimed, accepting the quest.

"Now back to the original purpose of my visit. You were going to reward me!"

"WHAT?! You are alive, aren't you? That is sufficient reward for a hero like you!"

"Your Majesty — I am no hero. I am a pirate! And I was promised a reward! If the emperor is to give me a gift, then he must give it to me, even if he is thrice enslaved. Such are the ironclad rules of Galactogon! Or do you wish to rewrite them? Do you have permission to do so? I think not. So let me speak with the Qualian emperor for a few minutes."

You dev bastards didn't anticipate this, did you? Let old Surgeon teach you a thing or two.

The second Anorxian blew his top and collapsed on the floor, leaving behind another loot crate. Her Majesty seemed irate.

"Ask for something else!" Another Anorxian waddled into the throne room. Does she have a warehouse full of them back there?

"It's my right — and it's inviolable. The emperor must give me my reward!"

The third Anorxian began to smoke, but this time the Queen managed herself. The robot did not blow. Instead, the Qualian Emperor rose from his throne and approached me. A gang of Anorxians entered the throne room and took the emperor by the hands, restraining him. One even grabbed his legs.

"I warn you, my mercenary — pay no attention to his pleas. Ask for your reward, receive it and go deal with the renegade child. Do you understand? If you do something that displeases me, our deal will be off. I will find a way to get the renegade without your

A CHECK FOR A BILLION

---

help."

"Do I have to wait much longer?" I plied my line. "My time's not limitless. A galaxy of booty awaits my plunder and I'm here talking to you."

There was a moist sucking sound — as if a boot had been pulled out of a muddy creek bed. The brainworm flopped to the floor, the darkness cleared from the emperor's eyes, they acquired clarity and sentience, and my stomach swooned and sank: Belmarad isn't dead as I supposed! He's simply locked out of his own mind. If I hand the child over to the Queen, the dark Uldan lord will return to Galactogon. I wonder if he's the kind to hold a grudge...

"Pirate Surgeon? What hap..." The emperor trailed off as he noticed the Anorxians holding him.

"I have been granted the right to receive a reward, oh Emperor of the Qualians. I wish to receive it from you personally. That is why I'm here. I wish to receive the KRIEG!" The emperor's eyes went wide with astonishment. Worried that he might ruin my ruse, I quickly added: "Do you know what the Vengeance does? I can see by your eyes that you know. Well, it was destroyed when I earned the reward I now ask of you. So now I need the KRIEG. It's the one gadget I'm sorely missing at the moment. Maybe it'll help me return here for another audience with you — who knows?"

How nice it is that the emperors in this game are governed by advanced AIs. As I watched, comprehension flashed deep in the NPC's eyes — and though broken by his cruel fate, he rallied — and again became the leader of his empire. Majestic, wise and, most importantly, with the highest security clearance in the land.

"I confirm your right to the reward you seek, Pirate Surgeon. If you really prefer the useless KRIEG instead of the planets you could ask for, have your way! My master of prisons shall bring it here. Remember this code, human. You cannot receive the KRIEG otherwise. Will there be something else?"

"Not at the moment. I will return when I earn the right to another reward."

One of the Anorxians picked up the brainworm from the floor and attached it back to the head of the emperor. There was an unpleasant sound and the Abyss flooded back into the local's eyes.

"What is the KRIEG?" The queen asked through the Anorxian. "For some reason, I can't access that memory."

"A device for my ship. It will make it faster," I lied immediately. "I have been looking for it for a long time, but the Qualians did not want to give it away. It's an Uldan device — stuff like that isn't available anymore."

The emperor approached his throne, put his hand on the armrest and a small screen slid out. A couple of clicks and a notification appeared before my eyes:

You have gained access to the KRIEG.
Your rapport with all the empires remains unchanged.
Current Rapport: 0.

CHAPTER
TWENTY-THREE

"DOESN'T LOOK LIKE MUCH OF A WEAPON TO ME."
The Uldan on Zubrail was in no hurry to accept
the task. He fumbled with the mysterious
KRIEG in his hands and frowned.

Frankly, I had my doubts too. The KRIEG turned out to be
a metal cube about half a meter tall, with two wires and one button.
A very smart-looking Qualian had handed it to me. One of those
creatures who've traded their social skills for a higher IQ. Giggling
awkwardly and constantly adjusting his glasses, the Precian
explained to me how to use the weapon. According to his
instructions, I was supposed to attach the wires to the planetary
spirit, push the button and just be happy that I could respawn
somewhere else. Because there'd be nothing left at all in a radius
of two hyper-minutes from the epicenter. Neither living nor dead.

Not even matter.

I conveyed all this to the Uldan, but he showed no interest. He seemed to have his doubts.

"Ask Eine! He will confirm that the KRIEG is dangerous," I pressed, trying to look convincing. Name-dropping the German had its effect — the Uldan looked down at the KRIEG.

"I want to see it in action," he said, handing the KRIEG back to me.

"No problem! Let's go see your planetary spirit! If you want to see it in action, you'll see it in action," I promised. I was in the most of fighting moods. I even descended from the dock to the ground, but then the bushes parted and four rhinos stepped out to the clearing. I quickly clambered back up to my ship.

Mission accomplished: One Last Shot.

"Enter the following sequence," Zubrail's resident Uldan gave up. He dictated the letters and digits to the riddle, I entered those into the cylinder, and the last green light went on. There was a click. They cylinder jerked and opened like a high-tech puzzle from a sci-fi horror movie. Like Lumara had said, cracking Belmarad's gift would be dangerous. Tiny explosives were packed just inside the casing. In the center, inside a glass bulb, lay a quite ordinary-looking piece of paper with numbers scrawled on it. It didn't take much time for Brainiac to decipher the coordinates. Once that was done, the Uldan kindly projected a giant 3D map of the galaxy in front of us. Judging by this map, the Zatrathi homeplanet was way out on the periphery.

A CHECK FOR A BILLION

"Two hyper-hours from the nearest discovered planet," Brainiac quickly estimated. "We would need a full cargo hold of elo to travel one way."

This was bad news indeed. It would be impossible to send a scout ahead — a smaller ship wouldn't have the fuel to make it. On top of this, I doubt I could accomplish much with just my orbship — and we wouldn't have the elo to get back.

"What is that?" Eunice asked peering closely at part of the map across the galaxy from us. While Brainiac and I pondered how to get to the 'X' marking the spot, my wife busied herself with photographing and recording Galactogon's projection. The star system that attracted her attention was as far from the galactic center as the Zatrathi planet.

"Nothing!" The Uldan waved his hand and that part of the map faded.

"Brainiac?"

"Don't worry, Captain. I managed to triangulate it. It is impossible to establish the coordinates, but we do have a vector."

"It would take two hours to fly there, no less!" Eunice interrupted with her habitual strictness. *"An error of even a hundredth of a degree would throw us light years off track. You two get distracted too easily. I'd get back to the task at hand, if I were you."*

"Scout it out in the battlesphere?" I suggested, returning to the problem.

"I have no reflectors," Eunice replied. "We'll be spotted."

"And they'll be sure to reinforce their defenses if they do," added Brainiac.

"As it stands, the static defenses in their home system might be too much for the battlesphere. We might not even be able to get close to the planet," said Eunice, finishing off my idea completely.

"In that case, we need a cruiser — and preferably several cruisers," I summed up our brainstorming session. "But where can we get them?"

I asked this rhetorically, yet the Universe took pity on me and answered. And so clearly, that the choice of allies became instantly obvious:

Attention all members of Jolly Roger 2.0!

The first Brotherhood assembly shall take place five hours from now. All Brotherhood officers are required to attend. The rendezvous point will be Barganil III, Barganil System.

The pirates had the forces and the will to plunder, they were hotheads and there were basically no players among them, so there'd be no need to wait for someone or haggle about random nonsense. Offer to split the loot with the NPCs and let them do the heavy lifting. Exactly what I needed most right now...It's decided then! I'll set out for the Zatrathi planet with the pirates, but first I'll need to do Wit-Verr's quest and deal with the Praline base.

Eunice took a rain check. According to her, I would have to complete Wit-Verr's mission on my own and preferably before the meeting. It wouldn't do for a major in the Brotherhood to show up otherwise. She did not say what she was planning to do without me, but I could say for certain that the battlesphere departed Zubrail before me.

A CHECK FOR A BILLION

At first glance, Wit-Verr's mission seemed like a cakewalk: fly in, fix the transmitter and be on my way. There was no reason to assume I'd encounter another ancient Uldan on the base. More likely, the transmitter had just broken or something. Some mundane malfunction.

And as a result of such thoughts, I was completely unprepared to discover six Zatrathi flying fortresses arranged in a circular garrison around the Praline system.

"We are being locked on by EM cannons! Our hyperdrive is being disrupted! I am detecting..."

Suddenly, *Warlock* went dead. There were no shots, no damage notifications. Simply the orbship lost power. Oddly enough though, my armor suit went on functioning as before. Everything on me read nominal. I activated the backup power circuit and waited for Brainiac to say something clever.

"Captain, it's a tractor beam!" he began. "We are being dragged into..."

Then he went dead again as did my ship around me. I had gotten so used to my orbship's speed and power that I forgot entirely about tractor beams! Properly operated, these could capture ships just as flycatchers caught torpedoes. If the tractor beam was large enough, it would depower the ship to boot. As it happened, we had emerged from hyperspace right under the stern of a flying fortress — as good as on a platter for the Zatrathi.

I looked around desperately. The self-destruct button was powered by a backup circuit that just died. Damn, damn, damn! These Zatrathi are a bunch of...well...Zatrathi!

Acceptance follows recognition and once I'd recognized

the situation we were in, I promptly got pissed. I won't give up without a fight! My armor suit's a legendary, my cargo hold's full of elo, I have several grenades and five starving cacodemons. Why I'll blow up the entire place if I feel like it! You Zatrathi should have just blasted me while I was out in space.

When the ship stopped shaking, I knew that we had been pulled inside. There followed an unpleasant sound, as if something metallic had been scraped along our hull. I cocked my blasters, summoned my cacodemons and prepared to throw myself at my enemies as soon as they appeared. Let the battle begin!

But the seconds ticked by and no one tried to breach our hull. To the contrary, the metal screeching stopped and I heard a polite knocking on my hull.

"Captain Surgeon, the elo has been delivered!" said a muffled voice in the common tongue. "We can provide you with technicians to repair any damaged modules or equipment you might have."

Having no idea what was going on, I didn't know what to reply and so I just waited, shifting from one foot to the other.

Another thirty seconds passed, but no one touched the orbship. Everything was quiet. The cacodemons began to whine. They were ready for a meal, yet it wasn't forthcoming. Realizing that perhaps I was doing something utterly stupid, I walked over to the control panel and opened a passage in the hull. I gestured to the cacodemons to stay in place. Let them cover me.

The orbship had been pulled into one of the hangars of the flying fortress. Around us, Zatrathi slugs went creeping on some errands, squads of warriors marched to and fro and even several black fogs drifted by. Everyone went about their business, paying no attention to me and my ship. The only ones interested in my person were a robot translator and a slug technician. They were standing by the ship with carts heaped full of elo.

I gulped, still unsure of what to say. Then I took several deep breaths, wishing I could pinch myself inside my armor suit. I shut my eyes as tightly as I could and opened my eyes wide. Nothing changed. The Zatrathi showed no aggression.

"We've been ordered to supply your orbship with anything you need," the robot translated for the slug. "Do you need help changing the elo? The energy blocking system consumes all the elo you have onboard. It must be replaced."

"Uh-huh," I nodded, shocked by the warm welcome. A few more slugs joined the technician. They disappeared into my ship, deftly carting in the elo and carting out the spent fuel.

"There are five hungry creatures on board. Shall we feed them?"

"Eh?!" I had no idea what they were talking about. When I realized he meant the cacodemons, all I managed was a feeble nod. "Sure...feed them."

What in the hell is going on here anyway? The cacodemons piled out of the orbship and threw themselves on a heap of elo that was brought up. In just a couple of minutes they gorged themselves until each was the size of a prize cow and then rolled aside with satiated looks.

"It's the Zatrathi, Captain!" Brainiac panicked as soon as he came back online. I tensed up, assuming that the technicians had begun digging around some sensitive ship system. I even

---

dashed back to the bridge deck but found no traces of trouble. The orbship remained whole and mine.

"What about the Zatrathi?" I asked.

"We are inside a flying fortress! Surrounded! By enemies! Battle Stations! Battle Stations! Shall I open fire?!"

"At what?! Hold your fire! The Zatrathi are our...allies... I think..." With this phrase I told Brainiac everything that I thought about this matter.

"What do you mean, 'allies?'" Brainiac almost stuttered.

The computer's amazement was no less than mine, yet the question still had to be answered. It's one thing to have to pick up your own jaw on the floor and another entirely when it's that of your subordinates.

"Oh just like that. I made a deal with the Queen. Until the deadline expires, the Zatrathi won't bother us." Or at least that's what I imagined had happened. I didn't bother to mention my doubts on the matter.

"But Captain...these are the enemies of all of Galactogon! How can we possibly work with them? Everyone will hate us."

"No they won't. Because we're not going to tell them. Do you know what a spy is?" The computer grunted an affirmative. "Welp, that's exactly what we are. Anyway, enough talking — let's get to work! Connect to this flying fortress and download everything you can get your digital digits on!"

Brainiac quickly warmed up to his new role. The snake crawled out with a network cable. The Zatrathi paid no attention to my engineer plugging into their ship's jack.

"I have full access!" Brainiac exclaimed. "I don't even need

---

to hack anything! Captain — what do you say we steal this fortress? I can pull it off! I swear!"

"Next time," I promised. "We have other business right now. Patch me through to the captain."

"I greet the messenger of Her will," the Relay said, clarifying my current status at the same time. Indeed, it seems the Queen had made an effort to hold up her side of our bargain. It looked like she was quite concerned about recovering that escaped brainworm. An interesting fact to take note of. "How may I serve you?"

"Is Praline under your control?"

"Yes, we are currently using it to cultivate shlocage for this entire sector.

"'Shlocage' seems to be the Zatrathi's chief source of nutrition," Brainiac explained helpfully.

"There used to be a pirate base on that planet. What happened to it?"

"It has been cleared. Such is Her will! Are you here for a long time? We can offer you and your crew some rest and recreation."

I hesitated to answer, because I did not know how long the maintenance of the ship would take and whether it was worth agreeing to the R&R. But my silence was taken for consent and a pair of slugs crawled over to *Warlock*'s hull. Unlike the engineer slugs, these were smaller and had some fancy tentacles dangling on their heads.

"The gerudo know what humans like and will be happy to serve the messenger with its tentacles."

It took me a bit to realize what he was talking about. And when I did realize it, I found myself at a loss for words. What is this 'gerudo' and 'tentacles' crap? I mean, I may not know the word 'gerudo' but I do know what tentacles are used for in hentai. It's not my thing, but I know it anyway.

"No, the R&R won't be necessary, thank you very much! Is the ship all right? May I take off?"

"Yes, messenger. We did not expect your appearance and assumed you were a threat. This is why you were brought in with the tractor beam. It will not happen again. We have recorded your orbship's transponder signal. We all hope that you will successfully fulfill the mission She has entrusted you!" said the captain and disconnected.

What have I gotten myself into?! Loud laughter rolled all over the ship. A longshot attempt to buy myself a few extra minutes of life during my audience with the Qualian Emperor had somehow turned into an alliance with the Zatrathi. And now they were offering me slugs with tentacles. What is happening to this game anyway?

To clear my conscience, I flew to Praline. I'd been promised loot from one of the warehouses — what if something was still down there?

Alas it was not to be. The Zatrathi really had cleared out every last bit of the place. Furthermore, there was now a crew of slugs working on demolishing what was left of the base. It seemed like they didn't even want to leave scrap raq behind.

Mission updated: A Praline Pirate.
Report to Wit-Verr that the base has been captured.

A CHECK FOR A BILLION

Praising myself for my foresight, I decided to test the waters. I needed to understand whether the new Zatrathi attitude towards me had been changed in only this one system or throughout all of Galactogon. In the latter case, I doubt I'd need any allies whatsoever. Eunice and I could calmly jump somewhere in the vicinity of the Zatrathi home system, I could load up on elo from her battlesphere and then head out on my own.

After rushing around the system and making sure that I did not arouse the attention of any of the flying fortresses, I popped into some of the Delvians' former core systems. Two of these had large stars, which the Queen wasn't 'mature' enough to devour yet. And although every time we emerged from hyperspace, Brainiac announced that we were being tracked and locked onto, as soon as the Zatrathi figured out who we were, they'd leave us alone. This suited me just fine.

The countdown to the pirates' assembly was winding down to zero, so I headed for Barganil. The system has changed noticeably since my last visit. The already hefty garrison had been reinforced with additional Arbiters and orbital stations, emblazoned with the Brotherhood's new, giant insignia. Wit-Verr had chosen this system as his new headquarters and seen to its defense.

I was assigned to dock #30, which struck me as odd. If this planet is the pirate capital, then you'd think they'd be a bit more deferential to a major of the Brotherhood. Brainiac began the descent — when I aborted it at the last moment. The system scan had just completed and I now had a list of all the cruisers in system — I didn't like it one bit. In particular, the presence of the cruisers *Alexandria*, *Ajaccio*, and *Watto.* Kiddo, the Corsican and Hilvar respectively.

I continued orbiting, as the dispatcher muttered with irritation. In addition to the aforementioned trio, there were another dozen or so ships here from the old Brotherhood. Mostly cruisers, but also several destroyers. In fact the entire system was abuzz with traffic — with fighters and scouts scrambling back and forth and driving the ground control operators to the verge of aneurisms.

And yet, the presence of pirates and players from the old Brotherhood was not the only news. Tucked away on the other side of the system from us — and therefore hidden behind the local star, which kept me from seeing it right away — was the main battle fleet of the Anorxian Empire. The Motherboard had deployed a portion of its navy to the pirate's assembly.

This was getting really interesting. What does the presence of all these guests mean?

As soon as *Warlock* landed, customs descended on us in full force. The pirate inspectors were quite thorough — after all, they knew all the smugglers' tricks. Snooping around, I noticed that Eunice's battlesphere was moored in the dock next to us. Judging by the loading crews bringing up elo, my wife had been on this planet for a while already and had long since passed her inspections.

A little while later, I found myself entering a sumptuous palace. The Bufondian, like the Corsican before him, liked to live ostentatiously.

"Major." The guard nodded to me, striking himself against his chest in a show of respect. I can't say it didn't feel nice to be saluted. You can't help but feel significant, your posture straightens against your will and you get the urge to clap the local on the shoulder in a fraternal kind of way. I even tossed my head to clear the sentiment.

The interior decor, its tasteless pomp, was already beginning to grate on me. I'd seen the same kitsch in the palace of the Brotherhood's former leader, as well as Hilvar's residence. The only major difference was the assembly hall. It was distinct in its simplicity, both in terms of decoration and furnishings. An immense, rectangular table occupied the center, with chairs all around it. The chairs were bolted to rails in the floor which moved at the touch of a button. Wit-Verr had ensured that no one could brandish a chair-leg like a club to beat their neighbor to death with.

Half an hour remained before the assembly. I was one of the first to arrive. The steward took me to my seat, which allowed me to get a good look at everyone who showed up. The first to appear were the rank and file pirates of note — the ones who had distinguished themselves from everyone else. Then came lieutenants and majors. Eunice appeared five minutes before the beginning, whispering about something with Kiddo. My former companion glanced at me and a fleeting shadow flashed across her face. Then the steward led the girls to their seats. Eunice was seated among the lieutenants, while Kiddo…Kiddo was ushered all the way to the head of the table.

Hilvar and the Corsican entered the hall one after another. They didn't bother concealing their ire — publicly wishing me a prompt death when they saw me. I saluted them in return, grinning widely as if they'd wished me good health and fortune. The steward didn't even lead them anywhere. They walked on their own to

Kiddo's right-hand side and sat down between her and the throne. Okeydokey. Looks like this whole trio now has seniority over me. This is bad.

Tryd and Gloom appeared in the doorway shoulder to shoulder and I expected them to get stuck like two stooges — but alas the door was wide enough for both to pass abreast. Finally, there came a flourish, and Wit-Verr himself entered to general whispering, walking solemnly and in the company of an intricate cube on wheels. Judging by its numerous stickers — this was some Anorxian aristocrat. The doors on both ends of the hall shut and the clicks of their locks indicated that the assembly had begun.

The new head of the Brotherhood, walked over to his throne with a toad's heavy gait, and waited as the Anorxian sat down on his right-hand side. He then scanned everyone assembled with a heavy gaze.

"I was gone a mere thirty years and in that time you lot managed to turn the dread Brotherhood into some kind of boys' fraternity. You have forgotten our true power! You have reduced us to a pimple on Galactogon's back! A couple of days ago, the empires agreed to squeeze us, wipe us out, and forget all about us!"

The hall erupted in a whisper of discontent but Wit-Verr extinguished it with a wave.

"Silence! Now you listen! I have returned and will restore us to our former glory. The empires have changed their minds and are ready to leave us alone."

Well sure. Didn't I just kill the Queen?

"This will give us time to grow strong, to make our

437

preparations. The Corsican and I spoke for a long time about where he took the Jolly Roger Brotherhood. What he turned it into. But I realized the most important thing — our strength lies in our unity! Therefore — in the name of fraternity — I will give the former leader a second chance!"

How commendable! And not a word about how it was the Corsican who stuck him in that black hole. I wonder how much the Delvian prince paid to get back into his former boss's good graces?

"I will now introduce you to my new generals! You know them well and you may trust them completely. The Corsican, Hilvar and Kiddo!"

The pirates began banging their fists on the table in unison, welcoming and approving the announcement. As for me, it came like a knee to the groin. Obviously I didn't expect anything good when I saw the three of them sit down next to the head of the table, but I consoled myself with the thought that this was nothing more than a tribute to their past merits and in no way a sign of their current positions. I now had three bosses that hated me — not the brightest prospect for a loner like me. Heck, Tryd was enough of a handful as things stood.

"They will be joined by new majors and new lieutenants!"

Wit-Verr listed the pirates I'd already met and then suddenly turned to me:

"Major Surgeon, report what you found at the Praline base!"

Everyone's attention turned to me. Smothering the urge to stand up and report officially, I replied as casually as possible:

"The Praline base no longer exists. There are six Zatrathi

flying fortresses in the system. The planet has been captured and the base itself has been dismantled. The third warehouse, which I was promised as a reward, is no more. I would like to request my due compensation for having accomplished a mission whose reward was not there to begin with. If you need proof that I was at the base, I have brought it with me."

"You snuck past six flying fortresses on your own? Now that is quite curiousss," Kiddo gibed, but stopped short from the look that Wit-Verr gave her.

"This is your first warning, general. I'm the one who decides what's 'quite curiousss' around here. Major, I recognize your claim for compensation."

A system notification appeared that I had received a transfer of GCs to my account. The pirate leader was quite generous: He had transferred ten million credits. Given my current financial state this amount was basically peanuts, and yet it would be an unheard-of sum for most of Galactogon's playerbase.

"Major Surgeon's report confirms my assumptions," continued Wit-Verr. "The Zatrathi have become too dangerous to ignore. Their offensive may has stopped for now, but in a month it will be even more powerful. The Queen will seek revenge and we will be the first in her crosshairs."

Wit-Verr shifted his heavy gaze on me. It boded nothing good at all.

Is he trying to suggest that I'm to blame? Has this frog lost his damn mind?!

"With his ill-conceived actions, Major Surgeon has imperiled the Brotherhood, imperiling us with a blow from a deadly and mighty force! Humans have already tried to kill the Queen. Each time, the monster discovered their leaders and wiped their star systems from the face of Galactogon. Now our turn has come. This is why I settled here. Let them rather destroy Barganil III than our home planets."

A murmur of approval met the pirate leader's words. A move worthy of a true chief. If misfortune is imminent — it is better to plan for the worst case, than let the blow fall on your head. I finally understood the indifferent reaction I got from Ash's people when I told them about the Queen's location. They already knew what would happen.

"I always said that this small fry is too unreliable to make major," Tryd muttered. "A lieutenant at best, and even that's too much."

"Sometimes it is worth admitting your mistakes." Wit-Verr never once looked away from me. "I was too generous in promoting Surgeon to major. His true rank is lieutenant. From now on it will be so. Steward — why have you seated a junior officer among the majors?"

Servants began to scurry around the hall, re-arranging the seating. They wanted to lift me along with the chair, unfastening it with a special key from the floor, but I quickly jumped to my feet. As the entire assembly laughed, my chair was moved to the very end of the officer part of the table. I found myself among the rank and file pirates who had distinguished themselves in battle.

I had never experienced such humiliation. Neither in Galactogon, nor in Runlustia, nor in real life. My face felt like it was burning and it was only thanks to the game's lack of detail that it didn't actually blush as red as a banner. I was unsure about what was making the Bufondian do this. Blood pulsed in my temples and a wave of anger swept away all my cooler thoughts. I stood there like an idiot, staring at my new place, and could not find the strength to walk over there and sit down. To accept the new place seemed the equivalent of accepting my shame and humiliation.

"Lieutenant, do you need a second invitation?" Wit-Verr continued. "Sit down!

The servants grabbed me by the elbows, but I jerked, pushing them away. The Brotherhood's token appeared in my hand. I looked at the piece of useless metal for a few moments, then threw it on the table, turned and headed for the closed doors. My time in the Jolly Roger had come to an end. I could have followed this up with an irate tirade but I decided to maintain my honor. Why waste it on empty words? We are men of action!

Wit-Verr grunted something over his shoulder and then announced:

"Take Surgeon to the brig. We will surrender him to the Queen. The orbship shall be disassembled for spare parts. Lieutenant Nurse, do as I command!"

CHAPTER TWENTY-FOUR

"STAY STILL," EUNICE ORDERED A BIT TOO LOUDLY as she tried to cuff the Rialto Bracelets on me. This was too much. Four manipulators had restrained my limbs and I could hardly move. I couldn't understand why the pirates were so angry. I just wanted to self-destruct with a Zatrathi grenade. True, I wanted to take as much of their stupid pirate mugs with me as I could, but those were details. Unfortunately, they were faster on the trigger. A beam shot out from the hall's ceiling, instantly defusing my grenade, and after a dozen seconds, Lumara's transmitter was also deactivated. Though, these dozen seconds were actually too much: When I ordered Brainiac to arrange a small Armageddon on the planet's surface and then blow up *Warlock* at the first attempt to capture her, the pirates burst into laughter in naïve carelessness. They did not think

---

that a person could contact the ship without an armor suit and through the assembly hall's jamming field. It was that much more pleasant for me to see Kiddo's face grow white and long as she began to receive reports from her people. Brainiac kindly made sure to blow up her personal frigate. Even after my transmitter was neutralized, I kept receiving notifications about my ship's guns leveling up. Brainiac really did let the pirates have it! *Lexus* was the next ship to head to respawn. The orbship computer had read my mind.

Still, sooner or later, all good things come to an end. Wit-Verr had fortified his residence very well. No matter how hard he tried, Brainiac couldn't overcome all the AA guns around the place. But I could be proud of him: The first fifty docks of Barganil III were no more. And neither were the ships that had been in them.

"Give me a knife," I asked in a whisper, watching my wife handcuff me. Mine had been sheathed in my body armor, and the pirates had confiscated it earlier.

"No way," whispered Eunice. "Why did you blow up my *Lexus*?! Spend a couple days in the brig. It will do you good."

"Are you having a laugh?" I asked with astonishment. "We have plans!"

"*I* have plans…You…you're just getting in the way. If I were on my own, I would have found the check a long time ago. Did you really think that the coordinates from the cylinder would be of help? It's a setup. Just like all the other ones before! I'm going to go on by myself from here. And you're not going to get in my way."

"What are you talking about?" I couldn't understand whether she was being serious or hamming it up for our audience.

443

A CHECK FOR A BILLION

However, I didn't have time to figure it out as the pirates began to jostle me toward the exit. Eunice turned sharply and returned to her place, earning the praise of the head pirate.

"Eunice?" I made one last attempt, but she didn't even turn her head in my direction, only exchanged glances with Kiddo.

"Shut yer yap and be on your way," Tryd suddenly appeared beside me. It seemed that the Delvian wanted to personally make sure that I would be delivered to my cell. Cursing, I took one last look at my wife — who looked perfectly content — and turned to go.

I was taken to a dark cell and shoved against the bench.

"Give me the keys and scram," said the Delvian to the guards, who did as ordered without an extra word. Making sure that we were alone, Tryd leaned closer and growled: "Now listen here, small fry! What I'm about to tell you doesn't leave your empty skull. In particular, don't you dare say word one about it to your female. Nod if you understand me and are ready to be silent."

"I got it," I replied and doubled over from the blow to my sternum. The breath knocked out of me, I gasped for air struggling against the debuffs that appeared.

"Are you stupid or just pretending? I said 'nod!'" Tryd growled. "Nod if you understand me and are prepared to keep what I'm about to tell you secret!"

This damn local. I regained my breath and glared at the fox with hatred. After a brief pause, I nodded.

You have agreed to the following obligation: 'Keep a secret.' Everything that Tryd tells you must remain between you

---

and him. You may not disclose this information in the game. If you violate your obligation, you will face a penalty of 100,000 GC.

"You didn't say anything about a fine." I did not like the notification and decided to stand up for my rights. "I refuse to comply with something I wasn't told of in advance! Especially a monetary fine."

"You will lose much more than just credits," said Tryd. "You will lose my respect."

"I would be happy to tell you where you can stick your respect, but my upbringing won't allow me."

I wanted to keep arguing with the fox, but common sense prevailed. At this point, I just wanted to quickly finish this entire affair.

Obligation updated: 'Keep a secret.' If you violate your obligations, you will lose rapport with Tryd.

"I don't care what you think of me. Our work is much more important. The chief sent you into exile for a reason. *You* have to find out who works for the Zatrathi Queen."

I was at a loss for words when I heard this. Not only had they just kicked me out, but I was supposed to do something for them too? Tryd interpreted my silence in his own way, deciding that I was waiting for him to go on:

"Someone within the Brotherhood is leaking information. The Queen seems to know exactly where our hidden bases and star systems are located. It was clear back when she gobbled up

A CHECK FOR A BILLION

Volta — she doesn't just show up at random. The Brotherhood can't grow strong as long as there's a rat among our ranks!"

New mission available: Secret Brother Seamus. Description: Wit-Verr suspects that one of the pirates is working with the Queen, passing her information about the pirate bases. Find the traitor and the evidence of their betrayal. Reward: Promotion to General of the Jolly Roger 2.0.

"Wit-Verr knew that you would not accept your humiliation and quit the Brotherhood instead. That was the entire plan. We won't know where you are and what you're doing and that will only make the rat worry. The rat will try to find you, and you will have a chance to catch it. Don't worry about your escape. The chief will ignore it, while the Queen only wants revenge."

I bit my tongue to keep myself from accidentally mentioning my new relationship with the Zatrathi. The pirates didn't need to know about it. Given how they're acting these days, the lot of them can go to hell! Still, I accepted the mission. Not to actually do it, but to escape from this place sooner. Tryd pulled out a long dagger and unfastened my handcuffs. The expression on the Delvian's muzzle was extremely sour.

"Now the business at hand. You have to kill me. We have to make it look like you attacked me and then vanished! And damn it all, this'll multiply my reputation by zero! Do you understand this, small fry?! Me! A space marine veteran with fifty years' experience will be cut down by a ninny pirate reject. If there was another way…But forget it. Find the traitor, Surgeon. Find the traitor and the evidence. Otherwise I will be disappointed in you. Now get on with it!"

Tryd tilted his head back, exposing his throat. He didn't have to ask twice — a sharp blow sent the pirate to rebirth. I had accumulated so much anger with this NPC that I could have torn him apart with my bare hands. And then glued him together and set him up like a totem on *Warlock's* bridge deck. Just to scare any intruders away.

A shimmering crate fell to the floor, containing nothing but a note:

"One more thing! Do not trust anyone. Your female is too close to Kiddo. They have business between them. Strange and mysterious business. Do this job on your own."

The warning unambiguously suggested whom I should consider rat candidate number one. Now I already knew that Kiddo was a giant rat, but I had been mistaken about the scale of it. In her blind desire to destroy the Qualians, she could go to great lengths. Including working with the Queen. As for Eunice…I didn't even want to think about it. Had she decided to show her true colors? Well…well…On the one hand, I should have expected it. After all, she had a storied gaming past. And she had always played solo. On the other hand…she should take care because otherwise she might get her teeth knocked out.

Undressing, I stuck the knife in my chest and returned to Zubrail. My wife's words had hurt me — they certainly found fertile ground in my mind. I had long begun to suspect that there was no

A CHECK FOR A BILLION

check on the planet that Belmarad had leaked to us, but I had kept this thought to myself.

In order to gain enough elo, I was forced to unload the orbship entirely. The raq, the extra seats, a bunch of the partitions. Any space capable of holding a container with elo was taken into account. I even left the cacodemons at the orbital station, sending them into stasis. Their pen offered ample space for more fuel.

"There should be enough for a return flight," Brainiac assured me, calculating our elo supply. "There is even a small reserve in case we need to make a couple of stops. Captain, I must say that I have never jumped so far. I am not sure we will handle the load."

"We'll have to risk it." There was no way out. I had to go check out the planet — if anything, because Eunice didn't believe me. "Make the calculations..."

The orbship did great. Several times during our flight the measured rumble of the engines stuttered, causing anxious muttering from the engineer, but on the whole our trip went by without a hitch and two hours and twenty minutes later, we appeared not far from a beautiful green planet with several tiny moons. A standard yellow dwarf shone at the center of the system and there were a couple of outer planets that stabilized it. And that was it.

No orbital stations, no flying fortresses, no vengeful Queen. Nothing at all. A scan revealed not so much as a stray fighter. Nor were there any dispatchers screaming at us when we appeared. The Zatrathi homeworld was like any other virgin planet, just discovered by the player.

"Captain, I am picking up facilities on the planet's surface. There is a city here!"

"Let's land then. We'll go check it out. Everyone be ready to deal with any air defenses!"

Until the last moment, I thought that they would start shooting at us and so first I ordered Brainiac to hang out in the higher orbit around the planet, then the middle one and only then enter the atmosphere. I figured it would be harder to intercept us that way, even if ground-based defenses would have an easier time of hitting us. However, we did not encounter any obstacles at all.

The planet's defenders did not seem concerned with the sparkling orb descending from the sky. Unable to locate a spaceport, we landed right in the middle of the central square of a huge metropolis. All the familiar types of Zatrathi came out to meet us: slugs, warriors, black fogs and even a couple of guards. Frozen in place and with their heads craned back, they watched our landing, without making any attempts to interfere.

The ship was surrounded on all sides. At first it was a little scary, but when the locals went on behaving like ordinary onlookers, I breathed a sigh of relief. The warriors' faces were funny looking to begin with, but now, distorted by their astonishment, they made me want to laugh outright. The Zatrathi touched the hull, chattered among themselves, shook their limbs and politely stepped aside to let those behind them take a look. When little Zatrathi kids began to appear, I realized that they were not afraid of me at all and that I could safely go outside. The children were drumming on the orbship, apparently having decided that it was some kind of toy. There was no aggression whatsoever. Only surprise and healthy curiosity.

I ventured outside and my appearance set off a commotion. The warriors rattled and clicked their mandibles, the slugs squealed and even the fogs made a strange humming. Everyone seemed surprised by the humanoid in the armor suit.

And yet I was far more surprised when, barely having set foot on the planet, I received a notification:

You are the first player to land on Haldon.
Do you wish to claim the planet for yourself?

Warning! Haldon has neither a planetary spirit, a binding point, nor a respawn point.

Everything sank inside of me. Eunice was right — there was no prize check here. Just like there was no Queen. I'd found a dummy planet full of Zatrathi civilians. They were exiled here many millennia ago. They bred, built megacities, established industry, but hadn't yet entered the space age.

On top of this, Brainiac couldn't understand their language. The natives understood neither the common tongue, nor Zatrathi, nor Uldan. They just clicked their mandibles, chattered, gurgled, and chirped without understanding what I was saying. Technologically, this planet was still in the steam age. No electronics to speak of, especially computers. It was time to head back. Especially once they began to bring presents to the orbship. I guess they decided that it was a god or the creator's messenger or something. Flowers, animal hides, some useless sculptures, precious crystals. The latter interested me and I picked up a couple for Eunice, causing an enthusiastic buzzing among the locals. However, they had nothing else to offer me. Neither elo, nor raq, nor some marginally useful device. Only flowers and crystals.

Still unwilling to believe in the tremendous failure of my mission to find the Zatrathi homeworld, I made several orbits around the planet, scanning it every possible way I could. Living creatures, forests, oceans and nothing more. It was indeed a dummy, a dead end.

"Brainiac, set course for Belket," I ordered, resigning myself to defeat. The time had come to play my strongest trump card.

"Lex, where are you right now?" The call from Eunice came through about twenty minutes before we were to emerge from hyperspace. "Drop everything and come to these coordinates. I just sent them to you. The Zatrathi Queen is unhappy about something and is assembling all her mercenaries. Just so you know, I'm working for her now and I've put in a word for you. She promised to give you a chance, so don't blow it. The Qualian players have been notified. They'll let our ships pass without any questions. The meeting is in two hours. I'll be waiting!"

I stared dumbly at the PDA for a moment. A note of triumph had sounded in my wife's voice. So that's the way it is...My wife believes that she hit the jackpot by switching to the Queen's side. This is starting to look quite interesting. I looked at the message pensively. The coordinates were in the capital system of the Qualian Empire. But I knew for sure that the Queen was not there.

"Orbship *Warlock*, prepare the ship for a full inspection!"

A CHECK FOR A BILLION

announced Belket's dispatcher. My relations with the Precians were a little strained, if you could call outright hostility 'strain,' and yet they were forced to accommodate me. As the Queenslayer, I had earned a month's worth of peace in Galactogon.

Taught by bitter experience, the orbship was subjected to an inspection both in orbit and on the surface. Apparently, someone had managed to leak one of the ways to infiltrate the planet. I stoically endured all the bureaucracy, only to find myself in the viceroy's office. And then my trump card finally appeared: the third adviser of the Precian Emperor.

"I was told that you wanted to see me." The Precian's tone suggested that he would be much happier doing anything at all other than speaking to me. "You have a minute."

"I'm tired of being an outcast. I want to join the Precian Empire."

Over my two-hour-long flight I had outlined our conversation and now I was sticking to my plan.

"You don't think it's too late?" the adviser smirked, yet added: "Do you know the conditions?"

"Turn over all the pirate bases so that you can wipe them out for good. Sure. I'm on board."

"You would betray your own Brotherhood?"

"The Brotherhood is no longer mine. I was stripped of my rank and expelled. Nothing else binds me to the pirates, so I can safely share any information I have."

"Yes, we were aware of this," said the adviser, admitting that he had a spy among the pirate brethren. I had no doubts about who that individual was.

"I am pleased that you have seen reason, yet, tell me, why did you insist on meeting with me? The viceroy would be happy to accept your allegiance."

"Because this is not the only reason I came here. I need the brainworm that I gave you."

"Why? It is an utterly useless creature. Even the captain of the flying fortress, whom we have interred in suspended animation, brought us more benefit than this empty-headed Relay."

"In that case, you won't lose anything by returning him to me."

"What do you offer in return?"

"The coordinates to a planet full of Zatrathi and the open Uldan cylinder as a bonus."

"So you found all the answers to the riddles?" The bureaucrat's mask almost cracked, revealing the curious archeologist underneath, but the adviser caught himself in time. "This is not enough. There are many planets in Galactogon. There is but one brainworm."

"The planet I speak of is one of a kind!"

"No!"

"Come on, adviser, you don't even know what to do with the brainworm…"

"But we know that you know what to do with it! I wish to see how important it is for you. The cylinder and the planet are trivial. I can feel it."

I hadn't anticipated this turn of events. I really did think that the planet would be enough.

"How about Wit-Verr? The Great Precian Empire will catch

the mighty pirate lord!"

"I will pretend that I never heard you say such an outrageous thing," the adviser darkened. "The Brotherhood of the Jolly Roger 2.0 has seen the light. Captain Wit-Verr has united all the pirates into a single force to fight against the Zatrathi. With the Anorxians' help we have entered into a cooperation agreement with him. And now you wish to shatter this fragile peace?"

Hearing this, I realized why the Motherboard's envoy had been at the pirate's assembly. The Anorxian had spoken for all the other empires.

"I will give you the orbship." It took an immense effort to utter this sentence.

"I do not need a ship that has already been thoroughly examined. Hansa reports that you have a battlesphere. If you want the brainworm, deliver her to us. I imagine that will be a fair trade."

"Deal!" I agreed after a brief deliberation and pulled out the access key. I had the same rights to Eunice's ship as she had to mine. By the way, I should probably revoke those. Who knows how she'll take this. "One condition. I need the brainworm right now!"

"After you deliver the battlesphere." The adviser tried to insist on his position, but I was adamant. I had no other option.

An hour and a half later, I was in orbit around the Qualian capital, undergoing yet another customs inspection. It was a good thing I'd left the brainworm back on Zubrail. A single thought occupied me at the moment: What am I going to tell Eunice about her battlesphere? The whole situation was growing pretty awkward. When I handed it over to the Precians, my PDA exploded with calls and messages from my wife, but I had ducked those, hoping to

---

have that conversation later.

"The emperor is ready to receive you." I was taken to the throne room. It had not changed much since last time, except that there was more security now. The Queen continued her conquest of Qualian hearts and minds, adding a dozen mind-controlled warriors to the emperor's retinue. There weren't many people in the hall, but the few that were there were very interesting indeed. There was not one NPC among them. Everyone here was a player. They wandered around, exchanging looks as if searching for acquaintances. It was a matter of time until I found some familiar faces: Vargen and Aalor. Liberium's two top officers were keeping to the shadows under the balconies, examining the new arrivals. I wonder if they had switched to the Zatrathi side before or after the recent battle..? Upon seeing me, the two cast me looks of utter contempt, but said nothing. Before entering the hall, the guard warned that any aggression would be punished by expulsion.

Nobody wanted to be kicked out, so Liberium's leaders stepped away from the main group. I wanted to follow them, just to mess with them and maybe see who they were paying attention to, but I didn't have time. The doors to the throne room opened, letting in the next batch of guests, and I immediately forgot all about Liberium. Kiddo entered the room, accompanied by my darling wife. There she is — the rat that Tryd had spoken of. If she's a general now, she won't be for long.

"Where is my *Lexus*?!" Eunice immediately set upon me, but the guards reacted quickly. I guess some notification appeared before her because she quickly stepped back holding out her hands in a conciliatory way: "Okay, okay! There won't be any problems! I was just kidding!"

She had no choice but to stand there pelting me with her irate looks. Kiddo approached me next.

"Howdy pardner! Let's talk straight — for old times' sake. You're the one leaking the bases' locations, right? We can be useful to each other."

"Um…" I didn't even know how to respond to such an opener. "Actually, I'm here to find evidence against you. 'Cause it's you that the pirates think is the rat."

"Me?" Marina asked with surprise. "Cut the crap. Tryd told me quite bluntly: 'Surgeon is acting strangely. He's risen too fast through the ranks. Someone needs to watch him.'"

"He told me the same thing," Eunice joined our conversation. "Tryd believes that it is you who are leaking the bases' locations. I wouldn't be surprised if he was right. Especially after the trick you pulled with my *Lexus*!"

"Oh don't start," I frowned, guiding the conversation back to the topic at hand. "You know, ladies, you're starting to bore me. I am here to find evidence of the mole's activity. That is, evidence that implicates you — former 'pardner.' And since this entire scene is starting to remind me of something from the theater of the absurd, here…"

I sent the ladies a description of my mission and looked at them expectantly.

"What do you say now?"

The ladies said nothing at all and simply sent me their own mission descriptions in reply. What the hell?

"Hey you…" I turned around and buttonholed a passing

player. "Do you have a pirate mission to find a rat?"

"Leave me alone, weirdo!" the player recoiled, jerking his arm away. "I don't have anything!"

My suspicions about the true purpose of the present assembly began to grow. All that was left was to verify them. Scanning around until I located Vargen, I bee-lined in his direction.

"Do you have a mission like this too?" I sent my mission description to the Liberium's leader. He froze for a few moments, then nodded and immediately turned to his XO:

"Aalor, let's go!"

The two walked over to the doors only to discover that they were locked. I looked around. There were only players in the hall now — even the emperor and the guards had disappeared. In total, I counted about fifty people and, gradually, everyone began to figure out that something was wrong. The players began looking around, talking to each other, gesturing, growing agitated. Vargen once again tried to yank the doors open to no avail.

"It's a trap: Respawn!" someone yelled.

It was not meant to be. As soon as a weapon appeared in a player's hands, a thin beam swept from the ceiling, turning the weapon into a useless piece of raq. The armor suit which Aalor tried to put on froze — stunned by an EM blast. A few seconds later, the player came tumbling out of it.

"What is this, some stupid NPC prank?" Kiddo and Eunice came up to us, and just then the door near the throne opened and in waddled the Anorxian with the brainworm from my last meeting. The Queen had appeared to her subjects.

"Greetings, my mercenaries! I am glad that you have

A CHECK FOR A BILLION

gathered at my first summons. The time has come for you to prove your loyalty. Meet the one who will lead you into the battle!"

The Anorxian stepped aside, letting in another creature. For the majority of the present players, the newcomer was no different than any other NPC, but for the Liberium boys, for Kiddo and Eunice and for me, he was a symbolic figure indeed: For the one who now examined his army from above, was also a general of the Jolly Roger Brotherhood 2.0.

Mission accomplished: Secret Brother Seamus. Tell Wit-Verr who the traitor is.

"This mangy, flea-bitten bag of bones," Kiddo cried out, finally realizing what was going on. "He's the one who advised me to make contact with the Zatrathi!"

"Attention everyone!" barked Tryd, and silence descended upon the hall. "The Queen has ordered me to recover a renegade Relay. The Precians have him, so this operation will be a serious one. The Queen has provided us with ten flying fortresses, the Qualians have added another five Arbiters, but our main strength is you! I want complete battle readiness in five hours. We will head out shortly thereafter. Whoever refuses or runs will forever forfeit our Queen's trust. In order to ensure that no one betrays us, a remote self-destruct system will be installed on each ship. If you run, you lose your ship. The installation is already underway!"

"You can't!"

"Who gave you permission?"

"I didn't agree to this!"

A wave of indignation swept across the hall, even as Brainiac screamed in my ear about a modification being made to *Warlock*'s mainframe. He was powerless to stop the procedure.

"You made your choice by switching allegiance to the Queen. If you thought that you could betray Her at any moment, you were mistaken! You should have thought harder earlier." Tryd was clearly enjoying the dismay he was causing among our ranks. "Join the fight and nothing will happen to your ships!"

Several players lost their tempers and rushed the Delvian, but the marine merely waved them off. Shimmering crates fell to the floor where the rebels had been. A screen slid out above us and showed the image of the solar system. Countless ships hung around the Qualian capital. Suddenly, two of the cruisers lit up in bright flashes.

"Who else wants to lose their ships?" Tryd asked menacingly. There were no more volunteers — the flogging had had its effect.

"Any more questions about your battlesphere?" I couldn't help but gibe at Eunice, who just shook her head in despair.

"The staging point has been loaded into your ships' computers," the Delvian continued. "Be there and be ready in two hours. Now you may go!"

The doors opened, but no one hurried away. Everyone was looking at Tryd, expecting him to announce that this was all just a prank and that the hidden cameras were there and there…After all, what the Queen was proposing here would force us to risk everything we had accumulated over our time playing Galactogon. In effect, we were forced to choose between our ships and our reputations. We could not save both. At least, not everyone.

"Any questions, Captain Kiddo?" Tryd fixed Marina with his stare, among the crowd of stunned players. "No? Then you have ten seconds to scram. Insubordination will be deemed a betrayal of Her to whom you swore your allegiance! Now hop to it!"

"You bastard," the girl said with hatred, then turned and left.

Well, now we know where Kiddo stands. Her ship was everything to her. Above all, it was her home, with which she'd never part. As for her reputation? It didn't mean that much to her after all. People like Kiddo would have no trouble enjoying the game while playing as the 'baddies.' I had no doubt about that.

One by one, the rest of the players began filing out in her wake. Defeated, shaken, unsure of what the future held in store for them.

"Surgeon, do you have any questions?" Four players remained in the throne room: Eunice, Vargen, Aalor and I. Liberium could not decide what was more important: Losing two more cruisers, which would be a substantial blow to the guild's naval forces, or a negative reputation with all the empires. For some reason I had no doubts about Vargen. For him, reputation was more important.

"Yes, actually," I said, before the Delvian could go on. "Only, not for you. I address the Queen: Where does Your Highness wish me to deliver the renegade Relay?"

"So you…" Eunice whispered, her eyes wide with surprise. She had thought I was here solely by the grace of her invitation.

"Hand it over to Tryd," replied the Queen through her synthoid.

"No!" I cried. "I have no reason to trust this rat. No one knows where his allegiance truly lies and whom he'll betray next. If you like working with his kind, that is your will, but I won't abide by it. I will have nothing to do with Tryd again. Have you no other representatives?"

"You're the same moron you ever were," the Delvian jerked his lip in derision. "Why did you remain silent? Everyone has already set out for the Precian Empire!"

"Why, I don't care about 'everyone!' I work alone. Plus I wanted to see who values their ship over their honor." I looked at Vargen. "Profit is not the only measure in this galaxy, Tryd. There are some who value their reputation more. This was a great way to see who exactly. So let me speak with another representative or tell me yourself where to bring the Relay."

"Very well, mercenary," the Queen replied. "Tryd shall give you the coordinates and travel with you as my guarantor to protect you from my minions. If you wish to speak of trust, I have none for you either. You have three hours. That is all!"

The Anorxian popped and sparked and collapsed to the floor, turning into a shimmering crate. The Queen did not like my conditions. I looked at the Delvian and could not resist asking:

"What did she promise you that you are willing to betray everyone? Do you really think she can bring Filta back?"

An evil scowl was Tryd's answer — while his explanation was a heavy punch. I crashed into a wall and began to get to my feet but Tryd was already upon me. He grabbed me in a headlock, dousing me with his stale breath.

"It's not for you to judge me, small fry. I do what I think is right. So shut up and do as you're ordered! Where is the renegade?"

"That's not for you to know!" I muttered, struggling with my dizziness. "We will meet in an hour where Volta used to be."

"Don't dare fail the Queen, you useless cur!" Tryd slammed me back into the wall. "You have an hour! Then I will personally destroy your ship! If you're late by even a second, you'll make my day!"

He walked out of the throne room, leaving me to Eunice's caring embrace. My wife opened her mouth to start interrogating me when Vargen suddenly interrupted:

"Do you need help?"

I was about to tell him where he could shove his help but bit my tongue. Help would actually come in handy right now. Not because there was a way to save our situation but because we could at least cause some trouble.

"Go to Barganil III and tell Wit-Verr that the rat is Tryd. That's my mission and I need it completed. Show him the video of what happened here. This is very important."

"We will do it," Vargen nodded and, after a little thought, held out his hand to me: "I propose we settle our past disputes. Without any ill feelings or fighting. Deal?"

"Deal," I agreed, shaking his hand in response. "No fighting, no ill feelings, but no friendship either. We know each other and we're both armed and neutral with one another. And that's it."

Vargen simply hummed understandingly. I had no doubts that he would rebuild and that Liberium would again regain its place in the guild rankings.

The two left without any further goodbyes, and I hoped that our roads wouldn't cross again in the future. Galactogon's big enough that maybe I won't have to see them again…Although who am I kidding?

Eunice was standing beside me and, as befits a wife, was breathing loudly through both nostrils. She couldn't really say anything — if I hadn't traded the *Lexus*, it'd have a Zatrathi bomb on it right now — and yet she couldn't just ignore my actions.

"Shall we go then?" I asked wearily. "We only have an hour. In theory, we should make it. We can talk while we're on our way. What's the point now…"

As soon as I got back into my armor suit, I heard Brainiac's wailing. The device that the Zatrathi had attached to *Warlock* was beyond my computer's understanding. Somehow, they had inserted a Zatrathi grenade into the mainframe and then connected it to the self-destruct mechanism. Brainiac had turned off the latter but could not remove the bomb. The explosion would be small and almost imperceptible, but it would also destroy my ship's computer forever. Brainiac was both powerless and terrified and therefore wailed in all the languages he knew about his somber fate.

It didn't take us long to get to Zubrail. I landed on the planet and tried to convince the Uldan to help my computer, but he refused to even hear me out. I have to solve my problems on my own, he said.

"So what, you're just going to hand over the Relay to the Zatrathi?" my wife asked, perplexed.

"No, and that's why you're coming with me. Do you know how to use this?"

A CHECK FOR A BILLION

I handed Eunice a small item. A look of understanding flashed across her face and my wife's armor suit disappeared, blending with the interior.

"Of course. You can count on me."

As agreed, Tryd's *Inevitable* was waiting for me at the rendezvous point. A shuttle brought the pirate over to *Warlock* with two officers who immediately began scanning my ship for any signs of ambush. I didn't even blink when the Delvian asked me where my female was. I'd kicked her off my ship, I said quite truthfully. I didn't mention that Eunice was actually out in space dangling from the orbship on a long tether. If the pirates naively believed that an inspection of my ship was enough, I wouldn't want to disappoint them.

"Enter the coordinates as follows…" said Tryd. He plunked down in my captain's chair and kicked his boots up onto the console. I swallowed my pride and ordered Brainiac to take down the dictated coordinates. It was hard for me to enter them — Tryd had insisted that I war Rialto Bracelets while he was on board.

All of a sudden, Tryd fell silent. His muzzle grew long and the Jolly Roger 2.0 icon flickering over his head vanished. No matter how hard I tried, I could not hide my smirk.

"You ratted me out?!" the fox growled, struggling with the urge to rush at me and tear me to shreds.

"What do you mean 'ratted?' You're the one who told me to find the rat. How was I supposed to know that the rat was so stupid that…"

I did not have time to finish the sentence — it's hard to talk as you're being slammed into a bulkhead. The former pirate loomed over me, a dagger in his hand ready to strike, but I found the composure to break into a grin:

"You're going to betray your Queen?"

The dagger plunged to its hilt into the floor beside my throat.

"I'll get you yet, small fry. Whatever hole you hide in, I will find you, and you will regret the day you appeared in Galactogon. The only thing that's keeping you alive is my word to the Queen, but she won't protect you forever!"

"The coordinates have been entered, hyperjump calculations are complete, hull integrity restored," Brainiac announced, adding in the passphrase that let me know that Eunice was back on board. "Flight time is forty minutes."

"Off we go then! Let's see the star map please," I ordered, hearing the flight time estimate. The Queen's homeplanet was located across the galaxy from where the invasion had started. It was on the opposite rim, a little past the Qualian Empire.

Tryd and his officers froze, going into standby mode. Of course, this did not mean that they took their eyes off me. A call came in on my PDA. The Rialto Bracelets could not prevent players from answering PDA calls. And yet Tryd, who was being played by a real human, would hear my conversation. Would he understand it?

"Lex, I'm ready. On the count of five…One…Two…"

Tryd lurched in my direction. As I suspected, he had somehow intercepted the call to my PDA and understood our —

players' — exchange.

"Three!"

No one was *actually* going to count to five. Eunice appeared right behind the Delvian and stuck him with an equine dose of tranquilizer. A most potent solution I had picked up during my travels. The pirate managed to brush her aside but he didn't have the strength to do anything else. His officers didn't even have time to move before Eunice blasted them into loot crates. Eunice hopped over to me and cut my handcuffs with a sharp blow. Having lost power, they crumbled to fine dust, freeing my hands.

"Hurry! He has a fast metabolism!" I warned, getting into my favorite armor suit and breathing out with relief as the medunit removed the bouquet of debuffs.

Tryd really turned out to be a staunch opponent. He categorically refused to lose consciousness, even after we took off his body armor and injected more tranquilizer. The fox wheezed, drooled, rolled his eyes, but remained conscious.

"We're in position!" Brainiac reported and the stars shortened to points on the screen. "We are being scanned. Green light — we have access to the system!"

I took out two Zatrathi grenades, stuck them into the fox's belt and pulled the pins.

"Game over, dipshit! Brainiac — take him to church!"

I will never forget the look on Tryd's face. No AI could simulate such a perfect blend of defeat and hatred. A hole appeared in the floor, and Tryd was flushed out to space where, for a mere second, he bloomed into a glittering fireball — and was gone.

The way of the traitor named Tryd had reached its end.

Only now did I get the chance to examine the system we were in: a giant star, of which there were but several in Galactogon, three lifeless gas giants for balance, one blue-green planet and one immense Queen — who was being tended to by thousands, if not tens of thousands of ships.

"We have been ordered to stay in place. A ship will come to pick up the renegade," Brainiac translated the dispatcher's orders. One of the myriad points began drifting in our direction.

"Captain, I am ready. Galactogon is more important than one ship. Even if I am that ship."

There was a pause. My next command was supposed to be as simple as pie, but I had to force myself to utter it. I understood the consequences very well. The Zatrathi drew closer and I finally committed:

"Go ahead! Take us to the planet!"

The sparkling orbship rushed toward the green dot. Even if the Zatrathi had been ready for such a dash, they could not have defended against it. *Warlock*'s reactor hummed at full power, while the shields absorbed the incoming plasma, at the very limits of their strength.

"Captain! I'm picking up a signal! The protective casing around the mainframe implant has been burned out…The Zatrathi are signaling the device…The next…"

There was a dull explosion somewhere inside the ship. My control console erupted in sparks and some of our screens went out. Ten seconds before entering the atmosphere, my faithful companion — with whom I had traveled far and wide and shared

A CHECK FOR A BILLION

so many adventures across the galaxy — had gone for good...

Goodbye, my friend! I will mourn you a long time — but to make sure that you didn't go in vain, I will mourn you later...

"Eunice, man the shields!" I suppressed the roaring in my ears and took control of my *Warlock*. At long last, the Zatrathi had made a mistake. They stopped shooting, thinking that in disabling my computer, they had disabled my ship. Normally, they would be right, and yet their hesitation still bought me the ten seconds I needed.

"We are entering the atmosphere! Altitude is 20,000 meters!" In addition to tending to the shields, Eunice managed to report our flight status. "Multiple targets starboard! I won't be able to fire the guns and do all the other stuff at the same time!"

"Don't worry — just work our shields. I'm diving in! Look for the entrance to the spirit's chamber!"

I wasn't planning on taking on the entire Zatrathi fleet. All my hopes rested on the speed and agility of my orbship. We were expected out in space, not planetside. By the time the Zatrathi would activate their atmospheric defenses, by the time they would track and lock onto us, a lot of time would have passed. In that case, we might just make it.

"Scan's done. The hall of the planetary spirit is three hundred kilometers to starboard! I'll highlight it in your HUD!"

A blue line appeared on the screen and I abruptly banked *Warlock* out and away from the dive. A squadron of enemy fighters stood between me and our objective. We had no firepower — the orangutan gunner had gone limp with Brainiac's demise and Eunice couldn't do everything at once.

468

"Eunice, baby, just hold the shields up," I begged, opening the throttle to full. *Warlock*'s hull could withstand a direct hit from six legendary-class torpedoes at once. What's a torpedo? A hunk of raq hurtling at high speed. What is a fighter? The same hunk of raq, only a little larger!

"What are you doing?!" screamed Eunice when I headed straight for the fighters. The Zatrathi maintained a tight formation, filling in the space between their fighters with their typical spikes. Somewhere in the back of my mind, I observed that this was the first time I'd seen the Zatrathi use their ships' protrusions for anything at all, but this did not distract me from my main target — the fighter in the center.

"Hold on!" I managed to yell, before the orbship shook significantly. Sparks and smoke appeared from somewhere, but we continued to race forward. The remnants of the Zatrathi fighter were just beginning to tumble away from our hull when we slammed right into the next enemy.

Our speed didn't drop even a little. Given our mass and resultant inertia, we had the advantage here. Four times we rammed the blockading fighters until the sky before us opened up and we broke free and left our enemies far behind...

"Fifty clicks! Slow down!"

The blue guideline ended abruptly at the foot of a huge pyramid. Suddenly something began rapping loudly on our hull and its durability began to plummet.

"Eunice?"

"It's not plasma! It's raq shells! Our shields won't stop them! Their AA mass drivers are pummeling us!"

A CHECK FOR A BILLION

In the air, we may as well have been in the palm of their hands — it was only a matter of adjusting the AA fire to our velocity. 'Not good,' I thought to myself and decided to risk another reckless maneuver. I didn't mind allowing their fighters to catch up to us, as long as it got us out of the AA guns' sights.

"Take it easy!" begged Eunice, clinging to her chair. I descended down to the very ground, at times scuffing the pavement with the bottom of my orbship, kicking up a long tail of sparks. The Zatrathi cities were arranged in an even grid with broad streets, so I didn't even have to diminish our speed. The only inconvenience were the incessant notifications about gained XP and drops in durability. We weren't losing it as quickly now as we had been with the AA fire, but it was still unpleasant. On the other hand, we kept smashing through monorails and other mass transit full of Zatrathi, which fed us XP and improved the quality of our hull. Brainiac would have gotten a kick out of this...

"Lex, there's the entrance! We've been hit!"

I grimaced — the fighters had caught up to us and knocked out three engines. We had only one left and that wouldn't be enough to slow us to a standstill.

"Get ready! It's about to hurt!"

I steered the orbship straight into the black entrance to the hall of the planetary spirit. The last engine burned out a few seconds before impact, but the Zatrathi could no longer prevent our inertia from carrying us to our goal.

The orbship slammed into the pyramid. Some kind of notification flashed past my eyes and the world lost its volume, furling itself into a dark tube...

"Lex...come on...wake up already! Wake up, Lex!"

I opened my eyes with difficulty — my entire field of view was chockfull of debuff icons. There was a click — Eunice switched out my medunit and several icons vanished — only to reappear again a couple seconds later. To be fair, there were fewer now, but still much too many. A new click and the emptied medunit rolled away along the floor.

"Lex, wake up! Come on, baby! This is the last one I got! Come back, please!" Eunice's voice grew tearful and plaintive.

"I think I'm back..." I managed hoarsely. My punctured chest punctuated my words with a gurgle of red foam and yet another debuff. The medunit again pumped all of its contents into me and flashed empty. But at least this gave me the strength to look around and curse mentally. The pyramid's entrance was gone: The orbship had blocked it completely, turning into a metal cork. Eunice cut a passage and pulled us out into the corridor, dragging us almost to the very entrance to the planetary spirit's chamber. Somehow she managed to do this despite suffering a fractured leg during our crash landing. Now, exhausted, she lay beside me, staring at the ceiling. I can't even imagine what mental fortitude still kept her here, holding on.

"Go on ahead — I'm spent." Eunice pulled out a blaster and aimed it at the orbship. Our metal cork began to jiggle. The welcoming party on the other side was desperate to reach us. A little more and a mob of warriors would break through and put an end to our raid. "I'll hold them back. The prize check has to be here. It can't be anywhere else!"

"Okay. But don't put off respawning too long," I nodded and

471

A CHECK FOR A BILLION

crawled forward.

As I reached the door, I heard a rattling behind me, the crash of falling debris and then the sound of gunfire. They had pulled the orbship out. I had to hurry!

Heaving myself over the threshold, I looked around. A huge chamber fifty meters wide. One side of it contained an ordinary planetary spirit crystal — on the other side of the hall was a shimmering item that looked very much like a scroll.

My heart skipped a beat. The prize check! Our raid's main objective, the subject of the wager, the goal of my entire gaming career in Galactogon. A mere twenty-five meters or so away from me. Behind me, I heard an explosion and Eunice's frame went gray in the party window. Another voluntary sacrifice. My wife had blown herself up to close the passage that led to me. I jerked toward the check but stopped. It dawned on me quite clearly that I wouldn't be able to make it both to the check and to the planetary spirit in time. I had to choose one or the other.

And suddenly I realized what I had to do. All the hints, clues and allusions arranged themselves into a single mosaic, forming one clear instruction. It was impossible to see it from the outside — you had to start at the very beginning and see the journey through to its final end as I just had. Eunice could not have understood. Without losing a moment, I crawled toward the spirit.

The shimmering scroll behind my back began to glow red, but I merely grunted. There'd be no fooling me this time! The door flew off its hinges and Zatrathi warriors burst into the hall. They chirred angrily and rushed toward me, wishing to pull me away from the crystal. I looked up at them and smiled exultantly, applying the

---

KRIEG wire terminals to the spirit's crystal:

"Boom, suckers!"

You have activated the KRIEG.

New title unlocked: Hero of Galactogon.

You have destroyed the Queen, ending the war with the Zatrathi once and for all.

Speak to any imperial representative to receive your reward.

Your sacrifice was not in vain, Brainiac. Thank you for having my back all this time.

EPILOGUE

"WHAT HAVE YOU DONE?! TELL ME?! WHAT HAVE YOU DONE, YOU ASSHOLE?!" Eunice's scream resounded throughout the forest, scaring the birds. They took off, flapping their wings with an offended air, but quickly calmed down, wheeled and retook their perches, watching the human's tantrum with interest.

"I blew up the Zatrathi planetary spirit," I said for the eleventh time, rolling my eyes. "That wasn't our check if it even was a check at all," I went on calmly persuading Eunice, not taking my eyes off the clouds.

I was lying supine on our dock on Zubrail, resting. At long last, our 'run or die' marathon had ended. Now I had absolutely nothing — not even a ship that would get me to the nearest planet. The race was over and we had won. At what price — was another question altogether.

"Why? What makes you think so?" My wife emotions were running amok. "I saw the video, the check was there! You ruined everything!"

"If that was a check, it wasn't for us," I repeated. "Remember the basic rule they told us when we first started? Remember how we would know if the scroll was for us?"

"What rule?" Eunice frowned, suppressing yet another outburst of frustration.

"I don't remember it verbatim, but the gist was that as soon as we set foot on the planet with the check, the system would warn us. And I mean immediately. You and I did our tour of Rrgord's planets using that same trick, remember?"

I looked away from the clouds and propped myself up on my elbow, looking at my wife.

"I remember," Eunice agreed reluctantly. "So you didn't get any notification?"

"Are you trying to say that you did?" My heart twitched. What if I'd made a terrible mistake..?

"No," she shook her head. "I didn't get one. But then where *is* our planet? They told us that the check would be on the Zatrathi homeworld! They couldn't have lied to us!"

Instead of answering, I just rolled my eyes again.

"Stop doing that!"

"Didn't you say you'd take care of everything on your own? What do you need me for?" I mocked Eunice, causing her to withdraw, embarrassed. She couldn't help but feel ashamed for how harshly she'd treated me earlier.

"Forgive me," she said at last, making a pleading gesture with her hands. I took pity on her and explained my thinking.

"Whoever said that the *Queen*'s homeworld should be the

Zatrathi homeworld?"

Eunice opened her mouth and immediately shut it.

"There...do you see now?" I smiled, and lay down to gaze at the sky, while my wife grappled with what I had just told her.

"Surgeon is correct," said a familiar voice beside us. It was Zubrail's resident Uldan. Eunice and I jumped up at the same time and stared at Galactogon's ancient progenitor. "Those whom you call the Zatrathi were not born on the Queen's homeplanet. My congratulations. You made the right choice, Surgeon, and you passed the test! I hereby recognize your right to be on Planet Zubrail!"

Access granted to Zubrail.

Attention search participant! You are currently on the planet with the prize check! You may find it in the hall of the planetary spirit!

"My god..." Eunice whispered, upon reading the same notification.

"Come with me. I wish to show you something." The Uldan waved his hand and the platform we were on parted, forming a broad path. We followed after him. "You proved that the fate of Galactogon was more important to you than a monetary reward. You proved that you are ready to fight to the very end. You proved that you are ready to sacrifice everything, even what you value most."

I guess he was talking about Brainiac. Some building flashed between the trees. I looked closer and froze. A rickety old hangar stood in the clearing. Above its wide, locked doors I read an inscription faded with time: 'Project #2373.' I swallowed hard, realizing the truth. Here, in this very hangar, many millennia ago, the first Zatrathi were born. *This* was their homeworld.

"I wished to see how determined you really were. That was why I pushed you to go see Mercaloun. I made sure that no one interfered with you. I eliminated any enemies that could get in your way. I wished to see whether you were worthy or not. Now I have the answers to these questions."

"Worthy of what exactly?" I asked, realizing that the Uldan wasn't speaking about the check. Something told me a new adventure lay around the corner.

"Worthy of a dangerous and important mission. But first look here."

The Uldan waved his hand and the thickets again parted, revealing a small platform on which stood a golden copy of my orbship. Against my will, my eyes welled with tears. *Warlock* was back — but my friend wasn't. It would be difficult to fly without him. It didn't matter that Brainiac was just a piece of code.

"Cap'n!" The snake popped out of the hull and rushed toward me, coiling around me in tight rings. "You're back, Cap'n! Glory to the creators! I'd already decided that we'd have to fly solo!"

"I decided to make you a present in case you succeeded in your quest. Before you set out to destroy the Queen, I made a copy of your orbship's AI," the Uldan petted the snake, avoiding my eyes. "The one you call 'Brainiac' is alive and well. He is inside the ship."

"Thank you," I said sincerely and, clearing my throat, asked: "You mentioned some sort of mission?"

477

A CHECK FOR A BILLION

"The Queen was not one of a kind. Soon the next creation of the Ancestors will appear and everything will start anew. You must travel to another universe, forever shutting the door to our world.

New mission available: In Search of the Ancestors. Requirements: Title of Hero of Galactogon.

"Later I will explain to you who the Ancestors are and what threat they pose to Galactogon. For now — come with me. Your reward awaits you in the hall of the planetary spirit. You have earned your billion."

END OF BOOK AND SERIES

January–April 2019

Dear Reader,

Thank you for being with me throughout these three books. The break between the first and second books turned out to be longer than expected. At one point, I even gave up believing that I would finish the series. But, gathering my strength, I finally did it. I can confidently say that I like the outcome. I hope you share my opinion.

Vasily Mahanenko

Want to be the first to know about our latest LitRPG, sci fi and fantasy titles from your favorite authors?

Subscribe to our *New Releases* newsletter:

http://eepurl.com/b7niIL

Thank you for reading *A Check for a Billion!*
If you like what you've read, check out other sci-fi, fantasy and
LitRPG novels published by Magic Dome Books:

Reality Benders LitRPG series by Michael Atamanov:
Countdown
External Threat
Game Changer
Web of Worlds
A Jump into the Unknown
Aces High

**The Dark Herbalist LitRPG series
by Michael Atamanov:**
Video Game Plotline Tester
Stay on the Wing
A Trap for the Potentate
Finding a Body

Perimeter Defense LitRPG series by Michael Atamanov:
Sector Eight
Beyond Death
New Contract
A Game with No Rules

**League of Losers LitRPG Series
by Michael Atamanov:**
A Cat and his Human

**The Way of the Shaman LitRPG series
by Vasily Mahanenko:**
Survival Quest
The Kartoss Gambit
The Secret of the Dark Forest
The Phantom Castle
The Karmadont Chess Set
Shaman's Revenge
Clans War

The Alchemist LitRPG series by Vasily Mahanenko:
City of the Dead
Forest of Desire
Tears of Alron

Dark Paladin LitRPG series by Vasily Mahanenko:
The Beginning
The Quest
Restart

Galactogon LitRPG series by Vasily Mahanenko:
Start the Game!
In Search of the Uldans
A Check for a Billion

Invasion LitRPG Series by Vasily Mahanenko:
A Second Chance
An Equation with one Unknown

World of the Changed LitRPG Series by Vasily Mahanenko:
No Mistakes
Pearl of the South

**The Bard from Barliona LitRPG series
by Eugenia Dmitrieva and Vasily Mahanenko:**
The Renegades
A Song of Shadow

Level Up LitRPG series by Dan Sugralinov:
Re-Start
Hero
The Final Trial
Level Up: The Knockout (with Max Lagno)
Level Up. The Knockout: Update (with Max Lagno)

Disgardium LitRPG series by Dan Sugralinov:
Class-A Threat
Apostle of the Sleeping Gods
The Destroying Plague
Resistance
Holy War

World 99 LitRPG Series by Dan Sugralinov:
Blood of Fate

Adam Online LitRPG Leries by Max Lagno:
Absolute Zero
City of Freedom

Interworld Network **LitRPG Series by Dmitry Bilik:**
The Time Master
Avatar of Light
The Dark Champion

Rogue Merchant **LitRPG Series by Roman Prokofiev:**
The Starlight Sword
The Gene of the Ancients

Project Stellar LitRPG Series by Roman Prokofiev:
The Incarnator
The Enchanter
The Tribute

Clan Dominance **LitRPG Series by Dem Mikhailov:**
The Sleepless Ones Book One
The Sleepless Ones Book Two
The Sleepless Ones Book Three

The Neuro **LitRPG series by Andrei Livadny:**
The Crystal Sphere
The Curse of Rion Castle
The Reapers

Phantom Server **LitRPG series by Andrei Livadny:**
Edge of Reality
The Outlaw
Black Sun

Respawn Trials **LitRPG Series by Andrei Livadny:**
Edge of the Abyss

The Expansion (The History of the Galaxy) **series
by A. Livadny:**
Blind Punch
The Shadow of Earth
Servobattalion

Point Apocalypse *(a near-future action thriller)*
by Alex Bobl

Moskau **by G. Zotov**
(a dystopian thriller)

El Diablo by G.Zotov
(a supernatural thriller)

Mirror World LitRPG series by Alexey Osadchuk:
Project Daily Grind
The Citadel
The Way of the Outcast
The Twilight Obelisk

Underdog LitRPG series by Alexey Osadchuk:
Dungeons of the Crooked Mountains
The Wastes
The Dark Continent
The Otherworld

An NPC's Path LitRPG series by Pavel Kornev:
The Dead Rogue
Kingdom of the Dead
Deadman's Retinue

The Sublime Electricity series by Pavel Kornev:
The Illustrious
The Heartless
The Fallen
The Dormant

Citadel World series by Kir Lukovkin:
The URANUS Code
The Secret of Atlantis

You're in Game!
(LitRPG Stories from Bestselling Authors)

You're in Game-2!
(More LitRPG stories set in your favorite worlds)

The Fairy Code by Kaitlyn Weiss:
Captive of the Shadows
Chosen of the Shadows

More books and series are coming out soon!

In order to have new books of the series translated faster, we need your help and support! Please consider leaving a review or spread the word by recommending *A Check for a Billion* to your friends and posting the link on social media. The more people buy the book, the sooner we'll be able to make new translations available.

Thank you!

Till next time!

www.ingramcontent.com/pod-product-compliance
Lightning Source LLC
Chambersburg PA
CBHW060756030726
47503CB00002B/272